PIERCED
Hearts

AHREN SANDERS

Editing: Kendra Gaither @ Kendra's Editing & Book Services
Cover Design: Letitia Hasser, RBA Designs

ISBN: 9781704811574

Table of Contents

Ahren's Ramblings...

A few years ago, someone on my team encouraged me to talk to an Editor at a large publishing house that was seeking submissions. I was terrified, self-conscious, and completely out of my element. My stories have always come to me organically and sometimes at inappropriate times (I'm looking at you, Hotshot and Fat Cat Liar... I was supposed to be chaperoning those kids, not holed in a corner typing furiously on my phone to lock in the ideas). But I decided to step out on a limb and throw caution to the wind.

The first step was to gather my thoughts and try to appear professional and organized. I outlined idea after idea, tossing my imaginative mind into different worlds and different stories that I wanted to create. It was during this time that the idea for the "Kendrick Boys" hit me. I immediately fell in love with Pierce Kendrick and his brother, Miller. But more so, Darby Graham's character owned a piece of my heart and I knew I had the ultimate soulmate for Pierce. The outline was rough, but the story was evolving. It took two years for me to get to Pierce and Darby in order to give them the attention and creative energy they needed.

Over this time, the Kendrick Boys no longer seemed like it fit the story, and this is how the "Southern Charmers" series was born. I think you will understand once you dive into the book and meet the guys.

What happened to that Editor and my submissions? Well, we scheduled a meeting! I got my chance to talk about my work, my ideas, my previous successes, and my learning experiences along the way. It was great! But my personal life and professional life were weaving together in a way that I knew I couldn't make any drastic changes. We kept the lines of communication open. Who knows what the future holds?

So, here we are. Pierced Hearts is done and in your hands. The format and telling is a throwback to my style, complete with loads of family and friends. This emotional, sexy, second-chance romance holds a place in my heart, and I hope you devour it, love it, and go back to re-read once you are done to experience it all over again.

I could not do this without the support, encouragement, and patience of my family. We're a small team, but the important thing is *we are a team* that somehow gets things done. I am a lucky lady.

Happy Reading!
Ahren

Pierced Hearts

Prologue

Darby

I turn off the engine, taking a moment to admire the landscape of my parents' property. Everything looks the same, but I couldn't feel more different. It's been a long time since I lived my life without a plan.

Out of the corner of my eye, I spot Lynda rolling Mom onto the terrace. Runner, my golden retriever, crawls halfway across the console, excited to finally be here.

"What do you think, boy? Ready for some changes?"

He barks his reply.

We jump out, and he races to the fields, checking out his new surroundings. My heart leaps when my mom stands, taking four steps away from her wheelchair, and extends her arms to me.

"Mama!"

"Get your skinny butt up here!" she haughtily calls back.

I cross the distance and almost collapse into her arms. It's been seven long weeks since her surgery. Seeing her stand and take those steps sends relief flooding through me. Of course, Dad, Lynda, my brother, Mom's physical therapist, and her doctor had all sent videos, but witnessing it in person makes it all the more real. She's fine.

"Looking good, old woman. Glad you fixed yourself. I was dreading coming back here to a lazy slug."

"Lazy my ass. I'll show you lazy when we're up at five-thirty in the morning."

"Oh, are we sleeping in tomorrow?" I tease, reaching out a hand to Lynda, who takes it affectionately.

"Smartass." Mom's arms tighten before she steps back, cupping my chin with her fingertips. "My Darby Rose is home."

The words are simple, but the meaning is clear. "I'm home."

There's a short twinkle in her eye before she looks me over, her hand falling to my waist and pinching my side. "You're even skinnier. I may have been drugged up last time you were home, but I remember you. Now, you're skin and bones."

Here we go. Let the ridiculing begin. "I'm not skin and bones. I needed to lose some weight. It's called getting fit."

"Look at these fancy clothes, Lynda. And that hair. Darby's always had such gorgeous, thick hair. I understand why she wears it up for work, but for a casual afternoon at home?"

"I think she looks lovely, Annie. Leave her alone."

I flash Lynda an appreciative smile, squeezing her hand once more before releasing it. Lynda has been my mom's best friend forever. I can't remember a time in my life when Lynda wasn't around. She and her husband, Ray, live close, and she has been a lifesaver to our family since Mom's fall. Without her, we'd be lost.

Eight weeks ago, Mom was riding her horse and had a horrible fall. Lynda was the first one to get to her since my brother was out of town. It took a day for doctors to give us all the answers. Mom had shattered her hip, fractured her pelvis, slipped a disc in her lower spine, and sprained her ankle. Lynda was at her side, giving me hourly updates until I could get from Charlotte to Charleston.

It was Lynda who calmed my hysteria and helped me arrange all that was needed when Mom left the hospital. My brother, Evin, and Dad handled all the medical professionals, while I worked on getting Mom's house ready, and her therapy, transportation, and caregivers set up. I barely remember the whirlwind of those few weeks, but Lynda was my family's rock.

Not to mention, she comes to my rescue when Mom gets on a roll.

"You would think she looks lovely. You love these fancy-schmancy, wide-legged trousers. I prefer something tighter that shows off her figure," Mom goes on.

"They're linen, Mom. They're cool, and they are comfortable for driving," I throw back.

"Speaking of driving. What the hell is that God-forsaken monstrosity you drove up in?"

"It's my new SUV. You know I needed something larger for the business, and I thought it would be easier for you to get in and out of than my old car."

She studies me for a second, and her eyes instantly fill with sympathy. A quiet understanding passes between us. A quick glance at Lynda tells me she's figured out the same thing. It has to be that motherly instinct that kicks in when a child is hiding something.

Or hiding from something.

"It's just a car. Let's not make a big deal," I try again.

"We'll go for a ride when your brother gets here. He'll help you unload. The shed is all set up."

"You sure you wouldn't prefer me staying in the house with you?"

"That's up to you, honey. You are welcome to your old room, but I figured you'd want some of your own space. I'm getting around well enough, and having you close will be fine."

I chew on my bottom lip, thinking about actually moving back in with my mom at thirty-three years old. Staying under her roof while visiting is a lot different than my current situation. For now, I've uprooted my life, coming home to be close to family while I figure out the next steps.

"Maybe the shed is best."

"Whatever you want. Let's get back in the house. Lynda and I have been dying to hear all about your new bakery space. Evin has been tight-lipped."

"Do you need your chair?" I start to grab it, and she shakes her head to stop me.

"Okay, let me get my purse and phone out of the car."

"See you inside." She and Lynda head to the back door, but not before she gives me another sympathetic glance.

I pay close attention to her steps and balance, which seem to be right on track. Then I think about the meaning behind her look. She's on to me. I'm not fooling anyone. It's been twelve years since I've spent any lengthy amount of time with my family in Charleston. I purposely lost all touch with my old life.

When I made the decision to come home and help Mom, I knew things had to change. I found a wonderful woman to lease my townhome, took care of my business and clients, packed what I needed, and made arrangements to store the rest. All of that was fairly simple with the help of my dad, brother, and best friend.

Then I went to work on me. It was easy to find a trainer, and with extreme commitment, I successfully lost twenty pounds, redefining my overly voluptuous curves into a leaner figure. The new hair and wardrobe came next. The purchase of the car was a bigger deal. Evin almost hemorrhaged when I told him how much I needed out of my portfolio to pay cash for the Infinity. He tried to talk me out of it but quit when I threatened to pull all my money and find a new money manager.

The vehicle is nice, but it's not really me. No more free-spirited, wild-haired, relaxed and easy Darby. That girl disappeared a long time ago. The new me is a sharp-minded business owner that most likely won't be recognized.

When I walked away from him, I gave him this part of my life. There was no choice. Charleston was his home, too, and he was making a hell of a lot of roots here that would have destroyed me if I'd stayed. Moving was easy. It was the years of self-torment and heartache that came afterward.

Pierced Hearts

I gave Pierce Kendrick my heart, my soul, and my beloved Charleston.

And he never even blinked.

Chapter 1

Pierce

Three Weeks Later

I lean casually against the brick column, drinking my coffee and watching the cars piling into the parking lot. Children and parents fuss with backpacks, lunch boxes, and what look like presents as they rush into the school. A few wave in recognition, but mostly, everyone looks panicked.

A flash of red catches my eyes as my Connie flies into the lot and nearly crashes into a post. I take a deep breath and go to help when she stomps around to the trunk, snapping at Cole and Maya to hurry and help her. They do as they're told, but both abandon their mission when they spot me coming.

"Dad!" Cole breaks out into a run, slamming into me. Maya is gentler, but her arms grip me tight.

"Hey, guys. What's going on?"

"Can some of you please come help me?"

Cole tenses at Connie's shout, and I recognize the irritation and exhaustion in her voice, which always results in her being a total bitch.

"Come on, kids. Let's help your mom."

Connie places two large shopping bags on the ground, never making eye contact. Her bad mood is even more apparent the closer I get.

"Hey, why don't you two go ahead and get inside? I'll help your mom with all this and meet you in the auditorium." Their faces fill with relief, and they don't even glance her way before taking off.

"What's the deal?" I cross my arms and prepare for the heat.

"What's the deal?" she sneers, her eyes coming to mine and flaming with anger. "The deal is Maya is eleven-years-old and needs a swift slap to get a lesson in manners. Cole didn't want to get up this morning, and I found out he snuck out of bed and played some fucking video game online until midnight. The teachers asked for volunteers to bring refreshments for the assembly, and since we were running so damn late, I had to swing through and get donuts, which means all the snooty-ass moms are going to have a shit fit that I brought unhealthy choices. Not to mention, it's teacher appreciation week, and today is gift day."

That explains all the bags.

"Okay, let's break this down. You slap my daughter, we're gonna have a problem. She's getting too old for a spanking, and if we need to punish her, we'll do it together. But you haul off and slap her, you'll answer to me."

The anger in her eyes begins to glow, her face twisting in disgust. I continue before she can respond. "You needed help with refreshments, you should have fucking called me. I would have picked them up. But, just saying, donuts are fine. Any snooty bitch that has a problem with it can go fuck themselves. As for Cole, I'll have a talk with him. He's losing his gaming system and his technology until the end of school."

"You think you have all the answers, don't you? I want to rip out the gaming system forever."

"School doesn't end for three weeks. That will feel like forever to a nine-year-old."

"You're gonna tell him. I'm sick of being the mean parent."

"I have no problem telling him. I have no problem disciplining our kids if you'd tell me what's going on before you're ready to have a rip-roaring brawl in the school parking lot. You need something, or there's a problem with our kids, you call me."

"We don't have time for this right now. It's already embarrassing enough for Maya that she's the only friend in her group with split parents. I'm not going to make it worse by arguing with you in public."

I bite back my reply because it's a never-ending battle with Connie when it comes to our kids and our situation. She claims it's humiliating and traumatic, blaming me. I've learned to shoulder the blame. But when it comes to my children, I've always put them first.

"I'll carry these." It's my way of shutting down the conversation.

We walk quietly into the school and find the kids grouped by grade in the auditorium. I follow Connie as she delivers the donuts to the refreshment area, which is overloaded with dozens and dozens of donuts.

She slices her eyes to me, and I don't hide my amused grin. "Shut up," she scowls.

"I'll talk to the kids tonight when I pick them up for the weekend. Cole will be easy; he knows he messed up. Maya, I'll figure it out," I tell her when we find a section against the wall to wait for the program to begin.

"Maya is about to start middle school and is prepubescent. She's going to be a royal pain for a while."

I cringe at the reminder my baby girl is close to not being a baby anymore. It's a constant battle, and I know she's much harsher to Connie, but I'm also more relaxed in my parenting style.

I put the bags I've been carrying on the floor, barely glancing inside. The assembly starts, and halfway through, an all too familiar scent fills the air around me. My head jerks from one side to the other, scanning every face in the room. I tell myself it's crazy. There's no way it could be, but I'd know that smell anywhere in the whole damn world. It's a tropical breeze—coconuts, lime, honey, and sea spray. And at the base is the faintest scent of Marc Jacobs perfume, a perfume I bought exactly six times in my life.

It's the unmistakable scent of Darby Graham.

I continue to look around, grunting when Connie elbows me in the ribs with a *'what the hell is wrong with you?'* glare. The rest of the program drags on like mud, each presentation seemingly longer than the last. When they finally announce the last fifth-grade award, my skin is crawling.

"Are you sick?" Connie has the decency to seem concerned.

"No, why?"

"I've seen you this jumpy four times in your life, and two of the times I was in labor."

I don't care enough to ask about the other two instances. And, thankfully, I'm saved when Maya comes at me from the side, crushing me with her excited screeches.

Cole joins next, and Connie positions us for pictures. The instant I crouch to the floor between my kids, that scent almost knocks me to my ass. It's everywhere. She's everywhere.

"Dad, you're looking a little pale." Cole places the back of his hand on my forehead.

"I'm good, buddy."

"Why don't we give your teachers their gifts so your dad can get out of this hot auditorium?" Connie gently pulls the kids away to give me air.

I yank the bags off the ground, ready to get the hell out of here.

It's then I spy it, the black card with the iridescent blue scroll. Dots, swirls, and the perfectly slanted initials DG lay in the middle of it all.

The emblem, the brand, the unforgettable blue.

My throat burns, my head spins, and my gut rolls over so quickly the coffee from earlier threatens to come up. The memory of the first time I saw this design assaults me.

Darby's spring break, senior year. She was lying on a lounge chair by the pool, and I was ready to pounce, to drag her back to our room until we left the next day. She started flipping through a notebook, and the picture caught my eye.

I grabbed the notebook, turned back to the page, and raised an eyebrow in question.

"It's a sketch. I may need a brand one day," she explained casually.

"And the blue?"

"That's not just any blue. It's a specialized blue. The kind of color that took layering and perfecting and is so unique it can't be duplicated."

"Why so perfected?"

"Because it's the color of your eyes."

That was it. I'd known for a while it was going to happen, but that was when I told her. She was going to marry me.

I swallow hard, staring at the business card until I have my thoughts remotely under control.

"Hey, what'd y'all get your teachers this year?" Cole and Maya look at their mom for answers.

"I picked up some of these new chocolates my boss has been raving about. They sell them at the shop by the office."

I jump to my feet, ripping the card, and tearing the delicate ribbons with it. "You need some cash?"

"Are you actually offering?"

"You usually have no problem taking my money. How much?" I try to sound normal, but the acid in my voice gives me away.

She goes back to glaring, and I feel like a dick with my kids as witnesses. I pull a few hundred-dollar-bills out of my wallet, fold them in half, and step closer to slide the money in her hand. "Do something nice for yourself this weekend while I have the kids, Connie. Thank you for picking up the end of the year gifts." My focus goes back to Maya and Cole. "We'll grill with Uncle Miller tonight."

There are murmurs of approval as I say goodbye and ignore Connie's inquisitive scowl.

When I get to my truck, my adrenaline is pumping so hard I'm light-headed. The card still tucked in my hand is like a burning poker on the skin. The fucking smell fills the cab of my truck, and I know she had her hands on those packages.

Chocolate was her specialty. That was twelve years ago.

I haven't touched a piece of chocolate since.

•—•—•—•—•

"Where are you?" Miller's shout is amplified throughout my truck.

"Going to be late."

"Why am I not fucking surprised? I thought you were going to leave this alone."

"I never said that."

"You agreed Friday night to let this shit lie."

"No, I drank beer and let you rant on about how this was nothing but a coincidence and trying to find her would be like opening a fatal war wound."

"I didn't get through to you at all. Waste of my damn breath."

"Miller, this is Darby we're talking about here."

Just saying her name sends a pang to my chest.

"Nothing has ever been just Darby to you. That's why I'm concerned. You've never had a clear head when it came to that chick."

"You used to love *'that chick'.*"

"Loved her and then loathed her. That bitch nearly destroyed you. Leave her in the past."

"You ever go to the depths of hell, you'll understand where I'm coming from. Until then, you need to back the fuck off and let me do what I need to do. If she's in this town, I deserve to know."

"And then what? Chase her down like the twenty-three-year-old pussy-whipped idiot that took the abuse the first time?"

Anger boils in my blood, and I swerve into the small parking lot to stop from turning around and heading back to the office to kick my brother's sorry ass.

"You're a fucking dick."

"I may be a dick, but I care about you. Sometimes, the truth hurts, and you telling me about this may be the only thing that saves you from spiraling down the black hole we dragged you out of."

That stings. Everything about this situation slices me up inside. He doesn't need to remind me of the past; I lived through it. I fucked up big time, and not a day goes by I'm not reminded of that. Lucky for me, I have two great kids that help ease the regret from mistakes that should have been avoided.

"You know what she meant to me and what we went through," I point out, grinding my teeth to keep from losing my cool.

"Just text me when you're on your way to a job site. I have some papers that need your signature." The line goes dead.

Having my older brother jump my ass is another fucking notch to add to an already shitty Monday. All weekend, my head was swimming with questions about Darby. Focus was impossible. For the first time ever, I asked Connie if I could drop the kids off early last night, lying about an early morning meeting that couldn't be rescheduled. It was another dick move because the kids were already in bad moods. Cole didn't like losing his video games, and Maya didn't like getting a lecture from her dad about respecting her mom. In order to try to cover my ass, we went shopping, and I stocked Connie's house with enough groceries to last a month.

One look at her when she opened the door proved she didn't believe my excuse, but she didn't push the issue. When I got home, I grabbed the scotch, opened my computer, and spent the next four hours glued to the internet. Then I sat staring into space, drinking more than I should have, thinking about what the hell I should do.

Every sensible thought told me to let this go. Self-preservation was at the top of the list. But my heart had other plans, and when I woke up this morning, the decision was made.

The reminder on my phone dings, and at the same time, an older man appears at the window of the storefront, unlocking the door and propping it open for the few customers waiting outside.

I'd hoped to be in the store alone so I could question the owner, but it looks like that's not going to happen. The combination of curious energy and caffeine overload has my nerves jacked up when I walk in.

Connie asked me to meet her here once for lunch at the deli tucked in the corner. That's a small portion of the interior. The rest is floor to ceiling shelves displaying local merchandise. Anything from handmade glassware to local artwork can be found here—not my kind of place.

It's impossible to miss the large display cooler next to the register. Candies and treats of all kinds line the top with samples set out in front of them. My heart hammers in my chest, setting my blood rushing faster at the items in the cooler. Small, delicate, beautifully decorated petit fours are stacked thick across an entire shelf.

My hands tingle with phantom cramps, thinking about the night Darby insisted I help her make those fucking petit fours for my mom's fiftieth birthday party. They were a pain in my ass, and I swore I'd never do that again.

"Can I help you?" A perky, upbeat voice slices through my thoughts, and I find a woman peering through the display at me.

"Just browsing. My kids mentioned your new selection of chocolate. We gave them to their teachers last week."

"We started carrying them ten days ago. The manager cleared out this whole display after last week's popularity. By Friday morning, we had a line out the door. It was crazy!"

"Must be good stuff."

"Would you like a sample?"

"Nah, I'm not a huge chocolate person."

Her eyes bulge at my statement, and it's a full two seconds before she shakes her head in disbelief. "That's too bad. It's not like regular chocolate. The baker has a specialty truffle that is flying off the shelves. We got a new delivery this morning."

At the mention of truffle, my heart actually stops beating. The words feel like sandpaper on my throat when I force myself to ask, "Does it have a name?"

"Funny you should ask. I figure it's something to do with the dark chocolate. It's Darose."

"Darose," I repeat.

Darby Rose... the name I chose the night she created it.

"Yes, if you ever change your mind, you should try a sample. We keep them back here."

"I'll remember that. How about a few of these cookies for my kids." I don't even know what I point to, but she nods and gets to work.

"You can check out at the end of the counter." She gestures to where the man who opened the door is working a register.

"Great choice," he says cheerfully, taking my money.

"Can you tell me more about the baker?" The words slip past my lips before I can stop them.

"I've known her family for years. She's quite the amazing baker, and having her back—" The statement dies when he glances up, recognition dawning in his eyes. He knows who I am. His movements become flustered as he shoves the box in a bag and hands me my change. "Her website tells all you need to know." He gazes over my shoulder to the next customer, effectively dismissing me.

When I get to my truck, I toss the bag in the passenger seat and slam my hand to my steering wheel. Anger builds from the bottom of my soul. I dissected every section and every word on her website at least a dozen times last night. *DB Creations.com* caters to the business owner interested in carrying the products and the consumer interested in learning more about how to request goods. There are a few snippets of information about Darby's background and training, never mentioning her by name. There is no personal information and specifically no mention of her leaving Charlotte and relocating her business to Charleston.

I glared at the 'contact DB creations' link for an hour, stewing over sending a message. What would I say? The last time we saw each other, we tore each other apart. It was brutal and savage, her cutting me so deep I couldn't stop myself from lashing out until we were both broken beyond repair. Then I walked away.

When I realized my mistake and went back to grovel at her feet, ready to take any form of punishment she could dish out, she was gone.

I'll never forget the way her parents looked at me the day I showed up at their house. Pity, sympathy, rage, confusion—all wrapped up together. They told me she'd gone to Charlotte. She left everything— her dreams, her land, her family. More importantly, she left me.

My pride was shattered, my heart broken, and the anger set in. Instead of going after her, I stayed. Then I fucked up, hurting a lot of people in the process, but was left with no choice but to take responsibility for my actions.

I never tried to contact her, never apologized for the things I'd said. My life took a new turn, and I forced myself to move on. It hurt like a motherfucker, but day-by-day, I adjusted to a world without Darby.

After all these years, who would have thought she'd return? But now, I have my definitive answer, which my gut already knew.

Darby Graham is back.

Chapter 2

Darby

"We have the weirdest parents on the planet." The dregs of sugar at the bottom of my glass make me gag. "And this is the last glass of sweet tea I drink forever."

"Heard both of those statements before." Evin leans back in his chair, tilting it on two legs and perching his feet on the table in an art he perfected a long time ago. I tried it twice and, both times, landed ass back, embarrassed as hell, and one time with a knot on my head.

"Why do two people who love each other this much get divorced?"

It's the same question I've had since I was twenty-five and my parents announced they were getting a divorce. I was in Charlotte and cried for three weeks before my mom and dad showed up together to explain. They never really set me clear, but I had to accept it. Since then, they have continued to not only be best friends and awesome parents, but they grew suspiciously closer. Proof of that is playing out in front of me as Dad guides Mom across the living room floor, holding her close as they dance. He swears it's the best therapy for her.

She agrees.

They talk softly, huddling close, and he holds her injured hip delicately. Edward Graham loves my mother, and she loves him, so why aren't they still married?

"I have a bar in the shed. Can we make a run for it?" I whisper.

"Lead the fucking way." His chair hits the floor hard, thudding as we stand.

"Ed, I think our children are trying to get away from us." Mom tosses her head our way.

"Let them go. I'll get you to bed safely." Dad winks at me.

I race outside the back door, my brother on my heels. Once we are safely inside the shed, I scream, "Make it stop!!!"

"Where's the booze?" is all I get out of him.

"Everywhere. Full liquor bar set up in the corner, and cold beer and wine are in the fridge."

"Where do I start?"

"How about pouring me a glass of wine? Get what you want."

"I'll open the Pinot if you get this straggler off of me."

I notice Runner is now full–up on his hind legs, paws on Evin's chest, and begging for attention. My poor brother is still in his work slacks and shirt, and my dog's breathing doggy breath with drool. I can't help but curl over in hysterics, laughing and clapping until my baby pushes him away and pounces on me.

Runner licks, cuddles, and wrestles until I have him half-pinned to the ground, shaking him like a ragdoll. He woofs in approval, lapping his tongue everywhere.

"He needs finishing school." Evin stands over me with two glasses of wine, watching with amusement.

"He has me. I'm as finished as they come."

"If you say so. Meet you on the deck." He steps over us, opening the door and whistling loud. Runner perks up, barely glancing at me for approval, and takes off outside.

I haul my ass off the floor, grab the bottle, and meet my brother on the deck. My butt hits the seat next to his, and I take the wine glass, almost inhaling the whole thing with the first gulp.

"Bliss." I exhale.

"She's not stupid," Evin says.

"I know, but considering she shouldn't drink on her meds, I don't want to rub it in her face. She's dying for a glass of wine, and Dad has explicitly told me he forbids it. I'm not getting in the middle of it. Plus, if she wants to judge my liquor lifestyle, she can bring her ass down the steps, across the lawn, and into the shed to ask me for a drink."

He chuckles, toasting my glass lightly. "Good to have you home."

"Thanks."

"She is better when you're here."

"That's questionable since she has critiqued every healthy meal fixed, quaffed at my attempt to do therapeutic yoga, and blown off the spa baths. She only shows appreciation when I bring home all my left-over items from the bakery."

"It's her way."

"I do kinda like being around. I've missed this place."

"It'd be nice if you stuck around." The good-natured mood of our conversation changes.

"I'm here for now."

"You're not fooling anyone, Darby. Sneaking out at four-thirty in the morning while it's still dark to go to work. The bakery is so hidden and non-descript no one knows it exists. Having your supplies delivered here and hauling them into town by yourself. Hiring a different delivery driver that meets you around the corner. Then sneaking back and hiding out with Mom until it's time for bed. It's been three weeks, and you act like a fugitive on the run."

"You're being overly dramatic. I've always worked early because

14

most of my deliveries need to be in the stores when they open. All the rest is schematics. It's called being efficient. And I don't hide out with Mom. I use my afternoons for my administrative business, and I like having her company. My contracts have specific outlines on my expectations."

"That may have been true in Charlotte, but I know for a fact you aren't signing contracts here. The stores you're working with have week-by-week agreements. I heard someone in the bank talking about how Mr. Rosen is dying to get your products in his restaurant."

"We've spoken. I can't overextend my capabilities right now. He wants daily desserts, and that's too much of a strain."

"Hire someone. Hell, hire two people part-time. You have the business in the pipeline that will justify the additional overhead."

"I'm not ready to take that on."

"No, you're not ready to make the commitment, which leads me back to asking, how long are you staying?"

I swig the rest of my wine, refill it, and try to find a way to answer him diplomatically. "I'm staying as long as Mom needs me."

"Mom's fine, Darby. You knew that the day you blew out of town. Home health was set up, therapy was scheduled, and she has a huge network here."

"I felt like she needed me. Why the inquisition? You're being borderline rude and kinda intrusive into my business."

"I'm not intrusive; I'm honest. When you came home, I made the decision to sit back and see how this was going to play out. But I don't like the way you've secluded yourself. It's not healthy."

"It's fine. No deadlines, no pressure, easy to enjoy lifestyle. This is invigorating."

"You're a fucking liar. Two months ago, you would have gawked at the idea of being a social hermit. Your social life was exhausting."

"There you go." I tip my wine to him to make my point. "I'm no longer exhausted."

"Don't take us for fools. We see right through your charade."

"There is no charade. I signed a lease on a bakery space, for God's sake."

"You signed a six-month lease."

"You, of all people, know I was in a rush. You're the one who had to view it for me. Signing a shorter lease was practical until I could get here and actually see if it would be sufficient."

His lips curl into a sly grin, and his eyes fill with a challenge. "How's it working out?"

"It's great. The location and size are perfect for what I want. The landlord is spectacular and kept all our business dealings private."

"Mmhmm." He sips his wine, keeping his eyes on me. My knees bounce nervously at the way he's staring. He's older than me by only four minutes, and the twin intuition has always been more dominant in his genes.

"Oh, fuck it." I snatch the bottle and drink straight from it, guzzling like an alcoholic junkie.

"Classy, Darb."

"It's your fault. I'm going to have to be drunk to deal with you."

"What if I told you the owner of the bakery approached me about selling the building? He's going to give you first rights to refusal, then contact a broker."

The wine lands like lead in the pit of my stomach, and I swallow a few times to keep it down. "I'm not sure I can stay," I admit with a whisper. "The next six months will be a trial run."

"You can't hide from him forever. It's been twelve years. We'd all hoped you'd moved on, but from the expression on your face, I can see it was wishful thinking."

My eyes sting as humiliation sears through my blood. It's embarrassing how even the mention of him from my brother makes me feel like twelve years was only yesterday. "He's the one who moved on. He moved right along, replacing me."

"I don't like the son of a bitch, but to his defense, you didn't give him a choice."

Tears well up and spill down my cheeks quicker than I can wipe them away. "You can't do this to me, Evin. I'm trying."

He takes the bottle out of one hand and my glass out of the other, placing them on the table between us. I suck in a deep breath, trying to control the overwhelming emotions swelling in my chest.

"Jesus, Darby, you still fucking love him."

"Always have. And I'm afraid I always will. There's no way to un-love Pierce. That's why I can't commit to staying in Charleston. The chance of seeing him every day is crippling," I choke out.

"I'm sorry." His voice is pained, and when I glance up, he's staring at me with so much remorse it hurts.

"It's okay, but can we not talk about this anymore? I'm here for at least six months, and then we'll see what happens."

He nods in agreement. We sit in silence a few minutes, the heaviness of the conversation slipping away.

"How about I open another bottle of wine that is free of backwash?"

16

I grab the bottle back and take a much lighter sip. "Help yourself. I'm gonna stick with this one."

He stands, reaching over to pat my shoulder. "Hopefully, we can convince you to stay."

"Not a chance if Mom and Dad don't stop with the googly-eyes and touchy-feely, lovey-dovey shit. It's grossing me out. Our parents have a more active sex life than I do."

He winces, his face taking on a distorted grimace. "On that note, I'm moving to whiskey."

I giggle into my bottle and try to remember the last time Evin and I had a real night together. It's been way too long.

No matter what happens in the next few months, I'm going to enjoy this time with my family. And, hopefully, avoid Pierce.

•—•—•—•—•

The beauty of running my own business and starting fresh is having some freedom to do whatever I want. Baking and creating delicacies have never felt like a job to me, but the administrative aspect has been my least favorite part. My OCD tendencies don't allow me to hire an assistant, and that's why I've decided to be more selective with my clientele in Charleston.

I used to work fifteen-hour days, but I did have some help. A few part-time employees helped make it work, and my business lawyer, who is also my best friend, was an asset.

Evin wasn't kidding; Mr. Rosen is dying to get my desserts in his restaurant. And he isn't alone. I scroll through my emails and groan at the number of responses I need to send.

"Bad news in the world of sweets?" Mom attempts to be funny.

"Kinda," I mutter, not paying attention to her.

"You're going to get premature wrinkles with that scowl. I'm too young to have a daughter that looks like a pug."

"Don't you need to take a nap? Or rest? Or do something that a woman who recently went through major surgery does that doesn't involve nagging the shit out of her daughter?'

"Nope, I'm all tapped up on rest. The therapist was easy on me today."

"Remind me to fire her tomorrow."

She takes the chair next to me, peering over my shoulder. "Fill me in."

"I'm wanted."

"Being wanted is a good thing. Billy said your stuff is flying out of his store."

"Yes, but look at my inbox. All these are requests to meet and discuss business proposals."

"Seems like a good problem to have."

"But I'm not ready to take on this much. My load is perfect right now. I've got it under control."

She takes my hand, pulling my attention from the computer screen. Concern is written all over her face. "You always have it under control, but would it be bad to have some help?"

"What do you mean?"

"Let me help you."

"I'm here to help you, not the other way around."

"And I love you for it. I love having our dinners every night and knowing you are close if there's a problem. But we both know I'm better and getting stronger every day. Cooking my dinners, cleaning the house, organizing my therapy and home healthcare—it's great. But it's coming to an end. Let me help."

"You can't come to the bakery all day, Mom. It's too much."

"No, but I can take some of the administrative work off your plate. I can check your emails, respond the way you want, and with a little training from Stephanie, maybe help with other stuff."

I sit stunned at her suggestion. "Are you proposing working for me? You hated working for Dad."

"First of all, I didn't work for your dad. I worked *with* your dad in our business. Secondly, I didn't hate it. I just wanted to keep control of the two rugrats we birthed, and he was needy."

"Evin was the rugrat. I was the angel," I correct her.

She pats my hand, smiling widely. "If you say so."

"You'd want to help me?"

"It would keep me busy. Since I'll probably never ride a horse again and my free time is about to drive me batty, it would be a good thing."

"What about me being here in the afternoons? Our time together?"

"If you had three more hours a day in the bakery, how much more could you produce?"

I do the calculations in my head and think about my ovens, the freezers, and the time I could work with creating new things. "Probably enough to take on three new businesses, with the understanding they had to be afternoon clients. No specialty orders at this point. Weekend orders will be delivered on Friday afternoons, and I'm keeping my Saturdays and Sundays free."

"Okay."

"And no huge celebration clients."

"Yet."

"None!" I emphasize loudly.

"I think you are underestimating your ability to handle new clients."

"I think you are underestimating what my current business load is. I am happy with petit fours, cookies, truffles, and chocolate-covered fruits, which, by the way, have to be refrigerated."

She tilts her head to the side, looking at the ceiling with squinted eyes, then looks to my computer with pursed lips. She repeats the notion a few times then blows out a breath. "Hmm, it's not exactly what I was thinking, but I guess I'll accept your job offer."

"There was no job offer!"

"I'm free to start training on Saturday, right after you drive me to the mall for new work clothes."

"Sweat pants and t-shirts are fine, you wench." I scowl, realizing I've been played to the nth degree by Annie Graham.

"Maybe after a few months, with my salary, I can afford a gas-guzzling, rich people, slick ride like yours."

"I didn't offer you a salary!"

"We'll see." She stands easily and breezes away, not a hint of pain in her hip or pelvis.

My phone rings, and I almost hit ignore before my mom calls over her shoulder, "You may want to answer Stephanie's call. She's excited about our new arrangement and ready to visit next week."

Fuck me.

My mom and best friend have just conspired against me and won.

Well-played, girls. Well-played.

Chapter 3
Pierce

"I'm sorry, but unless you have an appointment, I can't squeeze you in today. How about Friday?" The young receptionist is only doing her job, but I'm in no mood to deal.

"Darlin', do me a favor and call Evin. Tell him Pierce Kendrick is here to see him. He'll make time."

Her eyes bulge at the recognition of my name, and she bites her lower lip nervously. Kendrick Construction is a huge client at this bank, and most people know my family name. Dad handles most of this side of the business, but in the off chance I'm involved, I always go to a different branch. It was an unspoken pact between Evin and me.

We used to be friends and knew that the way things were going with Darby and me, we'd one day be brothers. The first time we saw each other after she left, I took one look at him and knew he knew what happened between us. He glared at me with a hatred that seared deep. No matter what had happened, he blamed me. From that day on, all ties were severed. On the few occasions we ran into each other, it was awkward and tense. I'm stepping over the line today for one reason only.

I need answers.

Hesitantly, she presses a button on her earpiece and turns her back, whispering. When she spins around, her face is pale and filled with confusion. "Mr. Graham has requested you meet him in the back parking lot next to his vehicle. He's parked in space number eleven."

I don't even say thanks, just flick a hand in acknowledgment and take off. It's easy to spot Evin's truck without looking at the space numbers. Large, black, extended cab, great for hauling a boat or hunting. It's the same exact model I drive.

He's leaning against the back tailgate, his arms crossed over his chest in a suit that was no doubt custom tailored. This is not surprising. Evin was meant to be in the corporate world. Even behind his sunglasses, I sense him sizing me up.

"Darby is back in town." I get straight to the point.

"Is that supposed to be a question?"

"No, it's a fucking statement. What I want to know is why?"

"She's visiting family."

"Don't bullshit me."

He remains silent.

"She's setting up her business here, planting roots back in Charleston. Don't deny it."

He rips his sunglasses off, and anger flames in his eyes. "Stay away from her."

For the first time, the thought that something is wrong hits me. "Is she okay?"

"Okay? You have the audacity to ask me that shit?"

"Answer the damn question, Evin. Is Darby all right?"

"You don't deserve answers. Stay away from her and let my family do what we need to do."

"What the fuck does that mean?"

"It means you did enough damage to last a lifetime, and everyone that loves her suffered. We're going to do what we need to do to bring her back. You do not get to ruin this for my family."

"In case you forgot, she's the one who left me."

His nostrils flare, and he takes a step into my space. "How are your kids, Pierce? What about Connie?"

"Back the fuck up and don't bring my kids into this."

"Then leave my sister alone. Let her be the memory you shoved into shit when you told her she was a selfish bitch."

He rips the wound wide open with the reminder of what I said to her that day. But there's something in his tone that doesn't sit well. "You're acting like that happened yesterday. It's been twelve goddamned years."

"Twelve years for you but not for her. If you ever cared even a little about her, leave her alone and let us take care of her."

My body goes tight, and my hands curl into fists at my side. Evin and I are about the same size, but I have the advantage of muscle. "Don't you dare say that shit to me. I fucking loved your sister."

"Well, then maybe you can dig up some of that compassion from your black heart and listen to me. Stay away."

"I'm giving you the courtesy of talking to me now. My next stop is to Edward and Annie."

He flinches, staring me down, and I know I've hit a nerve. Edward, Annie, and I always had a special relationship. Losing them hurt. One of the reasons I didn't keep in touch was the guilt of knowing how I treated Darby that day. Unlike Evin, on the occasions I've run into Edward or Annie, they've always been kind and cordial.

"Come on, Evin. You owe me this," I try again.

"Any favors I may have owed you disappeared the minute you knocked my sister up and then blamed her when she lost the baby."

My balance falters, and I stagger back, his words blaring in my head. "I didn't blame Darby. I wanted to help her. She didn't want me."

"Yet, you moved on quite well."

"Is that what she told you? That I blamed her?"

"It doesn't matter. Leave it alone." He shoves past me, his shoulder ramming mine roughly, sending me stumbling.

Instead of chasing after him to demand answers, I'm frozen in place, wondering what the hell just happened. More importantly, does Darby believe I blamed her?

•—•—•—•—•

"I'm scared, Pierce." She clung to me, burying her face in my shirt. "What happens if it's positive?"

"Then, we'll deal."

"It's too soon. We aren't ready. How did I let this happen?" Her body trembled, and she began to sob again. Moisture seeped through the material of my shirt and soaked into my skin.

"Shh," I tried to soothe her, kissing the top of her head over and over. "You're not alone here. We talked about having children. Maybe it's earlier than we planned."

Her head popped up, and my chest seized at her tear-stained cheeks and swollen eyes. My protective instincts kicked in, and I fought the urge to crush her to me, shield her from anything that brought fear to her beautiful face.

"I just graduated and don't even have a job yet! I live with my parents, and you share an apartment with your brother. We aren't exactly equipped to be parents right now."

"You do have a job, and we'll move into our own place."

"I make desserts and cakes for parties out of my mom's kitchen. That's hardly a job."

"People love your stuff. I'm one-third owner of a construction company. I'll build you a place to bake, and we'll expand your business. Together, we can do this."

Her light brown eyes began to glimmer, and the trembling lessened. "You'd build me a place to bake?"

"I'll build you anything you want."

"You're not mad?"

I threaded my fingers through the hair at the side of her head and gently caressed. "Do I look mad? I'm a man that loves you, and if you're having my baby, I'll shout from the rooftops."

"Our parents are going to freak."

"I'm not worried about our parents. They know where we're headed. I haven't hidden my plans."

"People will think we are getting married because of the baby."

23

"Those people can fuck themselves. We know the truth."

The timer on Darby's phone beeped, and she sucked in a deep breath, scooting away to grab the little white test on my vanity. She looked at me, the fear creeping back into her face, and I nodded in encouragement. Together, we both looked down at the little window that read 'pregnant'.

My world changed in that second, and this time, I didn't stop from crushing her to me. To any other twenty-three-year-old man, the news may have been devastating, but to me, it was everything. I held her tight, letting the reality of the news sink in. Darby and I were going to have a baby.

"I'll call my doctor tomorrow and make an appointment. It'll be best to have the confirmation and see how far along I am. There's no telling the date of conception."

I couldn't help the smile that spread across my lips. The day Darby finished her last final and the pressure was off, our relationship shifted. She left her apartment and moved back in with her parents, but there were no rules. We took weekend trips, we partied with friends, and she spent practically every night here with me. Our sex life had always been great, but it exploded. We both became insatiable and wild, finding new ways to drive the other insane. This baby could be the result of a wild night of fucking on every surface of my room, or the result of me rolling over in the morning and making love to her sweet and slow. Either way, it didn't matter because he or she was conceived out of love.

"Get the first appointment and let me know when to be there. I'm not missing a thing."

She wiggled out of my strong hold and lifted her hands from between us to frame my face. Her eyes were no longer swimming in tears, but shining translucent amber. "This is unreal."

"This is our life. Planned or unplanned, we're going to be kick-ass parents."

"Are you gloating?"

"Hell yes, I knocked up Darby Graham. Now, no one will ever be able to steal you away from me."

Her lips twitched until she had no choice but to smile with a giggle. "You're a crass caveman, but I guess there are worse baby daddies I could have chosen."

"Damn straight. You think we can get off this cold tile floor so I can carry you to bed and show you how a caveman celebrates?"

"Well, seeing as the damage is done, no need to stop now."

Just like that, my Darby was back. The weight of the situation wasn't lost, but in true Darby fashion, she was ready to deal. I shifted out

*from under her, and when I was steady on my feet, I slid one hand under
her knees, the other behind her back, and lifted her.*

"How much time do we have until Miller gets home?" She
skimmed her lips along the underside of my jaw.

"Don't fucking care."

*"You know, I have heard that pregnant women want sex all the
time. You better start working on your stamina."*

My eyes fly open, and I realize my hand is wrapped around my
dick, stroking lightly. Dreams of Darby stopped years ago, but this
morning, the memory of what happened next has my cock aching. The
scene plays out vividly.

*Her body naked, her thighs trembled against my cheeks as I ate
her like a starving man. She writhed against my mouth, begging for more,
and the sweet taste of her coming apart on my tongue was made even
sweeter by the fact she was pregnant.*

*Crawling up her body, I knelt above her, sinking my cock into her
soaking wet heat. Her muscles clamped down hard, tightening around me
until I felt my balls ready to constrict.*

*Her eyes were locked with mine, bright with satisfaction and
challenge. She was testing me, knowing from experience that I could
barely hold out when she locked her ankles around my waist and
squeezed my dick with her pussy, angling so I was deep inside her.*

My strokes turn furious as I remember everything about that
morning. Her moans, gasps, and screams so loud they shook the
windows. Forgetting about the baby, I'd pummeled into her so hard I
knew she would have bruises. It was wild, frantic, and crazy, with Darby
demanding I give her everything I had.

A deep growl rumbles from my throat as I come, knifing up and
feeling the streams hit my stomach.

"What the fuck, Pierce?" I bark into the dark room, unsure what
the hell is happening.

Am I losing my damn mind? Jerking off in the dark to the
memory of my pregnant girlfriend from over a decade ago? The same
girlfriend that I've spent all this time trying to forget.

When my breathing returns to normal, I haul myself out of bed
and go straight to the shower. There's no way I'm going back to sleep. I
go through the motions of my morning routine on autopilot, my mind
replaying the conversation with Evin over and over.

I'm on my second cup of coffee, staring aimlessly at my fridge
when the card catches my eye. It's a handmade gift from Cole for
Father's Day three years ago. There's a similar one from Maya when she

was his age. I scan over all the keepsakes the kids made through the years that are plastered over the surface.

Going to Evin was a mistake. Instead of getting answers, I'm even more confused. He kept referring to his family taking care of Darby, never mentioning a husband or kids. I always assumed she moved on at some point. It hurt like hell to think of her with someone else, but I had no right to judge, considering the situation I got myself in with Connie.

No one outside our families knew Darby was pregnant. We hadn't shared the news with our circle of friends. When she lost the baby, she decided not to tell anyone, saying it made it easier to move past the loss. That made our split even messier. Friends were forced to choose sides, and most of them chose mine, thinking she had turned into a fucking bitch. As much as I wanted to explain that she was going through a tough time, I kept my mouth shut.

She took off, and people tried to convince me it was for the best. Since I didn't know why she left and had no explanation, it was easier to let them believe whatever they wanted. Nothing changed the fact that I was a wreck.

"Any favors I may have owed you disappeared the minute you knocked my sister up and then blamed her when she lost the baby."

Twelve years have passed, yet it's like time is standing still.

"Fuck me." I drop my coffee mug in the sink and grab my keys. There's only one person in the world who can answer my questions, and I should have started with her in the first place.

My guess is she's staying at the farm, so that's where I'm heading.

Chapter 4

Darby

"You knew this could happen, sweetie. Don't act so shocked," Mom says breezily like she didn't just drop the bomb that Pierce showed up at the house this morning looking for me.

"I was prepared to run into him in public, not have him stroll casually up to my house like a welcome visitor."

"Don't know how you could run into him in public when you live like a recluse."

I disregard her remark and chew nervously on the inside of my cheek. "First, he shows up at Evin's work, and now, he comes there? Why, why, why???"

"My guess is he wants to talk to you."

"But why? How does he even know I'm back in Charleston?"

"That is a good question. I didn't ask him that. Our visit was cut short when Jessie showed up."

I swallow the groan at the thought of Jessie meeting Pierce. Jessie is Mom's twenty-something occupational therapist. She's tall, voluptuous, and not one part of her body has been touched by gravity. I've seen the way she looks at Evin and can only imagine what went through her mind when she got a glimpse of Pierce.

I have no right to jealousy, but old habits die hard. Even if I haven't laid eyes on him in... Wait! What did my mom say? "Did you say your visit was cut short, meaning you invited him in for a chat?"

"Oh, look at the time! I need to go... um... need to finish making these boxes. Don't forget to check your email. I sent you a few notes. See you tonight!" She hangs up before I can question her more.

"UGGGGGGGHHHH!" I scream into the dead air.

Runner lets out a weak 'woof' and rolls to his side, clearly irritated with being woken. There's a loud banging on the door that causes us both to jump, and this time he spurts up, clearly excited about having visitors.

I press the app on my phone that allows me to view the front parking area and the door. When I see the black truck parked in the first spot, I roll my eyes. There's no telling why Evin would come to the bakery in the middle of the day, but whatever the reason, it's most likely going to annoy me. Mom probably called him first, scared I was going to crumble apart, and he hightailed it over here.

The banging starts again, and I flip the deadbolt, speaking as I open the door. "No need to worry. I'm not curled on the floor in the fetal position, rocking back and forth. Just because I shed a few tears the other night doesn't mean—"

The words die on my lips, and my heart lodges in my throat. It's not Evin standing at my door.

Pierce Cole Kendrick.

His iridescent blue eyes pierce into me, and I'm motionless.

The image of the twenty-three-year-old I've held on to for all these years is nothing compared to the man standing in front of me.

It should be impossible, but he's even more gorgeous than ever. Time has been good to him. His dark, thick hair is messy and unruly like he doesn't care. The Kendrick Construction shirt stretches against his broad chest and shoulders, straining over his biceps. His cheeks, chin, and lips are covered with a light stubble that I know from experience is soft to the touch. He's tanned from working in the sun, and the color of his complexion sets off his mesmerizing blue eyes. My gaze rakes up and down, taking in every inch of him.

He's always towered over me. I loved the feeling of standing next to him and having that sense of protection. Today is different.

I feel the burn as he glowers down at me.

"Darby." Harsh, bitter, flat... not an ounce of emotion when he says my name.

A chill dances over my skin as time stands still, and I stare at the man I've loved for almost half my life. Pain stabs in my chest, and I clasp the door handle with all my might, hoping it will give me the support if my knees give out.

I open my mouth to respond, but it's hard to talk over the rock stuck in my throat.

"Darby, can I come in?" This time, there's a slice of warmth to his tone.

I step back, opening the door wider. He breezes by, the scent of his cologne lingering, and my grip on the door handle turns into a death clutch.

Runner picks up on the tension and nudges his body through the space, sniffing the area around Pierce. It doesn't take more than a few seconds for him to decide there's no threat, and he starts butting along Pierce's calves.

So much for a guard dog.

"Run, sit," I croak out, finding my voice.

Runner plops on his butt, swishing his tail and panting at Pierce expectantly.

"He friendly?" he asks right as Runner's paw jets out for attention.

"He's more of a hugger, but since you're a new face, he's trying to shake." Slowly, my senses are returning, and this time when I speak, it doesn't sound shaky.

Pierce crouches down and takes Runner's paw, pumps it up and down, then pats his head as he stands back up.

"What are you doing here, Pierce?"

His hands go to his hips, and his eyes sweep the room, passing over me and taking in the space. This was always a professional habit of his, looking around, sizing up the area, probably doing a mental calculation of the dimensions. To some people, this place may look small, but it's the perfect size for me. His eyes land on the massive cookie sheets packed with chocolate-covered fruit.

The silence grates on my already frazzled nerves. "It's National Nurses Day on Wednesday," I explain unnecessarily.

"That's why your mom was assembling all those little boxes."

I nod and blurt out, "Help yourself if you'd like one."

The heat flames back in his eyes. "I don't want your fucking fruit, Darby."

His words hit like a punch to the gut, but they also spark something inside my soul. I close the door, turn to face him, and square my shoulders, glaring. "Then what do you want, Pierce?"

"I want to know why you're back in town."

"You should have figured it out, seeing as you visited Mom this morning. She had a nasty accident, and I wanted to be close to her."

"She told me about the accident, and I'm sorry to hear it. But she also told me how well she's doing in her recovery. Doesn't explain your urgency to uproot your life and hightail it back to Charleston."

"I love my family, Pierce. Who are you to question what is urgent and what isn't?"

"Didn't you love your family twelve years ago when you hauled ass?"

Oh no, he's crazy if he thinks I'm going down this road with him right now. I've been preparing for years how to explain to him why I left, and today is not the day. It's going to be on my terms and not when he shows up to out of the blue. "How'd you find me?" I ask instead.

He reaches in his back pocket and flings one of my cards onto the steel prep table. "Saw your calling card."

"How'd you know it was mine? My name is nowhere on that."

"Yeah, it always seemed crazy to me that you branded your business without your name. But the design was a dead giveaway."

I suck in a deep breath and briefly close my eyes. How could I forget that he'd seen the rough draft? "You remembered."

"Of course, I fucking remembered."

"That doesn't explain how you found me."

"Your mom and Evin didn't give you away, if that's what you're thinking. They're locked up tight. I had to get creative. Tracked down your delivery service."

Dammit! I should never have changed my pick-up to this address.

"What I want to know is why you're being so secretive. Why not blast it to the masses that you're back and the name behind DG Creations? From what I can tell, only a select few know it's you."

"That's none of your business." There is no way I'm telling him the reasons behind my anonymity.

"Does it have anything to do with me? Because if so, you don't have to worry about me trashing your name. I left that shit behind a long time ago and moved on."

"Oh, trust me, I know you moved on," I spit out, not able to hold back the venom in my voice.

"What the hell is that supposed to mean?"

"Nothing, Pierce. Did you have anything you needed? Any other reason for stopping by than to let me know you've discovered I'm back in town?"

"Don't *'nothing, Pierce'* me. You don't get to dismiss me again. Tell me, Darby. Are you keeping your return under wraps because of me, because of us?"

I was right earlier. The image of the man I've held on to all these years is nothing like the man before me. This man is cold and brash, no sign of the lover who once was. The surprise of his arrival vanishes, and my defenses slide into place.

"No, Pierce, nothing I do anymore is because of you. You gave up that privilege a long time ago. I've been quiet about my return because I'm not sure I'm staying in Charleston," I yell.

"I didn't give up anything. You took it away. You stripped it from me, leaving my ass in the dust when you skipped town."

"You bounced back pretty quick, don't you think?"

"Bounced back? You think I bounced back? You don't know a goddamned thing about what happened to me."

"Maya Elise Kendrick is what happened to you!" I scream so loud Runner is at my side in a second. Heat sears my skin, fueling the fire of betrayal I've carried around. I can't stop the words that pour out of my mouth. "Maya Elise Kendrick, born September twenty-seventh, seven pounds, nineteen inches. Born to proud parents Pierce Kendrick and Constance Webber. Please join us welcoming this beautiful angel to the world." I quote the birth announcement verbatim.

The color drains from his face, and he drops his hands from his hips, opening his mouth, but I beat him to it. "Cole Matthew Kendrick, born January twenty-eighth, eight pounds, six ounces, twenty inches long. This handsome little guy joins proud parents Pierce and Constance and big sister Maya."

"What the *FUCK*!?!" He roars. "How do you know this shit?"

"I left here in tatters, Pierce. Broken, ashamed, hollow, and I went away for a reason. My brother drove up to Charlotte to break the news of her pregnancy. I found myself back in shambles. Then our dear, darling friend, Connie, followed the southern etiquette protocol and sent me a personal birth announcement—to my parents' house. She was kind enough to repeat the action a mere sixteen months later," I hiss, sarcasm dripping in my words.

"You have got to be shitting me."

"No. So you don't get to play the pity card because I do know a goddamned thing that happened to you. You got together with the one bitch in our group of friends that openly disrespected our relationship. I wasn't gone fourteen weeks before she was having your baby."

"I'm gonna kill her," he spews, slamming his hand down on the table with such force my pans clatter.

"Why? Why be mad now? You have the children you always wanted, and from what I hear, they are perfect kids."

"Leave my kids out of this."

"Fine. I didn't leave your ass in the dust and skip the town that I love easily. I was coming back—and I was prepared to beg, explain what happened. There was a sliver of hope that you'd understand."

"Understand what, Darby? What you did to me was unforgivable."

I flinch, wrapping my arms around my stomach to try to ease the pain slashing through me. He catches my actions, and for a brief second, there's a flicker of concern. I have to shut this down. "You're right; it was unforgivable. I was selfish and focused only on myself. But believe me when I tell you that I paid the price. There was no way for me to come back here and watch the man I thought I was going to marry live out his dream with a woman I could no longer stand. And that also tells you why I didn't make a big deal about being back. I'm still not sure I can live in the same town. You came in here wanting some answers, and you've got them."

He tears his hands through his hair, pacing a few times before pivoting and heading to the door. When he faces me, the color has returned to his face, and pure, unfiltered rage is pouring from his features.

"We're not done, Darby. Not by a long shot."

I try to tell him that we are very much done, but he's gone, the door slamming so hard the vibration shakes me.

What the hell did I do?

•—•—•—•—•

"And that is that." I toast my glass into the air in mock salute. "Five minutes alone with him, and I lose my cool, rip into him, insult the mother of his children, and let him know I was too weak to come back. I'm a real winner."

"What are you going to do?" Stephanie asks the million-dollar question everyone seems to want answered. She's patiently listened to me ramble on the phone for the last hour.

"I'm going to lament over my supremely bad choices and inability to control my emotions, and then I'm going to bed. Tomorrow, I'm going to show my face in public and hope like hell I don't embarrass myself."

"I'm going to re-arrange my calendar and be there sometime Thursday afternoon. You think you can be low key until then?"

For the first time in weeks, a surge of excitement shoots through me. Leaving my life in Charlotte was hard, but leaving Stephanie was devastating. She and her assistant, Scottie, were my lifelines. She is much more than my business lawyer and best friend. She is family.

"Low key is my middle name."

"Good, save your crazy for when I get there. We've got some things to discuss."

"Yeah," I pause, "about that..." I draw out dramatically.

"You still haven't told your family?"

"Nope, and I think they're going to put up a strong fight. Mom's doing everything she can to pull me into the community. Dad is remaining quiet, but he's shooting me looks that scream he's up to something, and you know about Evin."

"You left Charlotte hellbent on following through with this deal. Are you saying after a few weeks home, you're swaying?"

"I'm still thinking about the offer, Steph. It's a huge decision."

"No shit."

"Okay, we're not going to go over this again until you get here."

She goes quiet, and I can image her lounging on her sofa with her own glass of wine, the thoughtful look she gets in her eyes when she's got something to say.

"Say it."

"I usually don't condone spilling your guts to anyone because it always gets messy. But I'm proud of you, Darby. You gave it back as quick as he dished it out today. He's obviously still harboring resentment of your disappearance, but instead of taking it like a doormat, you blasted that shit right back."

"Thanks. I wish I'd found a better way of expressing my feelings other than reciting his children's birth statistics."

"Heat of the moment works for you. It always has."

"Can't wait until you get here."

"See you Thursday night."

We hang up, and I scoot lower on the sofa, curling into Runner and rubbing lightly on his belly. Stephanie's right. We have a ton to discuss, and all of it could mean enormous things for the expansion of DG Creations. The proposal on the table offers more than I could ever imagine, but it comes with sacrifices.

Stephanie knows where my apprehensions stem from. The one time in my life I made a sacrifice to benefit myself, I ended up losing Pierce. And I barely recovered.

But she's right about a few things. Pierce is harboring resentment and deserves the truth. And he's going to get it, on my terms. Then, hopefully, I'll find closure.

I force those thoughts out of my head and move to what happens tomorrow. I'm going to personally deliver the gifts to the hospital, taking my mom with me so she can be a part of it.

DG Creations was born in Charlotte, even though I worked on the concept for years here. Not many know it was birthed from the kitchen of Annie Graham and how long it took me to perfect some of the specialty recipes.

Tomorrow, everyone will know.

Because, ready or not, it's my homecoming debut.

Pierced Hearts

Chapter 5

Pierce

Someone's going to fucking pay.

Men scatter out of my way as I stalk to my truck and throw my hard hat to the ground with so much force it cracks. It doesn't faze me as this is not the only casualty of the day. My coffee pot didn't make it past the first pour, my bathroom mirror is splintered, and I'm pretty sure my administrative assistant is going to quit.

None of it matters right now because my anger is raging to the point of violence. I rip the phone off my hip and call the project manager who answers on the first ring.

"Did the brownstone project change their choices of marble last night?" I bark.

"Not that I know of," Joe answers cautiously.

"Funny then, because six of the fourteen units have the wrong countertops, vanities, and wet bar tops already installed. Not to mention, the backsplashes have been started."

"You have got to be shitting me!" he roars through the phone, his anger somewhat satisfying.

"I expect to see your ass here in the next fifteen minutes. Cancel your day until we find out what happened. That's a fucking order."

It's unlike me, but today, I want people to be raging. I want other's blood to be searing through their veins to the point of burning a hole in their gut. Maybe I'm a sadistic asshole, but there's no calming what is brewing inside.

I jump in my truck and drive around to the back of the job site. This is the last stage of the brownstones, and the area is practically deserted.

My mood has been crazed since walking out on Darby. My first instinct was to lay into Connie, but that wasn't an option. So, I poured myself into work, avoiding as much human contact as possible. Even a two-hour round with a punching bag didn't repress the anger inside. I stare out of my windshield and can't stop my brain from replaying the scene yesterday.

She was always beautiful, but the woman who swung that door open threatened to take me to my knees. Same amber eyes, same pouty lips, same gorgeous face—but that was the end to similarities.

She's bone-skinny, her dark hair was in a tight, tied ponytail, her skin pale, and her eyes were vacant. I know I took her off-guard, but for a minute, I thought she'd pass out.

My Darby was curvy in all the right ways, quick with a response, and sun-kissed by the outdoors, taking every chance to soak in the sunshine.

Still, she had the ability to make my pulse race and my dick hard with one glance. She's stunning.

The air in my truck begins to suffocate me, and I stagger out, pacing the abandoned area and kicking up every rock I find.

Never in a million years did I expect what happened. Now, I've opened Pandora's box and am so deep in questions it's going to drive me insane.

I love my kids and have done my best to give them a normal life. No matter what, it's not going to change the fact that they're never going to grow up in a traditional nuclear family. Darby was right; Connie was a tiger ready to pounce when word spread that Darby left town. She worked me hard, playing the role of the sympathetic friend. My mom warned me more than once to watch out for her, but I was stupid blind. Connie's advances became more and more assertive. She was a master manipulator, and I was in no shape to see the signs. I had sex with her twice, both times when we were partying, and both times with a condom.

That little barrier of latex didn't work, and she got pregnant. Unlike Darby, she had no problem spreading the news far and wide as soon as the doctor confirmed. I was forced to tell my parents with her sitting across the table, shining bright. Of course, Connie didn't know about what had happened with Darby, and the situation got ugly quick when my mom ran from the room in tears.

Connie expected a ring and a commitment, but the haze in my head finally cleared, and I saw through her.

That was the beginning of my life in hell. And I was such a fool I let her play me one more time. Cole was the result. No one on this earth, besides Connie and me, knows the circumstances leading to her pregnancy with Cole. We both lied our asses off to family and friends.

My head pounds at the memory, and I feel the churning before it hits, leaning to the side and throwing up the coffee I was able to consume.

"Shit, Pierce, get it together."

I didn't know it still existed, but the protective and possessive side of me kicked in when Darby spouted what Connie did to her. It's not a surprise she heard about the pregnancies. I suspected her family told her as soon as the news went viral. Darby may have slain me, but she didn't deserve that.

My thoughts are broken up when two trucks drive around the

corner, and my brother and dad park next to me.

"We need to talk!" Miller barks, stalking to me. "You're admin is in tears at the office, causing drama."

"Fire her," is my only response.

Dad comes to my side, his hand going to my shoulder. "Son, you okay?"

"Yes."

"We heard about the mishap with the countertops. You need to take a step back and let us handle it," Miller orders.

"Fine, but who's going to be responsible for the rest of the problems inside?"

"I got those," Dad assures me.

"I'm fine to handle things."

"No, you're not, and things are about to get worse." Miller spears me with a glacial glare and jumps back in his truck, driving off.

"Pierce, you need to cool down."

"I guess you know she's back?"

"Miller mentioned you had suspicions."

"My suspicions were correct."

"You chased her down yet?"

I sling my head to find him grinning.

"Yeah, I found her. It didn't go well. I was a dick, intentionally goading her."

"Your brother is still under a cloud of her fucking you over. He has no idea of everything that happened. You need to remember that."

"What did he mean, things are about to get worse?"

Dad lets go of my shoulder and pulls up a text on his phone.

Darby Graham just walked into the hospital with Annie. Get to Pierce, now.

I read through the rest and see that the auxiliary group is helping hand out small gift boxes to the nurses. Mom is sending play by plays to him about Darby.

"She made all the chocolates they're handing out today."

"No shit? She took her baking to the next level?" He's impressed.

"More than the next level. She owns a business that does very well. Her stuff is being sold in stores all around town."

"Does this mean she's back for good?"

"I don't know. We didn't get that far before I stormed out on her."

"Want to tell me what happened?"

"Not really because it's only going to solidify your opinion that I can't control my temper."

"I think I'll give you a pass, seeing as this is an intense situation."

I take a deep breath and blow it out slowly, then launch into the story. When I'm done, his face is red, his jaw locked tight, and his eyes are scorching with fury.

"She's the mother of my grandchildren, but that woman is a heartless bitch."

"Among other things," I agree.

"What are you going to do?"

"About Connie or Darby?"

"Both."

"I was going to take a few days to calm down before I said anything. For reasons she didn't explain, Darby was keeping her return quiet. But seeing as she's made a very public appearance, word is out. It won't take long for Connie to hear and come to me. What happens with that? Who knows, but she's going to know what I think about her stunt. As for Darby, not sure there is anything to do."

"You're wrong. There's a lot to do."

"What are you suggesting?"

"The woman who holds all the answers to your nightmares is ten miles away. Why are you standing here with me?"

His phone alerts with another text, and when he reads it, his lips twitch and his shoulders begin to shake. He flips it for me to see.

Annie is trying to set her up with every eligible doctor in this place. And from what I can tell, it's working. Where is Pierce?

"I'm gone." I shove his phone back in his chest and take off, hearing his laughter follow me.

I have no idea what I'm doing, but I'll start with an apology.

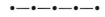

The heat beats down on my back as I check my watch for heart rate and time. My thighs and calves burn when I pick up the pace, trying to beat my own best record. *Thirty-three… thirty-two… thirty-one…* My feet cross over the sidewalk that ends my route right as the stopwatch hits thirty seconds.

I slow to a jog, rounding the corner, and curse under my breath when I spot Miller on the front porch. He's lounging on the swing, one foot on the floor, rocking back and forth. It crosses my mind to keep going, but my legs have other ideas and start to cramp.

"Were you being chased?" he asks from underneath the bill of his hat.

"Nope, beat my time."

"By?"

"Thirty seconds."

"Overachiever."

"Lazy ass. Maybe tomorrow you can join me."

"It's hot as balls out here. I'm not into self-torture."

"Why didn't you let yourself in?"

"Because when I turned the corner, Connie was beating on your door. I parked on the side street and waited until she left."

This doesn't explain why he didn't let himself in after she left, but my body is screaming at me for hydration, and I don't care what the reason is. The news that Connie was here kills my runner's high. I punch in the code on the lock and leave the door open for him to follow me to the kitchen.

"What are you doing here?"

"Did you see her?"

I arch my eyebrows, eying him as I gulp down a bottle of water.

"I'm going to assume you did since you decided to run five miles in ninety-four-degree heat."

"I saw her. She was the center of attention. It didn't seem appropriate to approach her and interrupt. Annie was busy telling everyone about DG Creations, and the one time I had my shot at getting her alone, Mom accosted me and yanked me into the volunteer lounge to give me the third degree."

What I don't tell him is that I purposely stayed out of sight to watch how she handled herself. I got a glimpse of the businesswoman and the hometown success in action. She didn't disappoint. Her smile radiated brightly, her words were laced with sincerity, and she accepted the compliments with grace. The shot I missed was when she went to the restroom, and I was fully prepared to chase her.

"Dad gave me the rundown of what happened yesterday."

"It's good I don't have to repeat it."

"How are you?"

I shrug, tossing the empty bottle in the trash and grabbing a new one to stall answering his question.

"I don't have a good feeling about this, man. It has disaster written all over it. You've got too much at stake to lose your mind again."

"I know that, Miller, but cut me some fucking slack."

"How about we head out of town this weekend? Blow off some steam and have a good time."

This is code for get drunk and get laid. Miller and I head out of town a few times a year for this sole purpose. It's easier to be discreet and keep our business private if we don't stand a chance of running into the women we fuck. In my case, there's a less likely chance word would get back to Connie than if I hooked up with someone local.

"Not this weekend. Cole has his end of the year baseball banquet."

He nods in understanding and moves to the fridge to get a beer, obviously planning to stay a while. Both our heads swing toward the front door when there's a jiggling sound, followed by a series of loud knocks.

"I'm going to sit this one out. Good luck." He twists the top off his bottle and tips it my way.

"Chicken shit."

"Connie's a cunt, and I'm on the verge of telling her that. Don't want to be the reason you have to go back to court."

"Appreciate it." I chuckle and head toward the sound of her shrieking my name.

The shrieking stops when she sees me approaching. Her eyes grow wide right before they narrow into slits.

"Where are my kids?" I open the door, glancing at the driveway to her empty car.

"*Our* kids are with my parents for dinner."

"Are they okay?"

"Of course."

"Do you need money?"

"No," she snarls with a hiss.

"Then there's no reason for you to be here." I make a move to close the door, and her arm darts out, stopping me. She makes a move to step inside, and I block the entrance. She was invited here when I bought the place, per the court order. She had every right to see where the kids would be spending their time. Otherwise, she doesn't invade my space.

"You want to talk, we'll talk outside." I sidestep her, giving her no choice but to back up.

"You're a piece of work. Is she in there? Is that why you're half-dressed, prancing out here with a smile on your face?"

"I've never pranced a day in my life."

"When the hell were you going to tell me she was back?"

"Who?"

"Don't play with me, Pierce. You know good and well Darby Graham is back in town."

"I heard about it."

"Heard about it? The whole fucking town has heard about it. Blaire said she breezed into the hospital today like she was royalty.

Floating around with her fancy clothes, expensive hair, and regal smile like she was the Queen of England."

"Is that right?"

"Fuck yeah, handing out her damn shitty ass chocolates and—" She stops, her face growing flush as realization clicks into place. "Those fucking chocolates. The assembly. You knew then!"

I give her a half-shoulder shrug.

"Is she in there?" Connie screeches, her control slipping.

"That's none of your business."

"I'm warning you not to screw with me, Pierce. Is she in there?"

"That sounds very much like a threat. It's none of your business who's in my house."

"It's my business if my children are here," she throws back.

"They aren't. You just pointed out they are at dinner with your parents. So why are you on my porch giving me shit about things that are none of your concern?"

The flush in her face grows to a flaming red, and as satisfying as it is, it's time to shut it down. "Is there a reason you're fired up about Darby's return?"

"I knew that bitch would come running right back to Charleston one day."

"I don't know the specifics, but considering her family lives here, she's probably been back plenty of times."

"Well, at least they had the decency to hide her from society and keep her away from you."

"We're done here." I take a step toward the door and freeze when her hand snakes around my bicep.

"Don't walk away from me."

"Get your fucking hands off me, Connie." My gaze drops to her hand and then back to her, fire searing through my bloodstream. As much as I try, I can't stop the words from spitting out. "Darby doesn't have a problem with society. They fucking love her. It was your shitty ass stunt that kept her away. You have no idea of the damage you did, sending her those birth announcements. I already told you I wasn't going to be a deadbeat dad, and we'd make our arrangement work for the best."

"Our arrangement? I was having your baby."

"I've taken responsibility for that since day one. I even owned up to the next colossal mistake of getting you pregnant twice."

She stumbles back, the ferocity of my words hitting her like a force of nature. "Did you just refer to Cole as a mistake?" she stutters.

"No, I said getting you pregnant was a mistake. Cole is a miracle. And don't act surprised. You didn't want more children."

"I didn't want more children with an asshole that refused to marry me! You used me."

"We. Are. Done." Any other response to that will put me in a deep hole I can't dig out of with even the best lawyers.

Connie recognizes the resolution in my tone, and her body language relaxes, her voice lowering. She knows she's gone too far. I never hid that I wasn't marrying her. After all I'd been through, the thought never crossed my mind. Everyone in her family put the pressure on, but when my blinders were lifted, it was never going to happen. Unfortunately for me, Connie didn't take the rejection well.

"Pierce, she broke you. I was there for everything and saw the wreckage. I sent her those announcements as revenge for you—"

"Bye, Connie." This time, I get into my house and slam the door.

She can scream all she wants, but I head to my room, ready to punch something. Miller walks into my bathroom right as I switch on the shower, and he's holding out a fresh beer.

"Get the whiskey," I order. "When I'm out of the shower, we're gonna talk. And make sure that bitch is gone."

He nods and disappears. I have no shame in sinking to the shower seat and letting the cool water beat down on me. Darby's face pops into my head. Even with everything that's happened, the thought of her has the ability to calm me after the shit show I've made of my life.

I'm fucked.

Chapter 6
Darby

I shouldn't find it at all surprising that my public appearance at the hospital and the news of my business brought in a lot of attention. Add in the arrival of Stephanie, and my quiet little routine in Charleston was flipped on its head. Mom's phone was blowing up, and she was all too eager to boast about my success.

And that is why Stephanie and I are staked out in my mom's kitchen, staring in horror.

"I need you to throw up," I whisper to Stephanie.

"Why?"

"We need an immediate excuse to leave."

"Why don't you throw up then?"

"Because Cruella De Vil will hand me a Pepto and tell me to freshen up. At least, if it's you, she'll have the manners to let us go. Once we get to the shed, we can grab Runner and escape."

"My gag reflexes don't work that way."

"Ugh," I groan, taking a huge swallow of my beer.

"Annie seems to have bounced back quite well. The way you were after her accident, I wasn't sure what her recovery would be like."

"Apparently, even the devil wasn't ready for her yet."

She bursts into laughter, nudging my shoulder with her own, well aware of the dynamics of Mom's and my relationship. Tonight is a perfect example. Mom sweet-talked us into joining her and Lynda for cocktails. She claimed it was a celebration of her being officially cleared off all medications. Since it's Friday night and Stephanie and I would most likely be drinking wine and gossiping at my place, we agreed.

Annie Graham conned me. She lied to her own daughter.

What was supposed to be a small gathering has turned into over a dozen women mingling around Mom's living room. My nerves are on overload because each glance they throw my way is filled with curiosity. The questions are coming. They're being polite, but no doubt they're ready to pounce.

"We're going to need something stronger than beer if we're going to survive a night with these ladies."

She goes to the bar, grabbing the bottle of vodka.

"Make mine a double," I instruct, ready to armor up for the night.

"I'll have what she's having." The low, sweet voice behind me immediately sends goosebumps over my skin.

I spin, coming face to face with the only other woman on this earth I wanted to call Mom. "Jill," barely comes out on a whisper, my throat closing. Before I can stop them, tears pool in my eyes and she becomes blurry.

"My Darby." She moves forward, then pauses, looking for approval.

I make the move, falling into her. She wraps her arms tight, embracing me warmly. "Oh, how I've missed my beautiful girl," she murmurs into my ear. "Still the prettiest girl in the world."

I choke back a sob, trembling from head to toe. Her hands rub up and down my back soothingly. It takes a few minutes for me to gain my composure, and she fully supports me, holding on until I'm ready to raise my head.

"I missed you, too, Jill. So much."

She gives me a sad smile, squeezing once. There's a muffled sniff behind me, and I turn to see my mom at Stephanie's side, both with wet, glistening eyes. Then I turn to find everyone staring. That's when I realize that all these ladies were keeping their distance for this reason. They were waiting for Jill to come in and break the ice.

Shame and guilt slam into me, and panic claws up my chest. I know for a fact that everyone thinks I left Charleston because of a huge argument and break-up with Pierce. They think I was running from a broken heart and acting on immaturity. It killed my family not to set the record straight, but my privacy was the priority.

I glance back to Jill and suck in a deep breath, praying my knees don't give out. Without hearing the words, her eyes communicate her understanding. "You know why, don't you?"

She nods.

Losing my baby put me on the verge of a breakdown, and I needed to deal. Unfortunately, I lost a lot more.

"I don't know the intimate details, but I know it's time to heal. Let it go," she says so only I can hear.

I blow out a long breath, step out of her hold, and swipe at my cheeks. "It's good to see you."

"Did you say you were making drinks, dear?" Jill speaks to Stephanie, who quickly goes back to what she was doing.

"I'll do my best to protect you from these inquiring minds, but promise me you'll call or come see me soon. You have grown into a truly striking woman and, from what I hear, a big success. I want to know all about it. Pierce wasn't the only one who loved you and lost you."

"I promise." Emotions threaten to resurface, so I clear my throat a few times and throw my mom a look to do something.

She picks up on the message. "Darby, can you check the appetizers in the oven and grab the trays from the refrigerator?"

"Sure, hope everyone is hungry," I announce loudly in the bubbliest voice I can muster up.

Stephanie hands Jill a drink and turns to the group, introducing herself. Thankfully, this douses any tension, and the room erupts in conversation. I do as my mom asked, happy for the few minutes to gather myself together.

Stephanie brings me a drink, clinking her glass to mine, and smiles reassuringly. "Drink up."

"Nothing like liquid encouragement to help rip off the Band-aid."

"I've got your back."

"Let's do this."

She trails me into the living room where we are swept up in the group. Luckily, Lynda starts a conversation about my business, which keeps the focus of questions on DG Creations.

Most of these women knew I was always into baking and chocolate creations, so it's easy for me to talk about. I glaze over the details of leaving, simply saying that Charlotte had an opportunity for me. Then I go on to explain the process of building my business. DG Creations is a small outfit, but it's financially solid.

Stephanie gushes about my reputation in Charlotte, which prompts Mom to jump in and prattle about my increasing popularity in Charleston. It becomes apparent Mom is embellishing and trying to overstate my status, but I let her go on because it's becoming hilarious.

Stephanie's face turns a deep shade of pink as she tries to hold back her laughter. I do the same until a very unladylike snort escapes.

"Darby Rose! Stop acting like a fool."

"Stop exaggerating. I bake goodies. It's hardly going to solve world peace."

She opens her mouth to argue, but Mrs. Winkle beats her to it. "I don't know about that. I heard the nurses talking about the chocolates you delivered. They went a long way in helping keep the peace at the hospital between the nurses and the administrators, who were at odds about schedule changes."

"I will admit that chocolate has magic powers, but so do nice gestures. That's all this was; the administrators did a nice gesture."

"You would certainly provide peace in my household if you'd chat with my husband about putting your desserts in his restaurant," Sandra Rosen pipes up.

"We have a meeting next week, Mrs. Rosen. I'm not able to provide large scale desserts right now, but I am going to give him some options."

"Thank you, Jesus. He's been griping about getting your toffee bars since he tasted one." She fans her face dramatically.

"Toffee bars are excellent, but the truffles will blow the roof off," Stephanie adds, winking at me.

My truffles are good, but she's an advocate because they bring in my largest profit margin. Since I make them with a specialty chocolate blend that is a secret recipe, we are able to set the price higher. They also take me days to finish.

"I've had your truffles. Of course, I didn't know at the time they were yours. I picked one up at Billy's place," Mrs. Asly boasts. "It was to die for."

"Thank you."

Out of the corner of my eyes, something flashes, and I look in time to catch Jill dabbing at the corner of her eye with a small smile on her lips. Pride is written on her expression. *"Proud of you,"* she mouths.

My heart swells, and I return her smile. She and I will never have what we once did, and that hurts. But for now, this is enough.

•—•—•—•—•

I wait with bated breath for someone to break the silence with any kind of reaction on my announcement that I've received an acquisition offer for DG Creations. Stephanie had the foresight to bring a few copies of the proposal, and Evin is reading through one, his eyes moving rapidly over the pages. He flips through and jerks his face to mine when he finds what any financial advisor and portfolio manager would be searching for.

"Is this solid?" His question is aimed at Stephanie.

"Solid as a rock. I've gone back and forth with the lead corporate lawyer for a while, tweaking. Best- and worst-case scenarios have been negotiated down to the minutest details." She transforms from the supportive, laid-back friend to the high demand, sharp-witted lawyer. "It's taken months of fine-tuning, but Darby and I felt the last round of changes were sufficient."

His gaze slowly moves to me, and I clasp my hands together tighter, swallowing hard. Hurt and confusion are plain in his expression.

"Don't be upset." I direct the statement at him but glance at my parents quickly and then back to him. "I'm still not sure this is the right move for me. It's a huge decision."

"That's an understatement. Guess this explains all the changes— the hair, the clothes, the new car. Not to mention the willingness to up and leave your existence in Charlotte without even a second thought. You've been contemplating this for months. We're a fly-by stop in your journey."

"Don't be a jerk, Evin. You know that's not true. I still haven't signed the papers. It's not a done deal."

"Why not, Darby? This offer sets you up financially, possibly for life. I may not know the legal side of things, but I'm intelligent enough to know Stephanie has taken every step to make sure you are protected."

"It's not about the money. You, of all people, know I'm doing fine on my own."

"Why not sign the papers?"

"Because DG Creations is my life."

"No, DG Creations is your expertise. You, Darby Graham, get to choose your life."

"To me, it's one in the same."

"What I want to know is how this came about? Since the inception of DG Creations nine years ago, you've refused to even have a storefront. Now, you may be joining forces with an exclusive hotel and resort chain?" Mom slides her copy of the proposal to the middle of the table, not bothering to open it.

"It's a case of being in the right place at the right time. I was hired to cater the desserts for an event last winter. One of the executives from Brasher Resorts was impressed and contacted me through the event planner. It started with a few innocent conversations, and when it got serious, I pulled Stephanie in."

"And you'd have to move to Colorado?" Dad asks.

"They want me at their largest resort in Aspen to start."

"What happens after Aspen?"

"If this goes as planned, we'll look at relocating me to the next resort."

"How will that work? You can't be in two places at once?"

My heart pounds harder, and the sick feeling of uncertainty settles deep in my stomach when I think about this part of the deal. "I'll have to train staff at each location. Part of the expansion would require me to teach others my recipes."

An uncomfortable silence hangs in the air, and I mentally note the questions running through their minds.

"It's not that DG Creations is your life; it's the fact that, once you sign those papers, you are handing it over?" Dad says as more of a question.

"That's what it feels like. But the other part is what if it fails? What if the idea bombs? Aspen will be the pilot program, and I'll be managing the whole process. Guests of this resort are high-rollers, and I'm a small-time girl—"

"Stop," Evin rumbles. "Don't diminish your self-worth. You've run a successful business for almost a decade. Being from a small town has nothing to do with your talent."

"What do you think I should do, Evin?"

He drops back in his chair and focuses on the ceiling, rolling his bottom lip between his teeth. Stephanie's hand squeezes my knee under the table in support, urging me to say more.

"I value your opinions. It's one of the many reasons I've held off on signing the papers."

"It all seems pretty straight forward. Brasher Resorts wants to buy your brand and own the rights to distribute and sell. It's an incredibly lucrative offer."

"It is," I agree.

"You know, if this was local, or even along the east coast, I'd hand you my pen to sign these papers right now. It sucks you'll be across the country."

"Think of it this way; I'll finally get to put my hospitality and management degree to use. You've always said Mom and Dad wasted their money on tuition since I decided to be a baker."

He cracks a small grin at our long-running joke. "Yeah, it's about time you use that degree."

"And I'm pretty sure that, buried deep somewhere in the articles of that contract, there is a family and friends discount clause for when you come to visit."

"I'd expect nothing less." His grin disappears, and his expression grows somber again. "In all seriousness, I'm proud of you, Darby. I'd like to look through this more carefully, but if you decide to take them up on their offer, they're the lucky ones."

"Thanks," I reply faintly, my eyes and nose stinging.

"I can help clarify any of the legal questions," Stephanie offers.

He dips his chin in appreciation.

"I'll stand by any decision you make," Dad adds. "I've always wanted to visit Aspen."

"Edward, what the hell am I going to do in Aspen? I doubt I'll ever ride a horse again. There's no way I can get on skis," Mom grumbles.

"Don't worry, baby. We'll find something to do to keep busy." He wiggles his eyebrows suggestively, bringing their linked hand to his lips.

Just like that, the mood in the room changes, and I gag loudly at the same time Evin groans. Stephanie giggles, encouraging them by clapping.

"On that note, we have our own news." Dad scoots back and gently scoops Mom to sit in his lap. "Do you want to tell them, Annie?"

"I'm not sure it's the right time. Darby's bombshell seems to have taken the air out of my sails."

Guilt smothers me, and I want to slink out of the room until Dad speaks up, eyeing me with a smile. "Not me. I knew she was world-class. She's also a smart cookie and will make the right decision. We raised both our children that way. It's time we drop our own bombshell."

She grasps his cheeks, kisses him softly, and then turns to us, beaming. "Edward and I are back together. He's moving home."

My jaw drops, but out of the corner of my eye, I catch Stephanie leap from her chair and start dancing in a circle. She's hooting enough to cover Evin and my silence. The shock wears off, and a little scream bubbles out, followed by a hiccup, and tears spring to my eyes. But, for the first time in so long, these are tears of happiness.

"It's about time." Evin takes the words right out of my mouth.

I watch my dad cradle Mom close, and a small part of my heart shifts back into place.

Pierced Hearts

Chapter 7

Pierce

Memories bounce in my brain as I stare at the darkened porch that I built for the Grahams. The whole place that Annie liked to refer to as the shed was already built when Darby decided it needed a front porch. Her dad had enough of the construction and cost and told her it wasn't going to happen. I made it happen, gathering every piece of material myself while bargaining with Miller and Evin to help me finish it.

She loved this shed, claiming it as her own, and I loved being able to give her what she wanted.

Lanterns come to life, illuminating the small area right as the door cracks open, and Darby slips through. Her hair is piled on top of her head, and her face is free of makeup. She comes to the railing wearing a black, silky pajama set that sets my blood on fire. Her nipples are poking through the material, her long legs are on display, her eyes are bright, and I swear I've never seen her so beautiful.

"Pierce, do you want to come up?" she calls into the dark quietly, not at all surprised I am here.

I take a few steps forward, sliding my hands into my jeans. "How'd you know it was me?"

She doesn't answer, giving the welcome hand gesture and disappearing behind the door again to leave me alone when I walk onto the porch. A few minutes later, she returns with two mugs of steaming coffee, this time in a robe that's clinched around her waist.

"Here." She hands me a cup. "I hope you still take it the same way."

"I do."

She moves to a chair and sits, crossing her legs when her robe slides away. As hard as I try, there's no stopping my eyes from landing on her bare skin. "How'd you know it was me?"

"I just knew."

"It's five a.m. Why are you awake?"

"I should ask you the same. Don't you sleep in on Sundays?" She evades my question.

"I came to apologize."

"Why?"

"Because of last week."

"You don't need to apologize to me. You didn't do anything out of character."

"Out of character? I came into your place, showed my ass, and stormed out."

"Yeah, you did, which is your character. You've always been protective of those you love. I shouldn't have brought up your children. You went into protection mode."

Fuck me! She thinks I was being protective of my children? "I wasn't mad about Maya and Cole."

She flinches at their names and directs her attention to the contents of her cup.

"I didn't like what Connie did to you."

"It's fine, Pierce. Life moves on."

"Does it?"

"Yes, it does." She sighs. "You moved on."

Her honesty fucking hurts, and I have no choice but to turn away and look to the darkness, knowing the sunlight will rise right above the east meadow soon. Memories of watching the sunrise from her bedroom window roll through my mind.

"I saw Jill Friday night. She looks wonderful," Darby offers.

"She told me about Annie's impromptu party. She also said she wasn't sure she should come. I think she's glad she did."

"I'm happy she changed her mind. It was nice to see her."

I nod, still staring out into nothing, unsure what to say. Mom was my date to the baseball banquet last night, and the instant she got in my truck, I knew something was up. She was hesitant to tell me about coming here Friday night, scared I'd feel somehow betrayed. It was the opposite. I'm glad she made the decision. Losing Darby was hard on her. The reasoning behind it was even worse. She begged me to chase after Darby, but she had no idea of the colossal damage I'd caused the day Darby and I broke up. Things I said were reprehensible, and of course, I was too much of a stubborn ass to admit it.

"Is that why you came to the hospital? To apologize?" Darby breaks into my thoughts.

I swing to face her. "You knew I was there?"

"I always know when you're close. I guess I was a little rusty at the bakery because of all the time that passed, but since then, yes, I know. That's how I knew to start the coffee before even coming to the porch." She sways her mug at me.

"I am sorry, Darby... about it all."

"Apology accepted. Unnecessary, but accepted."

I sip the coffee, thinking it's time for me to go. I did what I came to do.

"Apologies are weird, don't you think?" She sounds almost

wistful.

"Why do you say that?"

"Apologies are a few simple words that have such a tremendous impact. When said with the right amount of sincerity, they can change the course of everything. I have owed you an apology for a very long time. I have owed your family the same. It's a little late, but I'm sorry, too, Pierce, for everything that happened back then."

She comes to stand by me, leaning on the railing. Her words hang in the air. She's exactly right. Hearing her apologize has a tremendous impact that fuels my curiosity. Questions fire around in my brain, questions that were long ago buried because the answers wouldn't change the fate of my life. She left me.

That was that.

"I don't blame you for hating me, Pierce. You were right the other day. What I did to us was unforgivable. But I was young, lost, and immature. Letting all the time pass is one of my biggest regrets."

"Twelve years is a long time to hold on to regret."

"I'm afraid it's something I'll carry around for the rest of my life."

She twists to me, her light brown eyes glistening. My stomach turns, and my heart races at the raw, unfiltered sorrow and pain written on her face. For a brief second, I'm transported back in time to that afternoon—a younger Darby looking at me with the same expression she's wearing now. I'd walked away from her, but not before I called her a selfish bitch as my parting words. My anger got the best of me, and I'd lashed out harshly.

It isn't until right now, at this moment, that that anger finally starts to fade. "I didn't blame you, Darby. What happened wasn't your fault. Evin told me you think that—"

She puts a hand on my chest to stop me from finishing, and tears slide out of the corner of her eyes. "Evin has some very strong misconceptions about what happened between us. It's time I clear those up with him. But between you and me, we both know I am to blame for what happened afterward."

Even through the fabric of my shirt, I can feel the heat of her touch on my skin. My eyes drop, and she tries to yank her hand away, but my fingers fasten around her wrist and hold it to me. "Is that why you were crying the other night?"

"W-w-what?"

"When I showed up at your bakery, you said something about being curled in a fetal position and shedding tears."

"I assumed you were Evin when I opened that door. Mom had just told me about your visit, and it would be like him to come and check on me."

"I figured as much, but why were you crying in the first place?"

"A few nights earlier, he and I had a conversation that struck a chord. It really wasn't about you, if that's what you're thinking."

"I don't know what to think. Everything I thought was the truth for all these years seems to be a huge lie. You hauling ass out of town left a gaping hole in my life that I spent years trying to heal. You said some things that don't make sense."

"Please, don't do this."

"I want to let it go, but I can't. Why didn't you ever get married and have kids, Darby?"

She jerks back, her hand in mine trembling. I tighten my grip and stare into her eyes that are swimming in agony. It's impossible to miss the sadness and torment staring back at me. Then it hits me, all that Evin said, mixed with her own admissions. She never moved on. Darby has been drowning in misery and holding on to nothing but excruciating memories. Losing our baby was hard, but we had barely gotten used to the idea of being parents. That wasn't why she left.

Feelings and emotions that died long ago start to resurface, and my chest feels like it may explode. "Tell me," I urge her gently, setting my mug on the railing.

"Because I fell in love with my soulmate at seventeen-years-old. I could never love another man the way I loved you. There was never going to be anyone else for me. And when you started a family with another woman, my heart shattered into a billion tiny shards that never recovered."

"You broke up with me and skipped town!"

"You let me go!" she cries, her entire body shivering.

"You gave me no choice."

"There's always a choice, Pierce. You know that better than anyone." Bitterness bleeds into her statement, and I catch her defenses building.

My instincts kick in, and old habits click into place. I close the space between us, circle her waist, and crush my mouth to hers. She freezes for a split second before her hand wraps around my neck, and she dissolves into me. Her lips part, and my tongue slips through, finding hers easily. The taste of her chocolate and hazelnut creamer sends a shockwave buzzing through my system. For the first time in twelve years, I crave the taste and angle my head for more.

She whimpers, scraping her nails along my scalp, and rises on her tiptoes, giving me the signal. I let go of her hand on my chest and bend, lifting her so she wraps her arms and legs around me.

Her hips press into mine, and my dick is instantly rock-hard with the familiarity of our bodies locked together. My hands slide to cup her ass, holding her tight to me. Our lips stay fused and our tongues curl together, her low moans ringing in my ears.

Time stands still as the heat of her body coats over mine. My lips move urgently over hers, greedily demanding more. Nothing over the years has ever come close to the way Darby kisses. Adrenaline spikes in my veins as her tongue sweeps through my mouth.

My hands caress her ass, my hips rocking up, letting her feel what she's done to me. Her body responds by grinding down, and a small groan vibrates from her throat. She slants her neck, fisting my hair, giving me deeper access. Sparks of need fire off inside me, igniting a hunger that vanished all those years ago.

Her scent, her taste, the feel of her smooth skin—all of it invades my senses, and I'm ready to rip off her clothes and sink inside of her. As if she can read my thoughts, she tears her mouth away, her chest heaving, and lays her forehead against mine. I catch the look of horror right before she scrambles down and takes a huge step back. "We shouldn't have done that. It was a mistake."

"Give me a reason why." Her lips are swollen, her face flushed, and her body visibly wobbly. There is no way that was a mistake.

"I'll give you a hundred," she counters.

I widen my stance and cross my arms, waiting.

"You should go."

"We need to finish our conversation."

"Maybe we do, but now's not a good time."

As if on cue, her door opens and a blonde stands there, eyeing me knowingly. Runner trots out to Darby's side, licking her hand before bouncing over to me. Like last time, he sits, sweeping his tail over the porch, and paws at me. I crouch to shake his hand and pat his head, and he bumps my knee before heading down the steps and into the yard.

"Hi, I'm Stephanie." The blonde gives a half-wave.

"Pierce." I dip my chin her way.

"I kinda figured that out. Sorry to interrupt. Y'all can continue making out. I'll go back to bed if you want to bring it inside."

Darby drops her head, and the corners of my mouth twitch.

"Runner was ready to come outside."

"We get it, Steph," Darby snaps. "Pierce was just leaving."

"Actually, I was waiting for an answer."

Darby's eyes fly to Stephanie then back to me. Her spine straightens, and a mask of indifference clouds her face. "Are you going to make me say it?"

"Yes, I think you owe me that much."

"I've done my best to dig myself out of the hell I lived in for years. Loving you was the best and worst thing that ever happened to me. There's a piece that will always crave your forgiveness. But the one thing I can't forgive is Constance Webber. That's the number one reason, Pierce. You wanted me to say it, and I did."

With that, she's gone, running past Stephanie and into the house. I have no choice but to watch her, wondering how the hell I managed to go from one extreme to another.

"What the ever-loving fuck?"

"What did you expect?" Stephanie butts in. "You provoked her."

"Why is it that both times I've been around Darby, I'm left with more questions than answers? She's hiding something."

She disappears into the house and comes back, holding out a business card. "I go home this afternoon."

"What am I supposed to do with this?"

"My guess is you're going to want to call me in a few days. I have a blood sister, and I love her dearly. My love for Darby runs just as deep. That's why I'm giving you this card."

"Want to give me more to go on?"

"Yep, I want to give it all to you. If I could, I'd light the dynamite that's going to blow this powder keg up, but it's not my place. She's given you everything you need to know. Since you're a guy, I'm guessing it hasn't sunk in."

"That sounded mildly like an insult."

"It's still early. Give me a little time, and it will sound *definitely* like an insult."

"Darby left me. I was allowed to have a life."

"Oh, we know… Everyone who loves Darby knows all about your life. Since you are so dense, I'll throw you a clue. Outside of DG Creations, her family, and me, Darby never got on with her life after losing you. Think about that."

"Not sure why I'm feeling like the bad guy here."

"Just wait. I'm going to encourage her to talk to you. Once you hear her story, you'll understand."

"What's the fucking deal with her story? I lived through it."

"Dense…" She tsks, which pisses me off further.

"This is ridiculous. I'm going to talk to her." I step forward, but she blocks the door.

"You let her go, Pierce. She needed you more than anything, and you let her go."

"You have no fucking idea what happened."

"That's where you're wrong. I know everything. I'm warning you now; when she tells you her story, you're going to be in your own pit of hell."

"What the fuck am I supposed to do with that?" I throw my hands in the air.

"I honestly don't know. Any relationship I've ever had seems superficial compared to the love story Darby has shared. I never could understand why she never went past a first date with men over the years, until a few minutes ago. You touched her and it was clear. The connection you share is one for the ages."

I close my eyes and take a deep breath, focusing on not losing my temper. "She left me."

"I know that, and as she told you, she holds on to that remorse. However, you let her go."

Stephanie gives me no more, closing the door and leaving me standing there fuming. I pivot on my heel, rounding the shed where I parked down the lane. I haul myself into my truck, slam the door, and stare blankly ahead. Thoughts and memories rattle around my brain. Stephanie was right; the connection Darby and I share is still real. Although I should kick my own ass for even going there, it was no mistake. It's insane I'm even thinking about what happens next. I'm too fucking old to play games.

Darby's going to tell me what she's been hiding all these years. It's time the cryptic messages she's dropping come to an end.

I drive away with the taste of her still on my lips.

•—•—•—•—•

"Edward?"

"Pierce." He holds out his hand.

I shake it, looking over his shoulder to find his truck parked on the street in front.

"I'm alone," he clarifies.

"It's good to see you, but what are you doing here?"

"Can I come in?"

I step back, motioning for him to come in and follow him to the living room. His eyes dart around purposefully, checking out my house. "Nice place," he comments.

"Thanks."

"Those your children?" He points to the rows of pictures.

"They are."

He nods again, twisting his upper body and tipping his chin to the staircase. "How many bedrooms this place got?"

It seems like an odd question, but I answer anyway. "Four upstairs, the master down here. Three and a half baths."

"You got a big master bathroom?"

"I do."

"What about the closet?"

"It's big enough."

He purses his lips, leaning back for a glance into the kitchen. "Nice gourmet kitchen," he assesses.

"Edward, glad you approve of my place, but throw me a bone. What are you doing here?"

"Felt left out. You've visited every member of my family recently but me. Thought maybe I should rectify that."

"How'd you even know where to find me?"

"Annie and I are getting back together." It's a Graham trait to evade answering questions.

I jerk my head so fast my neck cracks. "That's great." The news of Annie and Edward splitting up was huge. They were the last two people on earth that anyone ever expected to divorce.

"Yeah, it took me eight years to get her to take me back. But now, I'm not wasting any time."

"Okay."

"Woke up this morning, she was still sleeping, and I decided to take my morning coffee on the terrace. I always loved that view and the peace and tranquility that comes along with it. I was thinking about how it's time to get our horses back from boarding, wondering about talking to Annie's doctor and the possibility of her riding because she misses it. My mind was all over the place. It's my quiet time."

"Okay…" I draw it out, having a good idea of where this could be headed.

"Dawn was breaking when I saw your truck driving toward the road. Runner was sniffing around, and my curiosity got the best of me. I took the dog back to the shed and walked into a mess."

"Is she okay?" My senses go on hyper-alert. I knew Darby was emotional, but she had Stephanie.

"Nope, not by a long shot. But that's not why I'm here."

"Edward, I get you're protective, but with all due respect, this is between Darby and me."

"It sure is. But that's not how this is going to work, and you know it. There's a lot of people involved in this."

"Why? I'm a thirty-five-year-old man and don't need a bunch of people in my business."

He crooks his eyebrows, and his eyes grow sharp right before they light with amusement. He bursts into laughter. "You're serious?"

"Dead serious."

"Son, that's plain stupid and hilarious."

"I don't see what's funny."

"No, I guess you don't. But I'm here to help you out. There's a buzz brewing, and you two are at the center of it all."

"That's unfortunate because there's nothing to talk about."

"Yet."

"Yet?"

"You're a dad now, so I know you get the protective burn that runs through your veins when you think about your children hurting."

"I do."

"Then you'll understand that I've had that burn scorching through me for a very long time. Not a day goes by that I don't want to strip that pain from my daughter."

"No offense, but you need to remember what happened back then."

"I know what happened. All of it. Every word exchanged, every tear that fell, every cry of regret, and even every drink you consumed to try to run from the heartbreak."

I'm shocked at the last part of his statement. "Why does everyone keep insinuating this was all my fault?"

"I don't think it was your fault. Sure, there were some things you could have done differently, but we all make mistakes."

"Is that why you're here, to throw my transgressions in my face?"

"Nope, I'm here to tell you I walked into a room this morning where my Darby Rose was tearing herself apart again, and it has to stop."

He's glaring at me with such fierce determination my chest hurts. "I'm not sure what to say to that."

"There's no telling what the future holds, but Annie and I know for certain Darby had an alternative reason for coming home. She loves her mom, but she's come for forgiveness and closure. Only then can she truly move on."

"What the hell is it with the Graham family? Why are all of you talking in circles around me? Someone needs to spit out what you all want to say."

"I'll tell you this. Darby left you for a good reason. A reason Annie and I supported one hundred percent. Evin wanted to go with her, and we practically had to tie him down to stop him from smothering her. She went away to get help."

"Help?" I force the word out, my heart now racing as the pain in my chest intensifies.

"Do you still love her, Pierce?"

I rock back at the bluntness of his question. "How can you ask me that?"

"I'm not going to lie. I thought you two were entirely too serious at a young age. Annie made me see reason. What I saw this morning was a glimpse of that spirit Darby had. She's sure as shit still in there somewhere, and I'm scared you're the only one that can bring her back. Hate to say it because I'd slay dragons for my daughter, but it's not me she wants to slay those dragons."

"I can not believe you are laying this on me. How can my life take such a fucked-up turn?"

"Remember, I said it took eight years for Annie to take me back?"

I nod, wondering what that has to do with anything right now.

"Eight years of hell, Pierce. It wasn't about getting my spot back in her bed. It was about getting my spot back as the man in her life. I did everything in my power, and it finally worked in my favor. There's no way to tell how this is going to play out with you and Darby, but I pray you don't have to go through eight more years."

"How screwed up would I be to walk back into the fires of hell that burned me so badly the first time? I don't know if I want her back." As soon as the words leave my mouth, I know they're a lie. My feet stumble to the chair, and I fall helplessly into it. "Fuck me. How did this happen?"

"It happened because there is only one Annie for me. There is only one Jill for Warren Kendrick, and I suspect there's only one Darby for Pierce Kendrick."

I scrub my hands over my face, unable to look at him.

"I think I'm going to arrange to have those horses returned in a few weeks. You around to help?" He asks the question with such ease as if he didn't just make me admit a life-changing realization.

"Huh?" I swing my eyes to him, dazed.

"Need help getting them back stabled and acclimated to our place. You around to help?"

"I'll let you know," is all I can find to say.

"I'll let myself out." He goes to the door and stops, twisting back to me. "For what it's worth, I'm pulling for you."

Then he's gone.

And I'm left waiting and wondering... again.

Pierced Hearts

Chapter 8

Darby

"Mr. Baldwin, I understand your urgency. If you can give me one week, I'll have an answer for you."

Did I just give a self-imposed timeline on my decision about joining Brasher Resorts? *Shit!*

"It's not that I want to pressure you, Darby, but we need to come to a conclusion on the building. If you want to buy it, the deal still stands," my landlord tells me.

"It's a very fair offer that is still under consideration, but there are a few things I must get straight first."

"Maybe I should call Evin," he wavers.

"No. Not unless you need to chat with him about something else. Evin helped orchestrate our lease agreement because I was in North Carolina. I'm here now, so there's no need to get him involved."

"I'll touch base next Tuesday."

"Thank you." I hang up and blow out a frustrated breath. My head pounds and I swear this day can't end soon enough. When I get home, Runner and I are going on a long walk before I sink into the tub and lock away the world.

It's been three days since I saw Pierce, but it feels like three minutes. The familiarity and comfort of being in his arms still surrounds me, and every night when I close my eyes, his face fills my mind. That kiss… that damn kiss…

Why didn't I stop it sooner? How did I end up draped around him like a horny tramp? Stephanie was right; there's no denying we still have a connection that scorches in my blood. But having a connection isn't going to erase the past, and it's best to remember that.

I go around to the trunk to grab the cooler and make my way into the restaurant where Mr. Rosen is waiting.

"Darby, I am glad you're here." He takes the cooler and ushers me through the restaurant to the kitchen.

"Thank you for giving me this opportunity. Hopefully, it will work out."

He beams and shows me to an area where he's cleaned off a table for me to set up a dessert tray display.

A few good things did come out of the clash with Pierce on Sunday. When he was gone and I finally calmed down, I knew the only way to keep sane was to stay busy. As soon as Stephanie left, I took my laptop and all my notes and walked over to Mom's, where we proceeded to fill my week up to levels of craziness. I called Mr. Rosen, and instead of meeting him today, we talked through a proposal where I'd come in and actually provide a personalized set-up of a few items for him to sell as specialty desserts tonight. It isn't a customary arrangement, but it gives me a chance to test what may do best with their clientele.

Between preparing for this, my regular daily quotas, and the added bonuses we promised to a few prospects, I've been working like crazy. Not to mention, Mom said invoices were being paid immediately because no one wanted to be dropped from my schedule for lack of payment.

This is good. It's the perfect distraction to keep me busy. And tonight may finally be the night I've pushed myself to exhaustion.

"What can I do to help?" he offers in an overly excited chirp. His wife was right; this man is thrilled to have my creations in his restaurant tonight. A small sense of pride rushes through me, and I point to the oversized bag I dropped on the end of the table.

"Grab the silver stands and the folder. I printed table cards with the descriptions of the desserts and the prices you set."

He does as I ask, sliding the cards into the swirly designed place-card holders. The display comes together beautifully, and he calls a few of the kitchen crew over for me to explain how to serve the desserts with specific toppings and sauces.

When I'm done, the head chef helps me unload my cooler and puts everything where he wants.

"How about a drink?" Mr. Rosen offers.

"I'll take some coffee."

"Perfect. Let's go."

We go back through the restaurant to the bar, and while he gets our coffee, I take the time to appreciate the décor. This is what's considered a fine dining establishment in Charleston, and the interior highlights the old-style architecture. I've known the Rosen family for most of my life, but he didn't open this specific restaurant until I was in Charlotte.

"Have you ever eaten here?" He slides a mug in front of me.

"Unfortunately, no. You opened after I moved, and when I come home, we prefer to do things low key at my parents' house. But I'd love to come for dinner one night."

"Any night you want. You don't even have to call ahead, just show up and tell the hostess you are my special guest. Anything you order is on the house."

"Not necessary, but I will be dining here soon."

He smiles gently and asks me the normal things about my business. I do the same, and pretty soon, we're on the subject of family. Mrs. Rosen had done a good job of updating me on their family on Friday night, but I listen intently as he brags about his grandchildren.

His face grows serious, and I brace myself for the question coming. "Did you ever want children, Darby?"

"I did. I still do. It hasn't happened yet."

He nods solemnly, and his eyes shoot over my shoulder, growing wide in recognition. I feel the presence behind me, but when I hear the voice, my stomach plummets.

"Darby?"

I twirl in my seat, coming face to face with Jill, Warren, and Miller Kendrick. Jill looks incredibly stylish in her navy jumpsuit. Then I notice Warren and Miller are not wearing their standard jeans and Kendrick Construction shirts. They're dressed up as well.

I mentally think through all the Kendrick birthdays, but none of them are close, so this must be some other sort of celebration. There isn't much time to think about it because, in a second, I'm engulfed in strong arms as Warren hugs me tight.

"Darby Rose," he grumbles in my ear. "All grown up and still pretty as a picture."

"Warren." I kiss his cheek when he sets me back on my feet.

"Are you having dinner here?" Jill gives me a short embrace.

"Not exactly. I provided the desserts tonight."

Mr. Rosen takes the opportunity to launch into the selections, and I catch the twinkle in Warren's eye when my chocolate raspberry tart is mentioned.

"Honey, it's your job to keep me from overeating to save room for dessert," he tells Jill.

All through this exchange, I can't miss the way Miller is glowering, nor the anger filling the small space between us. He hasn't said a word, but the tension in his body says it all. The best thing to do would be to shut this down and get away as quickly as possible without being rude.

"I shouldn't keep you from your reservations," I offer.

"Oh, we're early. I wanted to have a drink before dinner anyway. Maybe you could join us." Warren gestures toward the bar.

Miller's jaw gets tight, and his eyes flicker with annoyance, while Jill goes statue still, her face paling.

"I can't tonight, but maybe another time."

"We insist. Let us buy you a glass of wine."

"Honey, Darby is busy. Let's let her get back to her work." Jill's voice is nervous, and she grabs Warren's wrist.

"The annual Kendrick dinner. The Kendricks have been coming for years to celebrate the end of the school year with their grandchildren. We have a standing reservation," Mr. Rosen boasts beside me.

It all falls into place. Pierce is coming here with his children to meet the family. His... children... are... on ... their... way.

My vision gets blurry at the same time I dip down to grab my bag. My head bangs on the lower lip of the bar, and I groan at the pain radiating through me. There's going to be a knot on my scalp, but I can't think about that right now. I have to get out of here.

Jill reaches an arm around my elbow, bringing me up to her face, which is edged with compassion. "Are you okay?"

"Y-y-yes, thank you. I need to leave."

"Darby, I had no idea..." She trails off when Miller reaches around his mother and takes my hand. He speaks over me to Mr. Rosen.

"We're going out the back entrance."

Mr. Rosen nods, looking shaken, and I have no choice but to trudge behind Miller as he pulls me through the bar. My eyes do a sweep of the area, and I can't help the muffled scream that escapes at the scene in the front windows.

Pierce is there, climbing out of his truck, dressed in black slacks and a grey button-down shirt. He slams the door at the same time two children run into him, throwing their arms around him like he is the best thing in their world. Connie Webber follows with a foul expression, stabbing her finger in the air. But I can't tear my eyes from Pierce, who shelters his kids with his arms and turns them to the restaurant.

I think there's a crash of something near, and I realize Miller is now carrying me, hitting a door as he takes me out.

"I'm okay." It comes out so faint; I wonder if he can hear.

"I'm going to put you down. I'm going to go get your car and bring it back here so you can leave."

I shudder when he sets me to the ground. "I'm fine to walk around the building and drive myself." My voice cracks.

"I think you are a bitch, but I think less of Connie. She's going to worm her way into our night, been planting the seeds since she found out you breezed back into town. If she catches sight of you, it's going to be hell on wheels with Pierce. I'm doing this for my family. Give me your keys."

"No." I straighten my shoulders and look into the angriest blues eyes I've ever seen. They are full of hatred, disgust, and absolution.

"Goddammit, Darby, give me your keys. Pierce doesn't deserve the only dinner of the year that celebrates Maya and Cole's accomplishments to be marred with your stubbornness!"

At the mention of their names, I curl into myself and throw my arm around my stomach. My fingers go into the small pocket of the bag and hand over the fob. He leaves without a second look, apparently ready for me to be out if his sight.

Miller and I loved each other at one time. But when I was pregnant, everything changed. Pierce has no idea how his brother altered my way of thinking of leading our way into parenthood, and even then, I always loved Miller.

And he loved me.

Now, he detests me.

My Infinity flies around the corner less than two minutes later, and Miller leaps out, tossing my fob on the seat and stalking to me. "Get out of here, and if you have any decency, give him the night with his kids."

That striking pain hits my gut, but this time, I don't bowl over. There are a lot of things I want to spout back, but the only thing that comes out is, "Thank you."

He looks me over, shakes his head, and disappears through the back door of the restaurant, leaving me in humility.

I drive aimlessly home, emotions everywhere, but no tears. I can't do this anymore. It's a losing battle. My business can definitely keep afloat with the way things are going now. Solid income, great word of mouth, and now a presence in the social scene. It's all there.

But I'm done with the cloak and dagger. It's time to spill my guts.

After that, I'm signing the Brasher contract.

Pierced Hearts

Chapter 9

Pierce

The rage inside is already brewing before I round the corner and spot the Infinity parked on the street. Darby is nowhere in sight, so I pull into the driveway slowly in case she's waiting around back.

Nope.

No sign of her.

Maya is blowing up my phone with text messages. She wants to know what we're doing this summer since Miller mentioned us all going to Myrtle Beach. Then Connie joined in about the vacation. She felt like being with the kids was a family affair.

At dinner, Mom looked sick, Dad looked resigned, and I was the one to point out that work was important for bills to get paid. Needless to say, my kids' end of the year celebration was tainted with a total black cloud. That's why Miller worked hard to cover the uncomfortable vibe and may have oversold the idea of a summer vacation. It worked for a while.

Then the dessert presentation came to our table. I thought Connie was going to come out of her skin when offered Darby's selections. Dad overlooked everyone, ordered his favorites, and Mom tried to keep the peace.

I knew something had happened before I walked into the restaurant, but Miller kept shooting me looks that told me he'd explain later. As soon as Connie drove off, he unloaded.

I was torn between being thankful to him for stopping what could have been a nasty confrontation and wanting to kick his ass for being such a dick to Darby. She was clearly at a disadvantage in that situation. Once again, I found myself wanting to protect her, which pissed me off even more.

I grab my phone and see three missed calls from Connie. Against my better judgment, I return her call.

"Hey," she answers on the first ring.

"Are the kids okay?"

"Of course."

"What's going on?"

"It was a great dinner tonight, don't you think?"

"It's always a great dinner when my parents celebrate the kids."

"Thank you for including me."

"Didn't have a choice when you put me in a bind."

"Don't be a jerk. We had fun as a family."

"What do you need, Connie?" I walk around the corner of the house and stop dead.

"We should talk tomorrow."

"About what? We had all night together."

"Maybe we should discuss the living arrangements again."

"No. I need to go."

I hang up and stare at the sight from the sidelight of my porch. Darby is laid out on my oversized porch swing with her arms and legs curled around the pillows, asleep. The closer I get, I notice she's not actually curled around them; she's clutching them securely in a protective hold. The Darby I remember was always a bed hog. She loved to spread out—arms and legs everywhere. We'd fall asleep wrapped around each other and wake up with her all over the place. Many times, we'd wake up upside down because she'd turn over, and on instinct, I'd follow. It never bothered me because I liked that, even unconscious, we fit that way. Most mornings, I'd wake up before her and lie there, listening to her shallow breaths and feeling nothing but peace.

There's nothing peaceful about her position tonight. She looks small, frail, and afraid. I crouch down and put a hand to her shoulder to wake her. She darts up in a frenzy, searching the area until her eyes land on me. I hold my breath for a brief second and watch the cloud of doubt cover her expression. "I didn't mean to fall asleep."

"What are you doing here?"

"I came to talk to you," is all she says.

I stand, offering my hand, which she takes as I lead her into the house, turning on lights as I go. Her hand tenses in mine, but I take her straight to the kitchen, thinking she will be more comfortable.

The mistake rains down on me immediately as her hand snatches out of my grip, and I turn to see her white as a sheet, staring at the refrigerator. "Maybe we should go back to the porch."

"Why?"

"It's a safer place."

"Safer? What's wrong with right here?"

"I'm not sure I can do this in a room that's a shrine to your children with Connie."

The sudden blaze in her eyes pushes me to my limit. "Everywhere in here is a house for my kids."

"It was a mistake coming here tonight." She makes a move to run, and my reflexes kick in. I grab her by the waist, spinning her to face me.

"Are you that much of a fucking cunt you can't even look at my kids, the two people I love more than life?"

70

She flinches, bowing her head and sucking in deep. Guilt swamps me, and I immediately know I've gone too far. "Look, I've had a shitty night. I shouldn't have said that."

"No, you're right. I should have expected nothing less than your house to be filled with pictures and memories. Like I said, I shouldn't have come."

"Well, you did come here, so why don't we cut to the fucking chase and tell me why?"

"Please, let me go," she begs, trying to get loose.

"Tell me."

"I can't," she cries.

"What the fuck are you keeping from me?" I scream. "This shit has got to end. I let it go a long time ago and moved on! I have kids, Darby. That's a fact. This is their home, and you have no right to come in here and make snide comments—"

"I know that! I have no rights to you at all! I lost them the day I killed our baby!"

I let her go, tripping back until I hit the counter. "What?"

"I killed our baby." Her body trembles. "I did it!" she shrieks so loud my eardrums ring.

"You had a miscarriage. It fucking sucks, but it's not your fault. The doctors explained that."

Darby starts pacing in a circle robotically. "My worry and anxiety were the worst. You tried to help me see reason, but I was pessimistic, always worried and scared. Then I got used to the idea of having a baby at twenty-one years old because you chased every bit of that fear away. Excitement started to bloom, and the best part of it was that I was going to get everything I ever dreamed about. Marrying you and starting our family, I literally had it all. There was still a smidgen of doubt in the back of my mind, but I tried to beat it."

"Darby, a little doubt doesn't mean you killed our baby."

Her eyes lock with mine, and my blood turns to ice, chilling me all the way to my bones. Cold, flat, hard… the usual bright amber dies, and she stares at me with a lifeless expression. She may be staring at me, but she's not seeing me.

"I had a huge surprise for you and was thinking about bringing Jill in to help me. She's always been creative. It was the perfect excuse to plan a dinner with your family. I showed up early, hoping to catch her alone. Instead, I overheard Miller and your dad talking. Miller was convinced I got pregnant on purpose to trap you into marrying immediately. He said he knew we were serious, but he didn't see us going the distance. He couldn't understand why we'd been together since I was seventeen and avoided getting pregnant, then right after I graduated, I conveniently was knocked up. Jill piped in, agreeing that the timing was suspect. She had strong opinions about how unlikely we'd been careful enough, and starting a marriage based on a surprise pregnancy was doomed. Warren had stayed quiet, but when he spoke, his words are probably what broke me the most. He said it was good my family had money so I wouldn't come after yours."

A red haze clouds my vision, and I'm pretty sure I could rip my family to shreds with my bare hands right now. The chill that took over changes into a blistery fire, searing through my veins. A rage like I've never experienced brews to the surface, and it's all I can do not to punch something.

"What happened next?" I grind out harshly.

"Physically or mentally?"

"Both."

"I quietly slinked out of their house, called you and canceled dinner, told you I was feeling sick. You came to the shed and brought me something to eat and spent the night. Mentally, that smidgen of doubt grew into an avalanche of emotions. I no longer felt like I deserved to get the dream I'd been chasing since I was seventeen when Pierce Kendrick walked up to me at the gym and asked for my number. It was common knowledge that our age difference was the source of gossip, and no one could believe you'd date a girl that just graduated high school."

"I never gave a shit what people thought."

"You didn't, but it followed me for years. And here I was, strapping you down."

"Why didn't you tell me?"

"I was confused, hurt, and ashamed of myself for putting you in that position. You were perfect, and I loved you with everything I had. The last thing I wanted was to back you into a corner and make you choose between your family and me. And that's what would have happened. You would have unleashed fury on them to protect me. Instead of telling you, I tried to deal with it myself. Every day, my anxiety grew to new levels. I cried a lot, thinking again the baby was one huge mistake. Then I hated myself for thinking that way about something I loved so much that you gave me. It consumed me. My brain never shut down. It was all I could do to put on a brave face while trying to figure out how to deal. No one knew what was happening with me until it was too late."

She draws in a deep breath, her eyes scanning around the room and landing on the refrigerator. Her mind is a thousand miles away, and she's battling something big. When she turns back, I fight the urge to go her and yank her into my arms to erase the torture she's living in.

"As always, you were perfect during the ordeal. Even though you were devastated, you put me first. I couldn't deal with it. I couldn't look you in the eye every day, knowing I'd killed our baby. The guilt and shame were constantly clashing with the pain and sorrow. Because, when it was all said and done, I realized I wanted that baby. It didn't matter what your family thought, or if you ever married me, because I was meant to be a mom. The problem is, I figured that out too late. Then the hormones and never-ending emotions kicked into overdrive. You thought I was in a catatonic state because of the loss, but it was much more. There was no reasoning with me. I was convinced you'd find out and hate me. That added too much to my already fragile state, and I broke. I wouldn't say I was suicidal, but I was seriously unstable. My mom picked up on it and forced me to tell her what was happening. When she heard my story, she knew I needed help. I was already pushing you away and hated it. You'd been a rock of strength even in your own form of pain. I couldn't let myself bring you down to my level, so I picked a huge fight with you, giving you no choice but to break up with me. Then I left for Charlotte, where I went into counseling for severe depression."

"Jesus fucking Christ, Darby. Why in the hell didn't anyone tell me?"

"It wasn't malicious. It was on the recommendation of one of my counselors to work on me, and she was scared that, if you knew, I'd be more apt to worry about you."

"That's goddammed fucking bullshit, and you know it! I deserved to know. I was dying here, and no one thought to put me out of my misery? I'd have supported you. Hell, I'd have moved there myself to get you through each day."

She gives me a sad smile. "Always my hero, and that's why I couldn't tell you. You would have surrounded me with your protection and love, sheltering me from all the hurt."

"Is that so awful?"

"Of course not, but I had a very screwed up sense of reality. I went into a self-imposed exile, living a nightmare, but determined to rise up. It's not unusual for women who experience a miscarriage to delve into a depressive state, but my circumstances were different. During my time away, I also met with a gynecologist several times and forced myself to ask the hard questions. Since I was convinced I caused the miscarriage, it was important for me to know if children would be possible in our future. As you can imagine, she thought I was a bit loopy, but humored me. Turns out, physically, I'm fine. Slowly, things got better, and the state of my emotions evened out. It was time to come home, to beg for your forgiveness and hope you'd cloak me back in that protective armor."

Jesus, Jesus, Jesus... Fuck me. I swallow the bile rising in my throat, knowing exactly what's coming next.

"Then Evin showed up, unannounced, and my world crashed again, this time taking me to a place darker than I imagined. I barely thought about losing our son because the loss of you was greater."

"Son?"

"That was my surprise for you. I'd been antsy about finding out the sex early, so when I heard my sonographer was being shadowed with an intern, I volunteered for them to use me. It was too early to be one hundred percent accurate, but we gave it a shot."

In a rush, everything she says hits me with a force so strong I'm fighting for air. My chest and stomach seize at the same time, and I grip the edge of the counter for support.

That day with Evin...

"Answer the damn question, Evin. Is Darby all right?"

"You don't deserve answers. Stay away from her and let my family do what we need to do."

"What the fuck does that mean?"

"It means you did enough damage to last a lifetime, and everyone that loves her suffered. We're going to do what we need to do to bring her back. You do not get to ruin this for my family."

The conversation in the bakery...

"I left here in tatters, Pierce. Broken, ashamed, hollow, and I went away for a reason. My brother drove up to Charlotte to break the news of her pregnancy. I found myself back in shambles. Then our dear, darling friend, Connie, followed the southern etiquette protocol and sent me a personal birth announcement—to my parents' house. She was kind enough to repeat the action a mere sixteen months later."

"You have got to be shitting me."

"No. So you don't get to play the pity card because I do know a goddamned thing that happened to you. You got together with the one bitch in our group of friends that openly disrespected our relationship. I wasn't gone fourteen weeks before she was having your baby."

"I'm gonna kill her."

"Why? Why be mad now? You have the children you always wanted, and from what I hear, they are perfect kids."

"Leave my kids out of this."

"Fine. I didn't leave your ass in the dust and skip the town that I

love easily. I was coming back—and I was prepared to beg, explain what happened. There was a sliver of hope that you'd understand."

"Understand what, Darby? What you did to me was unforgivable."

"You're right. It was unforgivable. I was selfish and focused only on myself. But believe me when I tell you that I paid the price. There was no way for me to come back here and watch the man I thought I was going to marry living out his dream with a woman I could no longer stand. And that also tells you why I didn't make a big deal about being back. I'm still not sure I can live in the same town. You came in here wanting some answers, and you've got them."

Stephanie's warning...

"You let her go, Pierce. She needed you more than anything, and you let her go."

"You have no fucking idea what happened."

"That's where you're wrong. I know everything. I'm warning you now; when she tells you her story, you're going to be in your own pit of hell."

Edward's visit...

"I'll tell you this. Darby left you for a good reason. A reason Annie and I supported one hundred percent. Evin wanted to go with her, and we practically had to tie him down to stop him from smothering her. She went away to get help."

"You're a dad now, so I know you get the protective burn that runs through your veins when you think about your children hurting."

"I do."

"Then you'll understand that I've had that burn scorching through me for a very long time. Not a day goes by that I don't want to strip that pain from my daughter."

"No offense, but you need to remember what happened back then."

"I know what happened. All of it. Every word exchanged, every tear that fell, every cry of regret, and even every drink you consumed to try to run from the heartbreak."

Every word that Darby, Evin, Stephanie, and Edward said replays in my brain and slams into me like a hammer to the heart. It all makes sense. Years of hatred and blame seep out of my soul, and shame washes through me. Stephanie was right. So was my mom. I did let Darby go when I should have gone after her. She fucking needed me.

I rip my hands through my hair, feeling the blood pounding through my veins. I can't stop the rage that takes over, and I twist, throwing a fist through the wall. Self-hatred fuels me, and I explode in a roar. *"You should have come back to me!"*

She wraps her arms around herself defensively, and I realize how much of a madman I am right now. My whole body is shaking, and I need to check myself before I do something I'll regret.

Deep breaths, in and out. I clench my fists a few times then force myself to drop my hands to my sides. "You should have come back to me," I repeat.

"I couldn't. You were no longer mine."

"I was always yours."

"You were sleeping with the enemy! How can you say that?"

"There was no sleeping involved. I fucked her! I fucked her hard and fast. She was on her knees, face to the bed so I didn't have to look at her. Blew my load, went and sucked back a fifth of bourbon, and did it again. The second time, I made her face a wall, stick out her ass, and keep quiet. She wanted to suck my dick, so I let her. It was a way to dull the pain. No kissing, no foreplay, no feelings."

So much for calming down. Darby's face drains to deathly pale, and her body goes back to trembling. Tears pour out of her eyes that are burning with betrayal. Using her for a verbal punching bag is the last thing on my mind, but for some reason, I can't stop.

"Connie Webber marked me. I was an easy target when you left. You know our old crew; they were partiers. When you dipped out, she introduced me to a world of pot and booze that killed the pain every night. It was easier to live in a foggy haze than to face my world without you. It took her ten weeks to snake herself into my life, taking my grief and vulnerability and using it to her advantage. I didn't see it then, but she saw it crystal clear. I used condoms, Darby, but I should have doubled up on those fuckers. I also should have wrapped my own shit up and not let her take control. But that's what weed does. It mellowed me out so fucking much I handed that little plastic wrapper to her and let her slide it on. She knew she was pregnant within twenty-four hours of missing her period. And she was so goddamned ecstatic I knew I was fucked."

"I really think I should go." She starts to back away, looking around desperately, for what, I don't know.

"I think you should stay and hear how it all went down after that."

"I'm not sure I can."

"My family said that shit about you trapping me into marriage, but they should have saved their bullshit for what happened next. Connie thought she was getting a ring, a husband, and a grand mansion with me to pay for it all. She was dispelled of that notion lightning fast. What she got instead was the apartment next to Miller's and mine. My ass was working dawn until dusk, paying for most of her shit. It was easy to avoid her because she was living easy. She was pissed I wasn't around, but I did everything in my power for her when it came to the baby. When Maya was born, Miller moved out, and I turned his room into a nursery. My mom was around to help, but every night when I got home, I'd shower and go get my baby girl so Connie could get a full night's sleep. She had the days, and I had the nights. Connie kept going though. By this time, she'd turned into a full out bitch. Nothing I did was good enough. Her family put the pressure on, but I cut that line. Then, for the second time in my life, I got sloppy and stupid."

"Cole?" She flinches at his name.

"Didn't learn my lesson. But I loved my little girl and decided to let it go and try to form a cordial relationship with Connie. Things weren't perfect, but they were going better. She saw her opportunity and came after it. Bruce's bachelor party turned wild. He rented a party bus. We started the night at a sports bar and ended the night at a strip joint on the outskirts of town. Bruce was so pussy whipped; he immediately let Blaire know where we were. Thirty minutes later, the gaggle of women crashed in. Seeing as Blaire is Connie's best friend, Connie was right there with them. Maya was with Connie's mom for the night, and Connie was on a mission. I hadn't touched pot in over a year, but I was hammered. I avoided her most of the time, but when I went to the bathroom, she cornered me. Her face said it all. I tried to dodge her, but my inhibitions were hazy. She was persistent, and since I'd been staring at naked girls for an hour, I was horny.

"The thing about Connie is she has no shame. She dropped to her knees, slid the condom on, and then bent over. She actually thought I loved doing her doggy-style and never picked up on the fact that I didn't want to see her face. My son was conceived while I banged his mother over a toilet in the bathroom of a seedy strip club."

"Oh my God."

"I've never told anyone that, Darby. See, for all those months, I'd been living under the impression that her pregnancy with Maya was a complete and total accident. I can't prove it, but I've always believed that she did something to compromise the protection."

She's no longer pale but has turned a sickly green. The desperation in her eyes returns, and before I can ask if she's okay, she's in front of my sink, doubled over. I get to her in time to rescue her hair as she hurls over and over again. With each lurch of her body, my guilt rises. She heaves until nothing is left.

"Water," she rasps, taking her hair from me.

I grab a cold bottle from the fridge, open it, and slide it under her face.

"Thanks."

"I'm sorry, Darby. I've never in my life spewed the gory details of Connie before, and I shouldn't have started with you."

"No, it's okay. I'm okay, just give me a minute."

"I'm going to get a washcloth. Be right back."

She nods as more tears spill down her cheeks. I reluctantly leave her standing there crying and take the short walk to my room. I take a few minutes to mentally piece back together my control.

When I think it's been long enough for both of us to breathe easier, I return. And I'm alone. There's no sign of Darby anywhere. Her water bottle sits next to the sink, which is washed out.

I race to the door and see her truck's gone. She even repositioned the pillows on the swing cushion in their normal spots.

Anger rears up again, and I haul back, tossing the washcloth with all my strength. "Goddammit!" I scream into the night.

Chapter 10

Pierce

The waitress comes over, waving the coffee pot with a smile. I flick my hand, not even glancing her way, and keep my eyes on the door of the diner. I check my watch and see it's been exactly ten minutes since Dad and Miller texted to say they were on their way.

When the door opens, my mom walks through first, followed by my dad. He steps up next to her, possessively wrapping his arm around her waist in a simple gesture I've seen a million times in my life, but never did I understand the importance of it until this moment. It's not only about being proud to be by her side; it's about wanting to hold her—the feeling of having the woman you love nearby, and even the smallest touch from her can bring you to your knees.

Mom catches sight of me, and her steps falter, her mouth dropping open. Then I see it, the awareness that glazes in her eyes. She knows... She's been keeping the truth from me for all these years. Dad urges her forward, his own expression turning grim.

"Pierce, maybe this isn't the best place to have this conversation," she starts.

"Sit down. Miller is on his way."

They do as I ask, Dad ordering coffee for them but declining a menu. Mom fidgets, staring at the door with the look of a mother who will do anything to stop what is about to happen between her sons.

I don't have to see him to know he's here because she gives it away.

"Anyone want to tell me why we need to meet at a diner this early when we all saw each other last night?" Miller brushes past me, taking the chair to my left. "And why didn't we get a booth?"

"Because I'm not going to be here long, and I didn't want to have to throw your ass out of it when I get up to leave."

"Pierce, we should have this conversation somewhere else. Let's go to your place." Mom frets.

"My place isn't an option, considering there's more than one hole in the wall I already have to repair."

"Whoa, what the hell is going on here?" Miller picks up on the tension and looks between us.

"Twelve years ago, Darby arrived at the house for dinner and overheard a conversation where the three of you openly discussed her trapping me into marriage, insinuated she got pregnant on purpose, and rounded it out with comments about her going after my money."

"Son, that's not exactly how it went," Dad says.

"Really? You want to tell me how it went? What about you, Miller? Want to explain to me how you thought I'd picked up jailbait at seventeen and, even after four years together, still thought we weren't going to make it the distance."

"I didn't say that, man."

"What did you say?"

"It was twelve years ago. I don't remember exactly what I said."

"Well, twelve years pass by, and you've lived your life. I can understand how a short and simple conversation could fade from your mind. But not Darby. She's lived with those words scarring her to the point of believing them."

"She probably shouldn't have been eavesdropping then," he barks, and my hand jets out to wrap around his throat before he can react.

"Boys! Stop it right now!" Mom screeches, and the restaurant goes quiet.

Dad is out of his chair and has us both by the arms, hauling us out while Mom apologizes to the crowd as she follows behind. When he gets us to the parking lot, he steps in between and shoves us an arm's length apart.

"I knew her coming back would cause nothing but trouble. Look at you! You're acting like a lunatic," Miller seethes.

"That's because the woman I love came to me last night and bared her soul. You have no idea the seeds of doubt you planted in her mind that night."

"Why do you even care? She left you! She broke your heart, and now she's back to fuck you up worse."

"She left, but she didn't leave me. She was already skittish about the baby, scared out of her mind. Then she overheard your bullshit and thought the world was stacked against her. The doubts took over, and she made herself so sick she lost the baby. The blame pushed her into a deep depression that overwhelmed her. Yeah, she left, but she headed straight into the hands of doctors and therapists who pulled her back from the brink of suicide."

Mom's sharp cry fills the space, and Miller's body convulses. The fire of righteousness dies and is replaced with full-blown shock. Dad's hand lands on my chest, bunches my shirt, and he yanks me to him, knocking the air out of my lungs.

"Oh, fuck," he murmurs in my ear.

I was twenty-three the last time my dad hugged me like this, and at the time, it was what kept me standing when I learned Darby lost the baby. But today, his comfort does nothing to quash the disloyalty.

I push back out of his reach and look pointedly at my mom. "You knew. You knew what was happening with her, and that's why you pushed me to go after her."

"I had a feeling but didn't know for sure until a while later when Annie confided in me. There were never any details about her counseling, but I've always wondered what sent her over the edge. This morning, you confirmed it. She overheard something that sounded awful. But it wasn't as petty as it sounds, Pierce. She heard the worst and didn't stick around for the best. We shared our doubts, as we have every right to do. But then we shared our joy. You were having a baby, and the excitement outweighed the trepidation." Mom lays her hand on my arm.

"You're wrong. You had no right to have doubts because I didn't! She came over early that night to tell you we were having a boy. She wanted your help in surprising me."

Maybe I should have chosen my words more carefully, but seeing as I have lost my mind, it didn't happen. All the color drains from her face, and she begins to sway. Dad's at her side before her knees give out.

She grips in his arm and looks up with tears building. "A boy. She lost her boy."

Something passes between them that I don't understand, and his face goes hard. Warren Kendrick is usually a pretty relaxed man, but the stony look he throws my way makes me snap my jaw shut.

"Son, you need to get a hold of whatever is raging inside and remember who loves you. Everyone in this family adored Darby." He flicks his eyes to Miller then back to me. "We did wrong, and we didn't have a chance to make it right twelve years ago. But now we do."

The pompous dick in me stays alive and points to them. "Damn right. The first thing you need to do is get a hold of Annie and make an order so big it forces Darby into her bakery for days."

"Why?" Mom recovers quickly.

"Because since she ran out of my house last night after throwing her guts up, I can't find her. I want her where I know she's safe."

"We can do that. I can get to Annie."

"What are you going to do?" Miller dares to ask me.

"None of your fucking business. You stay out of my way, and I'll stay out of yours."

"Man, I had no idea what was happening with her head." He has the nerve to look guilty.

"Fuck you."

I spin, leaving them all gaping. Add another notch to my apology tour.

I jump in my truck, knowing someone may need to bail me out of jail if my next move doesn't go well.

•—•—•—•—•

It's eight o'clock before she finally drives up, and it's surprising she doesn't keep driving when she sees me sitting on her deck. I sip my beer and watch her climb out slowly, dragging a huge bag with her. She gives me one look and focuses on the ground as she makes her way to the shed.

"Hey." Her shoulders sag with exhaustion, and her voice is small and weak.

"Hey."

Her head pivots to both sides, and she leans to the side to look beyond the building. "Did you walk here?"

"Truck is parked around by the barn. I walked through with your dad earlier."

"Ah, the horses." She nods in understanding. "Did he ask you to come?"

"Not exactly."

"Why are you waiting on me?" She still is at the foot of the stairs, not approaching.

"Can I help you with that?" I point to the bag weighing down her arm.

"No, thanks. It's a bunch of business paperwork."

"Can I get you a glass of wine?"

"You brought wine?"

"Nope, but I saw some in your kitchen."

"You were in my house?"

I wave my beer as my answer.

"How did you get in?"

"Used the hidden key."

"My parents never moved that?"

"Apparently not."

"Good to know."

There's a beat of silence before she reluctantly trudges up the stairs. "Look, Pierce—"

"Where have you been?"

"I spent the day doing administrative work with Evin. We just finished dinner."

"What about when you left last night? You didn't come home."

"H-h-how do you know that?" she stutters.

"I came looking for you."

"Why?"

"Because you were sick, and I was worried."

"It was intense, but you don't need to worry. I'm okay now."

"Intense?" I raise an eyebrow.

"Okay, it was excruciating." Her shoulders slump lower, and her neck rolls back.

"Baby, you've always been breathtaking to me, even when exhausted, but you're dead on your feet. Why don't you go inside and change so we can have this conversation where you're more comfortable?"

She whips her face to mine, shock flaring in her expression. Then she twists and turns, looking around like she's confused. "This looks like the same shed. Last I checked, I still lived here. But for some reason, I feel like I've walked through to an alternate universe. Where's my dog?"

"Runner got quite the workout today. Last I saw, he was passed out on the living room rug."

Her fingers give out, and the bag makes a loud thud on the deck. "You took Runner with you?"

"Edward did."

"What's happening?"

"Go change. I'll get your wine." I stand.

"Aren't you furious with me?"

"Furious with a lot of things, but none of them are you."

"But—"

"Honey, please go change." I catch the trace of recognition in her eyes at the gentle tone of my voice, the same voice that was always my weapon of pushing her to get moving.

Thankfully, she listens and goes into the house. I grunt at the weight of the bag as I haul it inside and place it on her desk. Runner barely moves as I step over him and head to the kitchen, finding what I need.

A few minutes later, she reappears in the living room, and Runner instantly gets to his feet, pouncing over and almost knocking her down as she wobbles back on one leg.

"Runner, no!" comes out of my mouth before I can stop it, and both of them freeze.

"He's not going to trample me."

"He almost took you down."

She rolls her eyes and talks to the dog. "It's okay. He doesn't know how long we've been doing this. I can handle you."

He bumps against her jaw a few times then gets down, circling behind and plopping at her heels.

"That looks nice." Her chin jerks toward the glass of wine I'm holding.

"Get your ass over here, and it could be all yours."

Her lips crinkle in a small smile, and she comes my way, stretching her hand when she's close.

"I want one of those hugs."

The smile vanishes. "Not a good idea."

"It's a very good idea," I argue.

Her feet shuffle slowly, keeping her eyes on mine with uncertainty building. I place the wine on the counter and haul her the rest of the way, cradling her as close as possible. Immediately, her scent is everywhere, and my heart hammers in my chest, knowing she can feel it. "Fuck, Darby. I'm sorry, baby. Sorry to the bottom of my goddamn soul. I shouldn't have unleashed on you the way I did. It was a massive mistake on my part," I say softly into her hair.

Her body quivers against mine, but finally, she grabs hold of my waist and bundles my shirt. "I'm not sorry. At least, not about that. That was the part of our fight that actually gave me relief."

"Relief? There is no excuse for the way I spoke to you."

"No, but it was heat of the moment wrath. In the most bizarre way, it gave me peace of mind."

I rear back to see her face, and my own breath catches. "How?"

She sucks her bottom lip through her teeth, contemplating something, and then clutches my shirt firmer. "I thought you'd moved on, that you actually had feelings for her. It makes me an awful person to be relieved at the truth, and I should be ashamed. Maybe, one day, I will be. I mean, she is the mother of your children, and it is awful that I'm happy she—"

"I never moved on from you." I cut her off. "I was forced to get my shit together and face the music because it was about the welfare of my daughter and, later, my son. Last night was the first time in my life I said the gruesome details of how Connie got pregnant, and I got carried away. How fucked up is it that I've never even slept in the same bed or held the hand of the woman that had my kids?"

She winces painfully, and I catch the sadness creeping in. It's time to shift this conversation before we go too far again. "You said a lot of things, too."

"I did, and I should have been more delicate."

"Fuck no, you knew how to get my attention. There's a lot we need to talk about, but I have to know, do you still think it's your fault?"

"I don't know. I'll never know for sure, but I can't help but think my mental state, my confusion and anxiety, led to the result."

"I hate myself for letting you go through that alone."

"It was my choice."

"Which makes me think I need to be a part of your choices going forward."

Her eyes fill with misery. "We messed things up back then. Even now, knowing it's my fault, you were vulnerable to Connie. I pushed you into the mouth of a waiting shark. All the pain and heartache, all these years, it was caused by me."

"Baby, don't take that on your shoulders with everything else. I wish I could absorb every ounce of your pain. We're going to find a way to let it go, together."

Her lips part as what I've said sinks in. "There's no way to do that."

"There's a way. I may not be able to travel back in time, but I'm going to make things right."

"Things are right. We cleared the air and found closure."

"First steps."

"I can't stay here, Pierce. I know that now. The memories are painful, but the reality is devastating. You have children with another woman, and that's partially my fault. That will never change."

"No, but we'll make new memories, starting tonight." My hands sift through her hair, tilting her face to the side. I lower my mouth to hers, skimming my lips across hers, kissing from corner to corner. Unlike the other morning, I take my time, and when I slip my tongue through, it strokes hers gently. She tastes like chocolate and raspberries, and I'm instantly hard to taste more.

I walk her backward, supporting her weight, and keep our mouths joined. When we hit the doorway to the bedroom, I end the kiss, haul her into my arms, and sit on her bed.

"Pierce—" Her objection dies when I yank the neckline of her tank down and run my thumb over her nipple. "Ahhhh," she moans.

"Tonight, Darby. We make new memories tonight," I repeat.

It's easy to see she's waging a war in her head. Her body responds to my touch, her nipple hardening immediately, and her pulse racing. In the past, when Darby had doubts about anything, it was easier to get through to her with actions rather than words. It was the intensity of our connection that could break her uncertainties and ignite her faith in me and, more importantly, in us. I'm hoping that's still the case because she needs to understand that I've made a decision.

"You control this. Tell me when to stop. But right now, let me show you that you're the only woman I've ever loved."

Her expression changes; fiery, blazing heat blisters my skin as she gives a short nod. My hand travels under the satin of her bra, caressing her breast while my mouth covers hers. We kiss lazily, her fingers scraping the stubble on my cheeks, letting me control our pace.

A round of memories assaults my brain, more reminders of how Darby Graham owned me. Not once in all the years did I ever engage in the intimacy part of sex—the slow burn, small touches, expectations of what was happening—never with anyone else. Sex became fucking with one goal in mind, getting off. Always, no exceptions. I was generous, never taking without giving, but foreplay was quick, the fuck was usually hard, and the aftermath could get awkward.

Now, I can't get enough of her taste, the smoothness of her skin, the feel of her pressed close. There's a primal need brewing inside, but I force it down, wanting this piece of intimacy that's been missing.

Her breath hitches, and I break away to kiss along her jaw to her ear, nibbling lightly in a way that used to drive her crazy. She gasps, squirming in my lap, grinding against my dick. I lean us back, keeping her in my lap, propping on my elbow for support. She takes my hint, wiggling to remove her shirt and bra, and arches up. I take the invitation, dragging my lips over every inch of her perfect skin, and suck her nipple deep. She moans when I circle my tongue and scrape my teeth over the sensitive peak.

"More?" I know the answer before she even rasps her yes.

My hand slides into her shorts and instantly connects with her bare skin. "Fucking love that you still hate wearing panties."

"Only sometimes." Her response is low and breathy.

I glide two fingers along her slit, teasing and testing until they slide in easily. Her inner muscles clench hard.

"Shit, baby, you're tight." I pump them inside of her, twisting and scissoring, and she grinds her pussy down. Her breathing becomes ragged, her chest trembling under my mouth.

I pull her nipple through my lips, adjusting to watch her. She's so fucking hot, her neck arched, her mouth open, the sheen in her eyes as she writhes against me. This was supposed to be a starter, a little tease before I licked her pussy until she screamed my name. But fuck if I'm not going to make her come on my fingers.

My dick pulses, hard as steel and fully aware this is Darby. I surge farther and strum my fingertips in a rhythm. A slight brush over her clit, and she screams out, twisting into me, convulsing over and over. My cock throbs angrily against my stomach, the hunger inside barely contained. Any willpower or self-restraint I have is being tested. Her clutch on my fingers loosens, and I stroke her lightly as she comes down.

"Kiss me."

She brings her lips to mine, kissing me slowly, still trembling.

"Swear to God, watching you come for me is still the hottest thing I've ever seen. Glad you never lost that, baby."

She tenses, her nails digging into my shoulders as she buries her head in my neck. The air between us takes on a new vibe. She's retreating, and I can't let that happen. My hand slides out of her shorts, and I roll, balancing over her. The look on her face sends a chill down my spine. "What's wrong?"

"I didn't lose it. It's all yours, always has been."

The meaning behind her words slams into my chest. She said those exact words the night she gave me her virginity and so many times after. Always a pledge she belonged to me and only me.

"Never?" The question comes out sharp and clipped.

"Never, no one else. I couldn't do it."

A thousand questions flood my mind, but the answer is right in front of me. It's Darby. She never moved on. She held on to us and what we had for all those years.

My Darby...

Guilt and shame slash through my system. She picks up on it, cupping my chin and tracing a finger over my lips. My heart thunders in my chest. The possessive brute that disappeared long ago stirs and scorches through my veins.

"Always mine," I growl, barely able to control my voice.

"Yours," she confirms.

That's all it takes for my restraint to snap. I slam my mouth over hers, hauling us up. Both of us tear at clothes until we're naked and she's lying below me. Her eyes roam over my body, her hand darting out to grip my cock. The touch sends a jolt through me, and I'm ready to blow. Her pussy taunts me, my mouth-watering, but there's no time. I can't wait. Knowing I'm the only man to worship her body has me strung tight.

My hand covers hers, stroking twice before prying her fingers away, and I kneel between her thighs and hover over her. She reaches up, framing my face and bringing my lips a breath from hers. I glide through her slickness, pressing in slowly. Her eyes stay locked with mine, the copper glow burning deep in my soul. Inch by inch, she accepts me, stretching around my length as I sink deeper and deeper until she's taken me all in.

Darby is the only woman I've ever had flesh on flesh, and the sensation of her heat mixed with my need threatens my control. She tilts, angling her hips, silently telling me she's okay. Twelve years and no man has ever been inside her, pleasuring her, bringing her to the brink. Sparks sear my nerves, and my primal obsession comes alive.

There is no doubt in my mind; I'm not letting her go again.

I thrust in and out of her, slowly at first, picking up pace when her wisps of breath coat my lips. My cock swells thicker, my balls growing heavy with each stroke. Her knees drop, her ankles linking around my waist, and she heaves up.

"Stop holding back."

"Let me do this my way." I see the defiance forming in her gaze. Wild and insatiable, my Darby reappears. A throaty growl rumbles deep in my chest as she pounds into me from below.

"More," she commands, scraping her nails across my jaw and wrapping her arms around my neck.

I drive faster, harder, sweat dripping down my back as her groans ring in my ears. She screams my name when I hit the magic spot that always sends her over the edge. She breaks eye contact, pressing her neck deep into the mattress and arching into me. I lose sight of her face and the pleasure building.

"Look at me," I demand, cupping the back of her head and bringing her back into focus. "I need to see you. Every time I'm in you, I need to see you."

She understands immediately, licking her lips and squeezing her thighs. Her walls close in, grasping my cock until I can't hold back. I pound harder, her cries growing louder.

"God, don't stop!" she begs.

I couldn't if I wanted to because my entire body is ready to blow. "I need you there, baby," I grunt.

She yells out my name, her body shuddering against mine. That's all it takes to pull me there with her. A powerful explosion rocks over me as I pour into her until there's nothing left. My vision clears, and her face comes back into focus.

A small smile crosses her lips, but it's nothing compared to the liquid amber pools staring back. I recognize the glow, and my cock lurches. No downtime needed.

We're only getting started.

Chapter 11
Darby

It's going to be a good day.

And that has nothing to do with the fact that I had sex. It has everything to do with the fact that a thousand-pound weight is off my shoulders. Pierce and I cleared the air, and even if it was in the possibly most dangerous way for two people with our history, there are no regrets. My thoughts are interrupted when the phone rings, and I'm amazed when Stephanie's name pop up on my dash.

"What are you doing up this early?" I greet her.

"Your business is a pain in my ass."

Runner barks and moves his body to the console at the sound of her voice.

"What happened?"

"You made national news is what happened. Somehow, your little outfit in Charleston hit social media, and Brasher Resorts is chomping at the bit to get that contract and fly you to their headquarters for a formal announcement."

"Ooooookayyyyyy, is this bad news?"

"No, but since you don't have a public relations company, they think I'm your personal go-to gal. Their PR group is hounding me."

"Is a public announcement necessary?"

"What the hell is going on down there?" Her voice rises, and she ignores my question.

"Nothing out of the ordinary," I lie.

"You sound different."

"I sound normal. You're grouchy because you're up early."

"No, seriously, you sound different."

I sigh. "Fine, I was going to call you tonight and fill you in. Pierce knows everything."

"He knows?"

"Yes."

"Did you sign the contract before or after you told him?"

"I signed it after. Why?"

"What happened? There are some missing pieces here."

"There was an incident Tuesday night. I got caught in a bad position that almost ended with me coming face to face with Pierce, Connie, and their kids. I panicked."

"How did he take the news?"

"Too much for me to tell you on my way into work. It was messy, dramatic, and things got out of hand. But he showed up last night, and we talked things through. I think we're in a good place."

"That's it? Did you tell him about Brasher?"

"No, I didn't see any reason to."

"Did you get laid?"

"STEPHANIE! Why would you say that?"

Runner barks enthusiastically, giving me away.

There's a rustling of sorts, and I can picture her in her home office sifting through papers. "Never mind. I want all the details, but it's too early to discuss the reincarnation of your sex life. I'm going to call Brasher. Can you get to Aspen next week?"

"Push it off two weeks? There's a lot happening around here."

"Yep. They'd do anything to keep you on the line right now."

"Kinda late for that, considering the contract is signed. I'll give Mom a head's up that she's becoming a real assistant. Tell your contacts to call her with the details."

"Shit," she screams, the phone clattering down. A second passes before she responds, "Sorry, I'm back."

"You okay?"

"Yeah, but is Evin in the office today?"

"I suppose. He was going to scan the paperwork and have his assistant overnight them to you."

"Great, I have to go. Talk to you tonight." She hangs up in such a rush there's no time to say goodbye.

I pull into the garage by my building and let Runner out to go roam the grassy area across the small driveway. While he does this, I watch in the darkness with a smile on my face, leaning against the back door. For the first time in as long as I can remember, a feeling of contentment settles within me.

Runner does his thing, and out of nowhere, a light flickers on, blinding me for a second. I let out a little squeal, which has Runner racing to my side. Security lights beam all around the area, and a truck roars somewhere close. A few seconds later, that same truck pulls up in front of me. Pierce hops out, looking like a man who should be on a billboard, not a man that left my house at midnight to meet a moonlighting contractor.

"The security system is in place."

"This is what you had to do last night?"

"I don't like the thought of you here in the dark."

I roll my eyes and internally push down the butterflies fluttering alive in my stomach. "I'm fine."

"You are now, especially since your landlord agreed with me about the security measures."

"Should be interesting," I say under my breath and head to the door, only to find a new state-of-the-art keypad installed.

My key still works, but when I open the door, a loud beeping sounds. Pierce punches a few digits on the keypad and it stops.

"You should punch in the code after you open the door in case you feel danger. The same with the keypad on the inside."

"I'm not sure I'm a fan of you taking over my security. This place has been fine so far."

"Fine is great, but you being here in the dark doesn't sit well with me."

"I have Runner."

"The guard dog that would rather shake hands than attack?"

At the mention of his name, and seeing that my dog has now met Pierce a handful of times, Runner jumps up on his hind legs and goes full frontal with him. It takes a full three seconds before he starts licking the underside of Pierce's chin.

"My point is made. Runner is a lover."

"I don't know. I think he'll come around if anyone ever attacks me," I argue, throwing my hair up and reaching for my apron.

"He won't need to come around because I'll be the one to attack."

His statement causes my head to snap up from tying the apron strings, and I'm met with the Pierce Kendrick glowing blue eyes that could bring a woman down.

"Stop," I whisper, losing a little of my balance.

"Not a chance."

"What exactly are you doing here?"

"Giving you the run-down of the new security system, making sure you are safe, and in a few minutes, I'm gonna fuck you on that table."

A shiver runs up my spine, and my thighs clench as a flood of heat rushes south. "I'm working." I try to sound strong, but it comes out breathy.

"Do you always dress like that for a day of baking?"

"No." I prop my hand on my hip. "Today is Mrs. Asley's retirement luncheon, and Mom demanded I deliver the desserts."

"After we christen that table, I'll help you make up for the lost time."

"Don't you have a job?"

"Yep."

"Shouldn't you get to it?"

"I have lots of jobs. The most important this morning is you. The rest can wait."

"Pierce, you are insane. Go to work."

He works his lower lip through his teeth and searches my shelves. "Where would I find the caramel sauce you put on your brownies?"

"It's a chilled sauce."

He goes to the large fridge and yanks it open, reads through the dozen labels, and grabs a random bottle, setting it on the table. "This will have to do."

"Have to do for what?"

This time, when he meets my gaze, his eyes have transformed into liquid blue pools of lust and desire. Each step he takes closer, my skin tingles under the intensity of his stare.

"Why did you want the sauce, Pierce?"

"It's going on my breakfast."

"That's a double raspberry chocolate mixture, and you hate chocolate."

"Not anymore." He stops in front of me, his hand curling around my neck, his fingers sifting into my hair. "Chocolate was my addiction for a long time."

My breath hitches as he pulls me gently to him, sweeping his lips across mine. That fluttering in the pit of my stomach goes into overdrive, sending a tremor through my body, the double meaning behind his words winding around my heart.

"Addictions can be a very dangerous thing. Maybe it was time for a break," I whisper into his mouth.

"Worst mistake in my life was giving it up. I never stopped *craving* my chocolate."

"Maybe you should take it slow. You don't want to get sick of it."

"That's not going to happen."

The air around us thickens with sexual desire, and my knees threaten to give out.

"Darby," he rumbles.

"Hmm?"

"Get naked now." His hand slides slowly along my neck, over the exposed skin of my back, until he reaches the zipper and slowly draws it down. "On second thought, maybe I want you in this dress."

The seriousness of his tone tells me he's not kidding, and I move, slashing the knot out of the apron tie, yanking it over my head, and let the dress and apron fall to the ground. His eyes grow heated at the sight of my bright teal bra and hipsters that match the outrageous jeweled flip-flops.

"Breathtaking," he murmurs, right before he pounces and I'm off my feet.

The metal is cold against my skin, but I shiver for an entirely different reason. Pierce is studying me. His tongue runs along his bottom lip, and his gaze rakes up and down my body in a way I know he's memorizing it all.

"You got the honors last night. Today, it's my turn." He steps behind the table, the pads of his fingers skimming over my shoulder blades before he unclasps my bra and pulls it down over my shoulders and arms. The cool air hits my breasts, my nipples tingling as they instantly pebble. That's exactly where his eyes land when he rounds back. He grins, cocking an eyebrow. "I think we'll start right here."

He fits himself between my thighs, tips my chin, and brings my mouth to his. Our tongues touch, curling together, rolling in a familiar rhythm. He controls the speed, taking his time and exploring my mouth like we have all the time in the world. I lean into him, inhaling deeply, lost in the scent of him surrounding us and the promise of things to come that I barely feel his arm brush mine.

Freezing cold droplets fall onto my chest, breaking my haze, and I jerk away in surprise. The chocolate mixture drips down, covering my breast. Pierce's expression goes hot as he leans in, licking the trail and grunting his approval. The air grows thick as he repeats the process with the other side. The warmth of his mouth, combined with the cold of the sauce, is nothing short of exquisite.

Pierce and I had an explosive sex life, neither of us afraid to try new things or explore. Last night proved that our bodies are still in sync, knowing the other's desires. I couldn't miss the way he held back, but this morning, that is gone. There's an edge to him, a sense of dominance combined with the usual way he owns my body.

"Lay back, baby," he orders, sucking at the tender area behind my earlobe, and easing me down onto my elbows.

I nearly come off the table when he drizzles the mixture from breastbone to navel. He trails the pattern with his lips and tongue, covering every inch of my torso. My body is wound tight. Part of me wants this to last forever, and part of me is greedy for him to give me what I desperately need.

He squeezes my hips, bunching my panties and yanking them down my legs. I expect him to tease his fingers along my sensitive spots. Instead, he takes the bottle and dribbles chocolate everywhere as he raises his eyes to mine. "Last night, I was too fucking gone for you.

Deprived of your taste. This morning, I woke up craving what only you can give me."

He kneels, positions my knees on his shoulders, and holds my gaze as he slips his tongue through my folds.

"Oh my God!" My arms tremble at the shocking sensations shooting through my veins. He holds my legs open, licking, sucking, and lapping the chocolate dripping down.

I can't tear my eyes away from the erotic show playing out as he worships me. I'm close, so close that carnal need turns my stomach in knots, twisting and constricting until I can't take it anymore.

With all the strength I can find, I knife up, fist his hair, and buck into his face. Shamelessly, I chase the release. He pulls me close to the edge of the table, delving deeper, swirling inside and fucking me with his tongue until I'm gasping for air.

"Please," I beg, not recognizing the sultry voice coming from my throat. "Please, Pierce."

He knows what I need, changing pace and sucking hard. Stars explode behind my eyelids, and I scream hoarsely into the room, my orgasm ripping through like a bolt of lightning. He pries my legs apart in time to stand and catch me from tumbling over him. He fumbles between us, and I'm still convulsing when he positions my hips and slides in.

"Take me all the way, baby," he coaxes.

"Yesssss," comes out like a purr. Pierce was always large, but I swear he's grown. His thickness glides in and out until he rams a little harder, filling me. A whimper escapes, setting off a mini-orgasm as my body adjusts to his size.

His soft beard scrapes along my cheek as he grips my ass and increases his speed. I come down from my cloud long enough to remove his shirt and run my hands over the firm muscles of his neck, shoulders, chest, and arms. They ripple under my fingers, and I can't stop touching him, locking away the feel of his skin on my fingertips, the passion radiating between us. He rocks back and forth, kissing along my jaw.

"God, Darby, sliding into you, surrounded by your heat, sucking me deep; you have no idea what that does to me."

"Mmm," I moan, the coiling rebuilding at the base of my spine.

"Leaving you last night was torture. The whole time the system was being installed, all I thought about was this. Knowing it's only me. I woke up and immediately needed you."

"Yes," I whine when he speeds up.

"Let me see your face, beautiful."

I tilt his way, and my breath catches at the expression on his features. It hasn't changed in all these years.

Possession, hunger, desire bleeding into my flesh.

"I need you with me." He pumps harder, hitting my g-spot with each plunge. It takes less than a minute for me to hold on to him, shove my face in his throat, and shatter again. He's right there with me, flexing tight and emptying with a guttural groan.

I collapse, not moving, trying to catch my breath. A fleeting thought crosses my mind about the fact that he's now come in me multiple times. We touched on the subject last night, with him assuring me he's clean. His next words killed any worries I had about precautions outside of my pill.

"You are the only woman in this world that gets me. All of me. And I'm the only man that feels all of you. No barriers, no taking the time to stop and find a little plastic package. I'm done with that. I get you bareback. Nothing comes between us."

It was barbaric and crass, but deep down, I loved knowing that. Even the bitch who ruined my life never got to feel all of Pierce. So, this was us, having raw sex with no barriers and giving in to our desire.

"Baby, you with me?" he mumbles.

"Yeah." I sigh dreamily.

"Thought I might have lost you to space."

"It's possible, but I'm back now."

"Wanna share your thoughts?"

No, I do not want to tell him how it delights me that he gives me everything during sex. I think of something quick. "I'm pretty sure the health department would frown on us having sex on my prep table," I tell him with a giggle.

"Highly doubt anyone but a bitter shrew would think what we did was frown worthy." He kisses along my collarbone.

"I hate to do this, but I have to get to work."

He presses his head into my neck, nibbles a few more times, then brings me to my feet. "Go clean up."

I don't miss the look of loss and force my feet to hustle to the full bathroom in the back. Once I get there, I scream, "I look like I've been mauled by a bear! Or a serial murderer!" There are remnants of the deep red sauce streaked on my neck, chest, breasts, leading down my stomach, and—oh, God—my entire pelvis, hips, and inner thighs.

He's at the door in a second, holding my panties and bra, looking proud. "Want me to lick it off?"

"No, I have to shower!"

"Let's shower together." He points to the color staining his own throat. Then I notice it's splotched all over his shirt he has draped over his shoulder.

"Oh, good God, we are in trouble. You look the same. Please, tell me you have another shirt in your truck?"

"Maybe, but the difference is, I don't give a shit. You have to go to the party prim and proper. My job is a lot different."

"Get out of here." I push him away, slam the door, and do my best to shower off and salvage my makeup and hair. When I'm done, I groan at the fact that he only brought me my panties and bra, then decide to play his game, striding out confidently.

I freeze mid-step, my heart lodging in my throat. Pierce is shirtless, cracking eggs into a bowl surrounded by ingredients.

"Put on my shirt and come help me." He tips his chin to the small sitting area where my dress and his shirt are arranged over a chair.

I shrug on his shirt, switch on the ovens, and join him. "Are you making something specific?"

"Trying to get started on the almond torte."

"How'd you know about those?"

"Because Mom planned the menu."

"Explains why this became my priority of the day. Why don't you start on the cookies? The dough is already made in the fridge, and the cookie sheets are there." I point to the large plastic tub holding supplies.

He nods and gets to work alongside me, filling three trays with perfect rows of dough. As hard as I try, I can't concentrate with him standing so close, half-dressed, and the scent of him coating me. His arm brushes mine, and goosebumps pop across my skin. When I sneak a peek over at him, he's grinning smugly, keeping his eyes on the table.

"You need to put your shirt back on."

"I disagree."

"I can't focus."

"Because of my shirt?"

"Partly. You're half-naked."

"Would you prefer I was fully naked? That's not a problem." He begins to pull at his belt.

"Stop! You can't get naked or we'll get nothing accomplished."

He crooks an eyebrow, grinning wider. "On that, I totally disagree. I get a lot accomplished when naked."

My measuring spoons fall on the table, and I toss my head back to stare at the ceiling. "Do you want to explain to a bunch of meddlesome women why their desserts taste like cardboard?"

96

"I can guarantee, if I explained it, they'd know exactly why it tastes like cardboard."

"Pierce!"

He twirls me to him, his hands going under the shirt and cupping my ass firmly. "Baby, look at me."

I do as he asks, and my chest seizes at the playful glint in his eye. More memories batter my brain.

"I've missed teasing you." He takes the words right out of my mouth.

"Pierce." This time, his name comes out breathy and faint.

"I want you in my shirt because it will smell like you—your perfume, the sweet aroma of cookies, and the unmistakable scent of sex. All day, I want that clinging to my skin. Every man on my crew is going to know why my mood is fucking great."

"You want your employees to know you've been laid?"

"No, I want anyone who comes in contact with me to know I'm happy."

"You're happy?" I repeat, sounding like an idiot.

"There's a lot of shit swirling in my world, and I know you and I have a long way to go, but for the first time in over a decade, I woke up with a smile."

My insides melt into a puddle of sappy goo. I lift on my toes and run my lips across his. "I woke up with a smile, too," I admit. "Those women aren't going to miss your scent covering me."

"Is that a problem?"

"We don't want to give anyone the wrong impression."

"There is no wrong impression in this scenario. I told you last night; I'm not fucking this up again."

I refrain from reminding him that we can't erase the past. "We agreed to keep things light."

"*We* didn't. You said it, and I pretended to listen. My intentions are not light."

His declaration both thrills me and scares me. We can't go back in time and change things. Now would be a good time to tell him that this is never going to work, because if Brasher Resorts agrees to my timeline, I'll be moving in September. But something deep down keeps me from relaying this.

"I need to make some tortes." His sly grin is the sign he thinks he's got me, but this is my way of dodging any arguments.

He kisses me lightly, squeezes my butt, and then turns me back to the prep table. "How long on these cookies?"

"I'll know by smell when they get close."

"For those of us without a baker's nose, how long?"

"Check them in fifteen."

"I need to leave my assistant a message for when she gets into the office. I'll make the call outside and take Runner with me."

"Aren't you going to see her soon?"

"Doubtful since I'm not going to the office until after lunch."

"Going on-site?" I raise an eyebrow.

"Eventually. I'm going to spend some time with you this morning, then head to a project. I need her to message me Miller's schedule."

"Why not ask him?"

"Not in the mood to deal with him right now."

There's an edge to his tone that piques my curiosity. "Are you arguing?"

"Something like that."

"About me?"

"Why would you think that?"

"Because your eyes went from fun-loving to hard as stone, and also because he obviously hates me."

"He doesn't hate you; he has some misconceptions."

He throws my words about Evin back at me, and I decide not to pry. Instead, I nod and grab my mixing bowl. He leans in to kiss my cheek on his way out, calling for Runner to follow.

When the door shuts, closing me in, I blow out a deep breath and notice my hands are trembling.

The last thing either of us needs is more hurdles, but I have an idea this morning may have dumped us right in a world of complications.

Chapter 12

Pierce

"It's about time you call," Stephanie barks through the line. "I thought I was going to have to send Evin after your ass. That would not have been my first choice."

"What are you talking about?"

"Darby came to you two nights ago, and then you showed up at her place last night. Doesn't take a rocket scientist to know how that went. Heard it in her voice this morning. What the hell has taken so long?"

"Are you always this direct?"

"It's one of my many endearing qualities. Stop sugar-talking me and answer the question."

"I've been busy."

"And now?"

"You were right."

"I always am, but what point did I drive into your head?"

"I'm living in my own version of hell," I admit, the knot in my gut rolling.

"Thank fucking God. Did you knock the chip off your shoulder?"

"Someone should have told me. I didn't deserve to be kept in the dark."

"No, you didn't."

"Knowing the truth, and the events that happened afterward, makes me feel like shit."

"The bigger question is, are you going to be able to get past it?"

"In terms of why she left, yeah, I'm going to be able to deal. It's what I did to her."

Silence fills the line, and I check to see if we're still connected. "Stephanie?"

"I'm here, but I don't know what to say to that. You replaced her quickly."

"I never replaced her. She knows the reality of my situation, and it's not pretty."

"You knocked up the slut of your group. Can't imagine there's anything pretty about that. I've always told her it was a mistake, but Darby was convinced you replaced her. Good lord, you went and did it again, too."

"She knows the truth now." My mouth tastes like I've swallowed acid.

"Well, I'm glad you cleared things up. It's very good for both of you."

"That's it?"

"What do you want me to say?"

"I need to know what kind of fight I have on my hands here."

"What are you fighting for?"

"I'm fighting for Darby. For us. For the life we should have been living all these years. I want it all back."

"Does she know this?"

"She's in denial."

"She would be. You both bring a lot of baggage to the table, and yours have names and a mother that Darby hates."

I grit my teeth at hearing her refer to my kids as baggage. But it wouldn't be smart to piss off the person who holds the answers I need.

"I didn't say it's going to be easy, but what am I going up against in Charlotte? As her best friend and her lawyer, tell me what kind of life she has in Charlotte, because I sure as hell can't move, and the last thing I want to do is ask her to give up what she has there. Only you can help guide me."

The line goes silent again, and this time, my brain picks up on the unspoken words. It becomes clear. "She's not planning on going back to Charlotte, is she?"

"You need to talk to her."

"Dammit! Why the hell can't anyone—"

"Pierce," she cuts in, "I want to tell you more, but there's a very fine line between her lawyer and her friend. Answering that question pulls me over the professional line. You say you want her back? A lot of time has passed."

"You don't have to remind me of that."

"Do I have to remind you that you spent all of that time angry at her?"

"Do I have to remind you that I was kept in the fucking dark?"

"How can you be sure this isn't old feelings resurfacing and mixing with the heartache of knowing what she went through? Just because you had sex doesn't mean you have a future."

Her insinuation sends my blood pressure soaring. I bite the inside of my cheek to keep from lashing out. "Did you give me your number so you could bust my balls? You don't know the kind of man I am. If you did, you'd know sex has nothing to do with it."

"I'm hardly busting your balls. It's a legitimate question. Why do you want her back?"

"I love her."

"That's all you're going to give me?"

"That's all your gonna get."

"Fair enough, I guess that will do. I'm glad to know I didn't spend the last four hours wasting my time." She mumbles something under her breath, and the sound of papers rustling fills the line.

"Am I supposed to guess what that means?"

"No. You called for advice, and here's what I'm going to suggest. You need to talk to Darby and go into it with an open mind. She may have lived with the emotional scars of your history, but she threw herself into DG Creations and has built an amazing business. People took notice."

"People? What people?"

"Can't cross that line, Pierce. It has to come from her."

"I'm beginning to regret this phone call."

"Remember that chip on your shoulder I mentioned?" she goes on, ignoring my comment. "Ditch the attitude. I haven't heard the whole story from Darby, but from her brief details, along with a morning spent on the phone with Evin, I understand most of your conversations have escalated to explosive levels."

"That changed two nights ago."

"Good to know. I told you the morning we met that I saw the chemistry and connection. Let's hope that has the magic healing powers it's going to take. She's going to need that." Her voice grows softer, and I know immediately what she's referring to.

"Connie isn't going to touch this, Stephanie. I can assure you of that."

"Pierce, I'm going to go off-character here and step into your corner. I've already told you how close Darby is to me, but for some reason, I have a soft spot for you. Don't fool yourself into thinking you can shield Darby from the wrath that is going to rain down when news hits about your reunion. You said earlier it wasn't going to be easy, and you thought you were competing with Charlotte. Charlotte isn't in the equation; it's much more. Outside of Darby, you should start with Evin. You need him as an ally. From what I know, Darby set him straight the other day about what happened and told him that you never blamed her. I think that helped pave the way for forgiveness from him."

"Forgiveness? He was one of the people who kept her from me."

"He did what she asked, and you have to respect that."

"Fine," I grit out. Logically, she's right, but it stings like hell to think of what could have been prevented if Evin had talked to me.

"Then, I understand there's a problem with your brother."

"Miller won't be a problem."

"Outside of Darby, those two are the most important. Because you're both going to need all the support you can get when Connie throws down. I suspect that is going to involve your children."

I close my eyes and drop my chin to my chest, blowing out a deep breath. Stephanie doesn't even know Connie, and she has her pegged. "I'll start with Evin," I concede, suddenly exhausted.

"Good choice."

"Anything else?"

"Yeah, once you talk to Darby and Evin, you'll be calling me again. By that time, I can drop the smokescreen and we can make a plan."

"Two days, Stephanie. Two days is all it took for me to fall completely back in love with her. Losing her again isn't an option."

"Then, don't fuck this up."

The line goes dead, and I drop my phone on my desk. The stack of paperwork calling for my attention is going to have to wait. The scent of Darby clings to me, inducing more memories. I told Stephanie it took two days to fall back in love with her, but the truth is, I never fell out of love. A familiar pain seizes in my chest at not knowing what I'm up against. This may be the fight of my life, but like I said, losing her again isn't an option.

•—•—•—•—•

When I get out of my truck, I follow the sound of barking from behind the shed. Edward and Darby are tossing a rope-like toy back and forth, and Runner is going crazy trying to catch it mid-air. Annie stands on the porch with a drink in her hand and a smile on her face. She catches sight of me, her smile growing wider, and tips her drink in my direction. I jerk my chin and don't hesitate to head their way.

Darby gives in, throwing the rope high in the air for Runner, and when he catches it, he sprints to her, jumping in her arms and setting her off balance. They both go down, and I halt when she hits the ground hard, her body bouncing up.

"Runner, no!" I scream, racing to her, fitting myself between the overly excited dog and her body. He takes this as an invitation to play more and pounces on my back. "Runner, stop!"

Darby's eyes grow wide, and Runner stops moving, slinking to her side.

"Are you okay?" I scan over her face, neck, chest, and arms, cradling her head in my hand.

"I'm fine. We were playing."

"He took you down rough."

"We do this all the time."

"You could have been hurt."

"I braced."

"Baby, that dog could seriously crush you with that much momentum and strength."

"You're overreacting." Her eyes roll to the sky.

"Let me help you up." I slide my other arm around her waist and stand, taking her with me. When she's steady on her feet, I twist her. There's a spot of red seeping through her shirt, and I pull the material up to see a long scratch on her lower back.

"Pierce," she hisses, trying to wiggle away.

"Don't move."

"Put my shirt down. Did you forget my parents are here?"

"I'm inspecting a cut, not ripping your clothes off... yet." I throw in the last part where only she can hear.

Her face heats, and she slaps at my hand. Runner rounds our legs, butting up to me.

"You've hurt his feelings. He's not used to getting yelled at." She shifts, squatting down and giving the dog a hug. His eyes stay on me, and I swear that dog looks as if he's ready to cry. His sad expression hits me square in the chest. I kneel next to her and rub his head a few times.

"It's okay, boy, but you've got to be more careful." He actually nods in understanding, nuzzling his face in my palm.

"What are you doing here?" I don't miss the wince when she stands again.

"I told you I'd see you tonight."

"I guess I thought you'd call first or come after dark."

"Why would I do that?"

"Less chance of being seen."

"I'm not hiding anything, Darby. Are you?"

She glances down, to the sides, over my shoulder, and finally to me. Her eyes are filled with doubt and insecurity. "It's probably better for you."

"Let me worry about what's best for me."

"We don't want to give people the wrong impression."

I step back into her space, frame her face with my hands, and enjoy the look of shock when she realizes what's about to happen right before I lower my mouth to hers. She tenses, her body stone still as I run my lips across hers several times. My tongue darts out, and I groan at the taste of toffee and caramel. "You taste delicious," I murmur.

A throat clears behind us, and I nibble on her lower lip lightly before turning back to Edward and Annie. Edward's arm is around Annie's shoulders, and she is leaning into him with a look that takes me back in time. She's happy, relaxed, and completely unfazed with my show of affection.

"Pierce, you want to come inside for a drink?" Edward offers.

"Actually, I'm going to make Darby dinner. Can I take a rain check?"

"Sure," Annie answers, beaming bright.

"Runner, come on." I pat my thigh, and he trots ahead of us as I lead Darby back to the shed.

She remains quiet. Even after I've unloaded the groceries out of my truck and made my way around her kitchen, she's staring off into space.

"Darby, something on your mind?"

"I'm not sure what just happened. You drove up to my house, yelled at my dog, touched me tenderly, and then proceeded to kiss me in front of my parents."

"Play by play tells me you know exactly what happened."

"But why?"

"Why what? Which part?"

"All of it?"

"I came to make you dinner. Runner could have hurt you so, on instinct, I yelled, and I kissed you because this morning was a fuck of a long time ago. I missed you."

"You missed me?"

"That surprise you?"

"Well, yes, actually, it does."

"Have a seat, baby. Let me get you a drink." I go to her bar.

"This is weird."

"Don't make it weird. I want to make you dinner, talk about our days, then take you to bed where I plan to make sure *nothing* is weird."

She gives a few shakes of her head, raising her eyes to mine and taking a few seconds as the idea settles over her. "Okay, Pierce, tell me about your day."

I uncork the red wine and pour her a glass, taking it to her before going back to chopping vegetables. "It started out fantastic. I went to the office and had a mountain of paperwork to look over. My assistant didn't quit, which is an added bonus. Made a few phone calls, then hit the field."

"Is your assistant usually a flight risk?"

"Andi's a little sensitive."

"Which means you fly off the handle a lot?"

I chuckle, flashing her a grin, and dump my mushrooms and onions in a skillet. "Depends on who you ask."

She giggles, sipping her wine and coming around the island. "Can I help?"

"Yeah, you can get your ass back on a barstool and tell me about your day."

She grabs forks, knives, and napkins, sets her small table, and shuffles back to a stool, sliding on and twirling her glass between her fingers. Her teeth work over her bottom lip, which tells me she has something to ask. "You have something else on your mind?"

"Well, you didn't mention your kids. Did you talk to them?" It's not lost on me how she forces the question.

I tense, knowing this is going to be a delicate issue for a long time. "I did. Spoke to them twice. They're already planning the last week of school, asking to skip the final day."

"Understandable." She gulps her wine this time, avoiding my eyes.

Even though she brought it up, we're quickly heading into dangerous territory. "Tell me about your day."

A small grin forms on her lips. "It was interesting. I made it to the luncheon in time. Your cookies were a hit. Jill kept shooting looks my way, and my face was probably red the whole time."

"Mom doesn't know the meaning of subtle."

"I'm pretty certain, at one point, she actually sniffed me."

I bark out a laugh and drop the garlic butter in the pan, followed by the steaks. "Did you have fun?"

"It was nice, but I'm kinda sick of being the center of attention. This was Mrs. Asley's day, but I still found myself in the spotlight."

"People are proud of you, Darby. It'll die down soon." I glance over my shoulder to her.

"Yeah, you're right. But people are a little too curious."

I concentrate on searing the steak, tending to the vegetables, and getting everything plated before I move to the subject that has been eating at me since I hung up with Stephanie. "Let's eat." I grab a beer on my way to her table and almost hit my knees when she lets out a low, throaty groan on her first bite.

My cock springs to life, and I can't tear my eyes from her face. She's chewing slowly, and when she swallows, her gaze is burning into mine.

"Where did you learn to cook like this?"

"If you want to finish, you need to quit looking at me like that."

A sly grin forms on her lips as she puts another bite in her mouth and moans seductively. She's testing me and, any other time, I'd yank her up and fuck her on the sofa to take the edge off. Food be

105

damned. But I have a mission tonight. I drop into the chair and circle my fingers around her wrist. "Behave."

"Fine, I'll hold back all moans of appreciation until later."

"Good idea." I kiss the inside of her wrist and let it go, cutting into my steak. "I like what you've done with the shed. It's quite a showplace."

"Spoken like a true contractor," she teases. "You always were a sucker for the finer details."

This is the truth and one of the reasons why it took me so long to redesign my home. "When did you redecorate?"

She scrunches her eyebrows and counts down on her fingers. "I'm guessing four years ago. Mom and I were walking through a home design store, and I ran across that set of pillows." She points to the oversized pillows on her sofa with nautical designs. "They were the inspiration, and we knew right away this place could use a facelift. It took three months of shopping, comparing notes, and finally, it all came together. I drove down for a week, and we worked hard, but the end result was exactly as we pictured it."

"The two of you did it alone?"

"Not really. Stephanie came with me. Dad and Evin were hands-on, too. Dad had the cabinets painted, the new fixtures in place, and new counters installed before I got here."

"What about the double crown molding and the light fixtures."

"Boy, you don't miss anything."

"I built this place originally. I remember everything."

"Yeah, that was all us. Like I said, we worked hard."

It scalds inside, knowing I could have had a crew over here and finished in less than two days, but I keep it to myself. It's another reminder of how the Grahams distanced themselves.

"Evin teased it could no longer be named the shed, considering we made it into a coastal chic paradise, but I've never wanted to change the name."

"It is the nicest shed I've ever seen."

"Thanks, I enjoy it."

I take a long drag of my beer and push forward. "Do you think you'll decorate your new place in the same way?"

Her eyes widen, her skin pales, and the look on her face confirms what I feared.

"No, I don't think so," she whispers, setting her fork down.

"When are you leaving?"

"How did you know?"

"I had my suspicions, but no confirmation until this moment."

"Suspicions?"

"Small details that, alone, would raise questions, but once put together, they are glowing signs. You've got boxes stacked in your closet labeled personal items that you have yet to unpack. Today, in your bakery, I grabbed cookie sheets from a Rubbermaid storage bin when you have shelves lining your walls for all your supplies. I noticed Runner's tags on his collar don't reflect an address, only your phone number, and today, a request came across my desk that Mr. Baldwin is looking for bids to do renovations on the building you are leasing. The project notes don't include a bakery expansion."

"I guess your ability to seek the finer details isn't restricted to construction."

"Full disclosure, I also called Stephanie this morning."

This time, her eyes bulge, and panic washes over her features.

"She wouldn't tell me anything. Her loyalty to you is strong, which ironically gives me peace of mind that you have someone like her in your life."

"She's the best, but why did you call her?"

"I had my reasons. You know she gave me her card, told me I'd need her when the truth came out. She was right. I needed her, but unfortunately, we didn't get far."

She nods, not surprised. "I haven't had a chance to tell her what happened between us. We were supposed to talk tonight."

"I think I gave her the run-down, and she knows where I stand."

"I'm sure she loved that," she replies sadly.

"I'm right, aren't I? You're planning to leave?"

She nods again, and this time, a slice of pain slashes through my sides. Nothing could have prepared me for what she says next.

"Let me start at the beginning..."

For the next half-hour, I listen intently, hanging on to every word about how Darby created her business in Charlotte, built her clientele, and proceeded to impress the right people along the way. She stays on the topic of her business, but I pick up on the holes in the story where she pushed herself harder around the times my kids were born. When she gets to the event last November that led her straight into the direction of Brasher Resorts, my body tenses, knowing this is what Stephanie couldn't tell me about.

Darby talks about the job opportunity with as much enthusiasm as if she was talking about the weather, showing no emotion. The only time her voice hitches is when she mentions relocating across the country. That pain spreads through my body, intensifying so deep, my vision goes cloudy.

"Aspen?"

"Aspen," she confirms.

"When did you sign the contract?"

She fidgets, avoiding my question, and I'm forced to sit still, waiting her out. Finally, she admits, "Tuesday evening, I gave my commitment to Stephanie. Wednesday, I spent the day with Evin, going over financials and actually signing the contract with a notary and witness."

The weight of her answer pounds into my head, and I drop my chin to my chest, fighting for air. Tuesday night... The night she saw us at Rosen's. The first time she saw me with my kids... Miller's hateful words thrown at her... Connie... then her showing up at my place. The vulgar things I said in my kitchen. The way she ran, not returning home and going straight to Evin yesterday morning.

"Fucking shit." Reality crashes down, and absolutely everything Stephanie said clicks into place.

"Now, you know it all."

"You're leaving me again."

"That's not true, and you know it. I wasn't meant to come back to this town long term. You and I can never get back what we had."

"Why not? The past hurts like hell, but the thought of losing you again hurts worse." I pin her with my glare.

"As much as I wish that were true, it's not. There is no place for me in your life, Pierce." Her eyes glisten, and her lips tremble. "I'm sorry it's gone this far."

"That's bullshit, Darby. I love you."

Her body jerks forward. "You love me?"

"I told you this last night, but you refused to listen."

"You said a lot of things last night."

"Did you hear any of them?"

"Yes," she admits faintly.

"Then you heard me say I was going to make things right with us."

"You did, Pierce. Things are right, but it doesn't change anything."

Irritation spikes in my blood, and I grab our plates, taking them to the sink before I say something rash. She comes to my side, lightly gripping my chin and bringing my face to hers. "I understand if you want to leave. Let me handle the dishes."

I turn, taking her into my arms and crushing her body to mine. "I'm proud of you, Darby," I tell her the truth because, regardless of the emotional upheaval in my brain, she deserves to hear this. "But you need to know; I'm not giving up."

"Pierce—"

"No." The hesitation in her voice sets my nerves on edge. "You're not pushing me away this time."

"You have to understand—"

This time, I cut her off by closing my mouth over hers. Her tongue curls around mine without a fight, and she sinks against me. I kiss her gently, sending her a message. She's not convinced we can survive this, but there is no way in hell she's getting away from me again. Slowly, I break away, skimming my lips over hers and feeling the warm pants of her breath. "Baby, there's a change of plans. I do need to go home."

She stiffens, yanks back, and turns away, but not before I spot the disappointment on her face. "I understand," comes out shakily.

"I don't think you do. If we're going to Aspen in two weeks for you to meet with your new team, I need to start making arrangements tonight."

"We?"

"You don't think I'm letting you go across the country to make the biggest announcement of your career without me, do you?"

"Why would you do that? It's going to complicate things even more."

"It is, but clue in; things are going to be complicated until we figure this out."

"Pierce, figuring this out is an impossible scenario. It's doomed."

"A month ago, I would have agreed, but after last night, having you back, I know differently."

She blows out a ragged breath and face plants into my chest. "There is no way this is a good idea. Clearing the air and having phenomenal sex doesn't make our problems disappear. We have no future."

For the first time in an hour, I find myself grinning. "Phenomenal sex and the fact that I love you are two reasons we will have a future."

She mumbles something about bad decisions, delusional intentions, and insanity into my shirt. What she doesn't do is argue or move away.

Now, I need to figure out a way to pull off a miracle.

Pierced Hearts

Chapter 13

Darby

A small whimper of gratitude escapes as soon as my feet hit the warm soapy water. My nail technician smiles, sets the whirlpool function, and leaves me to soak. I settle back in the massaging chair and try to relax, shoving all thoughts of responsibility to the back of my mind.

It's hard to believe the shift my life has taken in the last ten days. My days were pretty normal, and Mom continually added a few new orders to my schedule, which didn't bother me. It was my evenings that became insane. While I've spent my days in the bakery, working with deliveries, and doing special drop-offs when needed, my nights have been a cyclone of meetings. Mostly with my family and Stephanie on speakerphone. Mom took to the role of my administrative assistant easily, but she slid into the role of my PR representative like a pro. She spent hours on the phone with the professional marketing and communications team at Brasher Resorts, outlining a plan for when our announcement goes public.

Brasher didn't blink an eye when I explained how important it was to let my community know what's happening. They spouted that my ability to form such close relationships with my clients was a high factoring reason in our impending partnership. With the help of a team of people, and my final approval, the press releases will be going live within the hour of my announcement in Aspen.

My local clients knew something big was happening because we had to decline event requests after August, and we stopped taking future orders more than thirty days out. I felt this was fair because we'd be loyal to our orders through the peak of tourist season in Charleston. And, hopefully, I'd be organized enough to get moving in time for peak season in Aspen. Expectations were loose, but I was up for the challenge.

All of it was more than I could dream of, except for one thing— Pierce. Since our conversation that night, he hasn't been back to the shed. That was nine nights ago. I knew better than to allow myself to hope there was something blooming. The next morning, he proved me right when he met me at the bakery and said he was picking his children up from school that afternoon and they were staying with him indefinitely.

He explained this was the beginning of their loosely arranged summer custody agreement. They would float back and forth between

Connie, Pierce, and the grandparents all summer, with a few camps thrown into the mix.

That hope I allowed to bloom died on the spot. This was exactly why I was serious when I told him we were doomed because nothing could ever work out in our favor. I tried to hide my disappointment, but he picked up on it. There was no repeat of sex on the prep table that morning, but there was a lot of kissing and more whispers of his commitment to make things right. Every night, he calls, and our conversations range from our days to filling in pieces of the last twelve years. It hasn't always been easy, reliving major experiences of our lives, but neither of us has shied away from the other's questions. The two subjects we have avoided are Connie and his children. Other than the casual mention of his life as a father, they are off-limits.

I know it makes me a total bitch, but I make a point to keep it that way. There are instances he starts a sentence and stops abruptly to change the subject. These are the times I know our lives can never head down a path for epic reconciliation. It's impossible. I've accepted that and am sure that he has, too. At least, that's what I keep telling myself. It helps soothe the ache that he never mentioned coming to Aspen with me again after I told him they scheduled the announcement for Monday. They've set up two solid days of meetings, and with the long travel days, I'm leaving early Sunday morning. He had no reaction whatsoever, which led me to assume he'd decided it wasn't a good idea to travel along.

One of the receptionists brings me a glass of champagne, which I accept gratefully. In preparation for my trip, Mom set up this day of pampering, starting with hair and makeup and ending the day at our favorite nail spa.

Most women like to sit in the center of the action, chatting with friends, greeting people they know when they walk in the door, and general socialization. In the past, I preferred this area because of the slight bit of privacy. Today, I'm looking for a few last hours of quiet. Not to mention, it gets exhausting trying to evade questions about my plans for DG Creations when I run into people.

The spa is busy for this time on a Friday afternoon, and as expected, most guests request the stations in the front and center. The bell attached to the door rings consistently with people coming and going, and I notice a cute blonde in her mid-twenties come in and speak to the receptionist, who points to an empty manicure station. She sits, smiling at her technician, and something strikes me as familiar about her I can't pinpoint. Her voice travels in the air, and I think I've heard it before.

My own technician comes back, carrying a tray of scrubs, lotions, and gels, and I forget all about the woman at the manicure station. I sip my champagne and grab my phone to check my email and see the string of texts from Stephanie.

She did a fabulous job! I'm not kidding. You look like a supermodel! This is going on your website.

No shit, those highlights are the new you! I can't stop staring.

Okay, I enlarged the picture, and your makeup is phenomenal. Those gold and green shadows are perfection on your eyes.

I smile at the phone, feeling a surge of confidence at her approval.

Me: Glad you like the makeup because, for what I paid for it, it's going to need to be a business expense. Make note for the accountant.

Stephanie: Seriously, you look too good to go home and play with your dog. You need to play with your man... Have you sent him this picture?

Me: He's not my man, and no, I didn't send it to him. You better not either!

Stephanie: Making no promises. Scottie was meeting with me when the text came through. His jaw hit the floor. You may have converted him.

This time, I snort out loud, and my technician glances at me with amusement.

"My lawyer is trying to make a joke," I chirp.

The entrance bell rings, but I'm too distracted thinking of a witty reply to look up. Just when the perfect reply comes to mind, a chill races down my spine. I peer to the wall of mirrors and catch a woman's profile as she bends over the display of polishes. There's no need to see her face to know who it is.

Constance Webber, with her best friend, Blaire. My eyes scan and see two pedicure chairs now open toward the front. For some reason, the blonde from earlier catches my eye, and I can't miss the change in her attitude. The smiley, bright-eyed woman is now sitting stone-faced, her jaw set hard, her eyes blank, and she's staring straight ahead. It strikes me as odd, but I don't have to wonder long because, on the way to their chairs, Connie stops by the woman and sneers down at her, speaking loud enough for everyone to hear.

"Andi, funny seeing you here, considering I'm still waiting on that email."

"I told you the last four times you asked. There is no information available."

"And I told you to find a way to get it."

I should look away, take measures to be invisible knowing Connie can't possibly recognize me. It's been a long time, and I'm a totally different person now. Hair, weight, shape, clothes, style... nothing about me is the same as the girl she once knew. But I can't tear my eyes from the woman as she attempts to ignore Connie, who badgers her.

My eyes dash around the area, and for a split second, they cross Blaire. There's a flicker of recognition, and she immediately bends forward to whisper something in Connie's ear. I act fast, grabbing my earbuds out of my purse and popping them discreetly in my ears, then lean back and smile my best smile down to my technician as she smears exfoliator over my calves and wraps them in a warm towel. "That feels wonderful," I tell her, not turning my head when the body stops beside my chair.

"Darby Graham," Connie snarls, venom pouring from her voice, and causing heads to turn our way. Once again, I notice the look on the blonde's face.

"Hello, Connie." I throw my best saccharine-sweet greeting her way.

"Heard you showed your face back in town."

"You heard right. Hello, Blaire." I add the same sugar to the woman who used to be my friend.

She has the decency to look uncomfortable and taps Connie on the shoulder, gesturing to the chairs up near the front. Connie shakes her head. "I think these two chairs will do fine. You don't mind, do you, Darby, if Blaire and I sit here? We have so much to discuss, and this area is much better to carry on girl talk."

"Oh, not at all." I wave to the chairs. "By all means, enjoy yourselves. I happen to be working." I tuck my hair behind one ear to show my earbud and go directly back to typing on my phone.

My technician gives the arch of my foot a deep push, bringing my attention to her, where she's raised an unhappy eyebrow. I jerk my head once to let her know I am fine and lift my glass for a refill. She speaks over her shoulder, and in a second, another employee is at my side, refilling my flute.

"I want a glass of that," Connie barks snidely.

"Sorry, Miss Graham is receiving the VIP package. I can offer you water or wine for a fee," the lady tells her, and I hiccup down the giggle.

"I'll have wine," Connie grates out, and I begin typing quickly on my phone, which has been vibrating like crazy for the last few minutes, all messages from Stephanie.

Me: Chill your ass down. Connie Webber and Blaire just walked in and proceeded to sit next to me. We can talk about my hair and makeup later.

Stephanie: Perfect fucking timing. I couldn't have planned this better. Wearing that outfit, looking like you do... this is the beginning of your sweet revenge. Do you need me to call?

Me: No, I've got this. Talk soon.

Stephanie's right about my outfit. I thought twice this morning about choosing the one-shouldered, asymmetrical, short romper, thinking it was too dressy. It's not completely formal, but the Gucci label and price tag make it a little much for a day of pampering in Charleston. However, catching a glimpse of envy in Connie's eye has made this the perfect choice.

I bring the flute to my lips and mindlessly swipe through emails, making sure to keep focused on my phone. I feel the heat of Connie's irritated stare and internally prepare.

She doesn't disappoint, talking loudly to Blaire about Maya and Cole's summer plans, their accomplishments, and taking every chance to brag about what wonderful children she and Pierce are raising. She drops his name so many times, I lose count, and it's everything I can do to keep my face expressionless as I read today's stock reports.

"Maya and Pierce decided...."

"Pierce and Cole built..."

"Our last family dinner..."

"The baseball banquet where Pierce..."

The tautness in my shoulder blades spreads high, taking over the tendons in my neck, and pretty soon, the vein in my forehead ticks. All the time, I keep my attention to my phone, throwing in a few exasperated sighs and ignoring her as if she isn't there. Blaire doesn't say much either.

My non-reaction pisses her off, and she moves onto more personal subjects.

"Our office has decided to do a health initiative, and I'm spearheading a group program. My first move is to eliminate all chocolate and sweets within the office. Then I'll petition the building manager. All that sugar, fat, and calories are gross. Even Pierce thinks so; he hates chocolate."

Not anymore, bitch. I think to myself, knowing he's a big fan of chocolate these days. This is a direct dig at me, and she's itching for a response.

I keep my mouth shut and swallow the cry of relief when the technician starts to paint my toenails. A few more minutes, and I'll be out of this chair and away from hell. My technician inspects the bottle I handed her earlier and curls a finger at me to bend closer.

"This is beautiful," she comments quietly.

"Thanks, it's one of a kind. It was made especially for me by a cosmetology company in Paris."

I don't have to look at her to feel the daggers piercing into my flesh when I sit back, dropping my earbuds in my purse. Connie takes this opportunity to ramble on more, and I restart the massage chair, hoping it will drown her out. No such luck.

I try another tactic, forcing my thoughts to the explosive night Pierce came to the shed. The way he kissed me, held me close, dominated my body in proof that it belonged to him. The words he whispered, the loving way he looked while moving inside me, all of it combined with the knowledge he never gave that to anyone else. Connie will never know what it's like to have Pierce's strong hands roaming over her in worship. She'll never feel the soft touch of his lips or the warmth of his embrace after him fucking her senseless.

I'm jarred out of my thoughts. A tingling sensation travels over my skin from head to toe, and my stomach dips low, curling and turning in a way that sends my heart racing. Call it subconscious spirit, or ESP, whatever it is; my mind is aware and alert, telling me to be ready. I'm so lost in the stir happening inside that I barely hear the ringing of the bell. But I can't miss the quiet hush that falls over the spa. The air leaves my lungs when I spot Pierce sauntering my way.

His bright blue eyes are locked on mine, filled with intent and purpose. He's wearing his jeans, Kendrick Construction shirt, work boots, and has his hat backward with his glasses perched on top.

God, a woman could fall in love with him based on his hotness alone.

My brain finally takes over, firing on all cylinders, and it hits me what's happening.

Connie...

Pierce...

Me...

The anger, the heartbreak, the jealousy, the betrayal, and the three of us all together with an audience. I may not know all the women in here, but the silence and gawking tell me they know Pierce.

He doesn't acknowledge anyone, doesn't break his stride, and doesn't take his eyes off me. There's confidence in his steps, and I know he's made a decision that's about to change both our lives. I swear sparks are crackling in the air the closer he gets.

He sidesteps Connie's chair without even a glance, wraps his hand around my neck, dips down, and crashes his mouth to mine. My body reacts on its own, pressing up into him and giving in to the kiss. His tongue strokes around mine, teasingly, then dives deeper as he slants my head for full access. It doesn't take long for my blood to race through my veins, the heat spreading through my body. This isn't a quick, happy-to-see-you kiss. It's much more. This is the kind of kiss a man gives a woman when he's making a statement.

That's what Pierce is doing. He's making a statement to me and to anyone watching.

I never saw myself as the kind of woman that would openly make out in public, but down in my soul, I need this.

My lungs fight for oxygen, and I slow down, breaking away. He doesn't let me go far, holding my face close.

"Baby, you're always gorgeous, but you look fucking amazing."

"Thanks," I whisper.

"The champagne would taste much better with some chocolate." He brushes his lips across mine once more and stands, keeping his back to Connie, whose fury is surrounding us. I steal a sideways glance and wonder if she's going to blow the roof off.

He takes my hand, inspecting my nails, and kisses along my knuckles. Then he glances at my feet, and I know immediately he approves of the color. I wasn't kidding when I told the technician the polish was one of a kind. It was created to match the electrifying blue in my logo design. "Very appropriate," he comments.

"Where the hell are our children?" Connie shrieks so loud the shrill sound vibrates in my ears.

He doesn't glance her way. "With your parents, as you requested, getting ready for the Art Festival tonight."

"You weren't supposed to drop them off until six."

"Your mom called and wanted them earlier."

"Any deviations in our children's schedule need to have my approval."

She puts emphasis on the words our children, still trying to get under my skin.

"When they're under my care, I make the decisions. They wanted to go to their grandparents' early. Never been a problem before, and it's not going to be a problem now." His voice is steady, but there's a sharp undertone that gives me a slight tremor. He's holding his patience by a string, and I'm not sure we need that kind of scene.

"How much has she had to drink?" he asks me.

"I don't know. I haven't been paying attention to her." It's a lie, and he knows it by the sly grin he flashes. But it does the trick of pissing her off more.

"You want to know something about me, ask me. Not your ex-girlfriend, cookie maker," she spits out.

Ex-girlfriend, cookie maker? That's the best she can come up with? I drain the rest of my champagne to try to hide my amusement, but she catches on.

"What the hell are you smiling about?" Her screech is annoying.

I shrug nonchalantly. "I graduated from cookies a long time ago."

He chuckles, squeezing my hand, and looks down at the technician. "How much longer?"

"All done." She sets up an oscillating fan in front of my feet. "Five minutes of drying time."

"You want another glass of champagne?" He motions to the empty glass.

"I'm driving."

"Not tonight, you aren't. We have dinner reservations. Evin and I will swing by and get your truck in the morning before the horses arrive."

I try to hide the shock at the mention of Evin helping him and the fact that he still is going to help with the horses. I figured he'd be wrapped up with his kids. But I'm not going to question him. "Okay, I'll wait until dinner for more champagne."

He kisses my hand once more before letting go and pulling out his wallet. He hands a credit card to the woman, telling her to take care of my services. Once again, it's in me to argue, but I hold back.

"Are you kidding me? The mother of your children is sitting right here, and you don't even offer to pay?"

There she goes with the children thing again. Suddenly, I don't feel guilty about his generosity.

"Nope. Because you're their mother is probably why you are sitting here. I pay handsomely each month for their care, and let's not forget your mortgage."

Oh lord, he's struck a nerve now. She jerks up, one hand snaking around his bicep and yanking. "How dare you insinuate that I take child support money for myself. And screw you for publicly announcing our personal business."

He doesn't budge, but his eyes fall to her hand. "Take your hand off me, Connie. Now," he demands in a voice low and scary.

The woman returns with his credit card, and he signs the slip, briefly showing me the tip he left. I nod approval.

"Baby, grab your stuff," he instructs me. "We're getting out of here."

I'm about to tell him I can't put my shoes on yet, but it's not necessary when he bends and scoops me out of the chair. There's a chorus of giggling and soft laughter that follows us out of the spa.

The blonde named Andi is laughing so hard her face is red. On our way out, he stops beside her, dips his chin in an appreciative nod, and then leaves without a word.

I was right earlier. Pierce came here today to make a statement, and he didn't hold back. To me, to Connie, to anyone who witnessed what went down. Pierce and Darby... Darby and Pierce... Any way you say it, he's staked his claim. He obviously doesn't think we're doomed.

Unfortunately, he may have also started World War III.

Pierced Hearts

Chapter 14

Darby

"Peirce!" His name leaves my lips on a strangled cry.

"More," he demands, pumping harder and lifting my hips to hold me in place. He doesn't let up, and when my eyes clear, my stomach twists and curls at the sight of him. A sheen of sweat covers his neck and chest. Every ridge and plane of his muscles are strained. I lick my lips, craving to run my tongue back over him.

His eyes flare, and I know he's remembering the same thing. My mouth around him, massaging his balls, swallowing deep. It had been a long time, but I hadn't lost my touch.

"Fucking addicted," he grates out. "On your knees, sucking my dick like a pro, taking me in so fucking deep I was banging the back of your throat. Ten seconds in, and I wanted to blow. Twelve fucking years I missed that. Knowing it's all mine."

I reach out and scale my nails down his chest. "All yours."

Saying Pierce is pleased about my celibacy is an understatement. His possessive nature is borderline obsessed.

What started slow and sweet turned frantic the instant he tried to slide out of my mouth, and I shook my head, working him harder. I needed to taste him, give him the same pleasure to drive him wild. He wanted to be inside me, but I didn't give in, pushing him over the edge as he erupted with a loud groan. I savored the few seconds of power it gave me.

Then I was flying through the air, tossed on my back, and he was between my legs, devouring me. He showed no mercy, and I came twice before he finally kissed his way up my body and slid inside me. It didn't take long until he had me screaming again.

"Give me another one." His fingers dig into my skin.

"Impossible."

Now, his eyes flame for a different reason. The challenge is there.

"Hands on the headboard, baby."

He picks up speed, slamming into me with such force, I know I'm going to come again. I close my eyes, thrilling waves shooting through my veins, feeling everything. He swells inside me, filling me more, and I moan at the sensations building.

"Watch, Darby. Look at me."

My eyes flutter open in time to see him trail a hand over my hipbone and run a finger along my slit where we're connected. He continues the movement, brushing my clit with each swipe. My hands grip the wood, and I arch into him, needing more.

"Oh my God." My body trembles, and he grins, knowing he's going to get what he wants.

My breathing is unsteady as I watch the scene. He's proving that he owns my pleasure. His hand dips lower, moving between us until he's rubbing a circle around my tight rim. My eyes grow wide, and he grins wickedly.

"Come for me, beautiful. Come on my cock." He drives in over and over, teasing me with his finger while I'm helpless to what's happening. I can't take it anymore.

"AHHHHHHHHHHHHH!" I yell, coming up off the bed. Fireworks cloud my mind as I shatter. He's with me this time, calling my name. Everything is a blur. My body goes limp, but he catches me, holding me close.

"Jesus, Darby." His voice comes out hoarse. "Every time, every single time with you is the best."

My heart soars, and I tilt my head to kiss him. He lurches inside of me, and I whine down his throat.

"I'll give you a little break." He nips my bottom lip.

After a few minutes, when I can move, I slip away from him. "I need to clean up."

"It's sexy as hell, knowing you're full of me."

My legs wobble when I stand, and he grins triumphantly. "You really are a caveman."

He swats my butt as I limp away.

A few minutes later, I shuffle back to the bedroom to find Pierce with his back against the headboard, sheets across his hips, and his eyes trained on Runner, who's laid out full length beside him. This leaves little space on my side of the bed.

"We're gonna have a problem."

"I don't need much room." I arrange my pillows and start to climb into bed.

"Stop."

"What do you suggest I do? He's used to sleeping with me."

"You need to figure something out. We don't have a night like we had, fuck like we fucked, and then sleep with a dog between us. The first night, I had to leave because I was installing your security system. The second night, I left to organize my life so I could take off to Aspen. This is the first time I've had you all night in twelve years. We need to find another place for Runner."

I go the hall closet and drag out the oversized dog bed that never gets used, and then throw it on the floor at the end of the bed. "Runner, down here," I coax him off, and he sniffs the unfamiliar bed, glancing at me, confused. "It's okay, lie down." He huffs, falls over, and rolls to his side.

"Better?" I prop my hands on my hips, pretending to be annoyed.

"I'll be better when you lose the clothes and get up here."

"I'm not losing the clothes because we need to talk."

"We can't talk naked?" He crooks an eyebrow.

"Not the way I want to." I crawl in and sit cross-legged next to him, wincing at the sting between my legs. "How'd you know what was happening at the salon? Did Stephanie message you?"

"Yes, but she was far down in line, and her message was a little more graphic in nature."

"What do you mean?"

"You want to talk about this tonight? We haven't seen each other in over a week."

"That's why we need to talk about it. You blindsided me today. I thought you finally saw my reasoning about our impossible reconciliation. Then you walked in, swept me off my feet—literally—and probably brought a world of hell upon yourself."

His lips form a hard line, and a flicker of irritation flames in his eyes. "Apparently, you do want to talk about this tonight."

"Of course, I do."

"First of all, I never agreed with your reasoning because this reconciliation has already happened. You're the only one who isn't seeing it. Secondly, my world has been hell for a long time, and today didn't add anything new. But I'm not living that life anymore, and I've been working my ass off this last week to make sure of it."

I take a deep breath, clap my hands together in my lap, and tell him, "Explain that."

"When you told me about Brasher's offer, I knew I couldn't ask you to give that up for me, but I'm not willing to lose you again. Stephanie had said something earlier that day that clicked into place, and I knew I had to be proactive. Connie's been a bitch since she found out you were back in town, or I should say, more of a bitch. That's why she was at dinner that night at Rosen's. She has no problem using my kids to her advantage. Maya and Cole had already hinted at coming to stay with me earlier than usual. The timing was perfect. It sucked I couldn't be with you, but in the long run, it was a good step in the right direction. When I have my kids, I'm in charge, and Connie knows to back off. It's one reason Maya has a phone. Connie can reach them, but my time is my time, and she knows better than to question me."

Like always, when his kids are mentioned, my body tenses and I clasp my hands stronger, digging my nails into the skin. "I wouldn't know anything about parenting, but I'm sure it's tough."

He studies my face and sighs. "We'll talk about that statement another time. Right now, I need to know you're focused on what I'm saying, not the fact that I have kids with another woman."

It would be easy to tell him that fact is never going to change, but I nod my understanding so he will go on.

"Being part owner in the company has a lot of perks, and one of them is adjusting my hours when needed. It's easy when they're in school. But the last few days, with school out, my mom helped me. I'd pick them up afternoons. We'd do our thing, and then they'd need their own time. They're independent kids. It fucking killed me staying away, but our nightly conversations became one of my favorite parts of the day."

"I liked them, too," I say, loving the way his eyes go soft.

"Outside of planning the trip to Aspen, first up was making amends with Evin. I called and asked for an appointment, and we met. Things weren't easy, but we both unloaded. In the end, we decided to bury the hatchet."

"What? You met with Evin? Why didn't he tell me?"

"Because he was step one in my plan, and out of respect, he gave me the time to get my shit together so I could tell you myself."

'That explains why he's going to help with the horses tomorrow."

"I'm pretty sure, if I didn't make the first move, Edward was going to throw us in a boxing ring and make us fight it out."

"Dad was involved?"

"I had to contact Annie to help with my travel, which meant Edward was blowing up my phone."

"I can't believe my entire family was keeping this from me."

"Don't get angry with them. I may have used emotional manipulation and asked them to let me get things straight on my end."

"And they fell for it?"

"I can be pretty convincing." I almost want to slap the smug grin off his face... almost.

"Go on."

"Evin, Edward, and Annie are all on the same page. Then it was time to cover my ass with Connie."

"Oh, God," I tense.

"I met with my lawyer. He's a smart guy and totally out of the gossip loop in Charleston. He knew a little about you from his wife, who, by the way, is a nurse at the hospital, but otherwise, he's clueless of our history. After I explained my concerns, he's now on call."

"Why would he need to be on call?"

"Because I'm in love with a woman, and the mother of my kids is not going to take that well. I'm not delusional and need to be prepared for anything. Connie's a wild card, and if she thinks of dragging my kids through the mud, then I'm prepared."

My heart sinks because this is exactly what I was trying to explain to him. We will never work. "Pierce, I think we need to be realistic. There are too many cards stacked against us."

"No, Darby, there aren't. What we have is a lot of balls in motion. And I'm getting ready for a fight."

I draw in a breath and decide to say it before I lose the courage. "I'm not strong enough for a fight. I'm about to enter into a new stage of my career, and your life doesn't allow you to be a part of it."

"Baby, you don't need to worry about anything because I'm strong enough to fight for both of us. You're going to kick ass, and I'm going to be there cheering you on. You stay focused, and I'm going to protect you from anything that threatens that."

"Protect me? That's why you showed up today."

"You had to know all that backstory to know what happened today. I told Connie last week I had a business trip out of town and would be leaving on Sunday. She didn't question me because my job is not her business. Connie's mom wanted the kids early. I already had plans to surprise you and take you to dinner. I knew you were spending the day getting ready for the trip, and when I was finishing up at my last site, my assistant, Andi, messaged me. She told me that Connie had approached a woman named Darby in the nail salon."

That's who she was! I knew I'd heard that voice before. She was talking in the background when Pierce called me the other day.

"Andi must have heard your name before. She perked up, felt the hostility, and thought to message me. Then my mom texted that she heard Connie was there. One by one, texts came in, and by the time Stephanie got me, I was in the parking lot. Connie is not going to make your life in Charleston hell unless she wants repercussions. I'm not hiding what you mean to me, and she saw today that her games are useless."

"Good lord, we're going to be on an episode of Jerry Springer."

"Not in my lifetime. She can act like a fool, show her ass, and try as hard as she wants, but she has nothing going for her."

"She has two things I don't," I confess.

His face goes pale, and I can see the turmoil building behind his eyes. He knows I'm right. "Give me time to prove this to you, Darby. Give me tonight, give me Aspen, give me these experiences we should have been celebrating all along. I need that. I need you."

The desperation in his words hits me square in the chest, and I unclasp my hands and fall over, hugging him tightly. "Okay."

He shifts me easily over his body and squeezes. "Trust me enough to stick with me."

I don't answer, burying my face into his neck. "I think you're crazy, but I'll jump on the bandwagon."

"Thank fucking God, because I wasn't taking no for an answer."

Chapter 15

Pierce

"I've got about a quarter of an ounce of patience left, which means there's not enough to deal with you." I gulp my whiskey, eyeing Miller over the rim of my glass.

He walks through my front door anyway, setting a full bottle on the coffee table in front of me. "Peace offering."

"Piss off. Unless you have the ability to time travel and give me the twelve years I missed with Darby, your offering is useless."

"Are you going to put all that shit on me? I have the right to my opinion, Pierce, even if it doesn't fit into your perfectly planned world. I was worried about you, had concerns, and voiced them to our parents when I thought we were alone. How the fuck was I supposed to know she was eavesdropping?"

A growl rumbles from low in my throat, and I glare at him. "Get out."

"No, this has gone on long enough."

"You used that ounce of patience. I repeat, get out."

"Not leaving here until you talk to me."

"Fuck me, Miller. I don't want to talk to you. I just hung up the phone with a highly pissed off Connie, who's raging so hard, there's no telling what she's going to do."

"You can't be shocked, considering the scene you caused yesterday. If you were going for low drama, you missed the mark."

It doesn't surprise me that Miller heard about the nail salon. Over half the town knows. Even with the aftermath, I'd do it all over again to see the look on Darby's face after I kissed her.

"Though I'd have paid money to watch it play out in front of Connie." He goes on with a soft chuckle. "For a man who's spent years keeping his private life a mystery, you certainly gave a good show. A lot of people took enjoyment in their front row seats."

"Glad I could provide the entertainment." I pour another shot as he sits across from me. "Why are you here?"

"Why are you shooting back whiskey by yourself on a Saturday night?"

"None of your business."

"Fair enough." He grabs the bottle he set on the table, unscrews the cap, and swigs straight from the bottle.

"Peace offering my ass."

"I got thirsty." He shrugs unapologetically.

"Seriously, Miller, go home. I'm not in the mood for you tonight."

"Too bad. I've given you enough time to stew over this shit. Darby comes back into town, and you're acting crazy. Going to war with your family, fighting with the mother of your children, taking off to unknown places, this is what I was afraid of."

"Do not come in here, spewing this shit to me tonight. I am not at war with Mom and Dad. They understand exactly where I'm coming from."

"What about me, Pierce? Don't I get to understand where you're coming from? Maybe you could explain it to me since I'm now the enemy."

"Why do you even care? You made up your mind and cast judgment a long time ago."

"Goddammit, Pierce! Talk to me."

I tilt my head to the side and look at my brother. Digging deep, I wonder what I would do if the roles were reversed? Images flood my mind of those first weeks after Darby left. He's the one that made sure I survived.

"Darby didn't get pregnant on purpose, Miller. The week before her finals, she got so stressed, she took an anxiety pill. We think it interacted with her birth control. She was mortified. It took me weeks to convince her it was meant to be."

"Why didn't you ever tell me?"

"It never crossed my mind because I never imagined you were such a dickhead. I thought you were happy for us."

He guzzles from the bottle again. "Tell me what happened."

Darby's face flashes in my mind at the same time Stephanie's advice comes back to me. I'm pissed at my brother, but he's still my brother, and I will need him to get through this.

Except for the frequent tugs of the liquor, he sits impassively as I tell him what happened from the time Darby knew she was pregnant until the time she returned over a month ago. By the time I'm done, he's leaning on his knees, his shoulders slumped and head hung low. "Jesus, what do I even say to this? How do we come back from it?"

"I don't know how you come back from it, but I'm seven hours away from picking up Darby to take off across the country where she can make the largest announcement of her career. I'll stand by her side, supporting her, knowing that's where I should have been all this time."

"What kind of announcement?"

"The kind that takes her business to a level she never dreamed of."

"Does this have anything to do with the two-hundred-thousand-dollar approval I had to sign and the rush permits Dad is asking for?"

"We'll see. Stephanie, Evin, and I are working on an angle."

"Give me more."

"You know Brasher Resorts?"

"The same Brasher that's rumored to be putting a boutique hotel over on Atlantic?"

"Yep."

"We're getting involved in that?"

"There's no we. I'm doing this on my own and hoping like fucking hell it works out."

"I'm on your side here, Pierce. Don't make me the enemy."

"You made yourself the enemy to Darby. Your actions have followed her for years, and the other night, you didn't do much to disavow your hatred for her. She lives with enough guilt and regret."

"What the hell? How did I become the criminal? I was on your side. You were my priority."

"I should have been fighting for her. I should have been the man she needed."

"Why are you doing this to yourself? I understand the curiosity and even the guilt that comes with knowing the truth. But what do you think is going to happen here?"

I do another shot and then look him square in the eye, knowing I can't make him understand, but also knowing he's going to know where I stand. "When Darby and I return, I'm facing the biggest fight of my life. She can't even hear about my kids without going pale and flinching in pain. Not to mention Connie. Obviously, that's a problem."

"It's more than a problem. What I can't get is why this is something you are even taking on. Everything about this reads disaster."

I slice my eyes to him, and his hands fly up in a surrender motion. "I'm not looking for a right hook, Pierce. I'm seriously confused. Flying across the country, thinking about how to introduce her to Maya and Cole, taking on Connie... all of it seems like overkill for an old girlfriend."

"The fact that you refer to her as an old girlfriend tells me you haven't been listening."

"I've heard every word, and my heart breaks for the two of you, but both of you have moved on. Her strolling back in town, looking like a supermodel, and setting up shop with her successful business isn't going to erase your history."

"Have you been talking to her?"

"No."

"Funny because you sound exactly like her. She thinks I'm insane and the past can't be forgotten. Her word was doomed."

"Well, Darby was always smarter than you."

"I didn't move on, not in the way I should have. The situation with Connie forced my hand to accept my life was going in a different direction than I planned, but I never moved on. I had my work, my children, my family, and a few friends. You and I had our weekends to goof off, get laid, and blow off steam. But that's all. I lived my life going through the motions. You were right; when I saw her again that morning in her bakery, it was like slicing open an old wound. Except it wasn't only my wound. It was hearing what Connie did all those years ago to Darby. As much as I hurt, nothing could have prepared me for the agony of what she went through when Connie sent those baby announcements. Then the truth came out, and I was done."

"What does that mean?"

"Edward Graham paid me a visit, and he knew, Miller. He knew where I stood even before I did." I glare at my brother to bring the point home. "He said there was only one Annie for him, only one Jill for Dad, and one Darby for me. I wanted to argue he was crazy, but I couldn't. Because it's the truth. Three weeks after I discovered she's back, and I'm wrapped so fucking tight around her, I can't see straight."

"Shit, you're really going to try and make this work?"

"I'm *going* to make this work. There's no other option. It's how I do it is the tricky part."

"Didn't you say she's not convinced there's a future?"

"She's definitely made it hard on me. I'm facing a few challenges."

"The kids?" He quirks an eyebrow in question.

"I have two kids that are innocent in all this, and it's my job to protect them and Darby while finding a way to bring everyone into the fold."

"Maya and Cole are easy going. They've adjusted to their life with separated parents."

"Yeah." I nod, pouring another shot.

"Is there something else?"

"Darby is moving to Aspen at the end of the summer." I take the shot, the words and the whiskey both scorching my throat.

"What the fuck?" he bites out.

"Like I said, she's making this hard on me. It's the reason we're going to Aspen tomorrow. DG Creations has been acquired by Brasher Resorts. There's a lot more there, but I don't have enough time to get into the details tonight. I think the picture will be clear when Brasher makes their announcement."

He stares at me in disbelief, his jaw working back and forth as this information settles. Then, a light sparks in his eyes as it dawns on him. "Son of a bitch, you're buying the building her bakery is in, aren't you?"

"Not just me. Evin is invested. He's working the deal on the banking and negotiation end. If Brasher does set up a location in Charleston, that would possibly allow for her to come back. Evin's very involved in this."

"Dad knows?"

"Yep."

"And y'all didn't think to mention it to me?"

"I pulled from my equity. If it goes bust, I take the hit. Not the two of you."

"Bullshit."

"It's done."

"Evin is helping you with this? When did you two start speaking again?"

"When I told him I love his sister and will do anything to get her back to Charleston. Like I mentioned, Stephanie, Evin, and I are working on an angle. Those two had already started talking before I was in the mix."

"I can't believe you and Evin Graham are going to be business partners."

"It's more than that. He knows that one day we're going to be family. You probably need to get used to that idea."

He blows out a breath, jerking his head a few times. "This is unbelievable."

"Miller, I'm not the only one that didn't move on. Darby may have a successful business, good friends, and her family, but that is it. From what I've been told, the only man in her life that's been around is Stephanie's assistant, who's openly gay and in a committed relationship. She never had another boyfriend or another lover."

"No shit? Twelve years?"

"No shit. She's always been mine."

"Damn." He takes another swig out of his bottle, looking ahead and squinting his eyes like he does when deep in thought. I watch as the realization sets in his mind as his body relaxes. "You got room for another member of your crew?"

"Why don't you try to make things right with Darby first?"

"Let's hope she's as forgiving to me as she was with you."

"Forgiving? If you think that, then you're dead wrong. I have a long way to go."

"Must have made some headway if you're traveling with her tomorrow. Any advice?"

"Nope, you're on your own. My form of persuasion comes with benefits."

He drops his head and rakes his hands through his hair. "Please, God, let us all work through this mess before you knock her up again." His tone is serious, but the twitch of his lips gives him away.

Usually, this would piss me off, but tonight, I find it hilarious. I throw my head back in laughter and hear him doing the same.

"The thought may have crossed my mind, but she's got too much at stake right now. Don't think Stephanie didn't say the same thing."

"I can't wait to meet Stephanie."

"She's different, but her priority is Darby, and that's what counts."

He chuckles again and pins with me with a look that grows serious. "I'm sorry, Pierce, for the role I played and for not encouraging you to go after her. I'm rooting for you this time."

"Good, man, because I'm going to need all the help I can get. Connie's up to something."

"Want to talk about it?"

I pour another round in my glass, knowing I'm going to need it to get through this story. "She's mad, she's unpredictable, and she threatened to ruin me. Then, in the next sentence, she told me she thinks it's best for Maya and Cole if we combine our households and give them a chance at a stable home life with both parents. She wants to move in."

His back goes straight, and a low whistle fills the air. "You've got to be shitting me."

"Nope, that's why this trip is important. At this point, she has no idea I'm going with Darby, but it's not going to be a secret for long. Connie's bound to do something drastic, and I have to be prepared."

"We got this, Pierce. She's not going to ruin this for you again."

The look of fierce determination on Miller's face gives me hope that he's right.

Chapter 16

Darby

Strong arms circle my waist and twirl me around. Before I can make a sound, Pierce's mouth crushes mine. One hand tangles in my hair, slanting my head to deepen the kiss. I sink into him, using his body as my anchor, and give in to his silent demand. All thoughts and reasoning disappear, and the world around us drifts away.

At this moment, I'm floating on a cloud of bliss, and being wrapped in his arms is exactly where I'm supposed to be. When I woke this morning, a wave of anxiety and uncertainty hit hard. I wondered again if I was making the right decision and if my small business was ready for this step. He took one look at me, folded his body around mine, and held tight. The safety and security of his embrace was all it took for my nerves to instantly relax.

The day turned into a whirlwind of introductions and meetings, and through it all, he's stayed close, never far from my side. A few minutes ago, I stood next to the CEO and CMO as they announced our partnership to bring DG Creations to the flagship Brasher Resort. It was an intimate announcement, highlighting my business connections and clients over the years. I had read through what Stephanie, Mom, and the Brasher PR team had put together, but this was the first time Pierce had heard. Personally, I thought it was embellished and could have been summed up with a few sentences. Mom didn't agree, so while I listened to the exaggerated tale of my success, Pierce stepped behind me, slid his hands on my hips, and held on. Out of the corner of my eye, I caught him staring at me, his blue eyes glowing with encouragement and pride.

I know I'm in trouble and going down a dangerous path, but with his lips on mine, nothing seems to matter. His tongue sweeps through my mouth, and faintly, I hear the familiar click of a cell phone, bringing me out of my haze. I break away and look to my side, gasping at the man aiming his cell phone a few feet away. Pierce lets out a rough growl and tightens his hold protectively at the same time I squeal, "Scottie!"

I try to wiggle free, but he only lets me go when Stephanie pops out from a column and whisper-yells, "Surprise," throwing her arms out.

I rush to them, pulling them from both sides until we're all locked together. "You guys came." Overwhelming emotions clog my throat.

"Of course, we came. This is the most excitement our office has ever had. You think I'm going to miss it?" Scottie leans back and cups my cheek. "You looked fabulous up there."

A blush creeps up my cheeks, and I pop a quick kiss on his lips in appreciation. There's a deep rumble behind us, and I turn to face a less than amused Pierce eyeing me.

"Did you know they were coming?"

"I knew about Stephanie."

"This is great." I release them, taking a step back and hitting the hard body. "Pierce, this is the one and only, Scottie."

They shake hands, and Scottie openly checks Pierce out. "I understand the picture clearly now. No one else stood a chance. That kiss was scorching hot, and it was in public. No telling what's happening when there's not an audience. I'd save myself for that, too."

Stephanie bursts into laughter while my face flames. Pierce chuckles, dropping his hand and kissing my temple. "I see what you were talking about now, babe. They are exactly alike."

"Inappropriate?"

"I like to refer to it as direct," Stephanie says.

Scottie swipes his screen and holds his phone for me to see the picture of Pierce and me he took a few minutes ago. He's right; it was hot. But even more than that, we look like a perfect fit and a couple in love.

"I'd like a copy of that," Pierce speaks up.

"While you two exchange numbers and pictures, I'm going to steal Darby for a few minutes," Stephanie announces.

Pierce kisses me again, this time lowering his lips to my ear. "Don't take long."

I nod and follow Stephanie to the bar set up for this reception. Once we have a glass of wine, we step to a corner with a wide view of the room. "Thank you for coming," I tell her.

"We literally just made it in time for the announcement. How'd the day go?"

I give her the run-down, pointing out some of the men and women I've met and their roles. She listens intently, asking a few questions. My phone vibrates in my clutch, and I hand her my glass to take the call.

"I'm glad you followed my advice and went with the black dress. It shows much better than that god-awful grey suit."

"Hi, Mom." I roll my eyes.

"I wasn't sure you could pull off those shoes, but they work, too."

"Glad you approve. I take it the video is on the website?"

"Yes, uploaded a few minutes ago. Your dad and I have been waiting anxiously."

"Isn't Dad at work?"

"I came down to the office. We streamed it for everyone to see. It was quite exciting."

"Of course, you did."

"Evin did the same thing at his office."

"Y'all are ridiculous."

"Well, I'd hate for all that work we put into cleaning you up to go to waste with a bad outfit."

"Seriously, Mom, how'd it look? Did I do okay?"

There are a few seconds of quiet before I hear a sniff and little cough. "You did perfectly, Darby. We are proud of you." At the crack in her voice, a lump forms in my throat.

"Mom." I turn partially to the wall to hide the tears springing to my eyes. "Thank you."

There's a shuffle, and then my dad is on the line. "Darby, your mama got something in her eye."

"I know the feeling," I say softly.

"You looked good up there."

"Thanks."

"You know what else looked good?"

"What?" I have a feeling I know where this is going.

"Pierce Kendrick standing at your back, watching you like there was no one else in the room."

"We're not going there, Dad."

"He told me you were resistant."

"I'm not resistant; I'm realistic. Can we put this conversation on hold, or maybe drop it altogether?"

"Sure." He chuckles. "We'll put it on hold. Did Stephanie get there?"

"Yes." I glance up at her grinning. "She and Scottie are here."

The sound of a small click signals he's getting another call. "That's Evin calling on my phone. Your mom will call you later."

"Okay, love you."

"You too."

"How are Annie and Edward?" Stephanie asks when I drop the phone back in my purse and take my drink.

"Great. Mom's relieved I didn't embarrass her with my outfit, and Dad focused on Pierce and the fact he was with me."

"Hmmm, you do look fantastic, but I have to admit, Pierce had his own audience."

"He does look handsome." My gaze drifts to where he's standing with Scottie, his hands in his pockets, casually rocking on his feet. The black suit and open-neck blue shirt tailor to his frame. When he walked out of the closet this morning, my mouth went dry at the sight.

"Yeah, handsome. That's exactly what every female in this room was thinking." She snorts.

A spike of jealousy hits me, and I sip the wine to avoid commenting but take the chance of roaming my eyes around the room. There are a few women openly ogling him.

"How long are you staying?" I bring my attention back to her.

"We're here for the rest of the trip. Annie sent me the agenda, and I'm attending your meetings in an official capacity. Tonight, we're celebrating. Scottie made reservations at a place he says is the hottest place to be seen in Aspen."

"How would he know that? Has he ever been to Aspen?"

"No, but he's spent countless hours researching online and scouring social media this last week. I'm pretty sure he did some shameless name-dropping to get us a reservation."

I giggle, wondering what we'll be walking into tonight. With Scottie, there is no telling. I start to say something about his eclectic preferences when her eyes dart over my shoulder, her mouth forming a firm line. I follow her line of sight to watch Pierce as he looks down at his phone and brings it to his ear. I don't have to question who's calling because he lifts his face, and the fury in his eyes tells it all.

His gaze locks with mine, and there's a second of warmth between us before his expression turns to stone. He jerks his chin to Scottie and stalks out of the room. Stephanie steps in close right as Scottie rushes to my side, wrapping an arm around my waist and urging me to lean into him.

"It's Connie," I rasp.

"Most likely," Stephanie agrees.

"I don't know what she sounds like, but that sounded like a pig squealing," Scottie chirps.

"He knew this was coming." Stephanie tries to sound strong.

"I guess he did."

"Let's sit." Scottie nudges me forward, but I shake my head.

"I'd rather stand."

"For what it's worth, I like him."

"How do you know?" I tear my eyes from the direction Pierce went. "You spent five minutes with him."

136

"One of my best traits is reading people. That man is insane about you. He may have been talking to me, but his focus was elsewhere."

"Whether or not that is true is arguable. You know what happened between us and why we can never work. His children are his life, and that woman comes with them."

He scoffs and glances at Stephanie. They share a look that I can't bring myself to care about. Seconds later, Pierce strolls back into the room. His face is blank, but the worry lines around his eyes give him away. Scottie steps aside, and Pierce stops in front of me, circling my waist and dropping his mouth for a quick kiss.

"Is everything okay?"

"Yep," he clips.

"What did she say?"

"I'm not sure since I tuned her out."

"She's pissed."

He shrugs.

"Pierce, seriously, what happened?"

"She fucked up big time."

"What does that mean?"

"Darby, she's not coming into your day. Let it go. Don't we have reservations to get ready for?"

My irritation spikes, and I swallow a gulp of wine. Then I glare at him, waiting.

"No, Darby. We're not—"

"What happened?" I demand lowly.

He blows out a breath, strengthens his hold, and shares, "I ignored her calls, knowing the kids are with my parents today. The only reason I answered the phone is because it was Andi at the office. It wasn't Andi calling; it was Connie. She showed up at the office, acting like a bitch."

"Oh my God, no."

"Yes, that's why she fucked up. There are witnesses to her behavior. One of the ladies in the office called the police."

I search for something to say, but Scottie beats me to it. "That's fantastic."

My head spins to find both of them smiling wide. "This is not funny."

"Actually, it is," Pierce chuckles himself.

"How can you say that? She interrupted your place of business with a tirade of craziness."

"That's why it's funny. I am thousands of miles away, and she instigated a situation that means she has to answer to the police. I didn't have anything to do with it."

His lawyer comes to mind, and I understand what he's saying. "Do you need to go home?"

"Fuck no. I told you, baby, I have this handled. The kids are safe and where they are supposed to be. My financial obligations are handled per court order, and I took a pre-planned vacation. She doesn't have a leg to stand on legally with our custody agreement."

It's on the tip of my tongue to remind him, again, that any relationship between us is too complicated. He reads my mind, his eyes growing dark, and he drops his forehead to mine. "Don't you dare say it. Don't even think it. Wipe that shit from your mind. I've got this handled."

I nod, giving in for the sake of saving the conversation until we are alone.

"As gorgeous as the two of you are huddled together, we are drawing attention. I think it's time to get me a drink and mingle," Scottie pipes up.

"I couldn't agree more. Let's go back to celebrating Darby." Pierce slides his hands down and squeezes my ass before twirling so I'm tucked to his side.

It happens so fast, I almost miss it, but I catch Stephanie winking at Pierce. My feet stumble over themselves at the subtle, yet approving gesture.

Now, I know I'm in trouble.

•—•—•—•—•

Cars line the driveway leading up to my parents' house when Pierce parks beside my SUV outside the shed. Instead of it being the two of us returning to Charleston, it's four. Stephanie and Scottie surprised me again when they announced they were coming home with me for a few days. Scottie insisted it was for the full tourist experience, but it felt off.

Now, I know why.

Music flows through the air, mixed with the sounds of laughter and chatter. Pierce takes my keys out of my hand and carries the suitcases inside, then returns to me, linking our hands and steering me around the shed. A few tents are scattered in the yard, and the terrace is filled with people.

Mom, Dad, and Evin are on the steps, and as soon as they see us, they start to cheer. Everyone follows suit, and I stand frozen in place. Stephanie and Scottie join in, screaming congratulations.

As if he feels my presence, Runner flies from somewhere behind the house, speeding my way. Pierce tenses when I rip my hand from his and hold out my arms for my dog.

Pierce moves behind me, and this time, when Runner jumps onto me, we don't go down but into the protective wall of Pierce's body. I give the dog a hug, but his attention is quickly taken when he sees Stephanie and Scottie. He wiggles free to greet them as well.

"Is it too late to take my dog and run?" I ask our little group, feeling the pressure of all eyes on us.

"Absolutely. I came for a party, and that's what I'm going to get," Scottie announces, flashing his megawatt smile my way and strutting forward.

"I can't believe you guys didn't warn me."

"I thought you'd catch on when I picked out your outfit." Stephanie waves her hand down my sundress.

"I thought we were preparing for Mom."

"And half the town. Now, come on." She takes off after Scottie, leaving me still pressed up to Pierce.

"What about you? Any chance you'll rescue me?" I practically beg, peering up at him.

He shakes his head with a mischievous grin.

"Not even if I promise chocolate raspberry sauce breakfasts on my prep table anytime you want?"

His eyes glitter with heat, giving me hope that I've got him until it fades into a humorous glint. "I think that tomorrow's breakfast menu is going to be more of a whipped cream type celebration."

My body does an all-over shiver, thinking about a repeat of this morning's whipped cream celebration and the long shower that followed. He takes advantage of my lust-filled memory and starts walking us forward. My parents, Evin, and Lynda get to us first, pulling us all into a large embrace.

The next few minutes are a blur as I'm passed around, engulfed in hugs, and congratulated until my head is spinning. Pierce lets me go but keeps a firm hold on my hand, greeting those that he knows.

It's surreal this is happening, and he senses when I need some air, guiding me a few feet away and explaining we're going to get a drink. When we're out of earshot, I sink into him.

"That was slightly embarrassing. You'd think I'd cured a disease for the way people are acting."

"What you've built is a big deal, Darby. It's time you realize it."

I peer up, and my breath hitches at the beauty of his eyes boring into mine. That one-of-a-kind blue is glowing so bright, it seeps into my skin, sending an electrifying current through my blood. "Kiss me," I blurt out, not caring who's around.

His lips tip up in a sexy grin before he brings his mouth down. He takes his time, sliding his tongue inside and stroking it with mine. The smell of his cologne fills my senses, and all the pressure dissolves as he kisses it away. A little moan escapes when he slowly pulls back, sucking my bottom lip between his teeth.

"You're incredible, Darby," he says against my mouth.

"So are you. Thank you for being with me these last few days," I whisper, his arms flexing around me.

"I'm always going to do anything in my power to make you happy."

There's an underlying meaning that seeps into his words, and my heart flips in my chest. "Pierce—"

"Baby, I'm going to ask you to do something for me right now. Something that isn't going to be easy, but it will mean the fucking world to me."

My body goes on alert, and my skin begins to prickle as I realize we aren't alone. Slowly, I turn in his arms, unsure what to expect. My knees wobble, and I begin to shake when I spot Warren, Jill, and a very somber Miller gaping at me. Jill and Warren's expressions are filled with love and gentleness. It's Miller who has me trembling. He's extremely overdressed for an afternoon like today, and he's carrying a gorgeous bouquet of calla lilies.

His face is grim, and his eyes are loaded with guilt and regret. He steps forward, looking like a man who's been through hell.

"Darby, I'm sorry for absolutely everything you went through and for any part I played in our loss all those years ago. You have to know that I never meant—"

"Stop," I croak, my mouth suddenly dry. The term *our loss* is a trigger that sets me off.

He winces, looking stricken, and raises his eyes to Pierce. I take a few breaths and can't stop what's happening. Somehow, I loosen the death grip Pierce has on me and launch myself at Miller, who drops the flowers, catching me easily. The first cry sounds like a strangled cat, and I can't help the outburst that follows. I hug Miller as tight as I can, a rush of emotions pouring out as I let go of the horrible things he said and finally forgive him.

Chapter 17

Pierce

"Mr. Kendrick, you wanted to see me." Andi stands in the doorway, wringing her hands.

"Come in."

She moves hesitantly across my office and slides into a chair, sitting ramrod straight. She keeps her eyes on the stack of folders in front of me.

"I want to thank you."

She raises her wide eyes to me. "You aren't going to yell at me, or fire me for what happened with Connie?"

"Tell me what happened."

I've already heard Dad and Miller's editions of what transpired, but neither of them was actually present. Andi goes into the story of how Connie stormed in with fire shooting from her eyes. After she pitched a fit only she's able to do, she snatched Andi's phone and called me. It was another woman in the office that called the police. "Mr. Kendrick, I wanted to force her out of the office and grab the phone back, but I was scared to get in a position where I touched her. She was unstable."

"You did the right thing. Do not fall to her level because she would have taken it to the extreme."

Her body deflates, and she relaxes in the chair.

"I need to know something else. How'd you know to contact me last Friday when you heard Darby's name?"

The relaxation is short, and she stiffens again. "I'd heard her name throughout the week." She stutters over her words.

"Don't be nervous. Tell me what you heard."

"Miller and Warren had an argument, and her name was mentioned loudly."

I take notice of how she calls them by their first names, but I can't get caught up in that right now. "And I was the source of their argument about Darby?"

She nods apprehensively.

"And you thought to call me based on that?"

"No." She blows out a nervous breath. "It was a combination of things. Annie Graham accidentally called here one morning, looking for you about the trip to Aspen, then Mrs. Jill came to join Warren for lunch, and they talked openly that day about taking Maya and Cole while you were with Darby in Aspen."

I rub my hand across my mouth to hide my grin. This place is a gossip cesspool.

"It may sound weird to you, but my women's instincts kicked in when I saw the way Connie sneered at Darby in that nail spa. I took a chance to message you."

"You did the right thing. You weren't the only person, but you were the first, so I thank you for that, too."

"O-o-okay." She draws out the word.

"But I do have something to talk to you about. Darby told me the things she heard Connie saying to you about getting her my schedule. Does that happen often?"

The single lift of her shoulders is my answer.

"That stops today. Connie doesn't get to abuse you. You have my permission to route her directly to my phone or voicemail. I'll be addressing that with her as well."

"I can do that."

"And, another thing; this is for you." I slide an envelope across the desk.

She hesitantly slips out the non-official, handwritten certificate, granting her a week off, with pay, for the following week.

"Really?!?" she squeals.

"Really. Officially, you were almost accosted by a crazy loon in my absence. Unofficially, you personally gave me a head's up about the woman in my life facing an uncomfortable situation. You deserve this. All I ask is that you get my schedule straight today and have someone in the office available for me to call into. I know it's short notice, but hopefully, someone will agree."

"No problem." She bounces.

"One more thing. I'm a dick, I'm a hothead, and I've been an asshole, but you do a good job, Andi."

She rolls her lips between her teeth and meets my eyes. "Thank you."

"Okay." I wave my hand. "Go back to work and make sure I can live without you for the next week."

She leaves but turns to me at the door. "Mr. Kendrick, I have a boyfriend, and he screws up a lot. But I swear, if he did what you did on Friday, I'd marry him and take his screw-ups. You were movie-star swoony."

Movie-star swoony? What the fuck is that? More like protection and possession to the point of madness.

"I think my romantic side died a long time ago."

The phone rings on her desk, and she races to grab it as Miller passes her on his way in. "Things good?"

"Yep."

"How's Darby this morning?"

"Hungover and facing a shitload of orders."

He grins widely. "The party was a success."

"You're gloating."

And, in a way, he should be. Darby's emotional response to his apology shook me to my core until I couldn't stand the sound of her cries and took her from his arms and back to the shed. We joined the party a while later, and she finally let loose. Miller, Dad, and I stole a few minutes to cover what had happened while we were gone, but I didn't stay away from her long.

Neither did my family, especially Miller. Apparently, Evin and Miller had words before our arrival and somehow decided to call a truce. Of course, Evin's side of things relied on Darby's reaction to Miller's apology. Since that went well, there was little tension.

By nine, the crowd had died down to my family, the Grahams, Stephanie, Scottie, Lynda, and Ray. This is when Annie kicked into gear. Edward popped bottles of champagne, and Darby went through our last few days in detail. Reliving it through her eyes was a different experience.

"I'm not sure gloating is the right word." The smug smile playing on his lips says differently.

"I'm almost caught up. Anything specific I should know?"

"We covered it all while you were away. Why did you come in early?"

"Because Darby went to work at daylight." I don't add that my morning plans of having Darby for breakfast went to shit with Stephanie sleeping on the sofa. Scottie stayed in the main house.

"Since you're all caught up, tell me about Aspen from your perspective."

"Nothing to tell. It was exactly as she described it. Brasher Resorts wanted her on their team and rolled out the red carpet. Her new kitchen is state of the art and larger than anything she's ever worked in, her business plan to get up and running is coming along, and they've given her a small staff to start."

"When do they want her in Aspen?"

My gut seizes at his question because the management team at Brasher only asked one thing out of Darby, and she couldn't say no. "They asked her to start on August fifteenth, which is three weeks earlier than their original date. She's refusing to do auto-transport and fly, deciding to drive herself and Runner across the country."

"Fuck, how far is that?"

"Somewhere close to two thousand miles. She's giving herself seven days travel time, since she'll have the dog, and she wants to be there a few days early to get settled. She's got it in her mind to ride out on August fourth or fifth."

His eyes connect with mine, and it's easy to tell he's thinking the same thing I am. School starts on August eighth. Since Cole started school, we have an ongoing tradition. The week leading up to the beginning of school is always my week. In the past, I've even given into Connie joining us for a few things in order to give the kids some normalcy. Nothing ever gets in the way of this.

Until now.

"How are you going to handle that?"

"Fuck if I know. There's no way she's driving across the country by herself, but I can't be in two places at one time. Somehow, I'll figure it out."

"If she knows your obligations with Cole and Maya, she'll agree to leave a few days later and log more driving hours in the day."

"Maybe, but it's also a landmine. This is exactly the kind of excuse she'll use to remind me that we can't overcome the obstacles in front of us."

He blows out a low whistle, and I also know too well what that means. "Go ahead and say it, Miller."

"No, because saying that I think you're fighting a losing battle may give you the impression that I'm not on your side. A few days ago, that was how I felt. But seeing you two last night changed my perspective. All I'm going to say is I hope you have a plan."

"There's a plan."

"Want to share?"

"Darby's going to leave Charleston. I wouldn't let her give up this opportunity for anything, especially me."

"That's doesn't sound like a plan. It sounds like you're going to lose her to Colorado and wherever else they send her next."

The image of Darby standing in my kitchen that night, crying as she relived the horrible events of what happened many years ago fills my head. There's the rage I felt toward Miller and the hurt she lived with for so long. Then, the image is replaced with her leaping in his arms last night as she let it all go. I was prepared to take on this challenge by myself, but he came through for me last night, proving he's on my side.

I reach down into my computer bag and retrieve a file, handing it to him.

"This information is highly confidential."

He opens it, scanning the first two pages of the document. When his eyes cut back to mine, he's hyper-alert. "It's not a rumor."

"Not to those in the know. Brasher Resorts bought the old hotel on Atlantic and has been quietly redesigning it. The plan is a boutique hotel unlike anything Charleston currently has to offer. I've personally seen the layout, construction, and renovation design. It's going to be out of this world."

"How'd you manage that?"

"Stephanie took me to one of her legal meetings with Brasher. Darby was occupied, and it was easy to sneak away."

"You snuck in?"

"Not exactly. Stephanie was invited."

"How does she play into this?"

I roll my bottom lip between my teeth, thinking how much Miller needs to know. "Let's just say Evin has been sitting on this information for a while. When I mentioned they were working an angle, this is a part of it."

"A hotel like you're describing is going to take years. Are you really pouring your investments and financial security into this? That's risky, even for you."

"Not exactly. Believe it or not, the building is solid. The old owner kept everything up to code. The construction is good, and very little permitting has to be done. Most of it is cosmetic and interior design. Brasher is contracting with a local group to create the gardens, landscaping, and water features. They have an aggressive timeline of next spring."

"That's virtually impossible."

"Not with the right amount of money and resources."

"This is why you bought that damn bakery! You're going to lure Darby back here." The light finally dawns as he puts it all together.

"Lure isn't the right term. I'm doing everything in my power to bring Darby home."

"You say Evin and Stephanie instigated this?"

"It's a long story, but yeah. Stephanie tells it like a fairytale coming to life with Darby and me reconnecting."

"You mean that hard-ass woman knows what fairytales are?"

"Apparently." I grin. "She says she has a soft spot for me."

"Lucky you."

"I'm not lucky yet. This is where the chips fall. Now, I have to persuade Darby we can have it all again. She knows nothing about this.

And Maya and Cole are a huge part of this decision. There has to be a lot of acceptance in order for any of this to work."

"They're good kids, Pierce."

"They are, but like I told you, Connie is going to make this hell on me. Now, you know it all."

"Yeah, I admit, the other night, I still didn't understand where your head was at, but it's all clear."

"Good, because we need to hit the brownstone project, then I'm headed to the bakery."

"I'll go to the bakery with you."

"Not today, you won't. I woke up with Stephanie on the sofa and Runner laid across the bottom of the bed. Needless to say, I need some alone time with Darby before I pick up the kids tonight."

●—●—●—●—●

"Where's your sister?"

Cole points to a group of girls huddled together. I give a loud whistle across the room, and Maya's head pops up. Even in the distance, I sense annoyance when her eyes meet mine. She takes her time gathering her bag, saying goodbye to her friends, and shuffling to us.

"Hey, baby." I try to wrap my arm around her shoulder, but she successfully dodges my attempt and goes straight out the door.

"She's been like this since Tuesday," Cole explains.

"Is there a reason?"

"She and Mom got into a fight, and they've both been critchy."

"Critchy? Is that a word?"

"It's like 'itchy' with the 'b' and cranky combined."

It takes a second to sink in. "You mean bitchy?"

"Yes, but Grandma said I shouldn't say that word."

"Grandma's right."

We get to the truck, and Maya's leaning against the back cab door with her arms crossed. "How about a hug for your dad?"

"Not in the mood." She cinches her ponytail and flips her hand in my direction.

Connie told me weeks ago about Maya's mood swings and the fact we were headed into prepubescent years. I wanted to think she was exaggerating, but today is proof.

"Cole, give us a second." I beep the locks, and he takes off to the other side. Maya makes a move to get in, but I spear her with a look that stops her hand mid-try.

"Want to share why you're wound up?"

"Not really."

"I respect your privacy, Maya, but I haven't seen you for a week.

Think you could give me a break and hug my neck?"

"Oh, I know all about why you haven't seen us for a week! Mom told us your business trip was a lie!" she spews with so much hate it's like staring at Connie.

"She told you it was a lie?"

"Yes. I know you ran off with your girlfriend."

"She told you that?"

"Yep." She pops the 'p' with such sass my blood boils.

"Is this why you didn't want to talk to me the last few nights that I called?"

Her silence is my answer.

"Hop in the truck. Let's get home where we can talk in private."

Once on the road, Cole fills the uncomfortable silence by filling me in on their first day of camp. Both are attending a S.T.E.A.M camp two days a week. Obviously, Cole is riding a high, while Maya is stewing over whatever Connie told her.

"Dad, what's that smell?" Cole jumps from one subject to the next.

"Got you guys something special." I pass the box of baked goods to them. Before I left the bakery this afternoon, Darby handed me the box with a small smile. She didn't say anything, but I knew they were for my kids.

"There are a few special truffles in there that your mom picked up for your teachers. She said her boss loved them, so I thought we should try."

It's underhanded, but mentioning their mom in a non-confrontational way will hopefully ease some of the tension fuming from Maya. I watch in the rearview mirror as she peeks in the box Cole has opened and pokes around until she finds a truffle. Her blue eyes bulge when she takes her first bite, and I think this is a good sign.

Maya goes straight to her room when we get home, and Cole helps me unload the groceries. He sits on a stool, watching me put things away and studying me.

"Got something on your mind?" I hand him a water and open one for myself.

"Your girlfriend is pretty."

"Thanks. I think so, too. When did you see her?"

"On Mom's computer."

"Did your mom tell you she was my girlfriend?"

"Not me. She told Maya when she thought I wasn't around. I saw the way you were holding her waist and standing close to her. I figured she was your girlfriend."

I nod and decide to get this conversation started. "Maya! Come down here. And bring your phone."

She stomps down the stairs, making an entrance and glowering at me as she takes the stool next to Cole.

"We need to talk."

Cole, being Cole, leans forward, ready to listen. Maya huffs out a breath and makes a gurgling noise from the back of her throat. I slice my eyes to her, lay my hands flat on the counter, and pin her with a hard glare. Slowly, the defiance starts to fade when she realizes her attitude is not going to work.

"I have met someone. Actually, that's not true. A woman I used to date has returned to town, and we've reconnected. This week, I traveled with her on a business trip."

"So, you don't deny you were with her?" Maya sneers.

"Why would I deny it?"

"Why didn't you tell us you were running off with some floozy?"

At the word floozy, a haze covers my eyes, and the image of Connie spouting this shit to my kids fills my head. It's all I can do to hold down the growl rumbling in my chest. "Where did you learn the term floozy?"

"Mom said it's a woman that is vulgar and disrespectful."

"Is that right? Well, from where I'm standing, you're being pretty damn vulgar and disrespectful to me. Does that make you a floozy?"

The color drains from her face, and her eyes pool with tears.

"Just so you know, that definition isn't entirely accurate. In a few years, I'll explain what a floozy is, and your mother should have more sense than that. But for your information, if anyone ever calls you a floozy, they will answer to me."

"Whatever. You still ran off with her." The attitude snaps back into place.

"The only reason I went was because it was your week with your mother, and it wouldn't affect my time with you."

"Yeah, right. Mom says—"

"Shut it, Maya. Let Dad talk." Cole snaps his head to her, and I see exactly why people say we're just alike.

"You shut it, little butt-kissing jerk of a—"

"STOP!" I roar, both of them cringing back. "Who the hell taught you to talk like that? Especially to your brother? I sure as hell didn't."

"It's not a big deal. It happens all the time," Cole mumbles.

"Not anymore. Don't let it happen again."

"Like you care. Mom says you are leaving us to go to live with your floo—" She stops herself.

"Your mom is wrong, and she's telling you things that should be discussed between adults."

"I'm not a baby."

"You're my baby."

She holds on to her anger, squaring her thin frame and facing me. "Fine, Dad, tell us about your girlfriend. Explain to us why you flew across the country to be with her, leaving us, and then made a fool of our family by making out with her all over social media."

At this point, my hand comes down hard on the counter, the slap echoing through the kitchen. "Give me your phone now," I demand.

She doesn't move, daring me. So much like Connie. My heart breaks that she's raising my daughter the way she is.

"Maya Elyse, give me your phone."

She still doesn't move.

I shake my head, knowing I'm about to ruin the life of a young girl who has been poisoned by her mother's hatred. "Fine, you had your chance." I pull out my own phone, log into our work account, and click on the link to her line.

She whips the phone out of her pocket and watches in horror. "What did you do?"

"I told you when you got that phone that it comes with responsibility. You had the chance to take responsibility and chose poorly. Now, you don't have anything but calling service."

"You erased everything!" she cries.

"Well, you saying that you saw me making a fool out of myself on social media means you were not abiding by our agreement."

"Mom said it was okay."

"That phone is owned and operated by Kendrick Construction. If your mom wants you on her line, take it up with her. She can pay for it."

Her mouth snaps shut, and she knows she's been beat. There is no way Connie is going to take on any extra expense.

"Now, do you want to talk reasonably about what's happening with me?"

"I do," Cole pipes in, looking bored with the whole outburst.

I give him a grateful grin and start again. "I'm seeing someone, and she means a lot to me. She knows all about you two. She's a great woman, and I hope you will give her a chance."

"She sure is pretty," he pipes in, and I have to hide my amusement at my son.

"She isn't anything like Mom." Maya finally sounds like my girl.

"Darby has nothing to do with your mom."

149

"Why can't you like Mom again?" Her lips tremble.

"Baby," I lower my voice and try to find the word to explain this, "your mom and I got the best gifts in the world when we had you, but we weren't meant to be together."

"Mom says you love this woman more than us, and we're going to be a nuisance."

"Well, she's wrong. That's why I wanted to tell you about Darby on my own terms. Maybe I should have pushed this conversation before I left town, but the timing didn't seem right."

"Darby is such a snazzy name." Cole surprises me.

"Snazzy?"

"Mom and Maya watch those silly talent shows. I'm suffering through life with women." He falls to the side dramatically, totally changing the mood of the conversation.

Maya starts to giggle, I find a smile, and Cole pretends to convulse on the countertop. It's a good place to end this discussion, for now.

"Okay, talk done. Cole, I need you to get the grill ready."

He scrambles away quickly, relieved to get away from the two of us. When he's outside, I look at Maya, who is struggling.

"Maya, no one will ever replace you."

She nods apprehensively.

"Come around here and help me start the salad."

She comes around and, instead of going to the refrigerator, throws herself at me, her arms around my waist. "Daddy, I'm confused. Mom is mad."

My mouth goes to her head, and I wrap my own arms around her shoulders. "You need to know I love you with all my heart. I'll talk to your mom."

She squeezes me and lets go. "Darby is a snazzy name," she mumbles.

Chapter 18

Darby

"Sweetie, I'm not sure you're in the state of mind to meet with her. Maybe you should give it a few days." I cup Pierce's cheek, running my thumb along his bottom lip.

"I'm rarely in the state of mind to deal with her, but it's got to happen."

When Pierce called last night after the kids were in bed, it was obvious something was wrong. He gave me a brief and vague version of what happened with Maya and Cole. I wanted to press for more details, but it didn't feel right.

It wasn't until he showed up at the bakery this afternoon that I knew how bad things were. One look at him told me he was struggling with his temper over Connie's tricks. He took Runner out while I finished what I was doing, and when they returned, he pulled us to my small sofa and started to unload.

Now, I'm fighting my own anger issues.

"She gave my daughter permission to upload Instagram, then dropped hints on how to dig around. Maya's a smart girl. She listened to her mom on the phone with Blaire, Googled you, and then did the research. Following your social presence, she got to Scottie's page and saw the picture of us kissing. That was something Connie hadn't seen, but Maya showed her."

"Is that when she called me a floozy?"

"Somewhere in the tirade."

"I'll talk to Scottie and ask him to delete the shot."

"Don't," he snaps. "I'm not living my life in hiding, Darby, and neither are you. Scottie has the right to post what he wants. Maya has no business on Instagram at her age."

"It sounds like Connie did enough to plant the seeds of curiosity in Maya's mind."

"She did more than that. She manipulated my fucking eleven-year-old."

"Pierce, I think that maybe we should look at the bigger picture here. You, the children, Connie, it's already a challenging situation. Adding me to the equation is only going to—"

"Don't finish that sentence. I swear to God, Darby, don't try and use this as another reason to convince yourself that we can't work."

"But don't you see the problem?"

"The problem is Connie, not you or me. For some crazy reason, she can't get it out of her head that I'm not hers. Out of respect and simplicity, I've never flaunted my personal life in her face, even though I've had plenty of women over the years."

My stomach lurches, and I flinch at the mention of his sex life. He explained to me about his and Miller's frequent trips out of town and his discretion when meeting local women, but it still makes me ill. I have no right to feel this way. "Let's not talk about that," I whisper.

"Baby, I didn't say that to make you sad. I'm saying it because there's never been anyone in my life. She knows I'm not celibate, but she hasn't ever been faced with seeing me with anyone. She took note of that and kept holding on, using my kids as leverage. Now that you're back in the picture, it's done. There is no one else in this world I'd go to battle over but you, and she knows it. Fuck, everyone knows it. Whatever she's conjured up in her head is dying fast, and she's drawing the lines with my kids in the middle. They're torn up over it."

"How do you know?"

"Maya admitted to being confused, so I decided to approach my relationship with you at a later time. But Cole had other ideas. He wouldn't shut up with questions about you. He already thought you were pretty, but when I explained why we were in Aspen, and you're the Darby behind DG Creations, he was out of his mind. Maya tried to act disinterested, but it was obvious she was curious."

"Her curiosity is understandable." I think of the poor girl whose mom has filled her head with unimaginable lies.

"What would you tell her?"

"I'm not the right person to ask."

"You were a young girl once. Give me advice on what to say to her."

"Pierce, don't ask me to do that. I'm not going to give you suggestions on how to raise your and Connie's daughter."

His jaw goes hard, and I know I've hit a nerve. He takes my hand in his, bringing it to his chest and clutching hard. "Darby, there are a lot of things in this world I can change, but that is not one of them."

"I know that, but it's not going away."

"I went to bed last night, wishing like hell you were by my side, and woke the same way. I spent twelve years without you, and now that I have you back, I'm not fucking around. I'm also a dad with a daughter who is at an influential age and has a mom who's a bitter bitch. Can you take Connie out of the picture long enough to help me?"

I close my eyes and think hard about what may help. "Keep telling her you love her and Cole. Don't ever let her hear you and Connie

152

fight because both will feel they need to take sides. Be honest with them, but be delicate with her. Puberty is hard, and she's going through a stage where emotions are uncontrollable. Connie should know this, but she's choosing to use it as a weapon. Make sure to surround them with stability when they're with you. Don't change your routine when you have them, and never ever let them think I'm more important." I finish and open my eyes to find him grinning.

"I think it will help when they meet you."

I jerk so fast, he has to reach out and catch me before I hit the floor. "Did you not hear what I said about keeping a routine? I'm not in the routine."

"You're in my routine."

"No, I am not."

"Meeting you will be a good thing."

"No, it won't! That will never happen." My loud pitch bounces off the walls, and sweat trickles down my back. I know what's coming and am helpless to stop it. This has only happened a few times in my life. The unmistakable spike in my pulse makes me dizzy.

"Jesus, Darby, you're pale as a ghost."

"It's hot in here." I fan my face and try to escape his hold. My heart races double time, and panic swells low in my chest. "Let me go."

"Baby, what's happening here?"

"Please." I squirm frantically.

"Breathe, Darby." His arms lock around me, forcing me to fall into him. I try to push away, but I'm trapped.

"Please, let me go," I beg into his shirt.

"Calm down, beautiful," he says gently into my ear, his arms loosening enough for his hands to massage my shoulders. "Breathe deep. I've got you."

Sharp pains throb in my temple, and dark spots cloud my vision. There's a loud ringing in my ears that drowns out his soothing words. Everything goes black, and I draw in quick breaths, trying to drown out the panic. After a few minutes, the familiar scent of everything Pierce fills my senses. It soaks into my skin, and sudden tranquility sweeps through me. He continues to massage my tight muscles, and the tension eases a bit. "I'm okay," I rasp hoarsely.

"Want to tell me why your heart's still thundering against my chest?"

"It's slowing."

We stay pressed close until I know my color has returned and my breathing is under control. He helps me straighten up, his hands moving to frame my face. "We need to talk about this."

"I'd rather not."

"I can still feel you trembling down to my bones. One minute, you're fine, and at the mention of meeting my kids..." He trails off, and a fresh wave of emotions washes over me as realization dawns on him. The bright blue in his eyes vanishes. "You have no plans to meet my kids, do you?"

I can't stand the disappointment in his voice. Guilt and shame lodge in the pit of my stomach. "I don't think I can."

"The thought of meeting them triggered a panic attack. How am I supposed to deal with that?"

"You aren't. I'm sorry it happened."

"How often does this happen?"

"Not often."

"When was the last time?"

"Pierce, I don't want to go over this now. You have enough going on."

"Darby, don't make me ask again. I need to know. When was the last time you had a panic attack?"

"The morning you came to visit me at the shed. That kiss, and then you demanding I tell you why it was a mistake."

His pupils flare, and he pulls his lips into a hard line. "Are these panic attacks brought on by other types of stress in your life? Or is it all based around Connie and my children?"

I drop my eyes in shame, not able to hold his gaze any longer.

"Fucking shit," he hisses, bringing his forehead to mine. "Baby, you're breaking my heart."

I can't respond because, if I did, it would be to say something ridiculously silly and juvenile about him breaking mine. With all that's happened in the last month, we've finally found a way to move forward. Finally, "I'm not ready to meet your children, and I'm not sure I'll ever be ready. And there isn't a point in confusing them, considering I'm moving. Why do that to them?" comes out.

"There's no confusion. They deserve to know the woman their dad has loved for most of his life. Before you try to spout your usual response that we're not going to work, you need to know that's not all, Darby. My kids deserve to know the woman I want to spend the *rest* of my life with."

If he wasn't holding my face, my jaw would drop. Instead, my eyes fly to his, and the air leaves my lungs. His eyes are blazing in a way that sends heat racing through my veins. Sincerity, passion, honesty— all glow back at me.

"Do you understand where I'm coming from now?"

I give a short nod.

He watches me with his lips curling smugly at the corners. "Now, I hate to leave with all this hanging in the air between us, but I have to go. When do Stephanie and Scottie leave?"

"Tomorrow morning."

"That gives them all night to listen to you ramble about why we can't be together, and hopefully, they can serve you enough wine to see things my way. I look forward to hearing your new excuses on Sunday night."

I begin to respond but find myself crushed to him, his tongue sliding urgently inside my mouth and silencing all protests.

•—•—•—•—•

"She is some piece of work!" Stephanie howls as I plop beside her on my sofa.

"It's not that funny. Pierce was irate," I grumble, not holding back my own irritation at the situation. I tried to act indifferent when he told me what happened when he showed up at the restaurant to meet Connie. It would only add fuel to his already boiling temper.

"Here, you need this." Scottie hands me a wine glass filled almost to the top with a bubbly pink concoction.

"What is it?"

"An experiment." He gives one to Stephanie and holds up his own glass in a solute motion. "Drink up."

I sip cautiously, knowing all too well that Scottie is a master mixologist but is known for his heavy pours. The tangy taste hits my taste buds, and I hum in appreciation. "This is lush."

"Of course, it is. Now, sit back, stop scrunching your face, and tell us all about it."

"She was drunk, Darby. Fucking lit like a fire and ready to go at it. Her so-called friends from work scattered and left her to me when I showed up at the restaurant. I was responsible for that bitch as she caused a scene. Then, she decided to play dirty, so fucked-up she thought she was being sexy. Grabbed my dick, sidled up to me, and offered herself in the goddamned bathroom—thinking that would ever happen again. I had to pay her damn tab, practically haul her out of there, and get her home. I considered putting her in a goddamned Uber but knew her ass was too drunk for even that."

I repeat his words from a few minutes ago. His voice shook when he called to tell me this. I worried about him driving, but even more, I worried about his state of mind when he got to his parents' to pick up Maya and Cole. There's no way he could tone down that type of rage.

"She grabbed him in public?" Scottie sounds appalled.

"That's what he said."

"This crazy bitch is klassy with a 'k'."

"Forget that part. What's with offering herself in the bathroom and it never happening again?" Stephanie's eyes dance with excitement and curiosity. She senses a juicy story.

"I'm not going into details, but let's just say Pierce and Connie's brief sexual encounters weren't exactly traditional and romantic."

"Scandalous," she chirps.

"More like sketchy and sleazy."

"What did he do next?" Scottie asks, scooting to the edge of the chair and bending forward.

"He said he left her at her front door, dodging more advances, and walked away with her screaming at him."

"She sounds unstable."

"Which is exactly why I can't be involved. Pierce doesn't need this type of stress in his life, and he won't listen to my reasoning. Even after this afternoon, when I had a mini-panic attack, he keeps pushing."

Their eyebrows shoot up, and their expressions are identical. "Something we need to know?" Stephanie's giggly mood turns serious. There's no way to miss the concern in her tone. She's well aware of what triggers my anxiety-induced panic attacks.

"I told Pierce today that I'm not interested in meeting his children."

"How'd he take it?" Scottie asks.

"He didn't say much, but I get the impression that he didn't accept it."

"Start from the beginning."

I take a large gulp of my drink and do as Stephanie demands, telling them about my visit from Pierce this afternoon. Neither of them moves a muscle, keeping their attention on me during the story. When I finish, they exchange a long glance, swing their heads back at the same time, and spear me with a glare that sends a shiver down my spine.

"Will you stop gaping at me and one of you say something?"

"What should we say?" Scottie asks cautiously.

"You two obviously have something on your mind."

"I wanted to hate him. No matter what Stephanie told me, when we showed up in Aspen, I was dead set on despising the bastard. He wasn't getting my forgiveness. All the time you stood in front of that room, I was torturing him in my mind. Then his hand slid around your waist, and I witnessed a miracle. You melted. My gorgeous Darby actually melted. To the untrained eye, it was invisible, but I saw the small quiver of your body, the flush of your cheeks, the sparkly light in your eye. It was one of the most beautiful things I've ever witnessed. My resentment toward him vanished. A few minutes later, after seeing him holding you and that kiss, I knew this was it for you. Forever. Being around you and Pierce the last week has been an experience unlike anything I ever imagined," Scottie says gently.

"He told you he never stopped loving you and wants to spend the rest of his life with you. He also said he's going to battle for you. That can't be easy for him," Stephanie adds.

"I didn't ask him for any of this. I never should have come back."

"You can try to lie, but we don't believe that for a second. I was scared to death of the fallout of your return to Charleston, but I took one look at Pierce Kendrick and knew I had come face to face with the man that would heal you and give you a future of happiness you deserve."

"You have to agree there's no longevity here. This thing with Pierce is supposed to be temporary. We cleared the air, admitted our mistakes, and found a way to have peace."

"Darby, you aren't stupid enough to believe that. To Pierce, there is nothing about this that's temporary. He's going for it again, and you're the only one standing in the way."

"That's not fair, Steph. There are obstacles everywhere. His daughter thinks I'm a floozy, and her mother is a making life hell on them because of me!"

"He's going to handle Connie. I have faith in that."

"What about Maya and Cole?"

"How much do you love him?" Scottie asks

"That's an odd question."

"Humor me."

"I love him more than I ever imagined possible. All these years, I held on to what we had. But this time is different. When we were in Aspen, I saw a side of Pierce I didn't know existed. He was always an affectionate boyfriend, but there was something about him that went even deeper. It's hard to explain."

"I've been your friend for a long time, Darby, and I've witnessed a side of you that *I didn't know existed*. In Aspen, it was easy to see why. You two belong together." There's tenderness in Stephanie's voice that she uses when she thinks I'm being unreasonable.

"Guys, I'm moving my business across the country."

"Yes, but what if you weren't? Would you be more apt to move forward with Pierce?"

"There's no what if. I am leaving."

"Are you going to drive away, leaving all memories behind, and forget about him?"

"That's not possible."

"You've convinced yourself a life with Pierce is impossible. Do you see yourself marrying and having children with a man you settle for?"

The thought of getting married and having children with another person causes my heart and stomach to seize at the same time. I can't look at either of them as my eyes and nose begin to sting.

"I didn't think so. But it seems you're dead-set on not only devastating him but torturing yourself. And we're not going to let that happen," Scottie speaks up.

"There is no chance here. You asked how much I love him. Well, I love him enough to stop making a mess of his life. He doesn't need to fight with Connie, Maya, or anyone over me. It's not fair to him."

"You're not paying attention if you think you're making a mess of his life. That man isn't going to stop, and you need to trust him to make the right calls when it comes to Connie and Maya."

"I'm mo—"

"Yes, we know all about you moving. Stop repeating it." Scottie flings his hand in the air dismissively. "But I'm guessing you didn't read your contract with the keen eye of a legal expert."

"No, I trusted you two to highlight the major points. That's what I pay you for."

"Good thing you did trust us because if you did read the finer points, you'd see that your move to Aspen doesn't have to be a permanent relocation."

"What are you saying?"

"He's saying I'm brilliant, and you will have options down the road. It's time for you to let go of all these shitty reservations and believe in Pierce," Stephanie states bluntly.

"Is that all you're going to tell me?"

"For now. Just know that we all love you and have nothing but your best interests in mind."

"I need more than that."

She gives me an icy hard stare that essentially shuts down the conversation.

"You're both suggesting I forget the fact that I'm moving my entire life across the country. Instead, I need to deepen my relationship with Pierce, meet his children—which makes me want to vomit—and trust that the impossible is going to work out, that there may actually be a future with the first and only man I've ever loved?"

"Yes, sounds right."

"Some friends y'all are. There's a psychiatrist out there that's going to make a fortune on me when my heart breaks this time."

"Nah, I have faith this time will be different." His eyes glimmer, and he winks at Stephanie.

A little voice in my head springs to life, reminding me these are two of my closest friends and most trusted people in the world. Through thick and thin, they've been by my side and would never do anything to hurt me. I blow out a loud breath, admitting defeat, and their faces break out with wide grins.

But I know what I'm doing tomorrow after I drop them at the airport. I'm going to lock myself in this shed and read through every line of that contract to find out exactly what my options are down the road.

Chapter 19

Pierce

Darby opens the door before I clear the last step, and my cock grows hard instantly at the sight of her. Her hair hangs down loosely in thick, shiny waves, and her skin sparkles brightly with the glitter in her body lotion. She's wearing the same black silky pajamas she wore the morning I showed up here, but this time, I can truly appreciate it in the daylight. It's a simple short set, probably not meant to be sexy, but the way it molds to her body, showcasing her long legs and hugging her waist, screams seduction. She flashes me a smile, her lips shimmering with her favorite lip gloss that I know tastes like raspberries.

"You're earlier than I expected."

"And you're fucking spectacular."

She sucks her lower lip between her teeth, her cheeks blushing. There is no doubt in my mind that I want to come home to this every day for the rest of my life and wake up to it every morning. Darby can push back and deny this thing between us, but it's time to break her resistance. A wave of possession and need crashes into me, and my primal instinct remerges.

I wrap my arm around her waist, lifting her gently, and cross the threshold into her place, kicking the door shut and reaching behind to click the lock. Runner greets me by rubbing along my calves but easily gets the hint that my attention is on Darby.

"Is everything okay?"

My hands go to her ass. "It took one look for everything shitty about my day to flee from my mind and my body to come alive." I thrust my hips, my dick pressing firmly against her. "Feel that? I need you."

She tries to step in the direction of her room, but my grip tightens. "Right here, right now, naked."

She studies me a brief second, her eyes glowing bright amber and burning into mine. She pulls the tank over her head, her nipples instantly pebbling. I bend in, lowering my head and sucking one into my mouth, rolling the tip of my tongue around the edge. Her hands grip my biceps, and she goes up on her toes, giving me easier access, and whimpers when I nibble lightly on the sensitive flesh. My lips kiss across her breastbone and do the same on the other side. Her soft skin is like velvet on my tongue.

Her breathing becomes louder, and one leg automatically slides up my thigh, hitching around my waist. She grinds slowly. My dick, now a steel rod, throbs against the friction. There's a coiling low in my groin, and I feel like a teenage boy about to fucking blow in my pants. It's only been a few days since I've been inside her, but it might as well be years with the way my cock is pulsing.

I give her nipple one last pull and look to find her watching me. Her eyes are filled with red-hot heat and desire that smolders through me. Knowing no other man on this earth has ever gotten this from Darby, and no other man ever will, drives my addiction.

One hand slips under the waistband of her shorts, around her hip, and along the crease of her thigh latched around me. My palm glides up and down her bare flesh, and her breath hitches when I slide two fingers inside.

"So fucking drenched, so fucking hot."

She keeps her gaze locked on mine as I tease her pussy, pumping my fingers in and out, and strum my thumb across her clit. My fingers curl inside her, finding the spot that always makes her shiver. Memories of the first time I slid my finger inside her race through my mind—the way her eyes brightened, her face flushed, and her tight pussy pulled me in. At twenty, I'd had my share of experience, but that first touch of her erased anyone before. Now, all these years later, the same feelings are there. Tonight is the night she understands.

Her body responds by jerking, and she clenches, bringing my fingers deep inside. Her eyes flutter closed, breaking our contact, and her neck falls to the side.

I suck a nipple back into my mouth and roll my tongue in the same rhythm as my fingers and thumb. She trembles as little goosebumps pop up. "Pierce," she screams loudly, my name echoing through the room and fueling the hunger for her as she comes undone.

I slow my movements, kissing every inch of flesh I can and feel her heart race against my lips. She melts in my arms, and I easily lift her again, taking the few steps to the table to lay her down. I rip the shorts from her body, kneel, and position her knees over my shoulders. "Just one taste." I kiss her inner thighs then run my tongue up and down her slit.

Her hands thread through my hair, and she squirms against my face, letting out a purr of pleasure. "I lied. One taste isn't enough. God, I missed you." It's my turn to moan in appreciation.

As insane as it sounds, the sweet flavor of chocolate and sugar coat my mouth. I know it's impossible, but my brain says differently. All these years, only one woman got this from me, and I knew with the first swipe of my tongue that Darby had ruined this for anyone else. My brief encounters never included oral sex after that. But now, I can't get enough.

Her fingers dig into my scalp, and she tilts her hips, urging me on. I angle my face so the stubble of my cheek rubs against her sensitive flesh, and swirl my tongue around. Her breath hitches and turns into soft pants as I feast on her. One hand glides over the cheek of her ass, my thumb gliding along the rim. My palm spreads out, pressing her to me, and I circle her clit with the tip of my tongue, gently sucking.

She's close, but the boiling inside is about to explode. I force myself away with one last kiss to her clit. Tearing my shirt over my head and ripping down my swim trunks, I lock eyes with her and feel the electricity surging through my system. My gorgeous woman is laid out with an expression that scorches straight to my fucking soul. That primal instinct rears again, and I slam into her with a possessive groan.

Her neck and back arch off the table, and she cries out at the invasion. I thrust hard, flicking her clit and watching as she tumbles over the edge. Her hips buck and pussy convulses, giving me an angle to drive harder.

"Oh my God, Pierce. Oh my God, oh my God..." she chants into the room.

I slow my movements, bend over, and circle my arms under her torso, easing her up to me. "Hold on to me, baby."

"I don't know if I can," she rasps hoarsely.

"Try."

She draws in a deep breath, locks her legs around my hips, her arms around my shoulders, and nuzzles her head in my neck.

I walk us to the hallway wall, pressing her back to it, using the support to my advantage. My hands go to her wrists and loosen their hold, linking our fingers together and pressing them over her head. My hips begin to rock again. "Look at me, gorgeous."

She does as I ask, and the sated look on her face threatens to bring me down. I swallow the growl and pump inside of her much slower. Her breath hitches as the lust returns to her gaze.

"Now that I have your full attention, you need to know a few things."

Her lips part when I thrust upward.

"This is all mine, Darby—the feel of you, the taste of you, the heat of your pussy clenching around me. It's all mine and no one else's."

Fire sparks in her eyes, and fuck me if she doesn't clamp her muscles so hard it shoots straight to my balls.

"Keep doing that, baby, because I'm a greedy man. I'm not leaving your pussy until you understand what I'm saying."

She has no choice but to release the pressure when I pivot my hips and ram upward. "Pierce..." The edge of her tone tells me I've hit

163

the right spot. I grip her hands tighter, press our chests close, and thrust until she's panting.

"I gave up on love a long time ago. You ruined me for any other woman. I should have chased you, should have been there. I'll regret it for the rest of my life. You've got a job and a beautiful life you've built. I want to be a part of it. I have kids, and nothing is going to change that, but we're going to find a way to make this work. I need you to get on-board."

She opens her mouth, but I sweep my lips across hers to stop the argument. "I know you're leaving, Darby, but it doesn't have to be forever. My job is to make it so when the time comes, you choose to return. And I don't mean to Charleston only. I mean, you return to me and what we have between us. This time, it's forever."

She bucks hard, fighting against me, and a fiery determination blazes from her eyes. "Don't make promises you can't keep."

"I would never do that to you. You have to trust me."

She flinches, and it's obvious she's now struggling with an internal battle in her mind. After a few seconds, the fight drains out of her and she melts, bringing her mouth to mine. "I can do that."

"I love you, Darby Rose. Always you."

"I love you, too."

My heart thunders in my chest and soars as I finally know I've gotten through. I close the millimeter of space, capturing her mouth with mine. She swivels her hips, rocking against me, and this time, I can't hold back.

"Come with me." My demand comes out harsh, and she grins against my lips.

Her thighs, knees, and ankles all constrict, and she rams down, sending fiery sensations shooting through my bones. A growl erupts low in my throat, and I explode, hearing her fall over the edge with me.

Not bad for round one.

•—•—•—•—•

A small nip on my neck rouses me, and I awaken to the view of Darby kissing a trail down my chest. She's still naked, hovering over me with her hair hanging like a curtain, shielding her face.

Her tongue licks around my navel, and my cock lurches to life, bouncing on my stomach.

"Go a little lower and I've got something for you." My voice is thick with sleep.

"I'll get there eventually. Figured you've had an hour to rest." She grins against my skin. "I've always loved the smell and taste of summer on you. It was one of my many favorites."

"The smell of sweat turns you on?"

Her head pops up, mischief filling her eyes. "No, the smell of suntan lotion mixed with salty air, the warmth of the sun on your skin from a day outdoors, all of it combined with you is what I love."

"And sex."

"Sex?" She quirks an eyebrow.

"All of that combined with sex. We smell like sex."

My chest tightens at the shrug of her shoulders as she lowers her lips back to my stomach. I do an ab crunch, cup her under the armpits, and bring her body to lay over mine. My fingers sift through her hair as I search her face. "Are you okay?"

"Of course."

"I was pretty rough with you earlier."

"No, you weren't, Pierce. We've talked about this before. I can handle it."

"The drive over here, I was pissed as hell. Took one look at you, and the shit I went through today faded. You did that. Something in me snapped, and I physically needed you."

"Do I want to know why your trip to the water park was awful?"

"Connie showed up and made a big deal about the family spending time together. Then, she proceeded to make things worse every time she opened her mouth. She openly thanked me for our time together on Friday night and for making sure she got home safely, all of this in front of the kids, who thought I was at a business dinner. When she took off her cover-up, her bikini was ridiculously inappropriate for a family water park. She strutted around like we were at a beach on Monte Carlo. Maya and Cole both found friends to hang with, leaving me to deal with her. I saw some clients and escaped just to be blindsided when she wrapped her arm around my waist and announced our kids were hungry and we should feed them. This was bullshit because they were nowhere to be found. She was trying to make a point."

"It sounds pathetic."

"Well, then Maya found us, and she actually was hungry, so I was forced to buy Connie lunch. She constantly made references to us as a family, sending the kids down a spiral of confusion. The only good thing that came out of it was, since Connie was already there and it's her night to get them, they went home with her. I missed out on an hour, but I came straight to you."

"There was no mention of Friday night at all?"

"Nothing other than her embellishing. I didn't care enough to ask how she got her car the next day. Tomorrow, I'm going to handle her."

I wait, anticipating her to throw back one of her illogical arguments. Instead, she shocks me by saying, "Okay."

"Okay?"

"I know you expect me to disagree, but I think it's best. This is no longer only about me. This is about sending mixed messages to your children, drawing lines on what you allow and the consequences when those boundaries are crossed, and your right to have a personal life. Connie can not control or dictate what happens with you."

"Glad to see you've come around." I grin.

"You can wipe that cocky grin off your face right now. The Pierce Kendrick fan club has gained two new members that ganged up on me Friday night and may have had an influence."

"Remind me to thank them. But I'd hardly say two people is a fan club."

"My family and your family—would that be enough to label it a fan club?"

My pulse picks up at the perceptive glint in her eyes.

She tries to roll over, but I drop my hands to her hips to hold her in place. "Where're you going?"

"I should find my clothes for this conversation."

"Not happening. Whatever you have to say can be discussed naked while lying on top of me."

"That gives you a huge advantage."

"I'll take any advantage I can. When it comes to you, I need to play dirty."

"Playing dirty is the perfect cliché."

"Depends. Tell me what I'm going against here."

"How about every single person in my life conspiring to bring me back home before I even start my new job?"

"I'm not sure I'd call it conspiring."

She slants her head, and a flicker of irritation sparks in her narrowed eyes.

Yep, we're definitely having this conversation with her naked and trapped to me. "Tell me what happened."

She blows out an incensed breath and starts. "Stephanie and Scottie are entirely too confident that things between us are going to progress. They had a rebuttal for every point I tried to make. True legal experts. Then, Scottie said something about my contract with Brasher. Stephanie shut down all my questions. It piqued my curiosity, so after I dropped them at the airport, I came home to comb through that damn contract."

Every muscle in my body goes rigid. Evin just mentioned the

clauses and addendums Stephanie added.

"Your body going stone still tells me you know what I'm about to say."

"Not true."

"Well, as it turns out, I hadn't seen the final one. I left my copy at Evin's office the day I signed with the notary present. He was supposed to make copies and overnight the original to Stephanie. I called him yesterday and asked him if we could go by his office to pick up my copy. He questioned my interest and, after I explained, said something along the lines of 'goddammit,' and hung up. Thirty minutes later, he was at my door, contract in hand and my parents in tow. I didn't have to hunt through the papers because he had tabbed the additional clauses added after I signed."

"I can honestly say I've never seen the contract."

"It's on my desk if you'd like to take a look. Those two really finagled an eleventh-hour deal. They did it the next morning, telling Brasher there were some new non-negotiable terms, but if met, they'd have a signed contract in a few hours. They lied on my behalf to make sure I had the option to come back to Charleston. Essentially, they did it so I could *return to you*."

She repeats the words I used when I had her pinned to the wall, and my poker face crumbles. "Baby, I—"

"Save it, Pierce. Evin came clean about telling you, too."

"The only reason I didn't tell you immediately is because of Evin's involvement with the bank, the local financing, and the confidentiality surrounding how he found out it was Brasher."

"I know and appreciate you looking out for my brother, but it's not fair these events were in motion behind my back. I've been independent for a long time, and that's not changing."

"I wouldn't say it's about making decisions; it was giving you options."

"The option to come home to my crazy parents, my overly intrusive twin brother, and the man I'm currently sleeping with? Y'all thought that was even an option?"

At the phrase '*the man I'm currently sleeping with*', my blood spikes, and a haze clouds my eyes. The next second, she's pinned under me, and I have her caged in with my arms and knees. "Your parents are crazy, but they're the kind of good crazy. Evin may be intrusive, but he wants his sister in his life full-time. And I'm not only the man you're currently sleeping with. I'm the only man on this earth who is ever getting that pleasure. You are my addiction and will be for the rest of my life. I'm not opposed to reminding you that, this time, you're not getting away from me."

"I'm willing to give this a shot."

I realize this decision was made before I even graced her doorstep tonight. She's had over a day to think about what's happening and knew we had options. But still, I tell her, "That was decided an hour ago against the wall."

Her lips curl into a sly grin, and she wiggles one leg loose, hitching it around my thigh to bring our hips flush. The tip of my dick glides along her slickness. "One thing you need to learn about the adult Darby is that threatening me with anything that involves sex is never a threat. We have a lot of years to make up for."

"Damn fucking right we do," I growl, sinking into her.

Chapter 20

Pierce

Connie's name flashes across my screen, and Darby slides the phone across her counter with a disgusted expression.

"Yeah?" I answer.

"How dare you tell my babies you're in love with that bitch?" The screech reaches around the room.

Darby rolls her eyes in dramatic fashion, making me chuckle.

"You asshole! Are you laughing at me?"

"I'm enjoying something that has nothing to do with you." Any other time, it would be way too early to fuel her, but considering my morning started over an hour ago with a naked Darby in my arms, my energy is high.

"Are you with her now?"

I don't justify her with an answer.

"We need to talk. Meet me tonight—"

"I tried this your way, and I'm not dealing with a repeat of Friday night. Tonight is out of the question. This morning, eight-thirty. I'll make this easy for you and meet you at the café."

"We are not hashing this out at a public café where my office is located. I'll come to your house tonight."

"Fuck no, Connie. You're not coming to my place."

"I have a job, Pierce." She spits out my name.

"You have a few hours before we meet. Get your mom over and go in early."

"I'm not going to inconvenience my parents."

"You want me to call mine? Mom is already up. She can be there in twenty minutes."

"You are a dick."

"Eight-thirty, don't be late." I disconnect.

Darby hands me a travel mug, shaking her head. "What?" I ask innocently.

"The café?"

"Figured I could help out with the morning order and deliver them for you."

"Let's go then." She turns to grab her things, not hiding her grin.

She and Runner pile into her SUV, and I follow them to the bakery while mentally adding to my daily to-do list. Darby didn't mention my purchase of the building her bakery is in last night, so I have to assume Evin didn't share that information. As much as I want to tell her, my plan includes keeping her in the dark a bit longer. She needs to concentrate on the next stages and not be thinking about nine months down the road. She's going to be an integral part of renovating the old bakery without knowing it.

When we park and get out, I take Runner over to the grassy area while she goes in to start the day. I give him some time and notice him curiously sniffing deeper into the wooded area. The security lights don't reach that far, so I call him twice before he reluctantly comes back with his tongue wagging.

Darby's thrown her hair in a bun, slipped on her apron, and is laying out the things I need for the cookies.

"The ovens are almost ready. You remember what to do?"

"Think I can manage. Come here." I lean back on her counter, and she walks into my arms, slinking her hands around my neck.

"I want you to spend the night at my place tonight." There's no missing the trace of unease that flits over her face.

"I'm not sure I'm ready for that."

"Baby, give it a chance. You need to be comfortable there."

Her expression gives her away. She's thinking of Connie, my kids, and my life without her. She has no idea of her stamp on what I created.

"I bought that huge porch swing because it reminded me of you."

She twitches, holding my eyes, but remains quiet.

"It caught my eye passing by a store one day, and I immediately remembered the time you saw one similar in Myrtle Beach. It held both of us as we laid outside that bed and breakfast, and you mentioned wanting one. That day, I turned my truck around, went inside, and ordered it. Everyone loves it. When we unfasten the hinges, it lays out enough for Maya and Cole to both lie on it. But, every time I look at it, it's a reminder of you."

Her breath catches, and her eyes widen, but I go on. "My kitchen was designed with you in my head. The counter space, the side work station, the appliances—all you."

"Pierce, that's insane."

"What's insane is I did it all unintentionally. When your dad visited me, he walked around and inspected everything intensely. The night I found you on the porch swing, a knot took root in my gut. It was a few days later that it all came crashing down. Everything I'd done had a piece of you. I bought the house because you loved the old neighborhood. I lived in a townhome next to Connie, and when the house went on the market, I didn't hesitate. It took two years to get the layout exactly the way I wanted, but when it came to the renovations and decorating, my subconscious took over."

"What about other women?"

"My house is for my family and me. Now, it's for you, too."

She face-plants into my chest. "All that time, I thought you..." Her voice fades away, and she quivers.

I rub up and down her back, giving her a few minutes for the emotional wave to pass. No one in my life knows what I told her. And the last time she was there, we had that huge fight. It's time we make new memories.

"Okay, I'll come over after work."

As if on cue, Runner whimpers.

"Bring him, too. He needs to get used to the neighborhood."

She nods into my chest, sniffing lightly.

"Not to push you too far, but I want you to meet Maya and Cole this weekend."

This time, her body goes rock-solid, and there's no missing the unsteady intake of breath.

"You knew this was coming."

"Let's see how today goes with Connie."

"It doesn't matter how it goes with her. I pick them up on Saturday afternoon. Let's do dinner Saturday night."

She sighs, and I pick up the undertone of relief. "Saturday night, I'm booked. It's the annual summer bizarre."

It slipped my mind that Annie registered DG Creations for the bizarre. She even wrangled Evin and Edward to help during the event. Darby's spot is going to be a huge draw. Almost every tourist and resident in Charleston shows up to the event at some point. It's one of the largest parties of the summer.

I make a mental note to look at the bizarre agenda and the events Maya and Cole enjoy. It's not the time to introduce them to Darby, but at least I can stop by to lend my support and still have the night with the kids.

"How about we talk to Edward and see about some horseback riding on Sunday afternoon? They'd enjoy that, and it may make you more comfortable being in your own environment."

She's quiet for too long, and I'm about to remind her she agreed to give this a chance when I hear a very bleak and faint, "Okay."

It's not exactly what I'd hoped for, but it's time to move on. "Baby, you have a huge log of orders, and I have cookies to bake." I try to lighten the mood.

She raises on her toes, bringing her lips to mine. "I love you."

171

●—•—•—•—•—●

Connie breezes into the storefront, smiling at people as she passes, but when she hits the table, her lips form a hard line.

"Did you at least get me a coffee?" She sits.

"Nope." I take the last bite of my chocolate chip cupcake and slide my plate to the side.

"Since you're obviously done, we can go somewhere else. Somewhere with a little more privacy."

"I don't need privacy."

Her face heats up as she leans in. "There are people here that work with me, and I prefer not to have our personal business as the source of office gossip."

"If you wanted discretion, you wouldn't have grabbed my dick in the middle of a restaurant on Friday night, and you would have chosen a better swimsuit to parade around in yesterday. You wanted a public statement, and you're going to get it." I don't attempt to lower my voice and notice a few heads turn our way.

The waitress appears, and Connie's fake smile returns as she attempts to keep up appearances. As soon as she's out of earshot, the venom returns.

"How fucking dare you? You're lucky I even showed up."

"If you didn't show, the next request would have come through my lawyer, which would require you shelling out four hundred dollars an hour to communicate through yours. Consider this a courtesy." Once again, I talk openly and hear the lady to our right smother a giggle.

Connie's face now flames. As much as I like pissing her off, it's time to move forward.

"Maya and Cole came to my house last Thursday under some pretty heavy confusion. Maya especially. I don't appreciate you filling their heads with lies about my relationship with Darby."

"I didn't fill their head with lies. We thought you were out of town on business, and then your picture was plastered all over the place with that woman. I told them the truth. If anything, you're responsible for this 'heavy confusion'." She air quotes the last words.

"Cut the bullshit, Connie."

The waitress arrives with her coffee and backs away uncomfortably.

"There's no bullshit, Pierce. You embarrassed your children, and you need to apologize. You're acting like a fool over an old girlfriend, and it's not fair to put Maya and Cole through it."

"How fair is it to let the kids think we're working on moving in together? Then, when they find out about Darby through your underhanded ways, convincing them she's replacing them?"

Her eyes grow wide, and her pupils flare angrily. "Living together is best for the children."

"That is never going to happen, and you know it. There was no doubt in my mind you were going to act like a bitch about Darby being back in my life, but I'm not going to let you poison our kids with your fucking antics. We've always had an agreement that the kids would be shielded from the truth about our past. But when you told Maya that Darby was replacing you and them, I was forced to stand in my kitchen, face my teary-eyed little girl, and delicately explain that her parents are never going to be together."

"Great example of parenting, Pierce. You want your kids to know they are the result of a casual relationship?"

"Don't go there and put this shit on me. You opened that door, and I handled the damage control."

"Damage control? You want to talk about damage control? How do you think it made them feel when they saw you hanging all over that bitch? They were devastated and humiliated."

"That's where you're wrong. You manipulated that situation, throwing it in their faces, and then used their vulnerability."

"Hardly the case. I was upfront and honest. You left me no choice but to tell them who that woman was."

"As much as you'd like to keep thinking this is about Darby, it isn't. It's about your choices in parenting and the way you are raising our kids when they're with you. Leaving your computer open, calling other women floozies, letting our eleven-year-old have apps on her phone that I don't approve of, and letting her see things she has no business seeing. Cole and Maya exchanged words in front of me that pissed me the hell off, and I'm not having it. They are kids, Connie, and you tried to turn them against me. Your plan rebounded."

"You do not get to question my parenting skills while you're out flaunting around town with that tramp. I'm not going to sit here and let you chastise me because your piece of ass returned and swallowed your dick."

The lady beside us openly gasps; I barely hear it over the roaring in my head. Heat and anger score through my veins with the familiar flood of disgust for this woman. The raging temper I'm known for boils close to the surface.

"Careful, Connie," I say through gritted teeth.

"Don't careful me, Pierce. I think it's pathetic you're willing to put your family through this over a woman that didn't want you in the first place."

"My family is perfectly fine, including my children, who now know about the woman their dad is in love with. I told you this isn't about Darby. This is about the way you've chosen to act lately. Throwing yourself at me in public places, showing up uninvited, and deliberately misleading Maya and Cole is a huge problem. I've been lenient over the years, but you need to know I'm not putting up with you dragging the kids through hell over your petty jealousy."

"Petty jealousy? I'm not jealous, especially over a woman that's leaving in a month. You're openly making a fool of yourself."

I can't help my lips twitching, thinking of the many times Darby said the same thing, only in a much sexier way. On that thought, I decide to stop back by the bakery on my way to work.

"Making a fool out of myself is not your problem. Nothing about my relationship with Darby is your business. I always have Maya and Cole's best interests at heart; they are my priority. Darby in my life doesn't change that we are parenting our children together. From now on, if you have something to say, you bring that shit to me. Don't funnel it through them."

"Fuck Darby in your life. I'm the mother of your children, and if you think I'm going to let her waltz in and—" Her voice steadily rises.

"Now, who's making a fool out of themselves?" I cut her off, standing. I've said what needed to be said, and it's time to go. She can bash Darby on her own time.

"Where are you going?" she seethes, the veins in her forehead popping.

"I've got places to be."

"This conversation is not over."

"You're right. I have two things to add. Maya's phone has been cut back to limited service. She no longer has access to adding apps or social media. She also understands that those privileges come when both her parents agree." I lean in and say the next part so only she can hear. "Secondly, I hate doggy-style, always have. When I'm with a woman, I want to see her face. Jack Daniels and weed don't equal a casual relationship. So, no, hopefully, Maya never finds out the truth."

Fire blazes in her eyes, and I flash her a quick grin before strolling away. The owner of the shop calls out his thanks for the morning delivery, and I swear there's a scream from the table I abandoned.

Perfect fucking exit.

Chapter 21
Darby

"Quit fretting. You're getting wrinkles," Mom instructs for the tenth time in as many minutes.

"Don't you have someone else to harass? I'm trying to make sense of all this stuff you threw on me." I thumb through the promotional display items that she brought with her. Apparently, as my assistant, she took it upon herself to work with the marketing team at Brasher Resorts and decided this was an excellent opportunity to advertise my new business venture.

"It's simple, Darby. Place them on the table and move on."

"It's not simple! They don't match my vision for the table. I had everything arranged in my head, and now I need to mesh my current decorations with all this stuff."

"Geez, I thought Evin was my perfectionist. You need to get a grip."

I stop short of pulling at my hair and slice my eyes to her in warning. "Go away."

"Nope, I'm hopin' this might cheer you up." She digs in her bag and pulls out something rolled up in a ball. When she shakes it out, my breath catches in my throat.

It's a black t-shirt with the DG Creations logo, and underneath, she's added 'est. Charleston S.C'. It's a simple shirt, but the meaning behind it is anything but simple. It's a reminder of my beginnings and much more. Familiar whistling sounds from behind, and I turn to see Evin, Dad, Lynda, Jill, Warren, and Miller walking our way wearing the same shirt with big smiles.

"I love it."

"Figured it was time you had something that relayed your roots."

All the irritation slips away, and I kiss her cheek. "Thank you, Mama."

"How about one of those for me?" Warren extends his arms, and I go to him.

"What are you guys doing here?"

"We're here to support our favorite girl," he booms.

"Whatever you do, don't put him in charge of the samples." Miller pulls me from his dad into his own hug.

I giggle at the pained expression that fills Warren's face.

"Thank you all for coming. I can't imagine this is what you wanted to do on your Saturday afternoon."

"This is exactly what we want to do on our Saturday, Darby." Jill squeezes my shoulder affectionately when I step back.

I can't help but feel the ping of sadness that Pierce is not here. He mentioned bringing the kids out later today, but we decided it was not the day for me to formally meet them. Actually, it was his decision, stating I'd be too busy. Internally, I was relieved at his decision because tomorrow's horseback riding 'date' is already giving me anxiety.

"You got a plan?" Evin eyes my unfinished display table.

"Yes, I need your help moving some things around." Suddenly, the additional materials aren't a big deal, and a table arrangement pops in my head.

The parents all announce they are going to walk around before the bizarre kicks off, leaving me to work with Miller and Evin.

"This is unlike any other exhibition booth I've ever seen," Miller comments, taking in the huge ice cream cooler displaying my refrigerated items.

Evin and I share a look and say at the same time, "Annie."

Miller jerks his chin in understanding.

"Mom badgered the chairman until we had this exact spot on the main drag. Somehow, she arranged all the refrigeration units, too. I was going with cookies and truffles until I knew we had them." I motion to the two standing coolers behind me.

"Explains the need for all this electrical."

"It's a little ostentatious, but she insisted on a full selection."

"Full selection, huh?" His eyes light up, peering in one of the coolers.

"Help yourself to whatever you'd like, Miller."

"Did you make any of those special truffles?"

I nod, pointing to the cooler, which has trays stacked on trays of the truffles. He doesn't hesitate to snatch two, shoving them into his mouth. "Mmmmm," he mumbles.

Evin reaches in, too, grabbing a chocolate covered banana and taking a huge bite. I raise an eyebrow at him, and he shrugs. "What? I ran today and need the potassium."

"Mmhmm." I grin at his hidden sweet tooth and go back to straightening the literature.

They carry on a conversation about the upcoming football season, Miller inviting Evin to join his Fantasy group. It strikes me how at ease they are around each other. I know from Pierce and Evin there was a lot of avoiding over the years—Evin always protecting me and my secret, and Miller protecting his brother. All of the Kendricks were living in the dark.

For so long, I thought exposing the reasons I left was humiliating and a sign of weakness. But now, it's the opposite. Everyone knowing has been uplifting in a way. There is regret, but it's slowly disappearing.

"Soooooo," Miller draws out with a sly smirk.

The recognizable teasing tone in his voice makes my skin prickle. My head jerks up in time to see them exchange a look.

"Soooo... what?"

"Tomorrow's the big day."

"Yes." My answer is sharper than intended. The smirk falls from his mouth, and his eyes fill with concern.

"Darby, it's going to be fine. They are great kids, mostly because of Pierce."

"You're their uncle, and they adore you. It's easy to think they're great. I've already been labeled a home-wrecking floozy that's going to snatch their dad away. Not to mention, I'm indirectly responsible for an eleven-year-old's phone privileges being monitored."

"You have to let that go. It had nothing to do with you," Evin explains again. At our lunch on Wednesday, I told him about Pierce wanting me to meet Maya and Cole and the conversation Pierce had with Connie. I hate my own lack of confidence, but the truth is that I'm slightly terrified of what may happen tomorrow.

"I agree with Evin. You're putting too much pressure on yourself. They may be my blood, but I'm telling you the truth. If it helps ease your mind, I stopped by Pierce's this morning, and they are excited about the horseback riding."

I nod absently, a feeling of sadness creeping in. This was the first morning in a week I hadn't woken up in a bed with Pierce in it. We alternated between our places this week. My first night at his house wasn't bad, but I was definitely tense. I tried to hide my discomfort, which was useless because he picked up on it right away. His solution was to make love to me on the kitchen island, erasing the bad memories of the last time I was there. It worked. He became obsessed with making me comfortable, and every time I started to sink, I found myself naked. Finally, I drew the line at having sex on the porch swing. He didn't seem to understand my hang-up, and I knew sometime in the near future, he would wear me down.

"Hey." Evin's hand waves in front of my face, bringing me out of my daze. "Did you hear us?"

"No, sorry, I was distracted. What did you say?"

"That you're not going to be alone tomorrow. We'll all be there to support you."

I blow out a loud breath. "As tempting as that sounds, I'm a grown woman, and there are some things I need to do on my own."

"Bullshit." He deadpans.

"Evin—"

"No, Darby. This is a family thing, and we're not letting you go down this road alone. Last time we did that, you ran off for twelve years."

"That's not fair."

"For what it's worth, I agree with Evin. My niece and nephew need to see upfront that we're a blended family."

My heart skips a beat at his reference. I don't argue anymore, giving them both an appreciative smile. My phone chimes with a reminder that the bizarre officially starts in fifteen minutes.

"Okay, guys, I need to give you a crash course in working the payment system because Mom will probably be flitting around every booth and forget she's supposed to be working."

They listen intently, assuring me they're comfortable. A squeaky honk followed by a buzzing gets closer. "What the fuck is she doing?" Evin sounds terrified as we watch Mom pull up on a bright purple scooter.

"Mom, what the hell?" I screech as she climbs off.

"I lost track of time, and your dad refused to let me run back, so I borrowed Tess's scooter. Evin, I need you to return this to booth twelve."

"There's no way in hell I'm driving that anywhere." He grunts.

She narrows her eyes in a way that silently says, *'we'll see about that'.*

There's no time to discuss the purple contraption now parked beside my tent because a wave of people crowds the streets, signaling the bizarre has officially started. I smooth my hands down my sundress, do one more quick check over things, and get ready to work.

Three hours later, my throat is raw from non-stop talking, and my feet are screaming at me. There hasn't been one break in the crowds, and my mom is perched like a proud peacock on her stool, upselling every customer. Lynda sits next to her, doing the same, except her style is subtler. Warren, Jill, Dad, and Evin are all busy as well, greeting people as they stop.

"We're out again! You got me ready, Evin?" Miller yells, coming through the crowd with an empty sample tray.

"I got it!" I hustle behind the tables and pull out a tray from the cooler, handing it to Miller.

"Get another one ready, Dar. The band's about to take a break, which means a bigger rush," he instructs me, and I get to work immediately. Jill jumps in to help me break up cookies and clusters we are using for the samples. It's amazing how everyone has fallen into a routine so easily. A stab of pain pierces my heart, thinking of the one person missing.

"You're killing it, sweet girl." Dad pats my back with an ear-to-ear grin, his eyes shining bright with pride.

"Thanks, Daddy."

"What's going on? We having a union break? Darby Rose, get your skinny butt back out front! You're the headliner, and I'm not paying you to crumble cookies," Mom yells to us, and I roll my eyes once again at her attempt to be funny.

I take another minute to restock the display cooler and then return to the front of the tent. Miller was right; when the band on the main stage takes a break, people swarm our tent. I'm doing my best to make my way through the crowd, accepting compliments and thanking the customers.

I'm mid-sentence when an icy chill washes over my skin with the response of being watched. My head swings in both directions, and when my eyes land on him, I stumble backward.

There's no denying the young boy staring at me is Cole Kendrick. All the breath leaves my lungs, and my heart races to the point of dizziness. I can't tear my gaze away, taking in the beauty of this boy. Cole is an exact replica of his dad, complete with the striking blue eyes. Eyes that are trained on me.

For the briefest of seconds, my mind goes to the baby I lost and if he'd look like the boy standing in front of me.

The answer is yes.

His lips curl into a boyish grin, and my hands begin to tremble. Panic knots in my stomach, winding its way up. Hot flashes hit my flesh, and sweat dribbles down the back of my neck.

Dear God, please don't let this happen right now. I pray silently.

"Cole!" Pierce's sharp voice cuts through the air as he shoulders through a few people and stops by his son's side. "What the hell are you thinking? You know you can't run off like that."

The noise of those around us fades away, and my hearing zones in on what's happening twenty feet away. Pierce's face is twisted, but Cole is unfazed, still smiling at me.

"Look, Dad. It's Darby."

Pierce's eyes follow the direction of his little finger, and when he spots me, his eyes grow wide. "Oh, fuck," he states, rushing my way. I know he's close, but I'm mesmerized by the young man that is the spitting image of his father.

"Darby, baby." Pierce wraps around me, pressing my head into his chest. "Breathe."

I do as he asks, sucking in air and squeezing my eyes tight. "He's you... He looks exactly like you," I rasp.

"Baby, I'm sorry. I was taking them to the library for the magic show. He slipped away."

"Shit," Evin hisses behind us, undoubtedly taking in the scene.

I snap out of my fog, shaking my head a few times, and realize how this must look. "It's okay." I step back, tip on my toes, and peer over Pierce's shoulder. Cole is standing close, his smile gone, and he's flanked by Maya, who is fidgeting nervously.

This is not how I expected to meet them, but it's up to me to make it comfortable. "Hi there." I sidestep Pierce and approach them slowly. "I'm Darby."

"Hey," Maya mumbles.

"I'm Cole." He bounces excitedly.

"This is a wonderful surprise."

"Hey there, Slugger." Miller breaks in.

"Uncle Miller!" Both their eyes light up.

"Want to try some?" He waves the tray of samples in front of them.

Cole takes one eagerly while Maya is a bit more reserved. Cole inhales his, groaning dramatically. Maya's eyes widen when she swallows.

"Oh my gosh, that is good," she gushes, and the compliment sends a thrill through me.

"Thanks. There's a lot more where that came from. Miller can help you pick something." I throw a thumb over my shoulder.

Their eyes slide to Pierce, who nods his approval. Miller throws me a glance full of support before ushering them away.

"You okay?" Evin asks worriedly.

"Yeah, I'm good."

He scans my face for signs of distress, no doubt ready to get me away if needed.

"Promise, I'm not going to break down," I assure him.

He nods, stepping away and leaving me with Pierce. "I thought you were set up on the other side of the fountain. That's why we came in this direction."

"It's okay," I say softly.

"Your face is still pale."

"I had a moment of reflection when I saw him. It made me think of..." There's no need to finish the sentence.

Pierce blows out a loud breath and yanks me back into him. His mouth comes to my ear. "Don't do that. Don't go back to what we lost. Think about what we have ahead of us."

"Okay." The calmness in my voice shocks me.

"Yeah, you good?" He bends back, cupping my chin gently.

"I think so. I mean, the range of emotions I've experienced in the last three minutes is certifiable, but I'm still standing."

A sexy grin spreads across his mouth, "God, I love you," he says right before he sweeps his lips over mine. I melt into him, the people around us forgotten.

"Hey, lovebirds! We're running a business here. Think you can join us?" My mom breaks into my kiss-induced fog.

I giggle, dropping my head back, and hold on to him.

"Dad! Look what Mrs. Annie gave us!" Cole shouts excitedly, dragging my attention to the tent. He's yanking a DG Creations shirt over his head, and my throat closes as Maya does the same.

"Oh my," I whisper, thankful Pierce is supporting me.

"We decided to skip the magician and help out here with the rest of the family," Maya calls to us.

Jill, Warren, and Miller are beaming while nodding approvingly.

"You got another one of those shirts, Annie?" Pierce jostles me in his arms, his own approval firm in his voice.

"Of course."

He drops his mouth to the column of my throat and kisses gently. "You heard the little lady. Let's get to work with our family."

•—•—•—•—•

"You're dead on your feet. Have a seat with me." Jill taps the lounge chair to her right.

"Gladly." I collapse, groaning as the cushion sucks me in.

"Would you like a margarita?" Lynda offers.

The answer is hell yes, but I look out over the pasture where Pierce, Warren, and my dad are leading the kids around on the horses. Is it appropriate for me to drink alcohol?

"Yes, she'll have one. Add a tequila topper, will you?" Jill decides for me.

"I'm not sure that's a good idea."

"It absolutely is. You've been working like the devil, and it's your weekend. Enjoy it."

Lynda hands me the large, salt-rimmed glass and sits at the foot of my chair. "Cheers!" she toasts, and we all join in chorus.

A loud 'yippee' sounds from the barn, and we all laugh at Mom, who is pumping her hands triumphantly in the air on the back of her favorite horse. Evin and Miller are walking behind them.

My anxiety spikes, but Lynda shakes her head when I move to get up. "She's good, Darby. Jessie has been working with her in therapy on what is acceptable."

"All right."

"How are you doing with all this?" Jill asks softly.

"The better question is, how do you think I'm doing? Two months ago, if you told me I'd be in this position, I'd have laughed hysterically."

"I think you're a champ. This is hard, but Pierce is very happy."

"I'm not sure if you've noticed, but he doesn't take resistance very well."

She feigns shock, popping her hand over her mouth in an exaggerated motion. "Pierce? My Pierce? The sweet little boy that bulldozed his way into this world and hasn't stopped since? The same darling that won't take no for an answer and has the temper of a caged lion when provoked? Not to mention, when he wants something, he stops at nothing? That Pierce?"

Lynda and I both giggle. "That would be him."

"I blame it solely on Warren. Both my boys inherited their father's tenacity and grit. Admittedly, Pierce is a bit more aggressive in his nature."

"Is aggressive your polite way of saying hot-blooded and headstrong?"

"Maybe a little." She winks.

"Darby, all joking aside, you didn't answer the question. How are you feeling about everything?" Lynda asks.

Damn Lynda and her intimate knowledge of the Grahams' evasion tactics. She eyes me gently, and I know there's no dodging this.

"I was nowhere near ready for this step. Pierce was determined to make it happen."

"It is a big step."

"Lynda, this is going to sound crazy, but meeting them makes it all too real. Obviously, I've always known he has children, but I was able to protect myself by insulating my life. Staying away was my solution. Returning to Charleston was always a temporary measure. I had a life and business in Charlotte that I could easily go back to. The Brasher offer was on the table, which was weighing heavily on my mind. In a way, I used Mom's accident as an excuse to come home, clear my head, and make decisions about my future. Never did I anticipate the turn of events with Pierce. As a matter of fact, I decided to take the Brasher offer the night I ran into your family at Rosen's." I briefly glance at Jill then back to Lynda. "Seeing Pierce, Connie, and the kids in the parking lot shattered that insulation I'd built. Any nagging thoughts of staying in Charleston died that night."

Jill's eyes widen and pool with tears. "That was a very tense night for all of us."

"Ironically, seeing all of you broke something in me, and I confronted Pierce with the truth. I guess you could say it set the ball in motion for where we are today."

"Sweetie, you carried those demons around for too long. It was time you told him," Lynda adds.

"Well, a lot was said that night, including his confession of how Connie got pregnant. It was not pretty."

"Warren and I have never understood how Pierce messed up so badly. He was in a terribly dark place, and no one could get through to him. We decided early on to do what is best for Maya and Cole."

"They're your grandchildren. Of course, you do what's best for them."

"Pierce is not going to let Connie do anything to ruin this second chance with you."

"Maybe not." I shrug nonchalantly.

"But?" Lynda pushes with an arched eyebrow.

"But what?"

"There's a 'but' in there."

"Not necessarily. Pierce has been completely honest about his dislike of Connie. *But* even knowing she got pregnant through carelessness doesn't change the fact that he has kids with her. And, I'm not sure I'm strong enough to put myself in a position that comes with that kind of responsibility."

"Give it a chance. You may be surprised. You're one of the strongest women I know." She reaches for my hand.

"Thank you for that. I think I'm doing pretty well, considering a few days ago, the mention of meeting his children prompted a panic attack. And, last night, coming face to face with Cole almost caused me to faint."

"The children loved being there last night. They thought it was amazing." Jill tries to sound upbeat.

"If you say so. Maya distanced herself and hasn't said ten words to me today. Cole is so much like Pierce; it's unreal."

"I'm picking up very mixed signals here. Pierce led me to believe you two had worked things out and talked about the future. Until this conversation, I was under the impression you wanted these things as well."

"I love Pierce with all my heart. I always have. Jill, he believes there is a future for us and is hellbent on proving it. I am willing to try, but I'm skeptical."

"Have you told him this?"

"A hundred times!" I semi-laugh. "He's not listening."

"You two are meant to be, Darby. He's never been as happy as he is with you. I'm not sure he'll survive if you leave him again."

I wince at the sting of her words. "I'm not a confused twenty-one-year-old with a head full of conflicting emotions anymore. There will be no sneaking away without an explanation. We know I'm about to launch a new stage of my career. He's supportive and excited for me. But the truth remains; his life, his career, and his family are here. The logical part of my brain is telling me to be realistic. I'm going into this with my eyes wide open."

"If Pierce didn't have children, would you still be hanging on to this realism?" Lynda squeezes the hand she holding.

I take a large sip of my drink, hoping the tequila will unravel the knot coiling in my stomach. "We'll never know the answer because, if Maya and Cole weren't in the picture, I would have returned twelve years ago and begged for my second chance." My gaze travels out to the back of our land, where everyone seems to be having a great time. The smiles on the kids' faces are visible from here.

"You know you can have a life, a career, and a family here, too, Darby." Lynda throws my words back at me. "We're all rooting for you."

"I love you for it. But, in reference to Pierce, I'm not sure it's the life he's envisioned."

"Maya and Cole are in an awkward position right now. Children are products of their environment, and we're all doing our best to guide them in the right direction. It's impossible to miss the way he feels about you. They witnessed that last night and then again today. It's going to be okay with them," Jill tries to assure me.

"I hope so because I hate thinking about Pierce hurting, but I'm being cautious. There's a lot more at stake for the grown-up versions of Darby and Pierce. His priorities are much different."

"I have a lot of regrets, Darby, thinking that maybe I could have prevented so much that happened."

"Jill..."

She holds up a finger, signaling she's not done. "No, Darby, I could have been there for you in a way you didn't expect. I know what you went through. My first two pregnancies resulted in miscarriages. One was far enough along to know the baby was a boy. It was a long time ago, but I remember each instance like it was yesterday. The feelings, the failure, the uncontrollable emotions that come like a force of nature. Warren was by my side, but bless his heart, he couldn't do much to help. I'm not sure the boys even know. We never talked about it once Miller was born."

That is not at all what I expected her to tell me. "I understand. It's not exactly a pleasant subject."

"No, it's not, but it's life."

"I'm sure, once you held him for the first time, the heartache healed—knowing you were able to carry a life inside you and bring him into the world. All the pain and despair would vanish, and you'd know you had this miracle. Or, at least, that's what I always pictured in my mind."

Her eyes fill with sympathy, and Lynda scoots a little closer, the mood growing somber.

"I'll admit that when the nurse placed Miller on my chest, the emotions were overwhelming. It in no way erased the past heartache, but it gave me a new appreciation for what I did have."

"And then you had Pierce."

"I did. Healthy pregnancies happen all the time after a miscarriage. You know that, right?" she informs me with hope in her voice.

"Oh, I know, but since I've been hung-up in love with the same man for over sixteen years, I never tried again. And, now, I'm not sure I will."

A heavy silence hangs in the air, and I take another large gulp to shut myself up and stop admitting things that should remain private. If I make eye contact with either of them, we'll probably all end up in tears.

Runner jogs up the steps, sniffs around my chair, and plops down with a loud doggy *huff*. His big brown eyes find mine before he closes them to rest.

"I'll amend that. My baby came in the form of a ball of fur." I take my hand from Lynda and rustle the top of his head.

Both women stay quiet, but their silence tells all.

Chapter 22

Pierce

"Got some great news." Miller strides in my office, flipping his phone in his hand.

"Did we win the Johnson bid?"

"Well, yes, but that's news for the afternoon meeting. This isn't about business."

"Hit me with it."

"Todd came through. The Kiawah Island house is ours in two weeks. Couldn't get Myrtle Beach, but this is a better deal."

I toss down my pen and lean back in my chair, trying to recall the details. Todd is an old college friend of Miller's, who came into some money and started a renovation-flipping business. He decided to keep a few of his properties for rentals. We've worked with him several times over the years, which gives us the perfect excuse to leave town for weeks at a time without Connie riding my ass. It's close enough to come home on the weekends for the kids, yet far enough we could live the life of bachelors without being watched. "Which place?"

"The five-five on the Beachwalk."

I whistle low. This isn't our typical two-bedroom condo deal. This is his beachfront mansion that rents for four-thousand a week during the tourist season. We worked on this place years ago during the renovations, and it's incredible.

"Did he cut us a deal? I'm not opposed to spending the money, but he charges a shit-ton for that rental. Not to mention, it's larger than what we need."

"Free in exchange for a few punch-list items."

"Punch-list?" This could go downhill very quickly if we're walking into a barter-exchange.

"He's emailing me a list, but the main thing is he's having a new outdoor kitchen installed, and he's going to be up in Chicago. The week was already free, and he needs someone to oversee it."

"Not a lot of work."

"No, and between the two of us, it won't be a problem. As for the size, I thought it was a good idea for everyone to have their own room this year, especially with the addition of Darby. We'll have a spare room if Mom, Dad, or any of the Grahams want to come for a few days."

"Good thinking. I'll tell Connie tonight when I drop the kids off."

"Let's hope to hell she doesn't mention joining us." He groans, remembering her insistence at Rosen's that night.

"To be honest, with everything happening, this trip slipped my mind. I didn't know if Todd would pull through, so I also haven't brought it up with the kids. Hopefully, this vacation will be exactly what everyone needs." Resentment seeps into my words.

His eyebrows shoot up, not missing the bitterness in my voice. "Something going on?"

My mood sinks, and the familiar unease returns. "The same shit that has been hanging over me for weeks. Connie is pissed, and when I say that, I mean she's *fucking pissed*, even by her standards."

"Well, you knew that. Last Monday, you slayed her ass."

"Normally, I'd be happy with her silent treatment, but her tactics have shifted. The kids couldn't contain their excitement over the weekend, and when they spoke to her last night, she killed it immediately. They had her on speaker. At the mention of working the booth and sampling all the treats, Connie went into a rant about the unhealthy effects of too much chocolate and the probability of getting fat. Maya's face fell, and all the color drained away. Then, she lectured them about the dangers of horseback riding and went as far as to tell them to have me sterilize their clothes because of the horse stench. At that point, Cole's shoulders slumped. Her hostility was so thick it sucked away their happiness. Before bed, I caught Maya deleting all the pictures she took over the weekend. Connie didn't even have to mention Darby's name to ruin their great time."

"I'm not sure you should share this with Darby."

"Hell no! That's another thing." The ping in my chest intensifies, as my mood grows angrier. "Did you feel the tension in the air last night? The atmosphere from when we arrived, to when we finished with the horses, was a complete one-eighty. Darby was reserved and detached. She pushed her margarita away when the kids were around, her conversations were quiet, and her own mood solemn. It was exactly the opposite of her on Saturday night."

"You should call your mom." Dad saunters in, taking the chair next to Miller.

"Why?"

"Because she rambled on and on last night. She's worried about you and Darby. Maybe you pushed this thing too fast."

Before he even said it, I knew it was coming. "I disagree. There's no way I could let Connie poison their minds about Darby. They needed to meet her."

"You have a point, but Saturday night, she was Darby Graham, the business owner and chocolate extraordinaire. She had to put on a show."

188

"You're wrong. You haven't been able to spend much time with her, but that woman on Saturday night is the same woman I fell back in love with the minute I saw her. When we were in Aspen, those people were falling over their feet to get time with her. In the community here, it's the same way."

"Well then, maybe us invading her space with Maya and Cole was too much. Riding the horses, playing games in her yard, chasing her dog, grilling on her parents' patio—all of it may have overwhelmed her. She definitely seemed uncomfortable."

"Jesus." I scrub my hands over my face. "I thought it would be simpler on her if we came to her."

"Pierce, I'm going to ask you something, and I want you to think long and hard before you answer me." He squares his shoulders in a move that takes me back to being a kid. "Back in the day, I don't remember Darby telling you no very often. You two were crazy in love, and she would do about anything in her power to take care of you. This woman you described sounds like she hasn't changed. Do you think you're taking advantage of her?"

A sharp pain throbs in my temple, and my blood singes. "Taking advantage of her? Because I want her to meet my children so I can ask her to marry me and begin the life we should have been living? You think that's taking advantage of her?"

"Pierce, Dad has a point," Miller interjects.

"Not a good one. You're crazy if you think that woman didn't tell me no. I'm an excellent negotiator. We were crazy in love, and now that she's back, I'm not willing to waste time. Why is that a bad thing?"

"It's obvious you're not wasting time. However, it isn't all about you. Darby has been thrust into a cyclone situation, and last night, we took away her safe place."

"I'm her safe place!" I erupt, slamming my fist on my desk. "Goddammit."

I can't miss the guilt that flares in Dad's eyes. He doesn't give me a chance to question before he's up and at my door. "Call your mama. I think that may help unwind the damage." Then he's gone.

"Damage? Who said anything about damage?"

"I don't think that was a suggestion. Obviously, Mom has some answers for you." Miller follows behind Dad, closing me in.

The person I want to talk to is Darby, but she's unavailable.

Reluctantly, I dial Mom, and she answers on the first ring, sounding anxious. "Honey, I'm glad you called."

"I think you have some stuff to share."

"Oh, Pierce, I don't have a good feeling about Darby..."

●—●—●—●—●

After her voicemail plays in my ear, I end the call and jump in my truck. Darby was supposed to be here an hour ago but never showed. She's not answering her calls or texts, and at this point, I'm ready to call her family. After the conversation with my mom, I'm not taking any chances.

It was news to me that Mom and Dad had suffered through losing two pregnancies before Miller was born. I wish I'd known that nugget of information twelve years ago while Darby was crumbling. But that's not what's been spinning in my mind all day. It's the way Darby responded to the news and almost everything else that was discussed.

When I pull down the lane, Darby's hunched in her trunk while Runner plays nearby. She's dressed in athletic clothes, her hair on top of her head and a faint sweat stain on her tight tank top.

She flashes me a bright smile and waves as I park. That smile sends a rush of relief over me.

"I was wondering what time you'd show up. I just got home myself," she sing-songs, crawling back in the trunk.

"Show up? I've been worried fucking sick about you," I growl, my hand itching to spank the ass perched in the air.

"Here we go!" She holds up her hand victoriously, waving her phone and popping the button for her trunk. "I knew it flew to the back somewhere." Her eyes go to her screen, and the grin falls from her face. "Eight missed calls and four text messages from you? Is everything okay?"

"Hell no! I've been blowing it up, trying to find you when you never showed at my house. You were supposed to be there at seven."

"I changed the plans. Didn't you get my messages?"

"What messages?"

"I left you a voicemail and sent you a text that I was going to try a spin class tonight since you were with your kids."

I rip my phone from my pocket and scroll through. "No messages, Darby," I say a little too forcefully, flipping my screen around so she can see.

Her eyes shoot me a warning as she hands me her phone with our text thread.

I'm going to try a new spin class Mom's therapist raved about. It's been too long since I've worked out. Let's change the plans to my place tonight. Beer is in the fridge, and I should be home around 8. Hope you had a wonderful time with the kids.

The message was sent at five-thirty, about the time Maya had my phone. Fuck me.

"I left the same voice message as well."

"Baby, I didn't get them. I've been fucking pacing the floors waiting on you. Why didn't you answer?"

"My elbow knocked over my purse, and everything went flying in different directions. I was searching for my phone when you arrived."

I tug her to me, holding tight. "I was worried."

"I'm sorry about the mix-up, but you're overreacting."

"Let's get inside." The words come out gravelly.

She dips backward, her eyes sweeping over my face and her lips pressing into a thin line. "Jill?"

I lift her off the ground and carry her with Runner at our sides.

"Put me down. I'm disgusting and need a shower," she demands, wiggling to get free.

I inhale deeply and shake my head. "You smell like chocolate and perfume to me."

"I still need a shower."

"We'll shower after we talk." I heft her up on the counter and fit my hips between her knees.

"This is unnecessary. Whatever you're muddling over is nothing but girl-talk."

"Did I fuck up by bringing Maya and Cole here?" I cut straight to the chase.

She draws in a breath and stares at me for a few seconds before shaking her head. "I don't think so. Did they say something?"

"No, they had a great time. I've always been able to read you like a sixth sense and knew something wasn't right. You withdrew from all of us, plainly uncomfortable."

The spark of pain followed by unmistakable guilt in her expression says it all.

"I did fuck up."

"No, you didn't."

"Stop lying." I slide my hand over her shoulders and circle her neck, running my thumbs along her jawline. She tries to look away, but I duck into her line of sight. "Baby, I've been aggressive, and I'm not going to apologize for that. It may make me an asshole, but my sights are set on our future and what I need to do to get us there. What I will apologize for is not seeing things more clearly from your perspective. You're still holding things back from me."

"I'm not," she denies.

"I'm going to break my own rules tonight and go back in time. We're going to clear up some things. If I think we're still not on the same page, then we'll do this often until you know it has always been you."

"This is totally uncalled for. You don't need to reassure me, and we don't need to take a trip down memory lane. There are two human beings on this earth that are undeniable proof that *it hasn't always been me.*" Her response is loaded with sarcasm and bitterness.

"I wasn't happy," I go on. "I wasn't happy about the pregnancies. With each of my kids, I held on to anger at myself. Are you with me?"

"I am, but we don't need to relive this."

"Here's another tidbit to add to the list of why I'm a dick. When the nurse handed them to me, the anger slowly went away, but my first thought was of the baby I lost with you. I allowed myself a split second to picture it and then came back to the hell that was my reality. This doesn't mean that I don't fucking love my kids. It means I gave myself the luxury of one second to wish they belonged to us."

I caress her jawline, watching the realization followed by relief wash over her face. Mom was right. She's lived with the assumption that Connie was able to give me something she couldn't and heal my pain.

"Oh, God, maybe I'm not ready for this." Her voice shudders.

"The heartache didn't go away, not once for me," I continue softly. "I didn't move on, and I didn't forget."

"We can stop now." The tears pooled in her eyes spill heavily down her cheeks.

"Not yet. I do listen to you, Darby, but the headstrong ass in me is insistent on tearing down your resistance. If I push too hard, you have to speak up in a way I can hear you because I'm a little deaf to your excuses."

"You don't say?" She cracks a sad smile.

"Another thing I need to make clear tonight. I not only want to marry you and spend the rest of my life with you; I want to have that family we talked about. I want more children with you. This is probably going to set you on a downward spiral, but I'm here to catch you. You agreed to give this life with me a shot."

She shakes her head, fear and dread spreading over her face and jumping straight to freak out mode. "No, you have to stop."

"You're too perfect to bury that dream. Consider this your notice to get ready. You go to Aspen and kill it. When the time comes to come home, I'll be ready."

She begins to shake, and I tense, ready for anything. She launches forward, colliding with my shoulder, and bursts into loud tears. "I am never, ever, in my life having a tequila laced heart-to-heart with your mom again," she sobs.

"Yeah, baby, you are. Because, apparently, that's when things get real, and my ass kicks into gear."

"Pierce, your ass kicked into gear the morning you showed up uninvited to my bakery to scream at me."

"True, but I was too slow and stupid to know how to proceed. Now, I'm brilliant in my pursuit."

She giggles through sobs, clutching stronger.

"We have one more thing before we shower." I kiss along the skin of her neck, her pulsing racing against my lips. "We have a rental on Kiawah Island in two weeks. It's going to be Miller, the kids, and me. I want you with us."

She freezes, every muscle in her body tensing. I don't have to see her face to picture her expression. An uncomfortable silence fills the air, and I wait impatiently for her.

"I can't," comes out raspy, and she clears her throat a few times. "I can't," she says clearly this time.

"That wasn't the answer I wanted."

She slides her hands to my chest and presses up, placing her forehead to mine. Her cheeks are tear-stained and flushed, and her red-rimmed eyes are filled with conflict. "You know I'm going to decline, right?"

"I'm figured you'd try."

"I'm going to speak in a way you can understand. This isn't only about the uncertainty of your family vacation with your kids. Pierce, I still have a small business to run. Orders are already on the calendar throughout the month. The bizarre was my last event, but there are a few other things around town I'm committed to. There is no way I can take off for a week and still fulfill my obligations."

I have to control the urge to argue with her. Dad is more than capable of handling our business while Miller and I leave for the week. Hell, it's not unusual for all three of us to be out of the office for a few days. I knew it would be hard for her but hoped she'd at least consider a way to make it happen.

"There's no way I'm leaving you for a whole week. We'll make something work."

"You're not listening."

"I hear you loud and clear, and I understand. We will figure out something."

She chews on her lip, deep in thought, flicking her eyes around. "If you're hearing me, then hear this. I'll drive down and spend the day on Saturday."

"I have a better idea. You come with us on Friday night and stay through Monday morning? Then maybe you could pull through with your orders on Monday and Tuesday and come back?"

She shakes her head with an amused expression. "I'll drive in Saturday morning, spend the day, and drive back that night. Take it or leave it."

"That's two hours of travel by yourself. It's ridiculous."

"Let's see how it goes with the kids sharing their dad on vacation."

I think her plan is shit but know this is a chance to prove I can see things from her perspective. My grunt is my response, and her face brightens with the victory.

I'll let her think she's won… for now.

Chapter 23

Darby

I drive down the sleepy street with my windows and sunroof open. The smell of salty air and sunshine breeze through the truck, and Runner's perched up with his head out the window, his tail wagging excitedly.

I'm right there with him. This neighborhood is gorgeous, and Pierce has spent two weeks hyping this place up in an attempt to get me to stay. I held my ground on this daily visit to test things out but secretly have been thrilled to spend the day at the beach. The phone rings, and I barely get out a 'hello' before Pierce is talking over me.

"Where are you?"

"Good morning to you, too."

"I'm standing in the foyer, staring out to an empty driveway. My morning is not going to be good until you pull in."

I take the turn, the large house coming into view. "Kinda like right now?"

The line goes dead, and he walks out the front door, marching toward me. He's wearing his running gear and his hat turned backward, looking every bit the sexy as sin man that makes my heart soar. I'm not even at a complete stop before he's slinging my door open, leaning in, and shifting my SUV into park. My seatbelt is released, and in less than five seconds, I'm in his arms, his mouth on mine.

His tongue takes over, the taste of clean spearmint filling my mouth. I wrap my arms around his shoulders, slanting my head and giving in to the familiar hunger that rushes through my body every time he touches me. He threads his fingers through my hair, thrusting his hips to mine. I whimper at the feel of his rock-hard length rubbing against me. He shifts us until my back hits metal, trapping me between his solid body and the edge of my doorframe.

My leg hooks around his waist, drawing him closer. I forget where we are, all logic flying of out my brain. His body heat surrounds me, soaking into my skin as he kisses me with the hunger of a starved man. His lips move urgently on mine, his tongue sweeping through my mouth as if we've been apart forever.

The thin material of his shorts and my loose dress do nothing to contain the way he rubs against me at the perfect angle, stroking me with his small thrusts.

"Didn't fucking like waking up without you," he growls into my mouth.

My only response is a low moan to the delicious friction happening.

Faintly, I hear a throat clear, though neither of us is slowing down. It isn't until Runner barks and whines close to my head that I snap back to reality.

"We have to stop." I break away, trying to catch my breath.

"The kids are still asleep, and I don't care about Miller."

"Maybe you don't, but I'm pretty sure my skirt is hiked up to my waist, and he's going to get an eyeful of my ass in a second."

"Shit." Pierce separates us a little, allowing my leg to drop and skirt to fall. His eyes roam over me, and a cocky grin split wide. "I'm going to fuck you in this dress at some point today."

"Not a chance in hell."

His eyes flame, and I know he's accepted this as a challenge.

"Good thing you're here, Darby. Pierce has been an ass," Miller calls from behind us.

I check my watch. "It's not even eight-thirty," I defend.

"I went to bed and woke up without you. My patience was wearing thin."

My heart swells and my stomach twists the same way it always does when he says things like this. "I'm here now."

Runner barks again, alerting us that's he's done waiting.

"Miller," Pierce looks over his shoulder, "will you walk Runner around and get him familiar?"

"Let him loose," he responds with a handclap.

Pierce unpins me, opening the back door while I go to the trunk. Runner almost falls over himself getting to Miller and then taking off into the side yard. I throw my beach bag over my shoulder and grab the large box filled with enough sugar and sweets to last most people a month.

"Jesus, baby, what's in there?" His eyebrows arch when he takes the box and peeks inside.

"I may have gone overboard. But I was nervous and thought maybe this stuff would help ease any tension."

"I think you'll see there isn't going to be any tension."

"Let's hope," I respond sincerely. Since our talk in my kitchen that night, I have been mentally preparing myself for today.

Pierce changed his strategy and took a much less aggressive approach. Connie was still pissed off at him and wasn't thrilled he wanted the kids for a full week at the beach, especially when she found out she wasn't included at all. After hearing Pierce's parting words that morning in the café, I expected her to slink back under her rock to lick her wounds. She didn't.

Her retaliation was keeping them with her the last two weeks and him having to jump through hoops to see them. Connie still relied on Jill and Warren to help with their childcare, so Pierce would work early mornings and got them for afternoons before he returned them at night. Twice, Connie arrived uninvited, joining them for dinner. This set Pierce off, but I suggested he lay his feelings for her aside and try to get along instead of glowering at her like a rabid dog. I had no idea if it would work, but in my mind, I wondered if Pierce's neutral attitude toward their mother would help lighten their confusion.

When it came to me, he took extra measures to make sure I was okay. Seeing as his children were spending every night with their mother, it gave us the opportunity to have our time. We alternated between houses and fell into a routine. Our routine. It was wonderful and scary at the same time. He gave me a glimpse into what could be if there was a chance for the future.

I loved it. I embraced it. And I made the decision I was going to own this with him.

So, while he prepared to bring them to Kiawah Island and give them an unbelievable summer vacation, I was planning on my own approach. For the first time in all these years, I wanted to be with Pierce and his children. Cole liked me; that was obvious. It was Maya I needed to move with cautiously.

Pierce takes my hand, balancing the box easily on one arm, and leads me inside. I'm immediately taken away by the house, noticing it is similar in style to my shed, only six times larger. The coastal décor is fun and chic, and the view of the outdoor living area leading to the beach is breathtaking.

I love it. He picks up on my approval, winking at me. "You haven't seen the best part yet." He takes us around a corner, and I cry out at the kitchen. It's massive, it's exquisite, and it's pristine. If I ever had this type of home, this is my kitchen.

"This is perfect!" I squeal, wrenching my hand from his and running to the first surface. "It's going to be exactly what we need."

"For this?" He places the box by me.

"Yes. How long before they wake up?"

"Hit or miss. Cole will barrel down the stairs when his stomach wakes him. Maya is a wild card. She likes her sleep."

I twist, throwing my hands around his neck. "How do you think they will react to homemade donuts?"

His fantastic blue eyes light to the color of the sky. Something passes across his features, something bright and beautiful that dips down to my soul.

"You want to be here," he concludes.

"I do. I want to make homemade donuts with you, eat a very unhealthy breakfast that we'll promise to work off chasing Runner on the beach and swimming until we're exhausted."

"You make a homemade breakfast with my kids, and then Miller is going to take them to the beach while you and I work it off in a different way."

"Stand back." I push against him lazily. "I'm here to spend the day with the Kendrick Family. You are going to have to control yourself."

"Not in a million years." He kisses me quickly, sucking my lip into his mouth.

"DAD! It's time for the beach!" Cole shouts, skidding into sight, and my stomach lurches. He looks and sounds so much like Pierce, it's uncanny.

"You trying to wake up your sister?" Pierce chuckles at his rumpled appearance.

"Hey, Darby!" He ignores his dad, coming to my side and giving me a one-armed hug.

"Hey, Cole."

He eyes the scene in front of him, me holding onto his dad, and he scrunches his nose. "Why are y'all dressed in real clothes? Aren't we going to the beach?"

"I went running, and Darby drove in, buddy. She's making breakfast before we head to the beach."

"Actually..." I raise a finger, and a loud slamming sounds from somewhere in the house.

"She's up." Cole grins triumphantly.

"I'll wait then." I leave the comfort of Pierce's hold and start unpacking the items.

Miller comes in the back door, Runner pouncing behind him. He looks at me with his blissful doggy eyes and stops to smell every inch of the new space. Cole calls his name, and he prances over, nudging his thigh before licking his hand.

"What's happening in here?" Miller goes to the coffee pot.

"Darby is spoiling us."

"Fanfuckingtastic." Miller grins over the rim of his mug.

"Here." I shove a box of cookies at Pierce, who helps me unload the rest. It's not long until we hear padding down the hall.

Maya comes into view, holding her phone. She looks drowsy, and her eyes barely meet mine before she head-plants into Pierce.

"Hand me your phone," he instructs, rubbing her back.

"Hi, Darby." She nestles into his side.

"Hey, Maya." I take the coffee mug Miller offers.

"Electronic free weekend officially starts now." Pierce slides her phone to the back of the counter.

"Mom wants you to call her," she mumbles.

"I will," he assures her, slicing his eyes to me.

"Your dad tells me you love donuts," I announce, pointing at my dough.

They both perk up, coming close.

"Can you help me?" I ask.

"What do we do?" Maya asks as Cole slides to her side.

"First, find me a pan for oil."

Miller jumps into action, grabbing me an extra-large pot. Pierce takes it and the oil I brought, starting the process. Cole and Maya roll out the dough, and when I suggest doing hand molds, they go crazy. I make sure the grease is ready, and Pierce steps up, helping them drop their creations. When they're done, I scoop them onto a drain plate and give them the option of regular glaze, chocolate, and raspberry.

"I want it all!" Cole exclaims.

"I do, too," Maya admits softly.

"Then you get it all." Pierce ruffles her hair.

"Anyone want fruit?" I open the fridge and find what I brought amongst the full and overflowing contents. It's hard to miss the two bottles of my favorite Chardonnay front and center, next to a stack of steaks.

The first sign he's going to try to convince me to stay. I peer over my shoulder and find Pierce's eyes glowing bright with mischief.

"Not going to work," I insist, handing him the bowl of fruit.

"We'll see."

"What's not going to work?" Cole sputters with a mouth full.

"Darby still thinks she's going home tonight." Pierce doesn't hold back.

Cole snorts, covering his mouth and mumbling, "Yeah, we'll see," mirroring his dad's words. Even Maya's lips tip into a small grin as she makes brief eye contact with me. Neither of them seems fazed or insulted their dad wants me here, and I'm now suspicious of what he has in store. I don't have to wait long for the next sign.

Runner bumps his nose to my knee and looks up at me expectantly. "It's time to feed you." I glance around for the plastic container of dog food I packed for the day.

"I've got it." Cole leaps off his stool and hops over to the pantry, pulling out two brand new dog bowls and an unopened bag of Runner's food.

"I'll get the water," Maya offers, and Cole hands her one of the bowls. They set up an area for Runner, and he butts his way in.

"Isn't that convenient?" I slice my eyes back to Pierce, who's now grinning arrogantly.

"Yep, convenient." He takes the last bite of his donut and pats his stomach. "It's a good thing we have all day to work off this breakfast." The wink he shoots me sets my pulse racing, and I know he's not referring to chasing Runner on the beach.

"I'll take over clean-up so everyone can get ready." Miller reaches for the remaining donut.

"I can help."

"I've got this. Besides, we all take turns. At some point, you'll get your chance."

Now, I know Miller is in on the 'convince Darby to stay' scheme. It's my turn to respond with the, "We'll see."

Cole snorts again, picking up on the sarcasm, and looks at his dad. "You're right. This is going to be fun."

I blow out an exaggerated breath and grab my bag. "Can someone point me in the direction of a bathroom to change?"

"Right this way." Pierce gestures behind him, in the opposite direction of where the kids came from earlier. He leads me to a bedroom, which I assume is the master from the size and view.

It's impossible not to stare out the French doors to the view of the ocean. "This is beautiful."

"Agreed." Pierce steps close behind me, brushing my hair to the side and bringing his lips to my ear. "Beautiful."

I lean into him, loving the way his soft scruff tickles my skin as he nibbles and kisses a path along my neck and shoulder. He eases the bag off my shoulder, tosses it to the side. Sliding his hand along the backside of my thigh, he takes my dress with it. He does the same thing on the other side until his palms cup the bare cheeks of my butt. "Thongs?"

"Not exactly, but close."

"Hmmm, as much as I wish I could see for myself, this has got to be quick."

I shake my head. "No, Pierce, we can't."

"Hell yes, we can."

"Miller and the kids are down the hall."

"The door is locked, and we'll be quiet. But I told you I was going to fuck you in this dress."

"I'll wear it for you at home."

In a split second, he's ripped the panties down, one hand coming to the front and dipping between my thighs.

"There is no way I'm able to have sex... Ahhhhhh..." I end on a moan when he strums his fingers along my slit.

"That's it, baby. Get ready," he says gently in my ear before his mouth goes back to my neck. "Give me a little space."

I part my thighs enough for him to slip a finger inside. The argument to stop dies on my lips when he begins the feather-light brushes on my clit. My body betrays me by clenching hard and rolling into him.

"Ride my hand, Darby," he commands roughly, adding a finger.

I'm unable to resist doing as he says. His hand dips, his finger curling and twisting in slow, skilled movements. I gasp when he grazes along the spot that ignites my insides. My hips buck, and he grins against my skin.

"Give it to me."

In no time at all, he brings me to the brink with expertise. I drop my head forward, squeezing my eyes, all my lower muscles clutching onto him as my orgasm rushes through me. My muted whimpers are barely audible over the ringing in my ears. There's a jerking movement at my back, but I'm still riding my high.

Slowly, he pulls his hand upward, circling my waist with his forearm and urging me forward a bit. "Tilt your hips a little. I've got you."

I arch back and swallow my cry as he slides into me. His cock is hard and hot, stretching me with every inch. In this position, my hips sway a little to adjust and instantly mold to him. He rocks in and out until he's fully seated, and his mouth comes back to my ear.

"I swore we'd never do this. I'd never fuck you from behind, always wanting to see you when I'm inside you. Help me out, baby." He picks up his pace, thrusting deep.

"Oh, God." My head falls back to his shoulder, and I grip his forearm for support. My eyes finally open, and I twist my neck to face him.

"Fucking gorgeous. When we're on that beach today, I'm going to be able to look up at this window and know you still have me coating your insides."

I love it when he gets wild like this. I filthy way he talks is his weapon of seduction and leaves me merciless to whatever he wants.

"Every inch of my dick is buried deep in your silky smooth pussy. You're coating me, too."

His words are fuel to an already blazing fire racing through my bloodstream. "Hmmmmm," I moan.

His eyes smolder with wild hunger, and he rams up, over and over. He loosens his hold on my waist, taking my wrist and raising my arm around his neck. "Baby, hold on to me. This is going to be quick. Swear to make it up later." His hand dives back under my dress, and his thumb flicks over my clit, again and again.

Tremors take over, and I clutch the back of his head, my mind growing fuzzy. Desire and need build low in my stomach, and I grind into him, wanting to feel the high together.

"Fuck, fuck, fuck... Now, baby, now." He slams up hard, bottoming out and growling. My vision goes spotty, and I erupt, feeling him pulsate and pour into me. This may be the single most erotic moment in my life. Standing in front of a window, in broad daylight, fucking like an animal where anyone could look up and see.

It's a thrill and a wave of pleasure different than anything I've experienced.

His chest heaves at my back, his heart thundering with mine. "Are you with me?" He nibbles on my earlobe, sending an aftershock rushing through.

"Oh yeah. The reply comes out breathily, and his blue eyes go liquid. He slowly inches out, twisting me so I'm locked to him.

"I love you."

"I certainly hope so, considering you just admitted to marking me like an animal."

His cocky grin returns, and he dips in to kiss me quickly before stepping back and ripping his shirt over his head. "Let's get changed."

I roll my bottom lip between my teeth, watching him disappear into the bathroom. Sheer naked perfection.

I pick up his shorts, my panties, and my bag from the floor, ready to follow him and clean up when a spark of color catches my eye. How did I miss that?

On the nightstand sits a beautiful arrangement of rare sunburst calla lilies mixed with white roses. "Pierce?"

"Yes?" His head pops out.

"Where'd the flowers come from?"

"Florist in town."

"Why are they in here?"

"Because that's your side of the bed."
I open my mouth to argue, but he's already backed out of sight.

Chapter 24

Pierce

"Five bedrooms, and you couldn't find a place for me to stay for two nights and enjoy the beach with my children?" Connie seethes.

"Nope."

"That's fucking rude, even for you."

"Connie, you have many weeks left this summer if you'd like to take the kids somewhere. This is my vacation."

"I can't exactly afford a luxury house on the ocean."

"Not my problem. You have a job. Do what you can do."

"My dad doesn't stuff my paychecks, so—"

"We're done here. You need something, message me. Maya will call you tomorrow." I end the call to more screeching and go to the counter where Maya's phone still lies. Once I make sure she shut off her location finder, I power it down.

"You good in here?" Miller sticks his head through the back door.

"Yeah, had to deal with her and didn't want the kids to hear."

"If you're done, you may want to get your ass back down to the beach."

"Are the kids okay?"

"They are fine. It's Darby getting the attention. She has an admirer or two."

"Son of a bitch." I'm on the move, jogging through the house, across the deck, and down the short walk to where our chairs are lined.

Maya is at the shoreline watching Cole and Runner play in the shallow surf. Darby is a few yards away, talking with two men who are crowding in on her.

"I was gone less than five minutes," I grind out.

"She's like a fucking beacon, man. I jumped in the water, and when I turned around, they were there."

I cross my arms, shooting laser beams their way and waiting for her to see me. One of them must say something funny because she throws her head back, roaring in laughter, and her chest pokes forward. My teeth grind together as her tits bounce. She props her hands on her hips, drawing my attention down her lean torso. Her multi-colored bikini sparkles in the sun and highlights every curve of her body. She's a fucking fantasy come true, and even from a distance, I can tell these guys are thinking the same thing.

A blinding red haze films over my eyes when one of the men reaches over and massages her shoulder, his elbow grazing over the swell of her breast. A possessive growl rumbles deep in my throat, and I'm storming toward them.

"Shit. Pierce, remember we're on a public beach," Miller says right as Darby glances my way.

Her smile glows brighter, and she says something to them, making them twist to look. One of them leans in closer to her, whispering something in her ear, and she nods. Our eyes stay locked, and when I'm close, she steps into me, flattening her hands on my chest. "I wondered how long it would take."

"Forty-five seconds from the time he hit the sand," one of them answers.

"Not that, Dave. His phone call," She responds cheerily, glancing back to them. "Pierce, this is Dave and Martin. Guys, this is Pierce and his brother, Miller."

They both jerk their chins in greeting. Miller grunts a hello. I glare at them, staring them down. They stare right back, both grinning smugly in a way that sets my blood on fire.

"Darby, sweetheart, as fun as it sounded to play our little joke, you may want to fill him in. He looks like a mated wolf that's about to kill his prey," Martin tells her, his self-righteous smile splitting wider.

"Pretty much. The territorial vibe is raging," Dave agrees.

Darby giggles and tries to step back, but I hold her to me firmly. "Dave and Martin are friends of mine from Charlotte, Pierce. I've known them for years. They happen to be vacationing here. We met through Scottie and his *partner*."

At the term partner, some of the tension eases, and Miller chuckles.

"That's her elusive way of saying we are no threat to you," Dave points out.

"Now is where you stop sneering like an animal and shake their hands," Darby tells me.

I keep one arm around her, offering my hand. "Nice to meet you."

"Scottie told us Darby had a new man in her life. We saw you online, but it's easy to understand why Darby lived like a nun now."

"Shut up!" Darby swats Martin's arm.

It's my turn to grin smugly. "Quite a coincidence running into each other on a beach in Kiawah Island."

"No kidding. We were sitting back there," Martin throws his thumb over his shoulder, "and I told Dave that Darby was picking up shells. I'd know that body and form anywhere."

At the last piece of information, the tension returns, and my grin turns into a frown.

"Martin was my masseuse," Darby clarifies.

"Wait, is that Runner?" Dave asks. Runner's supersonic hearing kicks in, and he dashes our way.

"You better brace, Dave. He's coming full force," Darby warns.

The dog barrels into their legs, hopping and barking while they both rub him down. "We were so excited to see Darby; we didn't even see him. Who is he playing with?"

"Those are Pierce's children, Maya and Cole."

At the mention of their names, both their heads pop up, their eyes casting between Darby and me. Shock settles on their faces at the realization of who I am. An uncomfortable silence stretches out until Darby speaks. "I'm guessing Scottie left that part out."

"Yeah, you could say so." Martin pats Runner one last time and stands straight, crossing his arms over his broad chest. All sense of joking from a minute ago is gone. There's no telling what he knows of our history, but it's evident he's trying to figure me out. "It seems you worked a miracle."

These men obviously had a place in her life in Charlotte. For them to know anything about me says they mean something to her, which is important to me.

"It's funny how life has a way of working out. I'm guessing you probably have some questions for Darby. Why don't you join us for dinner, and you can grill her on how I wore her down?"

Darby's fingers dig into my chest, and her breath hitches. They exchange a glance then agree. "We'd love to."

"I brought dessert," she adds.

"I've been craving a taste of your stuff for a long time." Dave smacks his lips appreciatively.

We agree on a time and say our goodbyes, the three of us and Runner joining Maya and Cole at the shoreline where they are studying the sand intently.

"What are you looking at?"

"We're looking for shark's teeth." Maya squints, leaning closer to a shell. "Neither of us has ever found one."

I glance over Darby's head at Miller, and he wiggles his eyebrows. He's the one who planted this in their heads, and I know exactly why.

"Lucky for y'all, Darby is the best shark's tooth collector I've ever known."

"I don't know about that, but I've found a few," she replies shyly.

"A few? You kicked all our asses when it came to finding those suckers," Miller throws back.

"Okay, I have a keen eye."

"Would you help us?" Maya asks sweetly, her eyes growing bright.

"Absolutely. Let's walk a bit."

My kids fall in step with her, Miller and I falling behind while Darby explains her best methods. After a few minutes, she stops, shaking her head. "This is better at low tide or early morning."

"Low tide isn't until seven-fifty-two p.m." Miller recites the information. "And we're grilling steaks tonight."

"Then we'll come in the morning," Cole decides. "Darby can teach us how to hunt then."

"That's a good idea," Maya agrees with a smile. "Dad can make breakfast."

Darby's eyes fly to mine, and I shrug innocently. We've all been dropping hints for Darby to stay, and each time, she declines, but her effort is wavering. Let's see what she comes up with this time.

"Guys, I appreciate the offer, but I'm not prepared to stay overnight."

"You're up," Cole and Maya say at the same time, running to the ocean. Miller stays behind to watch them as I take Darby's hand and head back toward the house.

"If you think we're going back into that house where you can seduce me to stay, I'm going to kill you!"

"That wasn't my intent, but I'm game if you can't help yourself."

"You're not going—" She gripes the rest of the way, and I enjoy her spirited argument with herself.

I guide us through the French doors of the master bedroom, taking a quick second to appreciate the spot I fucked her earlier, and lead her into the bathroom. I yank her to me, kissing her hard to shut her up. "Look around."

She twists and turns, her eyes fluttering in the space, passing over the vanity, the shower, the tub, the closet, while her hand in mine clutches harder. "When did you—? How—? Are those my pajamas?" she finishes.

"Yes, I packed you a bag. All the other stuff, we picked up while we were in town yesterday."

"You can't help yourself, can you? Was the shark tooth scheme yours, too?"

"Totally innocent on that one."

208

She scrunches her eyes and purses her lips together. "That was a clever one. Probably Miller."

"Are you having a nice time?"

"I am."

"Are you comfortable here with us?"

"Yes."

"Outside of my almost fit-of-jealousy-violence and my call with Connie, this day has been pretty perfect. Let's finish it out and wake up to do it again tomorrow."

She drops her neck back, exhales loudly, and shakes her head. "Fine, I'll stay the night. I can't believe I'm such a pushover."

"You're not a pushover. I'm persuasive. You should let me make all your decisions." I press my lips to her to hide my satisfied grin.

•—•—•—•—•

"Have I mentioned how glad I am you decided to stay another night?" I trace my tongue along Darby's jawline, kissing a trail to her earlobe.

She leans into me, her back pressing to my front, and sighs contently. "That was the idea all along, wasn't it? Pretend you agreed with my day trip plan, then gang up on me with a Kendrick sneak attack? I didn't stand a chance."

"It's no secret I wanted you here all weekend."

"I have to leave in the morning. No shenanigans tonight."

"No shenanigans."

Our bodies are warm from the sun, and I glance up to the vanity mirror, enjoying the reflection of us. Darby's wearing the black bikini I gifted her this morning. Maya actually found it when we were shopping on Friday afternoon, pointing out she thought it would be pretty on Darby.

The thought of Darby in the bathing suit wasn't only pretty, it was also hot. We went in and bought it.

We were right. When Darby walked out this morning in the suit, Miller's eyebrows shot up, and he sent me the *'are you crazy'* look. All day, I've been thinking of ways to get her out of this suit.

She slinks an arm around my neck, her fingernails scraping into my scalp, and locks eyes with me in the mirror. "What are you thinking about?"

"How I want to peel you out of this suit with my teeth."

"I'm afraid it's a little more complicated than it looks." She grins.

God, she's gorgeous. Two days in the sun has brought back her sun-kissed glow I remember from long ago. She's relaxed and happy, and it radiates from her.

"I'll figure out a way. I'm a very determined man." I nip on her ear, sliding my hand into the fabric and strumming through her slickness.

"Hmm, as nice at that sounds, you need to let me take a shower."

"Not without me."

"Yes, without you. We've already been promiscuous enough." She grinds her ass against my raging hard-on, jiggles out of my hold, and jumps out of reach. I watch in horror as she strips the top and bottoms in two swift moves, crashing my plans for later.

"Dream crusher." I palm my cock through my board shorts.

She smiles, her eyes glinting wickedly as she steps in the shower and turns her back to me.

I think about joining her but then think of the pleasure of punishing her later instead.

I force myself to leave the bathroom, throwing on a shirt and stopping to enjoy the view and loosen the ache in my cock. It almost works until a whiff of coconut body wash strays from the bathroom. I head to the kitchen, thinking of estimates, sales, football statistics— anything but Darby naked and wet in the shower without me.

A few minutes later, I'm busy chopping vegetables when Maya skulks in, handing me my phone. Her mood is a turnaround from when her mom called a while ago.

"Everything okay?"

She shrugs, pushing around the shark's teeth lining the countertop, looking miserable.

"Something on your mind, baby?"

"I think I lied to Mom, and when she finds out, she's going to be angry."

I stop chopping and lean against the counter, giving her my full attention. "What do you think you lied about?"

She glances nervously around the room. "Where's Darby?"

"In the shower. Is this about Darby?"

"Sort of. Mom had lots of questions and wanted to know everything we're doing."

"That's understandable. She misses you guys."

"I didn't tell her about Darby being here. I purposely left her out of the conversation."

"That's not lying."

"She wants to come here, and she asked me to talk to you. I told her I would try to convince you."

"Are you going to try?"

She slowly shakes her head. "We're all happy, especially you, and if she comes, I don't think anyone will be happy." Her voice cracks.

"Maya, come here." I hold out my arms, and she stumbles into them. "I don't consider that lying either.

"You kiss Darby and hold her hand. She smiles at you, and I swear you look like I've never seen. Dad, you really like her."

"I told you that already. She's special to me."

"Everyone likes her."

"That's true. She's very likable. A more important question is, do you like her?"

She nods into my stomach. "I do. I like her, too. And I love that she cares for you the way she does."

"You can't imagine how happy it makes me to hear that. Darby being in my life is going to be great for everyone. She's that kind of person, always has been."

"Can I ask you something?"

Something in her tone sets me on alert. "Yes, you can ask me anything. I may not always be able to answer, but let's hear it."

"If she's always been special to you, why hasn't she been around before?"

Her question is like a loaded punch to my gut, taking the air with it. I make a snap judgment call that hopefully won't come back to bite me in the ass. Moving my hand between us and tilting her chin to face me, I answer, "I messed up in a big way. Darby got sick and went away to Charlotte. It made me angry to the point I lost all reason. I let her go without knowing the details."

"She was sick?"

"In a way, yes."

"And you didn't go after her?"

"I was young and stupid, letting my emotions, pride, and temper control my actions. I fully regret that decision."

"But she's okay now?"

"She perfect, except for her enlightened stubborn streak."

This earns me a small smile. "Did you love her?"

I look into my daughter's dark, rich blue eyes that are swimming with questions and curiosity. I wish there was a way to stall this conversation for seven years, or maybe forever. But honesty has always been my style. "Always. I've always loved Darby Graham."

"You've never acted or spoken to Mom the way you do Darby," she points out. "Did you ever love her?"

Time to shut this down. Once again, honesty is my best policy. "Connie gave me you and Cole, and I respect her for giving me the chance to be your dad."

She reads through my statement, knowing the answer is no, I didn't love their mom. This may haunt me, but I can't think of any other way to explain. "Maya, you're a young girl, and this is a complex situation between adults. Your mom and I have separate lives that involve you and Cole. One day, she may meet someone special, and when that day comes, I hope you'll be open-minded and happy for her. Right now, be a kid, enjoy life as you know it, live in the moment, and quit worrying all the time. Let the adults handle the heavy stuff."

"Okay."

"Miller and I have to help Todd out with some projects. If you're feeling conflicted about your mom, maybe we can come to a compromise for her to do a day visit, and I'll stay out of your way."

She chews on her bottom lip and slowly shakes her head. "I like the way things are going now."

"All right, you want to jump back in the pool or help with dinner?"

"Darby's already showering?" she asks.

"Yes."

"I think I'll go shower, too, so I can hang out with her and help with dinner."

My heart hammers in my chest like I've run a marathon, and I hug her. "We'd like that."

She skips back down the hall, and I stare after her, feelings of contentment swirling inside.

Soft hands slide around my waist, and the scent of Darby surrounds me. "You're an excellent father," she says softly.

"You heard?"

"I got to the corner about the time you said I was special to you."

"You heard most of it then."

"I adore you, Pierce Kendrick. You are a fine, fine man."

Right now, I am invincible. At fucking last, my past and present lives have come together, proving there is a future. It's impulsive, crazy, and most likely going to create a freak-out, but at this moment, I'm only thinking about one thing and I'm not waiting.

I twist, my eyes falling on hers, sending jolts of electricity blazing and beating to every nerve ending. She sucks in a breath, gripping my waist. I drift my fingers through her hair, gently holding her to face me. She trembles, her eyes glowing to copper as she reads my thoughts.

At twenty-three, I made my intentions clear but lost it all. At thirty-five, I'm not making that mistake again. It may not be perfect as I always envisioned, but I'll make it up to her.

My lips glide across hers, and I finally say the words I've wanted to since I walked up to the gorgeous seventeen-year-old girl who stole my heart.

"Marry me."

Pierced Hearts

Chapter 25

Darby

"Mom!" I burst into the house, searching frantically around. "Mom!"

"In here," she calls from the kitchen, sounding oddly serene.

I rush in expecting the worst and screech to a stop when I spot Lynda and Jill sitting at the island, casually sipping what look like Mom's French Martinis. Mom is at the bar filling a shaker, her hair and make-up done, perfectly coifed. More importantly, she's not in a heap on the floor in agony or lying in bed surrounded by family.

Perfectly fucking fine... I've been set up.

"I'm going to kill Dad!" I scream.

"Quit being dramatic." Mom quirks her eyebrow and side-eyes Jill.

"Dramatic? He sent me a text saying to get home for an emergency. Then, he refused to answer my calls. The last fucking time I got a message like that, you were seriously injured." My gaze snaps to Lynda.

"For the record, I wasn't a fan of this plan," she tells me.

"Plan? What plan?" I rub my chest where my heart is still racing.

"You've been avoiding me, and Stephanie is locked up, so I had to take drastic measures." Mom shakes the container vigorously and pours two more glasses, setting them on the island. "Now, come sit."

I don't want to sit. I want to suck down that drink, scream a little more about how scared I was, and then find my dad to strangle him. These women are up to no good.

I should have been more alert, ready for this. Stephanie warned me that Mom was hounding her for personal details about my weekend. I'd evaded most of her inquisitions, dodging her all week. The only consolation is hearing Stephanie remained strong and didn't give anything away. As if she's reading my mind, she waves her phone in the air.

"I'm ready to get her on speakerphone if you try to run."

"Dirty play, especially for an old bat."

"Live and learn, babe. One of these days, when you have kids, you'll need these tricks in your arsenal to get to the bottom of things."

At the mention of kids, I jerk to catch Jill's lips curling into a knowing grin. Fucking Pierce, he told his mom. He's in on this.

As soon as I get out of this mess, he's getting an earful. He's lucky I don't drive to Kiawah and hand him his ass.

"You done stewing? We're waiting." Mom sighs as if I'm the nuisance here.

I stomp to them, slam my key and phone on the counter, and slump into the only seat left, which ironically is between Lynda and Jill. Deja vu rolls in the pit of my stomach, remembering the same position a few weeks ago when I lost my tongue and rattled on to them. I'm guessing this is going to be much the same but with martinis substituting margaritas.

I draw in a deep breath and decide to play along, pasting a smile, and saccharine-sweetly chirp, "If you ladies wanted to have an impromptu cocktail hour, I respond much better to invitations than sneak attacks."

"You'd have to talk to me to respond to an invitation," Mom points out. "And, so far, the only communication in days has been through technology. You've been home four days and are intentionally hiding. Don't think I didn't notice."

"I haven't been hiding. I've been busy. It's called work."

"Yes, Pierce is very unhappy you spent last night at the bakery. He asked me to offer my help if you're that swamped." Jill slides the lone martini my way.

"I didn't deliberately fall asleep at the bakery. I finished late, and it was supposed to be a power nap. Runner curled up with me, and the next thing I knew, Pierce was calling this morning."

"Cut the crap, Darby Rose. You're not an amateur. Long days and nights are your forte. We want to know how the weekend went." Mom scolds me like a child.

Why, oh why, do I love this woman?

"I already told each of you when you called. It was terrific."

"That is a very generic and PC answer," Lynda counters back.

"Whose side are you on?"

"Yours and Pierce's. This was a big deal, and terrific isn't going to cut it."

Dammit! Why do I have to love this woman, too? At least, she's gentler in her approach. Three sets of eyes bore into me, and I take a very unladylike gulp of the martini. "Fine, it was more than terrific. I drove up with nervous knots in the pit of my stomach. At one point, I'll admit to looking at the clock and calculating the hours until I'd be coming home. But in true Pierce style, he had other plans. You know I was ambushed, and my day trip turned into the weekend."

I tell them everything they want to know. Mom perks up at the mention of Martin and Dave, having met them several times. The dinners, the donuts with the kids, the days at the beach and pool, the games we played and movies we watched. Cole and Maya's success at hunting shells and shark teeth gets a proud smile from Jill. I don't mention the call with Connie that upset Maya because that is for Pierce to discuss. I also leave out the creative sexual escapades Pierce came up with when the kids weren't around and the fact that he blurted out, *"Marry me,"* in the middle of the kitchen, then took me to bed that night, making love to me tenderly and saying it over and over again.

He still doesn't have his answer, which has made him even crazier.

"That sounds more than terrific. You bonded with the children and showed them normalcy like they've never had before. Their father has never had a woman in his life, and the masquerade Connie plays is unhealthy. I've been a nervous wreck since you drove there. When I heard you were staying, there was concern he pushed too hard, but obviously not." Jill resembles a woman who's been given the best news in her life.

"Yes, I guess you're right if you put it that way. But this wasn't all Pierce. He graduated from his typical coaxing and dragged the whole Kendrick Clan in. Miller, Maya, Cole... they were the plotters."

"You are kidding!" She howls. "Pierce hasn't been very forthcoming, except for..." She trails off.

Shards of ice prickle my flesh, and I throw back the rest of my drink, jumping up to make another. Screw the mix. Maybe I should drink straight from the bottle. Then, I'm going to call Evin to save me from theses wolves.

"Except for what?" Mom presses.

"Well, Pierce... he is... his vision... Umm..." Jill's so tongue-tied I take pity on her.

"What she's trying to say is that Pierce was pleased with the outcome of our weekend and has set his sights on the future."

"Are we talking in politically correct jargon again? What does this mean?" Mom loses her patience.

"I think Pierce wants to marry me."

She stares at me blankly. "Everyone's known that forever. This is not news to anyone who's been watching. Did he finally ask?"

"In his own way."

"Hot damn!" She slaps her hand down with a loud clap and shoots the rest of her martini back. "It's about time."

"I haven't answered him."

Her eyes twinkle, and her lips curl into a playful grin. "That's okay. It took the boy long enough to do it; you can keep him on the hook for a while. Just don't make it another sixteen years."

"Mom, it's been a matter of weeks since we rekindled a relationship. This is too soon. A few great days with his children doesn't mean we need to rush anything."

"Pierce disagrees. When I spoke to him this morning, he was crawling out of his skin. I'm here to warn you; he says he's done waiting," Jill informs me with a hint of humor.

"I think it's safe to say we're all done waiting. Let's not drag it out too long, Darby." Lynda slides her empty glass toward me. "Now, let's have a drink of celebration."

"I'm on it. My girl can't make them right." Mom jumps up. "Gotta have the right portions to make that extra special pop."

"Yes, I can make them right," I defend. "And what do we have to celebrate?"

"Your 'in-his-own-way' proposal and eventual acceptance," Lynda answers.

"Not to mention, Darby's fantastic weekend with my family," Jill adds.

"And we never got to celebrate the record-breaking day at the bizarre a few weeks ago," Mom chimes in.

"You ladies need to get a life," I grumble, even though, secretly, I'm ecstatic with all these things, too.

"No, you, young lady, need to get an attitude adjustment. When you hit our age, you find the time to appreciate and celebrate everything good in this life," Mom snaps back.

I glance around at three of the women I love most in this world. It wasn't thirty minutes ago that I wanted to throttle each one of them, but that's the way it is. The nagging, nosiness, and inappropriate methods of butting into my life aren't going to change.

Reality explodes in my mind. Twelve years ago, they stood by and kept their mouths shut, letting me sort through things the way I thought best. And I lost so much.

This time around, they aren't going to let that happen. They're taking matters in hand. All the irritation I've been holding on to evaporates into thin air, and I swallow the sting at the base of my throat.

"Maybe we could celebrate my non-proposal from Pierce." I give in with a shy grin.

"That's a given, Darby. What I want to know is when can I expect grandchildren?"

This time, I can't stop myself, losing the last ounce of self-control. I slam back the drink my mom hands me and groan into the room.

●—●—●—●—●

"More," Pierce demands, squeezing my breasts so hard I whine.

"I can't," I reply breathlessly, my arms shaking as I balance on his chest.

"Ride me, baby. Give me another one." His hips slam up, and I cry out at the sensation.

"It's too much." I try to rock gently.

"Then say yes."

My eyes snap open, and I glare down, tempted to slap the cocky grin off his face. My exhaustion is gone, having been replaced with a new motivation. I press hard on his chest, strengthen my thighs on his, slip upward, and then slam down.

His grin falls, and his eyes blaze before rolling back in his head. "Fuck," he growls when I continue the movement over and over.

He swipes my nipples, sending pleasure everywhere, but I'm not giving in. His grunts grow louder as I pummel up and down, enjoying the view of watching him come undone. He tries to slow me by gripping my ribcage, but I stay focused.

"Say..." grunt... "fucking..." groan... "YES!" he screams when I reach behind and grab his balls.

"Maybe," I repeat again, referring to his constant insistence that I marry him. He's not happy with my non-commitment, and this is getting fun.

His jaw locks, the veins in his neck and forehead tick, and when he opens his eyes, they are smoldering. My energy intensifies as I drive harder, fucking him like never before. Control is mine, and it's a powerful drug that makes me want more.

He tries to roll us, but in this instant, I'm stronger, tightening my grip on his balls and thrusting forward with my hips. His teeth grind together, and he tries again only to howl when I scrape my nails, clenching every muscle in my body.

I'm sure the windows rattle and quake when he knifes up, screaming my name and jerking furiously. He thrusts up twice, and I'm crying out with him, giving into the fourth orgasm of the night. Sweat covers our bodies as he holds me close and unloads on shallow breaths.

"Welcome home, Pierce Kendrick," I say hoarsely, finding it hard to breathe.

"Thirty-five years old. Jerked off to the image of you in that bathing suit for four days, multiple times, preparing for this night. No mercy, no excuses, you were going to say yes. Then, I let you take over and lost my goddammed mind."

"Rookie mistake. I know how to play your game."

He bites, actually bites, not nips, nibbles, or snips, the tendon in my throat, and I yelp. His tongue moves along the area, kissing gently. "I want an answer."

"I want time."

"I want you."

"You have me."

"I want everything with you."

My heart melts, and I nuzzle into his neck. "I love you, Pierce. Give me some time."

"I want it all, Darby, and you are the only one who can give me that."

"Then, you'll wait... and maybe give me a real proposal," I throw in.

His head shoots up, and I know I've gotten through.

"If I kneel right now, worshipping you as I do, would that be the perfect proposal?"

"No, because I know your agenda. I need time, *and,*" I draw out, "we have more to conquer."

He scowls, clearly disapproving. "You aren't leaving this town without a ring on your finger. Six months in Aspen is going to be hard enough."

I take advantage of our position, leaning to the side and bringing him with me as we fall. "Baby, you just got home from a great vacation. Let's not focus on when I move."

"Temporarily move," he corrects.

A change of subject is in order. "Why don't we discuss you sic'ing your Mom on me last night?"

"I told you already, that had nothing to do with me. Annie was the ringleader. All I wanted was for Mom to offer to help you with anything so you didn't spend the fucking night in that bakery again."

I study him closely and decide he's telling the truth, or at least the half-truth.

"It wasn't intentional, and in a way, I did it for you. Well, as a surprise. With the exception of a few hours on Sunday to fill my orders for the Fourth of July events, I've arranged to be off through Wednesday."

His eyes light up, and like always, my heart melts at the blue beams staring back. The Fourth of July was always one of our favorite holidays. The Kendrick's have a huge bash that rivals most of the celebrations around town. Back in time, Kendrick Construction employees and all of our family and friends would start our day partying around the pool and break off when it got close to dusk. Miller always had the boat hitched and ready to go, and we'd ride out to watch the fireworks from the water. Sometimes, Miller brought a date; sometimes, he didn't. But Pierce and I always watched the fireworks with me on his lap, kissing and whispering.

His gaze grows soft, and I know he's remembering the same things.

"You know my parents upgraded that old boat. Bought one with a cabin." One side of his lip curls up.

"Why do you think I took the next day off?"

This earns me a full out, blinding smile.

Chapter 26

Pierce

I sip my beer and take in the scene of my parents' backyard. Runner lays snoring in the shade, worn out from a day of doggy entertainment. There is no telling how many treats and snacks that dog has been given. Next to Darby, this dog is one of the most popular guests of the day. In his own canine way, he's charmed everyone he's met.

Every year, Mom barks orders at us until Dad, Miller, and I have everything set up. It's a pain in the ass, and I've hated every second.

Until today. Today, I have a new appreciation for the grueling, backbreaking, and sweat-soaking hours of work.

The reason is the stunning brunette, shagging to the tunes of beach music with my Dad on the dance floor under a tent. They are surrounded by friends doing the same. Huge misting fans stand in the corners, but no one seems to care about the heat.

Edward dances with Annie, Evin with my mom, Miller with Maya, and Cole is cannonballing his way to a Guinness world record with a few other kids. The only thing keeping me from stealing Darby from Dad is the phone in my hand, weighing me down like a boulder. Connie is supposed to let me know when she's on the way to pick up the kids, and I want to have them ready to meet her at the front.

Not surprisingly, she's late, even after insisting she wanted them to spend the holiday with her family.

Edward shimmies Annie over to Miller, and they exchange partners, Maya's voice exploding in giggles when Edward takes her little hands in his and swings her out.

My girl is happy. She's having the time of her life.

I'm about to say fuck-it and join them when Runner jumps up, growling fiercely. I slash my head to him, then follow his line of sight to find Connie standing inside the back gate, glowering at the dance floor. He jets past me, over the pool deck, and through the crowd until he's circling Darby. She's also laughing but glances down and stops dead, crouching to him. Miller turns, sees Connie, and heads our way.

"Connie, stop," I say low enough for her to hear.

She shoots a death glare my way.

"You were supposed to let me know when you were coming."

"Wouldn't that be convenient?" she snaps.

"That was the point, to make it convenient."

"So you could make me the bad parent? Taking my kids away from the big party to spend the holiday with their own mother, instead of having the decency of inviting me?"

"Don't cause a scene, Connie."

"Why? Because Queen Darby may be embarrassed?" She throws her hand out to the direction of the dance floor.

"No, because our kids don't deserve it."

"We need to talk," she fumes, changing her direction toward my parents' patio doors.

"Don't," I bark.

"Why? Am I not allowed in the family home anymore? Jill and Warren have been brainwashed as well?"

"Hello, Connie," Mom soothes the air, appearing at my side.

"Jill."

"Pierce, why don't you take Connie to the kitchen, and I'll get the kids ready to go? They are very excited about going downtown with their mom for the festivities. It shouldn't take long."

I nod, noticing out of the corner of my eye, Evin and Miller already walking inside.

Connie opens her mouth to argue but has the manners to nod, stomping past us. I kiss my mom on the temple, whispering my thanks, and glance to see Darby with an encouraging smile as she twirls Maya around again to keep her distracted. Cole is still jumping in the pool without a care in the world.

Crisis averted.

I meet Connie in the kitchen, where she is glaring at Miller and Evin, who are at the table, drinking beer and shuffling cards. "Do they really need to be here?"

"I'm not focused on them. I'm wondering why you need to talk to me."

"I'm sick of being the bad parent," she claims.

"We've had this discussion before. You need reinforcement with discipline, you call. If you need help with implementing rules in your time, you call. Problems with the kids, *you call.*" I end on emphasis, trying to implement Darby's way of thinking in how I deal with her.

"You think you have all the answers, that our kids will adapt to a broken home easily when you introduce them to the old love of your life and things will be perfect over here. But you have no idea what's happening at my place. All they talk about is going on vacation, going to water parks, fancy dinners, and family parties. Today's the perfect example! There are a hundred people out there dancing, singing, swimming, eating... Our kids should have their mom and their dad here!" she screams, and Evin sends me a look that speaks for itself.

His sister will never be put in that position, ever.

"Connie, your parents have a pool, they take you all on a family vacation every year, and you have enough money to give them a day at the water park. What's important to them is spending quality time with you. We are not a broken home. You know this. Why bring it to me today?"

"I don't want Darby Graham in their life. If you're stupid enough to let her back into yours, that's your business. She ruined you once, she's leaving again, and my children don't need to witness the aftermath. This little fling you're introducing them to is not healthy. You want to focus this on our children, and that is what this is. Me protecting the kids."

I stare at her closely, trying to figure out if she's sincere or if she's baiting me. Either way, she needs reminding my life with Darby isn't going to affect my relationship with Maya and Cole. "Connie, this is not a fling. When Darby moves, it is not the end of our relationship. There will be no aftermath this time because I'm making it permanent. If you truly are concerned about their well-being, know I've got it covered on my end."

She holds my stare, and I watch as the meaning of my statement dawns on her. A spark of anger shimmers in her eyes right before they go cold. She, of all people, knows that trying to back me into a corner does not work.

The stare-down is broken when Cole comes racing in, throwing his arms around her middle. "Hey, Mom!"

"Hey there." She kisses the top of his head. "You having a good day?"

"The best! I beat all the other boys in the watermelon eating contest." He beams.

"That doesn't surprise me at all." She grins, ruffling his wet hair. "Where's your sister?"

"Right here. Hey, Mom." Maya comes in, her face still flushed from dancing.

"You guys ready to go?"

"Do we need to change?" Maya holds up her backpack.

Connie shakes her head. "We're meeting Blaire and the kids at the fountains."

"Awesome!" Cole punches his arm in the air. "I love the fountains."

"I'll walk you out." I start toward the front door.

They say their goodbyes, and Connie's face flames when they hug Miller and Evin. On the walk to the car, Maya cuddles to my side. "This was a great day, Dad. I don't think it's ever been this fun."

"You still have a lot of fun ahead of you. Be good for your mom, and help make sure Cole doesn't wander off."

"I will."

Connie doesn't look my way again, driving away without a word, while the kids wave their way out of sight.

"You buying her act?" Miller hands me a beer when I get back to the kitchen.

"Connie loves the kids, and I'd like to believe she's looking out for their welfare. But my gut says she's playing at something."

"Your gut is right. That woman is the green-eyed monster of jealousy. Easy to spot the second she stepped into the yard. She wants this life with you, and from what I've been told, she's been angling at it for years. Even before Darby left, she had her sights set. When you told her this wasn't a fling and things were moving toward permanent, I saw the hatred in her features. Stay on your toes, man. I get the feeling she's not giving up," Evin tells me.

"Darby tell you anything about my relationship with Connie?"

"She didn't give specifics, but I know it has something to do with impaired judgment and faulty condoms."

"That sums up my relationship perfectly."

"I hate to be a dick, but she's known for going to drastic lengths to get her way. Don't let your guard down," Miller advises.

I take a swig of the beer and nod, my eyes scanning the back yard to find Darby. She's now sitting on the edge of the pool next to Andi, staring up to the house.

"Evin, the instant Runner caught sight of Connie, he barreled straight for Darby. Have you ever seen him that protective before?"

"Once, when Darby was visiting, a snake was coiled on the porch at the shed. Runner saw it first and went crazy. Darby screamed her head off until Dad got there and took care of it. It was a cottonmouth."

"Good to know that dog can sense trouble."

"He's a big cuddler, but he's fiercely protective of her. My guess is he felt the vibe Connie was giving off."

"Connie's not going to be a problem. If you think that dog's protective, you have no idea what I'm capable of."

"Let's ditch the subject of that bitch and move onto something more important." Miller's voice is loaded with humor.

"What's on your mind?" I cock an eyebrow, slicing my eyes to him. Instantly, the hair on the back of my neck prickles at his shit-eating grin.

"Tell me how in the hell you managed to fuck up a proposal you've had sixteen years to prepare for?"

Evin drops his chin but not before I catch his lips twitching.

"I didn't fuck anything up."

"She say yes?" he pushes.

"She will."

"I'd say that is a fuck-up. Losing your touch."

"We're done here." I flick him the finger, leaving them both laughing as I go to Darby. Miller may have been joking, but he's right about one thing. I've had sixteen years to prepare.

My patience has worn off.

●—●—●—●—●

"God, I missed this," Darby mumbles, snuggling closer and twisting her naked body with mine.

"You're the one who refused to sneak off to my old room." My hand squeezes her ass.

"I wasn't talking about the sex, you feign. I was referring to the Fourth in Charleston. After we split up, I couldn't bring myself to come home for this holiday. All holidays were difficult, but this one always felt like it was our special time."

A sharp pain stabs in my chest, and I center on the full moon until it eases. "I know. This is the first time I've brought the boat out to watch the fireworks since then."

"Really?" She props her chin on my chest.

"That last summer, you were pregnant, and all I could think about was how the next year we'd be bringing our baby out here with us. Once you were gone, and after everything that happened, the thought of coming out here didn't appeal to me anymore."

"This is still just ours?"

"Yes, except for the fact that I finally got to fuck you under the stars like I wanted to all those years when Miller cockblocked me."

She smiles. "That is an added bonus."

"The added bonus is getting to strip you out of that black bikini."

Her leg glides higher, her knee scraping my cock, which stiffens on contact. "Careful," I warn.

She pulls her lip between her teeth and scales her fingertips along my length. "I don't want to be careful. I want this." She flashes a sexy grin, sliding her body down.

Shit, I want this, too. The thought of her mouth on my dick, kneeling between my legs is almost enough to unhinge me. She circles my nipple with her tongue, sucking it lightly, then kisses a trail across my chest to the other side.

I gave in to my own wants earlier, holding her as we watched the fireworks overhead, and the memories surrounded us. I couldn't help the overwhelming need to have her right here on the deck, fucking her hard until we ended up tangled together. But, now, I have an agenda.

Focus, Kendrick! I tell myself, threading my hands in her hair and easing her upward. She blinks a few times, her eyes locking with mine, and the hand on my bicep squeezing.

"I watched you for weeks, talking with your friends, stretching on the mats, bouncing on that fucking elliptical... Wherever you were, I had my eyes on you. Every guy in that gym had their sights set, but I made my intentions clear. Every day, I'd wait for you to come in. It became my obsession. *You* became my obsession. I knew you were young but didn't give a shit. It didn't matter that you made me wait ten months to have you for the first time. You were mine."

"Pierce—" she tries, but I brush my lips across hers.

"I could do this all night, reminisce about every day I've had you in my life and every day you were gone. It's burned in my brain. I may have lived without you, but I wasn't really living, not until that day in May when my heart started beating again because you were back." I roll us to our sides, face to face, and press close. "I'm a dick, an asshole, and a stupid motherfucker, but I'm not stupid enough to lose this chance. You are going to want to kill me at times, but you're never going to question how much I love you ever again. Our life together may have its ups and downs, but there's no choice but to have you by my side.

"Darby Rose Graham, I feel like I loved you before I knew you because that's how much a part of me you are. Every fiber in my soul will always belong to you. Please, put me out of my misery, take the chance on this life, and say you'll marry me."

She trembles, her lips quiver, and tears glitter in her eyes. The strong resistance she's held on to is waning. There's a chance I'm pushing too hard, but I keep going.

"You leaving was the worst time of my life, and it changed me. I turned into a hard, cold, bitter man. I'm not proud of that. But, each day, I wake up a better person because you healed me. You have reservations and want more time, and that's understandable. Your scars run deep. I wish I could give you that time, but the thought of losing another day is driving me crazy. Next year, I want to lay here with you, wrapped around me naked, on this boat, and finally call you Darby Kendrick."

At the mention of my name, she breaks. It's the most heartbreaking and beautiful thing at the same time. Tears well up, and she blinks rapidly, drawing in a ragged breath. When she locks her eyes with mine, a vice clenches around my heart.

"Yes."

A low, throaty growl rolls from the back of my throat. "Say it again," I demand, needing to hear it over and over.

"Yes, I will marry you, Pierce."

I tighten my grip on her scalp and bring her mouth to mine. "I'm going to take care of you."

"Right back at you." She grins, her tears wetting both our cheeks.

I roll to my back, bringing her with me. Without a word, she straddles my hips, positions herself, and slowly inches down my cock. A familiar bolt of lightning singes through my body.

The first time we made love.

The day we found out she was pregnant.

The night I showed at the shed.

Memory after memory rolls through my brain, all of them leading up to this moment. The final thought that races through my mind before she lowers her mouth to mine is if I can convince her to marry me in the next couple of weeks.

Is that too much to ask?

Chapter 27
Darby

I swing into Pierce's driveway, my stomach coiled in knots. His truck is already here, which means Cole and Maya are inside. I'd hoped to get here first and have time to set the stage, and possibly shoot back some liquid encouragement.

It's been ten days since Pierce and I got engaged, and we've sworn our families to secrecy until we tell the children. It was my advice for him to tell them alone in case they had questions or got upset. Of course, he didn't agree and wanted to do it as soon as possible. Our schedules have been crazy, and Connie planned a small vacation that took them away for almost a week.

Tonight's the night.

I twirl the ring on my finger, glancing down at the magnificent diamond solitaire surrounded by two outer bands of diamonds. Even though I haven't been wearing it often, trying to keep our news under wraps, it feels like it's a part of me. Runner paws up on the console and nudges my shoulder, whimpering. "Okay, boy, let's do this, but be ready to scram if tears ensue."

He nods as if he understands me, jumping into the driver's seat and trailing me out. I watch him sniff around the hedges and nearly jump out of my skin when I'm hoisted from behind. Pierce's soft stubble tickles my neck as his teeth nip at my ear. "You get it out of your system?"

"What?"

"We were in the living room and saw you pull around. I got tired of waiting for you to get out of your truck. I'm assuming you were in freak-out mode."

"I'm not sure it's all out of my system."

"Good thing I've got your back." He squeezes and places me back on my feet. "Come on, Runner. Let's go inside."

Runner's the first one up the back steps, waggling inside like he belongs.

"Darby's here," Pierce announces from the kitchen.

"We know, Dad. We saw her pull up." Cole calls back.

"Well, get your butt up and come greet her." Pierce keeps his arm draped around my shoulder.

Maya makes it to the kitchen first, coming to give me a hug and edging her dad out of the way. "Hey."

"How was your vacation?" I get out before Cole runs in, tackling my other side.

I'm completely engulfed with Kendricks, and my heart skips a beat. Could it be this easy? Was I worried over nothing?

"It was fun. We didn't go to the beach, but the mountains are cool," Cole answers, stepping back, clearly done with the affection.

"I love the mountains."

"Aren't you about to move to the mountains?" Maya unlatches from me as well, moving back a few feet.

"I guess you could say that. I'm going to be living at a ski resort. There are mountains everywhere."

"Dad says we're going to come to visit and learn to ski. He's going to try to bring us during Christmas break."

This is the first I've heard of it, but I'm not surprised. Pierce was not happy when I explained it would be impossible for me to come home for the holidays this year.

"That will be awesome." I lay my head on his chest.

"I'm gonna kill it on the slopes." Cole swishes his arms and juts his hips side to side to mimic being on skis.

"When are you leaving?" Maya looks shyly at Pierce, who tenses.

"In three weeks. That's why I was a little late today. I had to ship some things."

"I thought you were driving your stuff?" Cole's eyebrows pull together.

"I am driving what I can, but I still have to ship a ton of boxes."

"What about your furniture?"

"I'm moving into a fully furnished apartment on the property. My truck can only hold so much, and with Runner and whatever passenger I have, I won't have much room."

The mood changes, the reality of my situation hanging in the air. Pierce picks up on it, positioning me in front of him, pressing his front to my back, and linking our hands to wrap around my middle. His thumb runs across my ring. He does this often, as if he's making sure it's really there. They don't seem to notice the subtle action.

"Darby and I want to discuss something with you guys. Take a seat."

They climb on stools, fixated on him.

"Darby's move is not going to be permanent. We're hoping the opportunity to return here comes next spring, but we're unsure of the timeline."

"Cool!" Cole exclaims. "You're not going away for good?"

"No, but I'm sure my position will require some travel once I get established."

Maya's shoulders sink in obvious relief. "Thank goodness," she whispers.

"What's on your mind?" Pierce asks her.

"I was unsure if you were going to move, too."

"No, that thought never crossed my mind."

She visibly perks up. "You're coming back?" Her question is directed at me.

"That's the plan."

"There's more. When she comes back, Darby is going to move in here. I've asked Darby to marry me."

I hold my breath for their reaction, waiting for what comes next. This isn't exactly how I saw this conversation going. Thank God he's supporting me because my knees threaten to buckle.

They glance at each other and then back to us. "Like, she'll be around forever?" Cole blurts.

"Forever, buddy."

Cole looks back at Maya, and his little smile beams. "That's awesome."

Maya, on the other hand, is torn. Her gaze falls to where he's twirling my ring, and her face twists into an impassive expression that's hard to read. My stomach drops, and I try to wiggle free, but Pierce holds firm. "Give her a second," he murmurs.

She slowly raises her eyes to him, avoiding me. "Yeah, that's awesome."

The words are forced, and I want to leave them alone so she can voice her feelings freely. "Maybe I should go." Pierce won't loosen his grip, and beads of sweat pop up on my back. "Pierce, honey, you should have a few minutes with Maya."

"Baby, you okay?" he ignores me.

"Yes, it's... nothing."

Pierce's fatherly instincts must kick in because he reads her thoughts. "If you're worried about your mom, I'll take care of it."

All the worry written on her face disappears, and her mouth splits into a genuine smile. "Can I see your ring?"

I don't realize I'm holding my breath until my lungs burn, and I exhale softly, a weight lifting off my shoulders. Her loyalty to her mother is understandable, and I can't help but feel sorry for her.

Pierce doesn't release my arm, but he does stretch it over the counter, cupping my hand in her direction.

"That's beautiful," she raves, staring at it in awe.

"Thank you."

"How about you call your grandma and tell her we shared our news?" Pierce suggests to her.

"Oh, can I do it?" Cole jumps down and yanks the phone out of the cradle.

"Yeah, buddy. Maya, you should talk to her, too."

They go to the living room, talking over each other, and I sink into him.

"You're shaking." He spins me to face him.

"I hate Connie," I spew. "That poor girl was scared to death of her mother's reaction. Obviously, Connie is still messing with their heads."

"Like I said, I'll take care of Connie. You don't need to worry."

"I'm not worried about me. I'm worried about Maya."

His eyes grow warm, and his lips touch mine in a gentle kiss. "That means a lot to me."

"Dad! Grandma says we're celebrating! She wants a family dinner at Rosen's." Cole barges in, holding out the phone.

Pierce takes it right as mine rings in my pocket. I don't recognize the number but step away and answer it while Pierce talks to Jill.

The salesclerk on the line explains the issue, and I check my watch, assuring her I can be there before they close.

"Mom was ready to pounce. She's got a reservation at Rosen's tonight for all of us, including your family," Pierce informs me when I hang up.

"What time?"

"An hour."

"I'll need to meet you there. That was the supervisor at The UPS Store. There was an accident with one of my boxes, and they'd like me to come down and open it to see if anything is broken or damaged before loading it in the morning."

"We can all go by on the way to dinner."

"They close in twenty minutes, and you still need to shower. It shouldn't take long. I'll meet you at the restaurant."

His eyes grow annoyed, and he shakes his head. "I'm not showing up to celebrate my engagement without my fiancée. I'll push the reservation time. You go take care of it, come back, and we'll go to dinner together."

"Fine!" I throw my hand in defeat. "There's not time to argue. Get in the shower. I'll be back shortly."

I tip on my toes, give him a short kiss, and grab my key. Out of habit, I call for Runner.

"Leave him here. He's fine."

I nod, yelling a bye to the living room, and hurry to the truck.

The irony hits me as I pull onto the street. Rosen's is the place that started this all. It's the perfect place to celebrate.

●—●—●—●—●

"Darby, I knew you had nothing to worry about. Now, we plan a wedding," Stephanie says as Scottie's high-pitched squeal echoes through the car.

"Tell him I'm going to be deaf if he continues to screech like a banshee every time we mention getting married."

"I'll tell him when my own ears quit ringing."

"Y'all are not going to rain on my parade. This wedding is going to be fabulous," he yells again from the background.

"What are the chances of keeping him away from Mom and Jill for the foreseeable future?"

"Zilch, he's already called your mom twice today to see if the secret had been revealed."

"Ugh, that explains the texts to hurry for dinner. She's itching to openly discuss this. Most likely, the gossip chain has been activated."

"You can count on it. Call me tomorrow and we can—"

"What the hell?" I cut her off when Pierce's house comes into view. He, Maya, and Cole are wandering around the yard, a rope hanging from Cole's hand.

"What's up?"

I tell her what I'm seeing, and then I recognize the rope in Cole's hand. It's not a rope at all; it's a leash. "Oh my God! Runner!" I slam to a stop at the curb, switch the car off, and disconnect the phone to her shouts.

"What's wrong?" I run to the edge of the yard.

"Runner got out," Pierce tells me firmly.

"Runner got out? He doesn't do that."

"It was an accident," Maya replies faintly, her skin pale with streaks down her cheeks.

Cole locks eyes with me briefly, seeming equally as miserable.

"Runner! Runner!" I scream at the top of my lungs.

"Darby, calm down. We're going to find him." Pierce clasps my wrists, standing in front of me, and brings my attention to him.

"How long ago did he get out?" My voice is unsteady as I pivot in all directions, searching for his golden body. "You know how he likes to explore unfamiliar places. He hasn't been here enough to know your layout."

"He's been gone maybe fifteen minutes. I was in the shower."

A hushed cry gurgles from Maya as fresh tears roll down her cheeks.

There's no time to comfort her because the loud thumping of bass comes from a car rounding the corner. A young man is behind the wheel, and the sun hits a reflection of his phone in hand right as a flash of fur appears from around a huge tree across the street.

"Runner, stay!" I shout, but the sound of my voice sends him barreling toward me.

It happens fast. The boy looks up in time to slam on the brakes, but over-corrects, fishtailing into a large brick mailbox a few houses down.

There's the squeal of tires, the crunching of metal, the explosion of bricks going everywhere, then the unmistakable agonizing howl of Runner's doggy voice piercing my ears.

"NOOOOOOOOOOOOOOOOOOOOO!" My own earsplitting wail fills the air.

"Holy fucking shit," Pierce growls, but I can barely make out his words.

With superpower strength, I wedge my wrists free, shove him out of my way, and streak toward the wreckage. Twice, I almost trip, but I stay upright, dropping to my knees and skidding the last few inches to Runner's side. Pain rips through my knees, shins, and feet as the concrete tears my skin.

"Oh my God. Oh my God," I chant, tossing bricks aside to get to his head. Blood covers his back leg, an open gash cutting his hip.

I gently crawl over him, whispering his name. He strains his face in my direction. Sobs wrack my body, my arms circling his neck so I can nuzzle into him.

"Is he okay?" The young man appears at my side, and I glance at him.

Blood dribbles from his nose and mouth, his lip busted open. His eyes are wide in shock. "Are you okay?" I manage to croak.

"Yeah, I think so."

"Darby, scoot back so I can check him out," Pierce instructs me, but I shake my head in refusal.

"No."

"Baby, we need to see Runner's injuries. There's a lot of blood."

At the mention of blood, I go lightheaded, burying my face back in my dog's neck. Runner's tongue licks up the side of my cheek. "It's okay, sweet boy. I'm going to get you fixed up," I say to him.

A strong hand rubs up and down my back, Pierce moving me a few inches and whispering soft words to Runner.

236

"His tail thumped," Cole stammers in a shaky voice.

"I only see one cut. We need a towel," Pierce soothes.

"I have a blanket," the young man offers.

I suck in my tears and kneel back, running my hands everywhere to search for any more damage. Gently, we peel Runner forward to check his other side. The cut on his hip is the only visible wound.

"I'm going to pull my truck around so we can load him up."

I nod, not taking my eyes off Runner.

Pierce stands, and there's a loud hiccup, followed by wailing. I glance up to see a flicker of pain pass through his eyes as he scowls at Maya. My already broken heart aches for her.

"It was an accident." I try to help the situation, sticking up for her.

There's an eerie tension in the air. I take in the scene. Cole's gripping the leash with white knuckles and a look of panic. Maya is openly weeping. Both exhibit signs of shock at seeing an accident and a dog hit by a car. It's the blinding rage set on Pierce's face that turns my blood to ice. His eyes are cold and hard, his lips drawn in a taut line, and his eyebrows are pulled together sharply. He's pissed, and not in the general Pierce way of being pissed. He's holding on by a thread, ready to snap.

"Runner didn't sneak out on his own, did he?"

Pierce's eyes fly to mine, and I know the answer. Maya falls into her dad, crying uncontrollably and mumbling. It's hard to make out her words, but I pick up on a few statements.

"Mom said she's allergic."

"She said she'd die if we came home with dog hair on us..."

"She told me she'd take away..."

At this point, I tune her out, and the superpower strength from earlier returns. "Will you help me hoist him?" I ask the young driver.

"Yes, ma'am, but are you sure that's smart?" He frets.

"Just follow my lead." I look back at Runner and speak softly. "Okay, baby, we've done this before. You hang on to me."

I swear to God, my dog nods in understanding. He trusts me, putting his paws on my shoulders. I slip to crouching position, wrap my arms around his back, and surge up. The man jumps into motion, elevating Runner against me until I can anchor my arm under his hind legs while he whines in pain.

"Thanks." I try to sound grateful, but it comes out strangled and brash.

"Darby, give him to me." Pierce backs away from her, extending an arm.

"Get out of my way," I grate out.

I ignore him, trying to get to my car without wobbling my trembling dog. He runs ahead, opening the truck and adjusting the blanket as I lay Runner down and shut him in.

"Darby, you're in no condition to drive," he starts, and I throw my hand in his face.

"You have a mess to clean up here. That boy needs medical attention. It's smart to get a police report, and then you should let your neighbors know they have a demolished mailbox. After that, I suggest you get your daughter under control." Hate and anger boil to the surface. "She's proved today she's a wrecking ball that has no sense of what's right or wrong. I was ready to defend her!"

Guilt stretches over his features, but I'm too wired to care. "You were going to let me believe my dog escaped your house, which he has never done before!"

"I was going to tell you when we could discuss it in private. Word spread fast, and Connie got a hold of Maya while I was showering. There's no telling what she told her. We hadn't gotten that far when Cole ratted her out for shoving Runner out the door."

"That's because Cole has a heart and a good soul! He's you down to the bones. With what's happened today, it's hard to believe that girl shares your DNA. Wait a minute..." I bark out a cynical laugh, laced with wicked intent. "She's Connie Webber's daughter. That's where her malicious, conniving, and spiteful streak comes in."

His eyes grow stormy, his jaw clamping tight. The overprotective Pierce is about to make an appearance. "She's a girl, Darby. Don't dump her into the same category as her mother. She's misguided."

"Misguided? She almost killed my dog because of her mother's jealousy. That's not misguided; that's a fucking sociopath in the making! I have no idea the way you and Connie have chosen to parent all these years, but it's obvious your daughter has no moral compass or self-direction. You need to stop blaming it on her mother get a handle on that shit."

I yank open my door with so much force, pain shoots through my shoulder. The sting fuels my adrenaline, and I can't stop from lashing out again. "You say you want to build a family with me? Start a life, fresh and clean of the past? It's time you concentrate on the life and family you already have. There's not a chance in hell I'd bring a baby into a house where he or she could be harmed because your ex fuck buddy influences your kids the way she does."

He doesn't try to stop me from slamming the door and driving away. Hot tears pour down my face as I speed to the only after-hours vet I can think of. The impact of my outburst weighs on my chest, and my own guilt claws up my throat.

I'm pretty sure Runner is going to be all right, but the thought of being alone sends panic through me. I fumble with my steering wheel, scrolling through my emergency contacts.

"Darby? Where are y'all?" Evin answers on the first ring.

"I need you."

Chapter 28

Pierce

What a shit fucking night. On top of all the obvious, I can't stop Darby's words from rolling through my brain. Connie isn't what I'd consider my ex fuck buddy, but Darby was right about her influence over Maya. It's dangerous, and tonight could have ended under fatal circumstances.

Evin is waiting for me on the porch when I drive up. He's been my point of contact since he met Darby at the vet. Runner is going to be fine. He's bruised, and the gash on his hip needed stitches, which requires a cone on his head so he doesn't gnaw at them. But, otherwise, the vet saw no other damage.

By the time he got to them, she was solid and in control. She took the news well and insisted on driving home while he followed. I wish like hell I could have been with her, but I had to handle the mess left behind.

"You want a drink?" he offers.

"Yes, I want to down a bottle, but it won't help."

"She dozed off with the beast laid at her side. He's going to be groggy for a while, and the pain killers prescribed are going to make him loopy."

"As long as he's not in pain."

"I got her side of the story. Want to share yours?"

"In hindsight, I should have called Connie right away, but I figured tonight would be safe. Stupid decision. She got wind of our engagement and called Maya, in an outrage, while I was showering. Maya says she tried to ease the news by explaining some of the things I told her while we were at the beach and my previous relationship with Darby. Connie lost her mind, called me a liar and told our daughter that Darby is a home-wrecker. Maya is not equipped to deal with her mom's brand of crazy. One thing led to another, and after convincing her that Runner was a threat to Connie's health, Maya opened the door, pushed the dog outside, and the rest is history."

"Sounds intense."

"You have no idea. Losing Runner would have destroyed Darby." Her face pops into my head, the terrified yell that stopped my heart playing on a loop.

"How's the kid?"

"He's fine, but that's another story. His dad showed; he's a lawyer. Immediately, they shifted the blame."

"Shit."

"Yeah." I sigh.

"Her adrenaline crashed pretty hard. She's regretting a lot of what she said to you."

"She didn't hold back, but she had good reason. Jesus, Evin. It'll be a long time before I can forget the horror on her face and that bone-chilling scream. The image of her standing there, covered in blood, her dress ripped, cuts and bruises covering her legs."

"Runner is pretty special to her. He took the place of the baby she couldn't have."

I wince, rubbing the throbbing ache that's hammering against my ribs. "I better get inside."

"I told her you were coming. I also went ahead and moved the mattress to the floor in the living room. Runner's too drugged to jump up, and she's not leaving his side."

"Appreciate it. I owe you."

"No, you don't. I hope you can get this straightened out. Call me if you need me. Mom and Dad will be by in the morning to help." He swallows the last of his beer, flicks his fingers in the air, and leaves.

I watch him drive away and quietly let myself in. Darby is awake, watching the door with a weary grin. "Hey."

My feet take me straight to her side, where I squat to eye-level. "Hey, yourself."

"I heard you talking."

"Sorry if we woke you."

"I didn't know I'd see you tonight."

"Where else would I be?"

"Did you take them back to Connie?" I notice she doesn't use their names.

"They are with my parents. Cole is flipping out. Maya finally stopped crying. She realized her mother lied to her, used her to try to hurt you, and the guilt was too much. I didn't know someone so small could cry that many tears."

"We're small but mighty." She sifts her fingers through my hair. "Although, I'm paying for my herculean effort with every muscle."

"How about I help get you to the bed?"

"Can you help me get him down there? I could use a glass of wine."

I slide my hands between Runner's body and hers, grunting at his weight. "I can't believe you carried this beast. He weighs more than you."

"Close, but not quite." She fluffs the doggy bed laid beside the mattress.

I lay him down, and he huffs out a snort, which sounds distorted from inside the cone. There's a shaved patch where his stitches are visible, and thankfully, it's not nearly as bad as first believed from the amount of blood that soaked into Darby's clothes earlier. "Tomorrow should be interesting when the anesthesia wears off. He's not going to like that cone."

"He'll probably sleep a lot. The pain medication has a sedative."

I stand awkwardly as she pours a glass of wine, gets a beer, and brings them to sit on the edge of the sofa. There are no words for the guilt and blame weighing down my conscious.

"Have I ever told you how I found Runner? Or, should I say, how Runner found me?"

"No."

"I was at a party with Stephanie, and the hostess kept bragging about her dog's new litter. She showed us the puppies and explained there was one that wasn't going to make it. The puppy wasn't doing as well as the others, had stopped eating altogether, and wasn't showing signs of maturing. They expected him to pass soon. There was speculation he'd have blindness, have growth disabilities, never walk right, and certainly never run. He was more than the runt in the litter. As if he heard them planning his death, he looked up at me and weakly shuffled over. I held him that day and knew he had a chance. I bottle fed him that night, and he sucked it down like he was starving. It was a running joke that plants wouldn't survive under my care, so no one got their hopes up. But after two weeks of me going over and feeding him bottles daily, he perked up and started socializing. By week eight, I was attached, and he needed a home. Our first night at my place, I was a nervous wreck because taking care of a living being was a huge responsibility. He was asleep, and I snuck off to shower. When I came out of the bathroom, he was racing around my room, searching for me. Therefore, he's named Runner."

"And, today, you could have lost him."

"Yes, but I didn't. I know you're probably furious with me for overreacting."

My head snaps up. "You think I'm furious? I'm so fucking sorry it happened I want to punch something."

"Pierce, I said some awful things about your daughter, your ex, and your parenting. It was uncalled for."

She's calm, too calm, the familiar tune of resignation in her voice. "Don't, Darby. Don't you dare retreat. Everything you said was right, and you aren't the one who needs to apologize. Maya acted irresponsibly today, and her actions caused injuries. It doesn't matter if the injuries were to a dog; it was unacceptable. She was conniving and malicious, like you said, and the worst part is that I'm to blame."

"W-w-why do you say that?"

"Because, in a way, I've nurtured this behavior. You are right. I have to stop blaming it on Connie and get a handle on that shit. It's my job to parent her in the right direction and guide her to live by a moral compass."

"Obviously, her mother can't do that because she preyed on a wounded man in an effort to get what she wanted out of life," Darby says faintly.

"That's right, baby. She did, but I was living on the edge of destruction and played my part in that well. But I could live the rest of my life if you never refer to her as my 'ex' again."

She giggles even with her eyes brimming with tears. "I thought you'd want this back after I laid into you the way I did." She slips the ring to the tip of her finger, and I can't control the low rumbling growl that rises in my throat.

"Don't take that ring off. If I had it my way, I'd attach it to your finger permanently. This doesn't change what's happening between us. It's a wake-up call for me to open my eyes to the importance of teaching my kids the basics of right and wrong. You said something that hit home today."

"I said a lot of things in the heat of the moment."

"You said Cole is just like me, and he is because I know how to deal with boys. Maya is a reflection of her mother because I've allowed it. Tonight, when she was afraid of Connie's reaction to our engagement, you shook with anger at her fear of her mother. I need you to stick with me here because I'm getting to the bottom of this."

"Do you think something is happening in their house?"

"I think Connie has conditioned her in a way that she doesn't know how to think and stand up for herself."

"That's scary."

"It's going to end. You're not giving up on us."

"I don't see..." She trails off, and I can guess a hundred ways for her to finish that sentence.

"I need you, baby." Desperation bleeds into my statement. "I failed you today by not fulfilling my promise to protect you. I need to know you are still with me."

She has no resistance, wiggling the ring back down and reaching for me. I slide behind her, folding her into my body, careful of her wine. Dropping my mouth to her neck, I skim my tongue along the tendon and inhale her scent. There are many things left unsaid, but for now, I'll take this, knowing she's not giving up.

•—•—•—•—•

I wake at dawn when a hard object presses to my shoulder. My gaze slowly focuses on big, brown, sad eyes. Runner drills the cone into me a few times, and I pat his nose, shifting Darby off my chest.

"I've got you, boy." My legs protest when I press up and use the arm of the couch as leverage. "Jesus, I'm getting old," I mutter.

Runner wobbles, clearly in pain but needing to go outside. I pick him up and grunt again at his weight, knowing Darby shouldn't have carried him yesterday. He limps around, does his business, and then lays on his side, looking to me for help. I haul him up, take him inside, and search for the pills Darby mentioned.

"They're on the far counter next to his treats," she mumbles from the floor.

He's not persuaded, stealing the treat and hobbling back to her. I grab a bottle of water and go to lie next to her. Runner's already at her side, trying to dislodge himself from the cone, and she's talking softly.

"Here's the pill." I slide it into her hand and watch as she shoves it in his mouth, holds his mouth shut, and rubs his throat.

"That's harsh." I pity the dog.

"He's fine." Her face crumples in pain when she sits up, and I wish like hell I could stay here and take care of her today. But the sooner I get my shit sorted, the sooner I can get back here.

"I hate to say this, but I've got to go."

"I know," she replies sadly.

"Can you do me a favor and work from home today?"

"Yes, I can't stand in the bakery all day."

"Good." I snatch my phone from the floor and shoot off a quick text to my dad, detailing what I need. He responds quickly that it's taken care of. "They'll be here around eight-thirty."

"Who's they?"

"My dad and what I'm guessing is a small crew. They're going to set up a temporary ramp on your porch stairs to make it easier for Runner to get up and down. You can't lift him all day."

"Thank you."

Another text comes through, this one from Edward saying he saw me outside, and he and Annie are ready to head over when Darby wakes up.

"Your parents want to come by." I show her the message.

"It's not even fully daylight. It's too early to deal with my mom." She pouts.

Normally, I'd agree that it's too early for morning visitors, but today, I want Darby covered in case she needs anything. "Tomorrow morning, I'll push them off for a later hour, but today, I'd feel better with them helping until the ramp is built and Runner is more comfortable."

"If you're going to leave me here with them, you better get the coffee started."

"Not a problem."

"My mom has no business trying to get him up and down stairs or a ramp. Make that clear because she won't listen to me."

"I'll handle it."

"Fine, tell them to give us fifteen minutes."

I send the message back and help Darby off the floor, taking the time to look her over. She's wearing one of my t-shirts and a pair of panties that, at any other time, would be in a heap on the floor by now, but the scrapes and bruises marring her legs are a painful reminder that I have shit to handle.

She heads to the bathroom while I start the coffee and go to her closet to get dressed. The first thing I notice is the large void where the box of her personal items sat. I yank on my jeans and a shirt, taking inventory of other things missing. The ache in my chest returns with the reality staring me in the face. She'll be moving soon. I have to fix things before she leaves.

She waltzes in, her face freshly washed, hair in a ponytail, and slides on a pair of frayed jean shorts, tucking my shirt in the front. I'm taken back in time, years of memories assaulting my mind. But now, my eyes zero in on the ring on her finger, a ring she should have been wearing back then.

I go to her, curling an arm around her waist, and brush my lips across hers. "Keep the shorts on until I get back here. I'm having flashbacks I'd like to recreate."

She grins against my lips in response.

I hurry through my routine in the bathroom, and when I get back to the kitchen, Annie and Edward are already here. Runner snores loudly on the dog bed, unaware of all eyes on him.

"That shaved butt and cone head make him look like a space alien," Annie says.

Darby's eyebrows fly up, and she narrows her eyes, sending me a silent message that it's my job to deal with her mom.

"I need to get to my parents' before the kids wake up. There's a crew coming to install a ramp for Runner. Annie, I don't want you attempting to carry that dog or get him down the stairs. Let Edward

246

handle it."

"Don't boss me around, Pierce Kendrick. I'm fit as a fiddle," she sasses.

"That won't be a problem. I'll handle it." Edward cuts his eyes to her in warning.

Darby hands me a travel mug of coffee, tipping her face to mine for a quick kiss. "Good luck today. Check in when you have a chance."

I say my goodbyes, hiding my amusement at Annie's scowl. Darby may not want to admit it, but she's a lot like her mom when she doesn't get her way.

When I walk through the door at my parents', I find them in the kitchen waiting for me. "How are things?" Mom worries.

"Good. He's sleeping and most likely will be all day."

"How's Darby?"

"She's sporting some nasty scrapes, cuts, and bruises, but she seems fine."

"Is she still shaken up?"

"She's Darby. She calmed down, processed what happened, and we worked through it."

"She didn't dump you again, did she?" Dad throws in with a chuckle.

"She's learned she can't get rid of me." I leave out the fact she slipped the ring off her finger. "If I could get away with it, I'd kidnap her today and marry her."

Mom gasps. "If you steal this occasion from me, I'll never forgive you."

"I make no promises."

Feet pound on the stairs, Cole sprinting into the kitchen and straight to my side. "How's Runner?" is the first thing out of his mouth.

"He's better." I dig my phone out and show him the picture from this morning.

"He looks like a space alien." His eyes grow wide.

I smile at the reference, thinking of Annie. "He does."

"Can we go see him?"

"In a few days. He's on some heavy medicine. Once he's feeling better, we'll go over."

"What about Darby? When can we see Darby again?"

"Soon."

He accepts the answer, not hiding his disappointment.

"I'll see if we can do dinner on Sunday night when I pick you up from your Mom's," I add, hoping Darby will agree.

"Okay."

"Go wake your sister up. It's time to get ready for camp."

He sprints back out of the kitchen, yelling his good morning to Mom and Dad.

My phone rings, and at the sight of Connie's name, I hit ignore and start breakfast. This happens twice more before the texts pour in.

Why isn't Maya answering her phone?

Where are you?

I want to speak to my kids!

"Answer that woman before she calls my phone." Mom takes over the eggs.

The best route is to text her back, allowing a record of our conversations.

Maya no longer has a phone. It has been confiscated. We are at my parents' having breakfast. If you'd like to speak to them, I can have them call you on our way to camp.

Connie: You confiscated her phone? What are you, the police?

No, I'm her dad.

Connie: You have balls. Did you take her phone after she got upset over your engagement?

I took her phone after she made a poor and irresponsible decision that caused an accident and almost killed Darby's dog. Not to mention injured a man and resulted in thousands of dollars in damage. Maya and Cole witnessed every second of it. All of this because of your lies and manipulation. By the way, they know you're not allergic.

Nothing comes through for another minute, and I pocket the phone. The kids can call her in the car if they wish, but going forward, all communication from me will be in the form of writing or through our lawyers.

Chapter 29

Darby

Pierce is waiting out front when we arrive at Rosen's. He's wearing a basic white oxford, opened at the neck to show off his tan skin, and a pair of navy slacks that mold to him. He straightens, crossing his arms, and a shiver races up my spine at the sight. His eyes stay trained on me as he makes his way to open my door, hauling me out of the back seat.

"You're late," he gripes.

"Blame it on Mom."

"You should have let me pick you up."

"You should learn the art of patience."

His jaw clenches tight as his eyes trail slowly over me, my skin tingling under his gaze. Mom scheduled another day of beauty. This time, she and Lynda joined me, knowing that tonight is special.

His eyes meet mine, and I catch the smoldering desire right before his mouth crashes down, his tongue plunging inside. I fall into him, whimpering when his hands fist into my hair, slanting my head and diving deeper. He kisses me greedily, the contrast of his soft lips and hard strokes sending a shiver through my bones. I'm powerless to him in this moment. The world around us is forgotten. My brain blacks out the fact that we are on a busy sidewalk with strangers passing by. My family is no longer a few feet away, and his family is inside.

It's only us, and this is him, making his statement.

I grow lightheaded, twirling my tongue in rhythm with his. He growls down my throat approvingly as my nails dig into his side.

"We're going inside. Pierce, I'd appreciate it if you didn't ruffle her hair and makeup too much. We have pictures to take." Mom's request cuts through my haze, and I slowly float back down to reality.

Pierce sucks my bottom lip into his mouth once more before pulling away and pressing his forehead to mine. "You are stunning."

"You are, too."

We stay like this for several minutes, our bodies pressed close, his molten eyes locked with mine. Silently sharing our thoughts.

My heart swells and dives at the same time. It's been three weeks since the incident with Maya, and the results have taken a toll on him. He wasted no time jumping into action. The first thing he did is enforce the original custody agreement set in place years ago. No longer is there a loose schedule where the kids can float back and forth. It immediately went back week-to-week with each parent. Drop-offs and pick-ups are done in a public location or at one of the grandparents' houses. Pierce refuses to be alone with Connie without another adult present. He isn't going to risk his kids witnessing any type of argument or altercation, nor does he want to give Connie any ammunition to use in the privacy of her home. Anger toward her still scorches inside, and he can't look at her without thinking of the emotional damage she caused.

What I said to him that day scored deep. More than once, I've tried to explain my outburst was driven by shock and fear, but he feels differently. It awakened what he considered a huge, gaping, blind spot when it comes to his somewhat relaxed parenting style.

I haven't seen Maya or Cole since the day they watched me carry a bloody Runner to my truck and most likely heard the awful things I screamed at their dad. Since then, it's been a hectic balance of finishing the last of my orders, cleaning out the bakery, and packing the things to ship to Aspen.

He's had them all week, but Mom and I made an unexpected trip to Charlotte to handle personal business with my house and meet with Stephanie. He was not happy with my spontaneous trip, but it couldn't be helped.

"This week has been hell without you." He flexes his grip on my scalp.

"I missed you, too."

"I want you in my bed tonight."

"Let's see how dinner goes. I don't want to barge in on their last night with you for the week, especially since we're leaving tomorrow."

"You're going to see they want you with us. Cole is plotting his attack."

"That's because he's exactly like his father."

Pierce's lips curve into a sexy grin as he releases my head and laces his hand with mine. Together, we enter the restaurant, and the hostess is waiting to lead us to our table. Everyone is already seated. When Cole spots us, he's on his feet and in front of me in a flash. He flings himself into me, knocking me back on my heels. Luckily, Pierce steadies me before I collapse.

"Hi, Darby."

"Hey there." I take my hand from Pierce and wrap my arms around his little shoulders.

"How's Runner?"

"He's good, sweetie. Almost completely healed."

He moves back and lifts his big blue eyes to me, asking sweetly, "Can we see him before you leave?"

I whip my head around to find Pierce openly smiling. "I did warn you."

"Hi, Darby." Maya stands awkwardly beside Cole.

I step into her space and embrace her warmly. "Maya, you look beautiful tonight."

The compliment breaks the tension, and she hugs me in return, muttering her thanks.

"You're sitting between me and Dad," Cole announces, taking his seat.

Pierce's hand goes to the small of my back, steering me to my seat, while Maya takes the open chair on the other side of him.

"I smell an ambush," I whisper to Pierce.

"It's your last night in town. Are you going to break a little boy's heart by denying him?" Pierce doesn't lower his voice.

"Yeah, Darby, are you going to break my heart?" Cole mimics, sending a round of laughter spreading around the table.

"I need a drink."

Champagne arrives at my announcement, Mr. Rosen proudly popping the cork and pouring my flute first. He passes the bottle to a waiting server who begins filling the others. Warren raises his in the air. "To a very long-awaited and overdue celebration of your engagement. Congratulations."

The underlying meaning of his toast isn't lost on the adults at the table. The sound of crystal clinks around, Cole even tapping his glass of water to mine. I grin down to him and take a sip.

"Darby, I can only assume, with your upcoming nuptials, you'll be back in Charleston," Mr. Rosen says with a glint in his eye.

"Eventually, I'll make it back." The news of Brasher renovating their property here is still a closely guarded secret that can't be discussed openly. We've even kept the news from Maya and Cole. They only know I'm trying to get back in the spring. Once the news of our engagement was revealed, Pierce and I have both fielded questions. Our response has been vague that *'we're working out the details'*.

Rumors are swirling that Pierce is selling his share of the business and coming with me, leaving behind his kids to chase the girl that once dumped him. We suspect Connie started that one, trying to gain sympathy from a community that shunned her after the Runner incident.

"I expect to be the first name back on your client list." He crooks an eyebrow expectantly.

"You'll be one of the first to know," Mom interjects. "Now, tell us about your delicious specials." She gracefully takes the attention off me.

251

The rest of the night goes perfectly until the bill arrives. Warren and Dad argue over who's paying. Pierce covertly slips his credit card to the waiter, letting them bicker until he signs the slip and announces it's done. Dad scowls, throwing a dirty look his way and mumbling under his breath.

I excuse myself to the restroom, Maya asking to go with me. Mom and Jill exchange a glance and pass unspoken encouragement across the table.

Inside the restroom, I'm once again almost bowled over when Maya throws herself at me. "I am sorry for what I did! I'm an awful, terrible, horrendous person and deserve it if you hate me." She cries into my stomach. "I've wanted to apologize for a while, but Dad told me this had to be done in person."

A lump forms in my throat, and I swallow hard, trying to find my voice. My hands go to her back, soothing up and down until her cries soften and turn to short hiccups. My first instinct is to coddle her, dry her tears, and tell her all is forgiven and forgotten. It's a slippery slope because whatever I say or do in this situation could go back to Connie and mean hell for Pierce.

I think about Jill and Mom; what would they say? How would they handle this? What would Pierce want me to say?

"I hate to see you sad, Maya. It breaks your dad's heart when you're hurting."

"He hates me, too.

"He could never hate you. He loves you and Cole more than anything in the world."

"Not anymore. I messed up everything. Dad is mad, Cole won't quit telling me it's my fault you don't come around, and we're not even allowed to go to Grandma and Grandpa's unless it's Dad's week. All because of me."

"Maya, you need to talk to your dad about these things."

She peers up at me, her eyes bloodshot and filled with sadness. "He loves you. If you forgive me, he will too."

"His job as a parent is to love and protect you and Cole, always making sure you are taken care of. I imagine it's the hardest job in the world. You're confusing his forgiveness with his concern. There's a huge difference."

"You don't think he's mad at me?"

"No, I don't think he's capable of the kind of love he feels for you and anger at the same time. It's impossible for him."

"Even though he stayed mad with you all those years and still loved you."

My stomach seizes with the verbal sucker punch, and there's an almost inaudible growl from somewhere behind me.

"My circumstances are worlds apart from his adoration for you. Pierce Kendrick may be gruff and have the temper of a wet cat, but he will always love you, even when you mess up. That I can promise."

She seems to process this, color creeping back to her pale cheeks and her eyes clearing. "It's going to be okay?"

"Of course, it's going to be all right."

"Do you know my mom, Darby?"

This is the slippery slope I was trying to avoid. "I don't know her now, but I knew her years ago."

"She's... Well, she's..."

"Maya, anything you want to say about your mom should go to your dad. I'm not the person to talk to."

"No, what I'm trying to say is she loves Dad. She's always told us that, and I never understood why he didn't love her back. But I get it now. It's because of you. I overheard Grandma telling Uncle Miller that you being back is the answer to her prayers. She said that the love story was coming full circle. I'm not sure what that part means, but Dad is his happiest when you're around. I'm sorry I almost messed that up."

"Oh, Maya." I yank her back to me. "Everyone messes up. The important thing is to learn from our mistakes. It's a hard lesson, and if I can give you one piece of advice, it is that when you are unsure of what's the truth and what's not, go to an adult you trust. You may not like the answers, but it's part of growing up."

She nods, squeezing me tight. "I can do that, Darby."

"Okay. How about we use the restroom before your dad sends a search party?"

She grins, heading to a stall. The lock clicks, and I backstep around the corner to find Pierce, leaning against the wall.

"This is the ladies' restroom," I hiss.

"I fucking love you," he whispers back.

"Get out of here." I toss my hand in the direction of the door.

"You're spending the night."

"We will see. Now, get out of here!"

"I swear to God, if you try to say no, I'll haul you out of here kicking and screaming. No one will be surprised, and your mom will send the video to Scottie to post on Instagram."

"You forget I'm an expert at sneaking out the back."

I realize my mistake immediately when his eyes grow dark and his voice comes out strained. "You'll never get away from me again. What you just did for my daughter adds to the million reasons my stupid ass will go to the ends of the earth to bring you back to me. You're a part of us now, and I'm not fucking letting you forget it."

A toilet flushes, and I shove him, giving him a hard stare to leave before going back to the lavatory area. Maya comes out, her face almost free of splotches, and washes her hands. She looks at me through the mirror and giggles in a little girl pitch. "You should probably use the bathroom. It would stink if Dad throws you over his shoulders and you still have to pee."

My eyes bulge at the same time a loud, strangled cough comes from where I left Pierce standing. He pokes his head around the corner. "I'm going to stand outside the door long enough to escort both my girls back to the table. Maya, you okay?"

"Yeah, Dad, I'm good."

"Love you, baby girl." He gives her a smile, flashing me a look loaded with challenge, and disappears.

•—•—•—•—•

There are no tears left in me. Jill and Warren showed up early this morning. My parents, Evin, and Miller arrived in time for breakfast. Cole and Maya fluttered around, bragging on their efforts while I was fixated on how easy we all moved throughout the kitchen that Pierce had unintentionally built with me in mind.

Runner was almost one-hundred percent back to normal, but Cole and Maya babied him like crazy. He loved it.

My first outburst came when Pierce announced it was time for them to go back to Connie's. I helped them pack a few things, both their moods sinking low. When we said goodbye, Cole flung himself at me and buried his little head into my neck, sniffling.

That was all it took. I lost it. Maya joined us, and I ended up in a heap on the floor with Runner sprawled on top. Pierce had to peel everyone apart, and for the first time, I witnessed him cradling Cole in his arms and whispering in his ear until he calmed. Maya was teary-eyed but more reserved, though still clinging to me, kissing my cheek, and hurrying out the door.

My family left, giving me time with Jill, Warren, and Miller, while Pierce hit the noon deadline to return the kids to Connie.

This was another tear-fest but in the best way. Jill and Warren couldn't stop gushing, while Miller decided he was taking advantage of my family discount this season to hone his skiing skills.

We laughed, we joked, and when they left, I was composed. It gave me a few minutes to look around and reflect on everything. By the time Pierce returned, I was ready to go.

My family, Lynda, and Ray were waiting for us at the shed.

While Pierce and Evin loaded the car, Mom was her usual self, driving me crazy and insisting that the time on the road would give me a chance to start planning the wedding. She harped until Pierce came to my rescue and threatened to stop at a Justice of the Peace in Kentucky.

Everyone thought it was hilarious, except her. She's now shooting death glares his way.

"If you get hitched by the JOP, I'm going to hunt you down." Evin throws his arm around my shoulders.

"Why?"

"Because she'll laser in on me, and I'm nowhere near ready to get married."

"All the more reason to get her off my back and sic her on you."

"Hunt. You. Down. Darby," he repeats.

"Baby, it's time." Pierce slams the tailgate and whistles for Runner.

"I'll be there Labor Day." Evin turns me fully in his arms. "You'll be working, but it'll give me time to scope out the place."

"I'm going to miss you." My voice cracks.

"You're not going to have a chance to miss me. I'm on the permanent guest list, your money manager, and the brother who expects a nightly call."

"I love you."

"Get on the road." His own voice is hoarse. "You can make it to Nashville tonight."

I give him one last squeeze, kiss the underside of his jaw, and turn to my dad, who's waiting with open arms.

"Kick ass."

"I will, Daddy." His eyes grow warm and soft at the endearment.

"Okay, we're not going to have a mushy, gushy, tear-infested send-off." Mom yanks me from him into a hug. "Jill said this morning was humiliating the way you cried and carried on."

This is a lie. Jill said no such thing, but this is mom's way. She's never been one to show emotions in public.

"That's right. It was mortifying." The best thing to do is to go along with it.

"You'll be home before any of us have time to miss you," she adds. "Get going before you cause us to miss the beginning of the next NCIS."

"I wouldn't want to get in the way of you and your all-day marathon."

"Don't get smart. You know I have a thing for Mark Harmon."

"God, I'm crazy for even saying this, but I'm going to miss you, Mom."

Her chest spasms against mine, and she pulls away, dropping her sunglasses, but not before I catch the moisture in her eyes. Dad steps in, folding her into him.

Pierce makes his rounds while I say goodbye to Lynda and Ray.

"Pulling up here in April seems like a lifetime ago," I say with a sense of melancholy, scanning my parents' property as we drive away.

"You okay?"

"Yes, it's just amazing how things change. How I've changed."

"Do you think you've changed?"

"In a span of the last eight months, I've packed up to move twice. I relocated my business, started over only to join a hotel conglomerate, which is still unreal to me. I reconnected with you, got engaged, arranged to put my house on the market, and sometime in the future, I'll be a stepmom."

"You've always been a highflyer." He tugs my hand to his mouth and kisses my knuckles.

Runner *woofs* from the back seat and plops down, ready for his nap.

"You didn't tell me how your meeting with Mr. Baldwin went yesterday."

"It went fine. Quick and painless. He's not upset I'm ducking out on the last month. Apparently, whoever bought the building is eager to start renovations. He even gave me back my deposit and the last month's rent. You'll have to keep a watch for me to see what happens."

"I have fond memories of that place."

I smile to myself, thinking of all the things we did in there. "I hope they don't demolish it."

"Not likely since it's technically registered in the historic buildings category."

"I wasn't aware of that. If I had stayed, there would have had to be changes made. Wonder if they would have passed through permits."

"You have a very persuasive and creative fiancé that would have made it happen."

"You'd have had your hands full. My list would have been long."

His eyes cut to mine. "I'd like to hear what you would have done differently."

"We have days on the road. I'll bore you with my baker geek speak later. I want to know how it went with Connie and the drop-off."

His jaw locks, and he grips my hand tighter. "I gave Maya her phone back for the week, and she knows the rules. Connie threw it in my face that I'm breaking our week before school tradition, trying to stir the pot, but the kids didn't bite. She asked for money to buy supplies, and when I told her they had been ordered and I'd be taking them in on the first day of school, she went through the roof. Her parents witnessed it. I left without another word."

"I know you don't agree, but making this drive with me is probably not a good idea. You should be where your kids need you."

"This time is for us, and with all the shit flying around, there's no telling what I'm facing when I get back. On the positive side, I'll get the benefit of having them the first week of school for the first time in years."

At the mention of *'shit flying around'*, a knot coils in the pit of my stomach. Pierce isn't only dealing with Connie; he's dealing with angry neighbors who want their mailbox structure replaced with a very specific brick, and the father of the driver who hit Runner is arguing who's at fault. On top of all that, Kendrick Construction is about to launch into a new project.

"You should let me drive for a while."

"I drive," he states matter-of-factly.

"No need to be macho. I'm capable of driving across the country."

"It's not macho; it's a man thing. You're with me, I drive. Besides, you can sit there looking gorgeous and reserve your energy. You'll need it."

"Oh, really? Why is that?"

"I've mapped out the route, and we're passing through at least seven states. I plan on fucking you in all seven. You may need to get creative."

A rush of heat travels through my bloodstream, and I take my hand from his and slide it between his legs. My fingers outline the ridge of his cock, which hardens at the touch.

"Jesus, we're not even out of town yet, and I'm ready to pull over."

"Technically, we had sex in South Carolina this morning. You'll have to get us to Georgia." I continue to massage him. "And, since I haven't had car sex since I was twenty-one, you need to hurry."

He accelerates, his eyes slicing to me. "As soon as we hit the fucking state line, you're mine."

I lick my lips and moan, squeezing him gently. "You could use a little incentive."

257

I twist in my seat and hiss when a stabbing pain cuts into my calf. "What the hell is that?" A large bag I didn't notice with a plastic binder pokes out from under my purse.

"Something Annie told me to put up front."

I yank my hand back and pull the binder out. *DARBY'S WEDDING BOOK* is printed in bold black letters on the front. Color-coded tabs with labels and sheet protectors are clipped inside. The bag is loaded down with bridal magazines that have corresponding colored tabs with Mom's notes.

I thumb through the magazine on top and groan at her favored selections. "No, no, no! I am not wearing poof and tulle!"

"I have no clue what that means."

"It means my mom is trying to make me look like a bride from another generation."

"Guess she was serious about jump-starting the wedding planning on this trip."

A growl comes from the back of my throat when I read the letter she included. "She's already spoken to the minister at the church and reached out to a venue."

"That a problem?"

"We haven't set a date! I can't possibly plan a wedding right now. Who even knows when I'll be back in Charleston? The renovations on the resort may take longer than expected."

"The resort will be ready."

"You don't know that."

"I sure as hell do, considering Kendrick Construction is involved. I'll work my ass to the bone to have that hotel ready to open next spring. Knowing that the completion is the only thing standing between you coming home and marrying me is motivation enough to get it finished ahead of schedule."

I jerk back in surprise. "That's your new project?"

"That and a side gig I'm working on. We are one of the many contractors."

"Why didn't you tell me?"

"I was going to surprise you."

"My brother's involved with the financing, my fiancé is involved with the construction, and I'm now technically a partner with their hospitality team. This is all very weird."

"Think of it as coincidental."

I shove the binder and the magazine back in the bag and huff out dramatically.

"Can we go back to the hand-job part of our trip?"

"No, I need my phone." I snatch it from the console and open the browser.

"Why?"

"Because I'm going to teach the old bat a lesson."

I search through the google results, pick a random location, and forward the link via text to Mom with two simple words.

Back off.

A satisfied smile curls on my lips when the phone starts ringing less than a minute later, and I tap ignore.

"Let her stew on that."

"What did you do?"

"I found a Justice of the Peace in Kentucky and sent her the link."

He returns my smile, shaking his head. "Just say the word, and I'll get us there tonight."

Chapter 30
Pierce

"This is it!" Darby announces, spinning with her arms wide around her new industrial kitchen.

The area is massive, easily three times the size of what she was working with at home. Recognizable faces of her new team filter in from the adjoining kitchen and swarm her, throwing out questions.

News of her arrival spread, and for the two days we've been here, we've been inundated with visitors at her new place. I can't count the number of invitations we've turned down to go out and introduce Darby to her new city. These people have encompassed her, welcoming us both and working to make her a member of their crew. A part of me is glad she has this support system. Another part of me wants to steal her back, lock us in her apartment, and continue to fuck her on every possible surface. Unfortunately, that's going to have to wait because I'm leaving for the airport soon.

While Darby fields questions, I take the opportunity to walk the space, taking inventory of everything and snapping pictures. With what she's shared with me, and seeing this for myself, ideas for my design begin to come together. Mr. Baldwin sold me the whole building, not only the space she was using, so my plans include expansion.

"Are you almost ready?" She presses into my back, linking her arms around my waist.

"Do we need to unpack those?" The boxes she shipped are stacked in a corner.

"I have all next week to get that stuff arranged."

"Let's go then."

She gives a quick wave to those still lingering, and we head out. The drive to the airport is quiet, and the closer we get, the lead grows heavier in my stomach. I just got her back, and all too soon, I'm losing her again. The circumstances may be different, but the reality of her being far away is sitting heavy on my mind.

"I'm going to be fine. There's no need to worry about me." She clutches my hand.

"I didn't say anything different."

"No, but the grinding of your teeth and strain in your neck are dead giveaways."

"This isn't how I pictured our life together starting, me hopping on a red-eye back to South Carolina and leaving you in Colorado."

"You almost sound angry."

"I'm pissed at myself. If I would have handled things differently back in May, we could be in a very different position right now."

She stays quiet, and when I glance over, she's staring forward, working through something in her head. An uneasy silence fills the space, and when she turns, her face is filled with sadness. "I would have probably turned them down. If the timing was different, and we'd have reconciled even a few days earlier, confessing all that we know now, there's no way I would have left you. I'd have given up the largest opportunity of my career to have our life together."

Her admission cuts me even deeper. "Baby, that's not what I meant."

"I know it sucks. My heart is breaking with each mile we get closer to the airport. This is a huge risk for me. I've left everyone I know and love to chase a dream. When you get on that plane, it's my dog and me. No friends, no family, not even an emergency contact that doesn't require a cross-country trek. I'm scared to death, my confidence is on shaky ground, and the man I've spent most of my life loving will be thousands of miles away. Not to mention, my place in your new life is causing a war with the mother of your children, which I knew was going to happen."

I swerve at the impact of her words. "Jesus, Darby. Why didn't you tell me any of this?"

"Because I don't get to play a victim. It's hard to garner sympathy when it's my decisions that led me here."

"You're not a victim, nor do you need sympathy. You need the fact that you're amazing drilled into your head until you believe it."

"What I need is the assurance you can handle this because my biggest fear is you realizing you made a mistake and can't deal with the distance. You've convinced yourself that Brasher is going to automatically relocate me home, which is most likely true according to the terms of my agreement, but what about in the meantime? The six months or longer I'm out here?"

Fuck no.

I notice the exit in time to veer off, driving to the back of the first parking lot in view. She starts to protest, but I'm quicker, releasing her seatbelt, hauling her over into my lap, and trapping her to me. "There will never be a time I consider this a mistake. It was a dick move to bring it up."

"I'm being dramatic because I'm emotional about you leaving."

"That could be part of it, but the bigger issue here is if I've given you any reason to doubt where I stand when it comes to you."

"No, but your uphill battle is only beginning."

"I'm strong enough to handle what's waiting for me at home. You have a job to do out here. Kick ass, stay strong, and when the time comes, get home to me. You can't keep me away for long. I'll be back in a few weeks. I'll be making this commute for as long as it takes."

She frames my face with her hands and brings her quivering lips to mine. "I love you."

My chest constricts, and I sift my hands through her hair, twirling the smooth strands around my fingers. "If there was any way to reschedule my flight, we'd be headed back to your place."

"I know. It gives us something to look forward to."

●—●—●—●—●

"Is this shit ever going to stop?" Miller's clipped question ratchets up my own frustration.

"Not soon enough."

"I'll have a bottle waiting at your house when you get home. Don't worry about the kids. We'll be fine."

"Thanks, man. I owe you. Don't forget to grab Maya's phone, especially tonight. Connie's going to be unpredictable."

"Got it." He disconnects as a text chimes.

Darby: Good luck. I'll be here when you're ready to talk.

Me: I got this. Call you tonight.

I try to keep things light because the last thing I want is Darby worried. After her revelation last weekend, it's important for her to focus on what's in front of her, not what's happening here.

I spot my lawyer exiting his car and go to meet him. "Pierce." He offers his hand.

"John, thanks for all your work on this."

"My line of work is rarely known as a ball of fun, but I don't envy you today."

"Yeah, that's why I called in the big guns. Dealing with Connie has become an issue best dealt with professionals." He dips his chin in understanding and leads the way into the law office.

The receptionist gestures to a large conference room, where Connie is seated with her lawyer. Her eyes are trained on me, glowing with immense anger. I ignore her, taking a seat across the table.

Her lawyer begins immediately. "Mr. Kendrick, we understand you have an urgent matter involving the children that couldn't wait."

"It better be urgent. I had to take the afternoon off work," Connie snips.

John opens a folder and passes around the documents I forwarded to him earlier this week. "These are copies of what Mr. Kendrick has requested this meeting for."

"Oh, for God's sake, can we cut to the chase so we're not paying these lawyers for every word?" Connie rips the papers from the table. "What the hell is this?"

John motions with his fingers for me to go on. "The first is a three-thousand-dollar veterinary bill on the dog that was hit. The next invoice is for the thousand dollars it's going to take to replace my neighbor's mailbox. If you flip again, there is a notice from the driver of the car that had the collision. His father thinks we should pay half of the damages to his son's car."

"Why the hell are you bringing all this to me?"

"It was your demand and instructions that led to the accident. You are partially responsible."

"The hell I am. This happened on your watch. It's your responsibility."

"I was in the shower, in my home, with the kids locked in. There was no danger. Then you called, lost your temper, and directed our daughter to do something, threatening her if she didn't."

"That's such crap. I'm not stupid enough to believe you're going to have to pay for any of this. That boy was texting and driving. He's at fault no matter what his father wants to believe. His insurance is supposed to pay for all damages, including the mailbox. I'm not paying shit toward your girlfriend's dog nor the accident."

John hands me another sheet. "Just to be clear, you are refusing to help cover any of these costs?"

"Yes," she snarls.

"Well, here is the breakdown from our custody agreement the judge signed off on. Over the years, we deviated away from this with a loose arrangement where the kids could float, but that is no longer a possibility. We've already reverted to the split living arrangement recommended. Starting this month, I will no longer be paying extra to cover your mortgage even after these bills are paid in full."

Her face flames red, and she snatches the paper, scanning it. "Is he really able to pull the support he's been paying? How am I supposed to survive?" She looks to her lawyer with an edge of panic in her voice.

"I went back and logged all of the extra money I've been giving you. Outside of all the financial extras, I've covered their insurance, their extra-curricular activities, their clothing, school supplies, and countless other things. You rarely have to open your wallet. In addition to child support, your supplemental income has been generous. That's ready for the judge if necessary."

"Don't you dare talk to me like I'm a freeloader. These are our children you're referring to. You live in a swanky mini-mansion in an exclusive part of town and own a portion of a very profitable business. Yet, you shoved me in a mediocre townhome, and I work paycheck to paycheck. No judge is going to take your side."

"Keep telling yourself that if you want. Your townhome is anything but mediocre; you chose that community based on the zip code and prestige. Don't forget, I lived next door for many years. And, last I knew from court papers, you make a generous salary."

"You brought me here today to discuss money?"

"No, there are a few other things. Maya's pediatrician gave me a referral to a child psychologist."

"You want her to see a shrink?"

"I'm concerned about Maya. It's evident in the last few months that your influence over Maya is dangerous and, in my opinion, borderline harassment. She's at an age where guidance is important."

"Harassment? How did you come up with that one?"

"You're using her to get back at me, and she's not equipped to handle the pressure and confusion."

"You are a piece of work. I've gone through hell for years, been humiliated by you, and tried to raise our two kids while you lived your bachelor lifestyle. All I ever wanted was what was best for us as a family, and you refused to try. The instant that woman breezed back into town, you're suddenly a family man that has high morals and standards. Two months back, and she's sporting a diamond that could fund a small country. How dare you do this to me?"

John's hand lands on my arm, and he gives me a weary warning. He's well aware of my temper and animosity toward Connie. I suck in a deep breath and give him the signal I'm under control.

"Connie, I gave up my bachelor lifestyle long before you entered the picture, and you know that. Darby was my life, and then things changed. I've never made you any promises, nor did I do anything to lead you on. At the risk of sounding like a bastard, you knew the stakes back then. My love for Darby has nothing to do with me being a good father. I want what's best for the kids, and your recent actions prove you have a different agenda."

"I'm not going to go under scrutiny for being a single mom who wanted to make things work with my children's father!"

"You knew there was no chance of that."

"Connie, I think we should stop now," her lawyer advises.

"I can't believe we're even here right now, all because of your damn girlfriend and her mangy dog." She ignores him.

"My fiancée," I correct her.

"It's not my fault the dog ran off and caused a damn accident."

"Connie, your actions almost killed Runner and could have seriously hurt that young man. You've gone to great lengths to manipulate our kids. Your anger could have killed someone, and you spread that shit through our little girl. I'm taking that seriously. This goes much deeper. I've been warning you for a while that you need to reel in your attitude, and that we need to focus on raising Maya and Cole. You continued to fill their heads with falsehoods, and now, you've put them in a position to where they don't know right from wrong."

"Bullshit. This is all about that bitch."

"That right there is a single example of the reason we're here. You place the fault anywhere but on yourself. I take full responsibility for being blind all these years to what is happening under your roof. That's not the case anymore. Darby doesn't factor into this unless you count your hatred for the woman in my life. A part of me wonders if you'd be acting this way if I was marrying someone besides Darby. Would you despise them, too?"

The fire in her eyes is my answer. It's time to wrap this up.

"The bricks for the mailbox had to be specially ordered, and they arrived this week. Maya and I will be rebuilding the mailbox this weekend. I probably know the answer, but I'll throw it out there anyway. You are welcome to stop by and help. It will be a good step toward proving to the kids we can be civilized."

"Are you kidding me? You own a construction company and can easily have one of your crews do that job. Why is she doing manual labor?"

"Because she's learning there are consequences to her actions."

"You're punishing her."

"No, I'm teaching her a lesson."

She rolls her eyes. "Fucking ridiculous."

"Suit yourself. One last thing. I'd like to take the kids out of town during their Christmas break."

"Let me guess? Aspen?"

"Yes."

"The answer is hell no. Their first time on a plane is not going to be to fly across the country to see her."

"I think we're done for today," John speaks up. "We'll discuss any plans for travel at a future date."

He and I stand, him shaking the other lawyer's hand before going. John waits until we are at my truck before speaking.

"I hope your generosity over the years doesn't come back to bite you in the ass."

"Me too."

"It's none of my business, but humor me. Why did you decide to give her all that extra money?"

"Out of guilt and obligation to Maya and Cole. I guess it was my way of compensating for not loving their mom."

"You know that you aren't going to have to pay for the damages to that kid's car. He was at fault."

"I know, but Connie needed to see how serious this is. You heard her. She can't see past my relationship with Darby and understand I'm focused on the wellbeing of our kids. She's always been cunning and conniving; hell, she even made a play to move into my house. It can't go on."

"I'm going to piss you off here, but it's my job to be objective. You've been dormant in parenting with Connie for a long time, so the boundary lines were blurred. Now, you're speeding at full throttle to establish what should have been happening all along. Darby reentering your life lit a fire under your ass. It's important to keep your attention on the welfare of Maya and Cole and steer clear of any references to your personal life when it comes to Connie—no matter how hard it is—because that woman sitting across from you today is the epitome of a woman scorned. She's pissed, and she's likely to keep lashing out. You're going to need to get a grip on that Kendrick temper you're known for. Stay on the straight and narrow and find an outlet for your anger. If this goes back to a judge, we need everything solid."

I nod, hearing him loud and clear. Lose the attitude.

"Call me if you need me, which will probably be soon." He slaps me on the shoulder and leaves.

I hope he's wrong and that I won't need him soon. But it's highly unlikely.

Chapter 31

Darby

"Let's head home. I'm beat." Runner sits dutifully at my feet while I strap his leash to his collar. He trots his way through the park while I wave to a few familiar faces and call out my greetings.

This has become our routine. Several afternoons a week, we come here so he can release some energy. He's used to having space. My place only has a small yard, but he's adapted well.

In the five weeks we've been here, my world has shifted on its axis. Being a part of Brasher is nothing short of spectacular. Everyone from management to my team has made me feel welcome. I thought it would be hard, working with a large crew and managing the demands, but it isn't. There was a small period of adjustment, not handling all the financials, but since I'm included in all managerial meetings, the reports are given to me weekly. And that suits me because I can concentrate on running my kitchen.

Three days after Pierce left, I couldn't stand the boredom and threw myself into work. They were happy to have me start earlier than expected. They already have a full-time baker, and everyone knew I was brought in for my specialties. So far, it's been a hit. Technically, it's not tourist season in Aspen. Between the festivals and outdoor enthusiasts, Brasher keeps a packed resort, which has been great because I've been able to stay busy.

Evin did come for a long weekend, and I cut back my schedule to spend time with him. We were invited to go hiking, and I stupidly thought it would be fun. He had a great time. It took me days to recover from abusing my muscles.

There hasn't been time to feel lonely, except when Pierce and I have our nightly call. He's been busier than ever, and the weeks he doesn't have the kids, he's pushing long days, too. The Charleston Brasher Hotel and whatever side project he has are in full swing, and he's exhausted.

The good news is that it seems he and Connie are at an impasse. There have been no more tense situations, and the kids are thriving in school. Maya's visit with the child psychologist seemingly went well, and while the psychologist couldn't disclose much about their private conversation, she assured Pierce that Maya is in a normal mental space for a girl her age. She's dealing with feelings toward her parents but nothing out of the ordinary for an almost twelve-year-old entering middle school.

The times I've spoken to them, they've been happy.

I'm lost in my thoughts, not paying attention, when Runner yanks on the leash, lunging forward and whining excitedly. A movement in the distance catches my eye, and I stop, frozen to the spot. The ringing in my ears pulses to the rhythm of my heart at the beautiful man striding across the walkway. I drop the leash, and we race to Pierce. He barely has time to brace before I'm attached to his front while my dog is at his side. My mouth covers his face, kissing everywhere before landing on his lips.

The instant our tongues meet, electrifying sparks race through my system. His taste, his scent, his touch, all of it soaks into me. My mouth presses harder to his, my hands going to his scalp and tugging on his hair. The soft bristle of his beard rubs along my cheeks and chin, and I moan in appreciation. His arms clutch around my middle, supporting me as I kiss him greedily, unable to control myself.

His chest vibrates against mine in a low rumble. "God, I fucking miss you." He tears away too quickly, leaving me panting.

"What are you doing here? I thought your meeting was on Wednesday."

"I came early to surprise you."

"I love your surprises." I smile against his lips.

Runner decides he's done waiting for his greeting, bumping into us over and over. Pierce sets me on my feet and crouches to give him a rubdown. It's then I get a good look at him, and my heartbeat speeds for a different reason. Something's off. His eyes and face show signs of exhaustion and stress from more than endless hours working and now a cross-country flight.

"You okay?" I run my fingers over the top of his head.

"I am now. In about a minute, I'll be even better." He stands, grabbing my hand, while Runner takes off in the direction of my door.

I want to ask him more about what's bothering him, but the instant we're inside, all conscious thought flies out of my brain. He attacks, pinning me against the wall and ripping my sweater over my head. His fingers flick the clasp of my bra, leaving goosebumps as he slowly slides it down my arms. His eyes darken and blister into my skin as he stares at my naked chest. He strums his thumbs over my nipples until they're hard and aching. Need and desire ignite from deep inside, coursing in my veins.

His lips and tongue brush tenderly around one nipple while he continues to caress the other. I arch into him, silently begging for more. He sucks and nips, teasing and tormenting until I'm winded and dizzy with lust. My calf hooks around his hip, pulling him closer so I can grind against the hardened outline of his cock.

"Baby, if you do that, I'm going to blow in my jeans."

"You're torturing me."

His hand travels down my side, sliding under the waistband of my pants and directly beneath my panties. I gasp as one finger slips inside and curls, joined immediately by another.

"Soaked. For weeks, all I could think about how is hot this is, knowing it's all mine."

"Yes." I clench around his fingers.

"You want more?"

"Please," I beg shamelessly,

He pumps them in and out, twisting and rolling, while his mouth goes back to my nipple. Pressure builds low in my spine, my hips grinding down on his hand.

"Fuck my fingers, baby. I can't hold out much longer. My dick is throbbing for you."

"I want you inside me."

"You can have me as soon as I feel you come apart."

"No... ahhhh..." I moan when he hits the perfect spot. All it takes is one swipe of his thumb across my clit, and the pressure explodes, tiny dots popping in my vision as I have my first Pierce induced orgasm in what seems like forever. He continues his movements until I'm trembling and writhing.

My head hits the wall, and a cold rush of air coats my overheated skin when he jerks my leggings down. "Help me out, baby."

I toe off my shoes and lift my legs for him to remove the rest of my clothes. The clouds of ecstasy clear my brain, and I reach for him, tossing his shirt behind us. I get his belt, button, and zipper undone quickly then slide his jeans and boxers low enough for him to spring free. My hand grips around his hard length, stroking a few times before he stops me.

"Can't do that," he grates out, bending to grab my ass. "Jump up."

I hop, circling my arms on his shoulders, and cry out when he plunges into me. The short pinch of pain turns to pleasure as my body accepts the invasion, stretching to welcome his frantic thrusts.

"Can't fucking help myself. I told myself I was going to go slow, worship your body. Kiss you, lick you, make you so crazy you'd know how I feel without you. Then one look, walking across that damn parking lot, and I was gone."

Power surges through me that I have this kind of control over him. "More," I demand, bouncing to meet him stroke for stroke.

His blue eyes liquefy as a wicked grin crosses his lips. "You want it hard?"

"Yes."

"Gladly." He drives up, again and again, pounding into me with such force my sight goes hazy and my toes curl.

I close my eyes and drop my head to his shoulder, clinging to him and fighting the sensations rippling their way through my body. It would be easy to let go, fall over the edge again, but I don't want this to end. Every part of me is alive with his movements, and each thrust grows more intense. My brain becomes hyper-aware of his body holding mine. The heat of his hard-muscled chest rubbing the tender flesh of my nipples, the crashing of his hipbones to mine, the way his fingers are digging into the curves of my ass.

A low, slow moan escapes from my throat, encouraging him further. "Let me see your face, beautiful."

My neck is heavy, but I lay my head back, thankful for the support of the wall.

"So tight, wet, and ready for me."

"Please," I beg, not sure what I'm pleading for.

"More what? Harder? Faster? You want to come all over me?"

"Y-y-y-eeee-ssss."

His gaze locks with mine, and the smoldering heat scorches, lighting my insides on fire. He brings his mouth to mine, outlining my lips with his tongue. His hips rock with short, swift movements, allowing me to catch my breath.

"When I woke up, my dick was ready. Knowing that, before the day was over, I'd be buried in you was too much. I took care of myself, picturing your perfect lips wrapped around my cock. It didn't do anything to take the edge off, so I did it again in the shower, this time thinking of that morning in Kiawah, you in that dress as I drilled you from behind. That still wasn't enough, but I found the self-restraint to wait."

I'm distracted by his words, his dirty thoughts, and the warmth of his breath as his lips move against mine. He's got me under a spell, and then I realize he's pulled almost fully out, the ridge of his crown slipping along my sensitive and slick entrance. His blue eyes share a split second of warning before he slams into me, showing no mercy. He gives me what I asked for—harder, faster, rougher. It's raw and savage, pounding to my bones.

I can't hold out. My nails dig into his shoulder, and I use every last ounce of strength to clamp my inner muscles around his cock. He sinks his teeth into my neck, and I shatter.

A million bolts of energy fire through my veins, lighting me up. His own roar sounds distant, cutting through the ringing in my ears. He throbs, pulses, and releases inside of me, continuing to thrust and bringing me to another earth-shattering climax.

It's too much. I try to cry out, but my throat is raw from muted screams. All I can do is ride spasm after spasm of immense pleasure rushing through me. My heart hammers to the same rhythm as his as I slowly float back to reality.

He stays hard inside me, still pulsing, showing no signs of a man who just fucked me senseless.

"Tell me you're okay." His voice is hoarse and gruff.

"I'm better than okay."

"It's you. I lose all control. It's unexplainable the need I have for you."

Another tremble races down my backbone. "I love it when you get this way."

He raises his face to me, his eyebrows raised in question. "Baby, I fucked you like an animal against a wall and came so hard my brain rattled."

"It's not the first time and hopefully not the last."

His mouth splits into a wide grin, and he sweeps his lips across mine. "We have twenty-four hours until Dad and Miller fly in. I'll see what I can do. Let's try the bed next time."

"Okay, but there's one problem. I'm pretty sure I can't walk."

His face lights up, his eyes filled with pride as he bursts into laughter.

●—•—●—•—●

"Finally, I get to see where the magic is made." Miller waltzes into the kitchen casually.

"I thought you were in meetings this evening?"

"Nah, I was dismissed early."

"Dismissed, meaning you bailed?"

"Same thing, right?" He wiggles his eyebrows, grinning.

"And, instead of spending your time enjoying the gorgeous city of Aspen, you came to watch me decorate truffles?"

"Yep, I wanted to see you in action. Besides, we have the big party tonight."

"Well, you missed prime time. An hour ago, this place was insane, all to get ready for the party."

"Where is everyone?"

"Once we cleaned up, their shifts ended. All I have to do is finish these, and I'm done, too."

"Need help?"

"Not unless you want to take responsibility for the presentation and appearance of an eight-hundred-dollar tray of truffles."

His eyes bulge, and he throws his hands out. "No, thanks."

I chuckle and meticulously drizzle the chocolate sauce over the pieces.

"Nice kitchen. Do you like it?"

"What's not to like? It's large, pristine, and efficient. We have been able to produce substantial quantities, and there's plenty of room to move around."

"That sounds mildly clinical."

"I will admit that a little more personality would make this space inviting. The industrial ambiance isn't my style."

"What would you do differently?"

"Nothing in terms of the appliances and general set-up. Pops of color on the walls, a few pictures, maybe something besides standard recessed lighting. But this is a corporate kitchen."

"Yeah, I guess you're right." He glances around attentively with a look I know well. It's the look of a contractor working through an idea in his head.

"I didn't think your contract included the kitchen renovations."

"It doesn't. This was pure curiosity."

We stay quiet for a few minutes until my own curiosity wins out. "Has he heard from her?"

Miller shrugs, avoiding my eyes. My mood plummets because he's not going to be forthcoming.

"How mad was she?" I try again.

"We're not going to talk about her."

"Apparently, that's the Kendrick theme because Pierce is avoiding the subject as well. He's hiding something and obviously upset."

"He misses you, that's all."

"I get that, but this is beyond the surface of missing me. He's protecting me from something. I may have been gone for a long time, but I didn't lose my touch of sensing when something's wrong with him."

"You should talk to him."

"Instead, I'm talking to you."

He blows out a breath, scrubbing his hand through his hair, and focusing back to me. He doesn't have to say a word; it's written on his face.

"She's gone crazy, hasn't she?"

The 'she' being Connie. Today, Brasher Resorts finally made a public announcement about opening their southern location next spring. Typically, this would have been an exciting occasion because the secret is out. Pierce arranged for his mother to take Maya and Cole to school this morning so we could tell them together. I knew from the gazillion text messages that the City of Charleston was ecstatic with this news. They may be calling it a boutique resort, but they have huge plans for it.

"All I know is Pierce won't take her calls, and her messages are loaded with hatred."

"I guess the impasse is over."

"Yeah, her knowing about the resort means she knows you have a job and will be coming back home. My guess is she ignored Pierce when he told her your move was temporary. Now, it's a reality. She's on a rampage."

My hands shake so bad, I screw up the glaze on a few of the truffles. "Here, these are yours." I hand them to him.

"Jesus, woman," he garbles with a mouthful of chocolate. "These are fucking fantastic."

"That's why we can charge what we do."

"Lucky for me, my future sister-in-law is the mastermind."

His reference helps my spirits, and I go back to dribbling curlicues.

"Darby, Pierce is going to handle this situation with Connie."

"You sound exactly like him." I don't look up from my work.

"He doesn't want you to worry. I'm not asking you to lie—"

"It's okay, Miller. I'm not going to tell him about this conversation. I'm hoping he shares."

I know there is more to this, but I don't have a chance to ask because Pierce and Warren stride in.

"I want whatever that is." Warren steals the last chocolate from Miller's hand and pops it into his mouth.

Pierce crowds close. "You almost done, baby?"

"Soon. How were the meetings?"

"Meetings are meetings. We're on schedule and budget, so our asses aren't on the line. Can't say the same for the other companies. Where's your ring?" He eyes my hand, scowling.

"Tucked in a safe place."

"I'd rather it be on your finger."

"I don't usually wear it to work, especially when my days are like today."

"That's ridiculous."

"You're cute when you pout."

"We're going to head back to Darby's to get ready for tonight," Warren announces. "I'll take Runner on a quick walk, too."

I shoot him a grateful smile on their way out. Buzzing sounds from Pierce's pocket, but he makes no move. I don't ask questions until it happens again a few minutes later.

"Any reason you're not answering your phone?"

"There's no one I need to talk to."

"Could be Maya."

"It's not Maya."

"Well, it could be important," I try again.

"If it's important they'll leave a message."

I bite my tongue and work quietly, sighing in relief when the last truffle looks perfect. They go into the fridge until the wait staff picks them up later. Pierce watches me, but it's clear he's lost in thought.

I hang up my apron, tug my hair loose from the bun, and walk to him, wrapping my arms around his waist. "Talk to me."

"About what?"

"I know something is spinning in your brain. You're keeping secrets."

"No secrets, just working through things."

"Things like Connie having another shit-fit now that she knows my return is imminent?"

The wrinkles in his forehead crease, and his eyes go cold. "We're not talking about her."

"We don't have to talk about her, but we do need to talk about you. Tell me what's on your mind."

I hold his gaze, silently telling him I'm not backing down. He blows out a frustrated sigh and drapes his arms around my shoulders. "She's definitely not happy."

"Outside of the obvious, what's been happening this week?"

"The messages started when she found out I was in Aspen. She accused me of being an irresponsible father and all the other bullshit she could come up with. Today, when she found out about the new hotel, it tipped her scales of insanity. It may have finally hit her that you and I are going to get married and build our lives in Charleston."

"A lot of people have been questioning how we were going to make this work. It's a relief to finally be able to talk openly."

"Yeah, but she's not like most people. I can only guess she assumed you'd have to give up your career and business to marry me, and in her whacked mind, she was waiting for our relationship to fail. Now, I can't get a read on what she's thinking about us, but she's made it clear she's out for blood."

A cold chill races across my skin, and I grasp him tighter. "What does that mean?"

"Only time will tell, but she's starting with money. She's assuming this job with Brasher is a goldmine and financially beneficial to me."

"She's demanding money?"

"The last message I bothered to check was financially driven. Who knows what the others say? None of that matters. My financial situation is locked. I pull a salary, and bonuses are based on company success, similar to the other executive team. She can take me back to court, but it won't matter. John and I already prepared for that scenario."

This is not a surprise. Pierce and I discussed our finances a while ago. Even though she's not a family attorney, Stephanie was pretty confident Connie wouldn't be able to demand more payment from Pierce. But it doesn't matter because Pierce's investments and portfolio are strong. "You're holding something back."

"I'm concerned about my kids."

"That's understandable. Why won't you talk to me about it?"

"Because you have much bigger things happening."

The memory of our trip to the airport weeks ago snaps in my head, remembering the emotional vulnerability that came out. He's keeping all this to himself to protect me. "Please, don't shut me out. I'm your partner. You can't keep telling me only the good things happening and keep the bad hidden. That's not how this works."

He searches my face, dragging his lip through his teeth. I know I've made my point when his stormy eyes clear and he nods. "Okay."

"Okay?"

"But, for now, this conversation is over. We have a celebratory party to get ready for. She's not ruining that for us."

"Agreed."

"Before we go, are you absolutely sure I can't fuck you on that table?" He waggles his eyebrows suggestively.

I slap his chest, shaking my head furiously. "No! Let's get you out of here before someone hears you."

He sweeps my feet off the ground and spins me around, his lips against mine. The heaviness evaporates but not before I make a mental note to call my mom tomorrow.

It's time she goes on Connie watch.

Chapter 32

Pierce

Connie: Our plans changed. The kids will not be able to join you today.

Each time I reread the message, my blood boils hotter. This was expected, but there was hope she'd follow through. Plans changed my ass. Technically, it's her week, so I can't do shit, but seeing as it's Thanksgiving, we agreed that I could have Maya and Cole for a few hours. In return, I would do the same at Christmas while they were with me.

Not only did she do this on purpose, she played me. I was headed back to Aspen for the holiday. The only thing that could change my plans was the chance to have time with the kids today and enjoy it with my family.

She's waiting for a response, wanting me to explode. As much as my fingers are itching to blow up her phone, it's not worth it. She doesn't get that satisfaction. A simple response should do the trick.

Thanks for letting me know.

Then, I shoot off a quick message to Maya, telling her we'll have our own version of Thanksgiving Sunday night. She responds with a heart. A fucking heart.

Gotta love the life of communicating through emojis.

As if she can sense something is wrong, Darby's name pops up on my screen.

"Hey."

"She reneged on the deal."

"How'd you know?"

"Connie's not exactly reliable, and it was too much to hope she'd quit her ploy for revenge for a day. Please, tell me you didn't ream her ass."

"You'd be proud."

"Good boy."

"Boy?"

She laughs, and the sweet sound strips the tension from my body. "God, I miss you."

"How much do you miss me?" The sweet is gone, replaced with a sexy rasp that speaks directly to my cock.

"Like a starved man who hasn't seen his fiancée in nine weeks."

"Like a man that would fly across the country for a booty call?"

"Booty call?"

"Well... I made contingency arrangements with the speculation Connie would pull this."

"And this contingency plan has to do with a booty call?"

"Kinda."

"I'm listening."

"You know, our concierge is also a travel coordinator. She waved her wand, reached out to a contact, and viola. You now have a ticket waiting for you if you're interested. Flight leaves at seven, so you can still make it to Jill and Warren's for dinner."

I'm on the move, barging to my closet and throwing a bag together in record time while she chatters away. "Pierce, are you listening?"

"Didn't hear a word you said after a ticket's waiting for me."

"That means you're coming?"

"Hell yes. I'm fucking lucky you're presumptuous."

"It's called proactive."

"Still a lucky man."

"I need to warn you; this place is nuts. Booked to full capacity, and guests are raving about the slopes being perfect. I've never seen anything like it."

"It won't bother me."

"Pierce, that isn't the only thing guests are raving about." The tone of her voice drops, and I stop, a rush of adrenaline speeding through my system. I know this tone.

"You did it," I state, aware of what she's going to say.

"I did it."

"Give me the details, baby."

"I can't share exact numbers yet because there is still a week left, but preliminary numbers show we surpassed the budgeted goal by thirty-four percent. DG Creations officially had the largest month of my career."

"I knew you could do it. This is only the beginning." I picture the beaming excitement on her face.

"I was going to wait and surprise you, but it was impossible to keep inside."

"Makes this trip all the more special."

"I'll meet you in baggage."

"I don't want you driving in the snow at midnight."

"I won't be. I have a Brasher driver and car tonight. It's one of the perks of being management and working the holiday weekend."

I know how hard Darby's been working and hasn't had a full day off in three weeks. On top of the resort's normal business, she's had weddings, parties, and preparation for this weekend. Most mornings, she starts at daylight and doesn't end until well after dark. I'm not happy about the long hours, but she was working toward a goal. A goal she crushed.

"Pierce, are you really okay about this thing with the kids?"

"I'm good. There's no doubt they are disappointed, but we'll get through it."

"I need to get back to the kitchen. Call me when you get to your gate."

"Done."

"Love you." She disconnects.

I do a walk through my house, making sure everything is locked, grab my bag, and hit my truck. I'm the last to arrive and find Annie and Mom in the kitchen. Mom's face falls when she notices it's only me.

"She-devil strikes again," Annie mumbles.

"We knew to expect this," I point out.

"Yeah."

"Look at the bright side. We won't be shuttling back and forth at Christmas."

"I guess." Mom half-shrugs.

"Mom, you knew this was probably going to happen."

"Yes, but I was hoping she'd stop the battle for one day. She has to know this will backfire. And Maya and Cole, not seeing their mom on Christmas, I can't even imagine." She shudders dramatically.

"What do you suggest I do? Chase her down and beg her to give me a few hours today? Can you imagine the satisfaction she'd get out of that? It's best I play it cool."

"You're right. We've come too far. You're doing the right thing by going the legal route and letting the lawyers handle this."

"Mom, make no mistake. Connie wants money and vindication. John told me Connie's lawyer presented him with a market housing report comparing the value of my home to Connie's."

"What did she hope to gain by that?" Annie scoffs.

"Most likely to show that I have equity? Try to go after it? Who knows how her mind works?"

"Are you going to have to sell your house?"

"Not because of Connie. If Darby wants something different, then absolutely."

"You shouldn't spoil her so much. She's turning into quite a diva."

I raise an eyebrow and stare Annie down.

"No, really, Pierce. Her ego is growing by the day. I tried to call her this morning, and she rushed me off the phone. Doesn't even have time for her mama on a holiday. What kind of daughter did I raise?" She's throwing in the dramatics to hide her hurt feelings.

Mom coughs to conceal her laugh, covering her mouth with her hand.

"Annie, they are expecting to serve Thanksgiving dinner to over a thousand people today."

"It's a buffet, and it's not like she's doing the cooking."

"No, but she's responsible for a portion of the desserts."

"Whatever. She's lying to me, too, telling me she had a meeting. No manager schedules a meeting today."

I'm not as polite as my mom and don't cover my smile at Annie's grouchiness. "Annie, she didn't lie to you. She got word this morning. She did it."

Her sullen expression lights up, and her eyes gleam. "She did it," she repeats, knowing what I'm referring to.

I fill them in on my conversation and plans to fly out tonight. "Now that you are up to speed with my life, I'm going out back."

Dad, Miller, Edward, and Evin are sitting out under the outdoor cabana, drinking beer and watching football. All of their eyes roam behind me. Miller shakes his head in disgust, but no one says anything about me being alone. "The beer is stocked." He tips his bottle.

I grab one, sit by Evin, and clink my bottle to his. "Darby call you yet?"

"Not yet, figured we'd touch base before she goes to the employee dinner tonight."

I repeat the story and my travel plans. Similar to the incident in the kitchen, Darby's news overshadows the frustration with Connie's trick.

"You really think the hotel here will be ready by spring?" Warren's question strikes me as odd coming off the news I shared.

"Yes."

"And she'll be back."

"That's the plan."

"You think she'll always have to work this grueling schedule around the holidays?"

"Knowing Darby, she'll volunteer to put in the hours, especially until she has a solid team in place."

He nods thoughtfully, squinting his eyes and dragging his hand over his chin.

"What are you getting at, Dad?" Evin breaks in.

"She's not getting any younger, and seeing as the holidays next year are going to be crazy, I'm thinking Pierce needs to get busy on making me and Annie a grandchild."

The beer lodges in my throat, and I choke, the burn working its way down painfully. Evin slaps me on the back, maybe a little too hard, until I catch my breath.

"Don't you think I need to get her down the aisle first?"

"Y'all bucked that tradition once; why hold out for it now?"

"Jesus." Evin drops his head.

Miller and Dad erupt in laughter, and I stare at Edward. He's serious. Dead serious. His lips may be twitching, but his eyes give away his intent.

"You want me to get her pregnant? Now?"

"Now's as good a time as any." He ticks his fingers, mouthing something, then looks back at me. "I figure, if you do the job right, we'll have a baby next August. That'll work for us."

Like I said… he's dead fucking serious.

"We're the same age. She has plenty of time." Evin sounds panicked at the thought of his dad encouraging me to get Darby pregnant without being married—again.

"We're working on you next," Edward tells him.

"You're on your own here. I'm not wading into this clusterfuck," Evin utters.

Nothing about Darby being pregnant terrifies me. It didn't scare me twelve years ago, and it doesn't scare me now. What does put me on edge is thinking about her carrying my baby so far away. I'd be a madman.

"Maybe I should have this conversation with Darby."

"Having a conversation with Darby means you give her time to process and come back with an argument. It took you weeks to get her to accept your proposal."

At this reminder, all the men burst into laughter. I grind my teeth, knowing I'll never live that down. They take aim at me every chance they get.

"My point is, don't discuss anything with her because we'll lose time that we don't have. You obviously know what you're doing when it comes to the biology involved, so I need you to make this happen, like tonight."

He didn't say Connie's name, but the reference to her pregnancies is there. He's not insulting me; he's driving home his point. Edward Graham is playing hardball. I chug the rest of my beer before responding. "You're giving me permission to knock up your daughter? Are you drunk?"

"Sober as a goat. I figure, this time around, you're not letting her get away. Which means we're stuck with you forever. It's time to make yourself useful."

"Jesus Christ, what's happening here?" I mumble under my breath.

"It's a little late to look afraid. Darby has always wanted to be a mom. If it happens sooner than she planned, she'll adapt. It's a win-win."

"You can stop talking now. I'm pretty sure this is not a conversation to have my future father-in-law."

"Probably not, but you need a push."

I eye the cooler, considering calling an Uber to take me to the airport. Getting drunk may be the only way to get me through this afternoon.

"At least, tell me you'll consider what I've said."

"I'm not agreeing to that out loud. Darby would castrate me." I fling him a look like he's crazy. Or crazier.

"Speaking of Darby, let's pretend this conversation never happened. I'll act surprised when you make the announcement."

"I'm already scrubbing my brain and hoping I don't have nightmares for the rest of my life." Evin rubs circles on his temple.

"Just for the record, Jill and I would love a baby in August," Dad throws in his first words since this insane conversation started.

"I'm going to get the fryer ready for the turkey." Miller rounds the cabana and stops on my other side. "A piece of advice."

The amusement in his voice sends a prickle over my skin. He's having far too much fun with this. "No, I don't want any advice from you."

"Too bad, because now that he's planted the seed, I'm on board. But you need to get it out of your head. It'll mess with your success."

"What the hell are you talking about?"

"With your track record, it's best you keep not trying. Avoid pregnancy at all costs. Stick with that mindset and put in the extra effort." He smiles wide, thinking he's clever and proud of himself.

Evin chuckles behind me.

I have the decency to yank Miller's phone out of his pocket before I send him flying into the pool.

Take that, shithead.

•—•—•—•—•

"This is a much better plan." Darby nestles in between my legs, leaning back against my chest. "No wonder the brochures always include couples in front of a sparkling fire pit."

"It wasn't my idea to ski today."

"I wanted to get the whole experience and see what all the hype is about. Apparently, I need a lot more practice. My butt is going to be black and blue. You made it look easy."

"I used my athleticism to my advantage."

"You've been doing that a lot since you arrived." She wiggles in exactly the right spot to graze against my balls. I'm hard instantly.

"You're athletic where it counts." I thrust my hips so she can feel what she's done.

"Maybe we should try again tomorrow morning?"

"Baby, you spent more time on your ass and back than you did actually standing. I can think of much better things to do when you're on your ass and back."

She whips her head to the side, giving me a dirty look. "You're making fun of me. You think it's funny I made a fool of myself."

I take a sip, hoping to hide my grin.

"Oh my God, stop smiling." My attempt fails.

"You were adorable and highly entertaining. I have video to prove it."

"I'm going to take lessons. Next time you're here, I'm going to ski like a pro."

"You're not taking lessons unless you find a female instructor." Her instructor from today pops into my head. He enjoyed picking her up off the ground too much.

Her eyes narrow into slits. "Why is that?"

"That guy today couldn't take his eyes off of you and not because it was his job. It was easy to tell what he was thinking. Darby, you want to learn, I'll help you next time."

"He was a boy! And I was a marshmallow."

"Even under all those layers, you can't hide your level of sexy. He noticed. Since you've never had any other man in your life, you haven't been introduced to the playboy lifestyle. And that's what that guy lives. No doubt he gets a laid a lot."

"I'm not naïve, and you honestly can't think any of those *boys* would hit on me."

"Any man with a pulse, who thought they had a shot, would hit on you. Let's not give them the opportunity."

"You're ridiculous." She turns back to face the fire. "I'll find a female instructor."

I kiss over the soft knit of her cap and brush my lips on the shell of her ear. "I'm protective and jealous, always have been when it comes to you. Don't act like it's a surprise."

She relaxes with a short nod. The small band on the outdoor terrace begins to play, and people file out from the lobby. Darby was right; the resort is a new experience this trip. It's not only the difference in appearance with the onset of winter but the whole atmosphere. Every member of the Brasher staff has perfected the art of making their guests happy.

"Pierce, would you consider putting in a fire pit in your backyard?"

"For you, I'd do anything. Tell me where you want it, and I'll build it next week." My hand covers hers with my fingers going to her ring.

"Did I tell you that, when Dave and Martin found out Stephanie, Scottie, and Billy were coming for New Year's, they invited themselves?"

"Are they staying with you?"

"We'll have to make it work. The resort is full, and there are two weddings that week. It's going to be crazy, but I can't wait to see them."

"Speaking of weddings..." I let my words hang out there.

She sits up, twisting to the side, and swings her legs over my thigh so we're almost facing. Her eyes sparkle, and it's not because of the firelight. My heart thumps, hoping she's going to tell me what I want to hear.

"Yes, speaking of weddings. I think it's time we plan ours."

"Thank fuck." I lay my forehead against hers. "My patience is waning."

"I've picked up on every one of your not-so-subtle hints."

"Good, I thought I was losing my touch."

"It was too fun to keep you hanging. But, seeing as we need to make a decision quickly, I have to quit playing with you."

A dozen ideas come to mind of how she's going to pay for her little game, but they will have to wait. "What decision do we have to make?"

"Do you like it here?"

"This resort? It's gorgeous."

"What if we got married here?"

"If this is what you want."

"I was thinking around next Christmas when all the decorations are up. This place will be a winter wonderland of twinkling white lights, snow-covered grounds, and extraordinary scenery."

I barely hear her over the siren in my ears and the pounding in my chest. For the briefest second, I think of Edward's request to have a baby in the family late next summer. The thought goes to the bottom of my list of things already wrong with what she's suggested.

"We are not getting married next Christmas, next Thanksgiving, or anywhere near the next holiday season. I'll be generous and give you until May." I shut her down gruffly.

"You want me to plan a wedding by May?"

"Like I said, generous. I'm not waiting longer than that."

"You're going to deny me my dream wedding under the lights with the backdrop of snow-covered mountains?"

"I'll bring you back and renew our vows. But the answer is fuck no."

"You're not going to wait, huh?" Her lips tick until a coy smirk spreads across her mouth.

"I've waited my entire life. Your time is up."

She openly laughs. "When you put it that way, I guess I'll have to settle for the third weekend in May, under the twinkling lights of the grand gardens, with the backdrop of the water in Charleston."

I know exactly the spot she's referring to—the grand gardens Brasher is creating on the new property. "You're serious?"

"Every time I pass the scale model in the lobby, I'm infatuated with the landscape. It's a huge risk to have an outdoor wedding, and my mom will probably have a coronary. I went to our event planner and talked through the idea. She assured me of all the options in place for weather problems. That was all the convincing it took. They are saving the date for me to get your approval."

"Were you trying to piss me off by baiting me with the Christmas season?"

"I prefer to think of it as toying with you."

"I think your ass is going to be black and blue for a different reason tomorrow."

"Before you get grumpy, let me tell you more good news. The costs aren't bad considering my position with the organization."

"Cost wouldn't be a problem anyway. Between your dad and me, it's covered."

Her eyes glimmer bright as she kisses me quickly. "We have a date and a location. I'll have easy access to the event coordinator here. Looks like you're getting your wedding."

"The wedding isn't the issue; it's the wife I'm waiting for."

Her gaze goes over my shoulder, and she waves to someone. A few seconds later, a waiter appears, handing us two flutes of champagne. He dips his chin, offering us his congratulations before hustling back to the bar.

"What should we toast first?" she asks, raising her glass.

"Us. Being here. Missing you for so long and you knowing how to make everything right in my world."

"I like that." She clinks, taking a sip. "Now, we have one more thing to discuss."

"What's that?"

"You wouldn't happen to know why my parents have decided to turn my old bedroom into a nursery, would you?"

"No."

She quirks an eyebrow, not buying my answer. "No, you don't know, or no, you're not going to tell me?"

"I'm not going to tell you. I'm going to show you."

Realization dawns on her, and she head-plants into my chest. Pretty soon, she's vibrating with laughter. The sweet sound fills the air, and I immediately think that Edward's idea may not be so bad.

Chapter 33
Darby

Something is wrong... very, very wrong. I clench and unclench my hands to try and stop the trembling. My mind is buzzing, and my heart is knocking against my ribcage.

Someone should have called me by now. Instead, all of my calls are going straight to voicemail and texts unanswered. Even Lynda and Ray aren't responding.

Runner picks up on my anxiety, circling my legs a few times before sitting at my feet with his own miserable face.

"I don't know anything, boy. Everyone is ignoring me, which means this is bad," I tell him with a quick head pat.

In the six weeks since Pierce visited, things in Charleston have heated up between him and Connie. She didn't react well when she found out he flew out here, realizing her attempt to ruin his weekend was foiled. That was only the beginning. My mom and Jill were ecstatic about my wedding plans and didn't hide their excitement. It didn't take long for word to spread, and our guest list was growing by the day.

Connie didn't take this news well either, sharing her feelings with anyone who would listen, including pushing her opinions and disgust onto Maya and Cole. Pierce said they started to retreat into shells, and he was pissed and doing everything in his power to keep the air clear and the mood light. According to him, they responded well during their weeks with him but reverted once they went back to Connie's.

We agreed he needed to stick around for the holidays and be accessible at all times. This meant we didn't get to have any kind of Christmas or New Year's celebration, which made him downright savage.

His hatred for Connie was approaching nuclear levels.

Due to my grueling schedule, my parents and Evin flew out to spend a few days before Christmas, and Stephanie and the crew still came for New Years. I missed Pierce fiercely but tried to keep my spirits up. He didn't need my misery piled on top of his worries.

He stuck to his guns, making plans for Christmas, which included multiple family visits, parties, drop-ins, and a full Kendrick-Graham combined celebration.

This set Connie on a rampage. She wants more than blood; she's going after his heart. Her plan is to take away his kids.

Today is the day Pierce had to go before a judge and listen to her tear him apart and argue for full custody. She also wanted financial support to cover this, including more absurd demands.

None of us are surprised about her quest to suck money because that's never stopped. But the mention of him taking full custody rocked through the Kendrick family. John wasn't concerned with her plight, explaining Pierce had a better chance of being granted full custody in any court. Connie's seven months of craziness was about to be exposed to a judge.

Even with John's reassurances, all of them are still on edge. Pierce's blasé indifference is an act. As hard as I try, he won't reveal where his headspace is.

I check my phone again, noting it's now six-thirty in Charleston. At this point, I'm beyond restless.

The phone rings, and I jump five feet off the ground at the shrill sound. My heart plummets at the caller. "We still have nothing," I tell Stephanie.

"It's been too damn long."

"I know that! I'm going insane over here. What the hell did that looney-toon bitch do now?"

"You have nothing?"

"Not a fucking thing. My entire family has ghosted. The only thing I know is that the city of Charleston is not under attack, on fire, or broken off into the ocean. I've checked the internet for any kind of news that would explain why no one is communicating with me."

"I'm going to make some calls. Sit tight. Maybe I can get some intel from my contacts."

"There is no sitting tight. My nerves are shot. Let me know if you get anything."

"On it." She hangs up, and I take the chance of dialing my brother for the tenth time.

"Hold on," he cuts me off. I open my mouth to scream, but it dies in my throat when the raging roar pierces in his background, followed by the sound of shattering glass.

I know that rage, that roar, and the agonizing source of its pain. My blood turns to ice, sending a bone-chilling pain all the way to my toes. It takes a minute for my brain to kick in, but when it does, I'm on the move. It doesn't matter what's happened. Pierce needs me.

"Darby?" The grave and strained voice of my brother sends another round of pain. The twin bond hits me hard.

"Evin, what has happened?"

"We're trying to piece it all together. Why don't I call you back?"

"If you think I'm going to let you keep this from me, you're fucking insane. Tell me."

"Long story short, Maya and Cole are missing."

I stumble, falling into the wall, while a sharp pain slices my chest. "W-w-hat?"

"They were scheduled to take the bus to Connie's parents' house after school. Neither child ever got to their house. We have confirmed they were on the bus and think, since Maya gets dropped first, she waited for Cole."

"Then what?"

"The police have mentioned them running away."

"The police? Why hasn't anyone called me?"

"Calm down, Darby. We're all holding on the best we can. There isn't much you can do."

"I'm still a part of this family! Just because I'm not there doesn't mean I'm helpless! Pierce is my fiancé!" My shouts bounce off the walls, and Runner barks at my distress.

"You don't understand. This isn't about you. All of us are trying to keep Pierce from going to jail."

"Oh my God... Pierce..." The image of his broken expression fills my head. "What happened in that room today?"

"That's the least of our worries right now. We have to figure out why Maya and Cole would disappear."

"Have they tried tracking Maya's phone?"

"Wouldn't do any good. She left it at home today."

"Is that where you are now?"

"Yes, but not for long. I'm headed out to search as soon as the police finish talking."

"Evin," the crack in my voice burns down my throat, "they get off the bus at four-thirty. That's hours ago. It's dark and cold."

"We know this."

"I'm coming. I'll be on the next flight and let you know when to pick me up at the airport. If you can't, I'll get a cab. Do not tell Pierce you spoke to me. He has bigger things to worry about, and if he knows I'm on a plane, he may have a heart attack."

"You don't want me to tell him you're coming?"

"No, he'll drive himself mad. If he calls, I'll tell him, but until then, let him concentrate. I've got to go."

I hang up and dive into action. An hour later, Runner and I are pulling up to Renee's house. Renee is the Brasher event planner, and over the last few weeks, we've become close while working on the details of my wedding.

"This means the world to me." I unload Runner and haul his things into the house, grateful she has a fenced yard. He immediately starts exploring.

"Anything, Darby. We'll be fine, promise," she assures me with a sympathetic smile.

I give her a quick hug and avoid chasing after Runner for fear of breaking down in tears.

Once back on the road, I call Stephanie and explain what's happening. She takes the news calmly. Too calmly. A nerve twitches in my neck.

"Stephanie, what's going on?"

"How far are you from the airport?"

"Twenty minutes."

"Call me when you're through security and safely seated. I'm not sharing this shit while you're driving."

There's no time to argue because the line goes dead. By the time I'm through security, my heart is racing so fast I'm a quivering mess.

The first thing I do is send Pierce a text with a simple I love you. Then I call her back.

"First of all, you need to know I've spoken to Annie, and I'm on my way, too."

"Oh, God, did something happen?"

"No news on the kids. They're scouring the city—bus stations, schools, friends, all family homes, etc. Someone is at every house in case they show up, and the police have units searching as well. I'll help with the search, but mainly, I'm coming as your best friend and your lawyer."

"Why?"

"I hesitate to tell you this because my priority is your mindset, including your mental and emotional stability. But as your best friend, it needs to come from me. I thought about contacting John directly, but he's bound by privilege. After a little digging, I found someone that would talk. Today was a verbal bloodbath. Connie's goal was to crucify Pierce, and she almost succeeded."

"What did she do?" The possibilities are endless with her.

"Constance Webber modeled herself as the emotionally abused victim and painted a very unfavorable picture of the Pierce Kendrick from thirteen years ago. She went through all her woes, getting pregnant and him refusing to acknowledge her as a fixture in his life, his refusal to live under the same roof, to try and make their family work... You can guess all the bullshit she spewed."

"Didn't he get to defend himself? While some of that may be technically true, there is so much background to his decisions. He lived next door until both kids were in school then worked his ass off for two years to build them a home. He's more than financially responsible, and he's an exemplary father."

"Oh, yeah, he had his say, and my source says he executed his explanations and argument well. Then, Connie went after you and he lost his mind."

I drop my head and curl into a ball, trying to shield myself from anyone who may be near. "Tell me the rest."

She pauses too long. "It's okay," I assure her.

"She exaggerated her role in his life of being a trusted confidant while falling in love with him. It sounds like a well-orchestrated effort, tears, sniffles, outbursts, shaking like a leaf—all the elements of a woman devastated. She claims to be in therapy for emotional and psychological depression because of his treatment of her."

"Is that even a real diagnosis?"

"Who knows?"

"Did the judge buy this? Surely, he's an expert on emotional manipulation in his profession."

"She brought up you leaving, blaming you for his recreational drug use and excessive drinking. Connie used you as her bargaining chip, claiming that him marrying you was dangerous and detrimental to the kids. Her lawyer thinks he has found the hole to make you responsible for Pierce losing custody of his children. Not to mention, she publicly blasted him by claiming he never wanted the kids in the first place.

"He went back at her with the pregnancies being results of drunken hook-ups and her tampering with the condoms."

"Oh fuck, oh fuck, oh fuck..." I chant until my chest boils from holding my anger inside.

"You promised to hold it together."

"I'm together, but I knew this was going to happen."

"Darby! Now is not the time for self-righteousness contemplation. That man is drowning in pain, and he's still trying to protect you from it. You can't honestly be thinking of your fucking reservations about your relationship."

"Yes, I am! But not in the way you're implying. I am thinking about my reservations and how he crushed them. He is still trying to protect me, which stops tonight. He's done fighting that bitch behind my back. Pierce may be strong, and fierce, and possibly on the edge of insanity right now, but he's still out of his league. There is only one way to fight a woman scorned, and that's with another woman scorned."

"I'm glad to hear the fiery spirit, and that woman definitely deserves an ass-kicking. Try to keep that adrenaline pumping until you get here because you may need it."

"That won't be a problem."

"There's something else you need to know, and it's the reason everyone is crowding Pierce to keep him from going to jail. The police searched Connie's house for any signs of the kids and found the notes with her strategy. It read like a screenplay, equipped with highlights of when to bring on the tears, the cries, the screams. Lower your voice, raise your voice... when to look at the judge for sympathy... It was like she was preparing for the role of a lifetime. And, Darby, when I say it was detailed, it was precise."

"You can stop now." I grouse, my heart cracking for a new reason. She doesn't have to verbalize it. I know. Pierce is known for a temper, but he'd only get violent if his family or I were threatened.

And that's what's happened. Connie set it up for Maya to find and read those notes. Instead of Maya retaliating by lashing out at her dad, she took Cole and ran away.

My flight doesn't leave for another hour, and with the layover, it's going to take too long. "Stephanie, we need to make miracles happen."

"I figured we did. Have any ideas?"

I've made quite a reputation for my business and myself over the last five months, working my ass off along the way. "It's time to pull some favors and take advantage of my position," I tell her, already on my feet and headed out of the commercial terminal.

Chapter 34

Pierce

I stare at my phone on the counter, willing it to ring with some kind of news. Instead, it lies there like a ticking time bomb, taunting me into further desperation. The three people I love most in this world are out there somewhere, and I have no idea where.

Evin admitted he spoke to Darby, and she is coming. Only, he told me after her phone was shut off and she was somewhere in the sky. Annie looked into possible flights she'd be on, and the options had her going anywhere from LA, Chicago, Dallas, or Nashville before getting here. Darby acted on impulse, boarded a plane to get home and get back to me. Her last communication with Evin by text was to either be by my side or searching for Maya and Cole. She didn't give him her arrival time either.

I should have called her the second this nightmare began. It should have come from me what was happening. Instead, I was too preoccupied, trying to find the kids and manage the situation while simultaneously guarding Darby against the horrors of the day. She has no idea what she is walking into.

We were with the judge when Connie got the call from her parents that the kids never arrived after school. The fear on her face sent an evil slither throughout me immediately. Snatched, kidnapped, injured... all of those were a possibility. It never occurred to me they would run away until the pieces came together, and witnesses told the police Maya and Cole walked away from that bus stop together, perfectly healthy, and went in the direction of town. What happened after that is unknown.

We've searched everywhere, and as far as I know, everyone we know is on the lookout. Miller and Evin haven't let me out of their sight, and thankfully, they were close when the police shared what they found at Connie's. One look at her was all it took for me to know she'd planted that for Maya to read. Unable to take the heat, she flung herself at me, dramatically apologizing over and over, sobbing real tears. Her parents stood by like zombies, unable to believe Connie would do something that malicious.

Miller and an officer removed her from me before I had the chance to physically react.

A strong hand grips my shoulder, and Evin jars me from my thoughts. "She'll be here soon."

"You heard from her?" I lunge for my phone.

"Not exactly. It's the twin thing."

"Fuck." I scrub my hand across my forehead. "Wish you had something more than DNA telepathy."

"Dad messaged. He took the golf cart out and did another round on the property. Still nothing, but he's covering his ground."

"It's three in the morning."

"He and Mom are restless. They want to feel like they're helping."

"Appreciate it. I'm about ready to hit the streets again, regardless of what the police advised."

A series of short, shrill beeps come from the code on the front door. My heart picks up speed, and Miller leaps to his feet, all of us sharing a look filled with hope it's the kids.

The door swings open, and the sight of Darby standing there slams into me with such force I'm momentarily struck immobile. She treads to me cautiously, holding my eyes captive, telling me a story without a word. She knows... She knows everything.

When she's less than a foot away, I drop to my knees, yanking her to me. Her hands flatten on my scalp, and she caresses softly. "Guys, we need a moment."

"You get your minutes, and then your ass is going to answer to me. Don't you ever pull a stunt like this again," Evin growls.

"Why don't you tone down your overinflated testosterone and come with me. I'll explain everything." Stephanie's voice filters into the room, but I can't pull my head from Darby's clutches.

The room clears, and Darby sinks down, laying her forehead to mine. "Any news?"

"Nothing."

"We'll find them."

"You know she caused this."

"I know."

I run kisses across her lips, inhaling sharply to fill my senses with her scent. "How do I make this better?"

"We will make it better. You're not alone in this anymore. We'll deal with her after we find Maya and Cole."

"I'll deal with her."

"You don't understand. No more fighting this battle without me by your side. Constance Webber stole my happiness once. She's not going to do it again. And I'm not going to let her ruin the lives of those beautiful children. Get it through your stubborn head; I'm not fragile. Whatever the fall-out of this is, we'll deal together. As a family."

It's all I can do to remain upright on my knees. Her eyes are clear. No clouds of hesitation, no panic, no distress. They are bright, alert, and full of love. The hint of betrayal she always tried to hide is gone. I was prepared to spend the rest of my life working that betrayal out of her system, but she did it on her own. She's also communicating she knows what the future holds. I'm not going to let this happen ever again. I want my kids full time, and she's prepared to take that on—to raise my children in a house of love, even though they are the result of the darkest years of her life.

"Pierce, let's go find them. Then we can process what happens next."

I nod, gripping her tighter, unwilling to let her go. "Not knowing where you were these last few hours has been torture. I should have called you, filled you in, but don't do that to me again."

"Don't do it to any of us," Evin booms, still irritated, stomping back into the room.

I help her to her feet and stand, feeling the exhaustion in my bones.

"Quick version, to catch Pierce up. Once I remembered the Brasher private jet, things went into overdrive. I barely had time to coordinate my arrival with Stephanie's. We knew everyone was busy here, and I didn't want to distract from the important issues. What's done is done, and here I am. Let's move on."

"Unless you have a superpower, we're at a standstill. The police are searching, but our efforts of driving up and down the streets have been useless."

"Let's go to the shed."

"I've checked the shed personally. Mom and Dad have been through the house, their basement, the stables, and Dad is currently patrolling in the golf cart. If you want, he'll go to the shed," Evin responds.

"Call him and Mom and tell them to shut down for the night and pretend to go to bed. If Maya and Cole are there, they need to feel like it's a safe place."

"Why are you convinced they are there?" I wonder. "They've never been in the shed. The times we've spent at your parents' were at the stables and the main house."

"I'm not convinced, but it's a hunch. Just go with it."

Miller passes us, dangling his keys. "Let's roll. Better than sitting here fucking watching the clock."

"I'll stay behind," Stephanie offers.

We pile into Miller's truck, and on the way to the Graham's, Darby explains the theory Stephanie and she worked through. Actually, it's more like Stephanie beat down doors until she got a hold of a detective friend that works with runaways. Maya and Cole aren't runaways. They are confused, young children. Maya is twelve now and most likely knows enough about the biology of how babies are made. If she's heard Connie ranting and read the papers, she's probably figured out that she and Cole weren't planned.

The fiery burning lead in my stomach scorches hotter, thinking about the way Connie unashamedly performed today. If Maya overheard any of that, there's no telling where her mind is. I have a feeling this is what a detective will be telling us tomorrow morning when he shows.

Annie and Edward's house is dark when we drive around the far side of the property.

"You two wait here," Darby tells our brothers, taking my hand and leading me quietly across the yard.

"Let me go in first," she whispers, using the hidden key.

"I'm with you."

"Then hang back a few steps. You're a very scary shadow."

She creeps inside, moving through the rooms, expertly maneuvering around the furniture. At the entrance to the bedroom, she stops, stands, and in the darkness, I can make out the flash of her white teeth as she grins.

I join her to find two shapes under the covers. My arm jets around her waist while the other braces on the doorframe as everything seeps out of my body. I send a silent prayer to God.

"May I?" Darby mutters softly.

All I can do is nod, unable to look away. She sidles up to the bed and lays a hand on the small form who jumps. "It's Darby."

"Darby?" Maya's little voice is skeptical. "You're here?"

"Yes, sweet girl. I have your dad with me. Can I sit down?"

Maya scoots, and Darby lowers herself. "Can I turn on the light?"

There's a rustling of movement before the room is bathed in dim light. Cole pops up his face, darting his eyes around, and when he spots Darby, he launches across the bed. "Darby!"

Maya knifes up, joining him in her arms, and I can't stand back anymore. I step forward, covering all of them with my body and arms.

"Daddy, we're sorry. We didn't mean to ruin your life!" Maya cries, and fuck me if I can't respond over the stinging in my throat.

"Oh, Maya, you are so, so wrong. You didn't ruin your dad's life. You two are everything to him," Darby soothes.

"That's not true. It's because of us he didn't marry you and have your own children," she continues.

My loathing of Connie heightens to impossible notches. "Maya, that's not true."

"Can y'all look at me?" Darby asks gently.

They give her a little space, and she glances at me briefly before cupping both their cheeks. "I am marrying your dad." She sucks in a deep breath in warning of what's coming. "And your dad and I did have our own child. He didn't make it. You are way too young to understand the details, but the important thing is that you know you had nothing to do with it."

Maya's face goes pale because she understands completely.

"We're in a lot of trouble, aren't we?" Cole's blue eyes are wide and scared.

"You scared the shit out of everyone. What were you thinking?" I control the tremor in my voice.

"It's my fault. I convinced him to come with me. It wasn't the plan to run away."

"You weren't running away?"

"Not really. I just wanted to get away, and I didn't think it through. Then I got scared. We didn't have anywhere else to go. We got here, and I decided to find Mrs. Annie in the morning. I don't know how else to explain it."

"Why don't you try?"

"How about we message Miller and spread the word we've found them and they're fine. Then we need to let Connie know."

At the mention of Connie, Maya's face goes stark white. Cole slides a few inches closer to Darby. "Maya, we know what's been happening at your mom's. She's not taking you away from me," I try to assure her.

Their shoulders slump, relief extending across their faces. Boots pound up the stairs and through the space, Miller and Evin rushing in.

"Thank God," they clip.

"Get Annie and Edward, and let Mom and Dad know we're going home." I take another look at Maya and Cole, dislodge myself from our huddle, and leave to make the call to Connie.

Pierced Hearts

Chapter 35
Darby

All eyes are on me as I descend the stairs with Jill. Maya and Cole are asleep, both of them seemingly unscathed after the events of the day. Pierce stands across the room, as far away as possible from where Connie sits with her parents. He holds his hand out to me, and I signal to give me a second. The room is uncomfortably silent, the tension thick. My parents went home, but Evin refused to leave while Connie was still here. Even with the traumatic events of what happened, his focus is on me.

I go to the kitchen, open a bottle of wine, and pour three generous glasses, taking two to Jill and Stephanie. It may only be daybreak, but we deserve this. I take Pierce's elbow and lead him to sit across from the Webbers.

Mr. And Mrs. Webber are flanked on each side of Connie, slumped in exhaustion and fatigued. Their loyalty to Connie is being tested since they learned her quest for revenge. Apparently, once the truth came out, they saw a different side to their daughter. It was obvious they were terrified over the children missing, but they were even more upset when Maya told her version of what she had witnessed, overheard, and read with her mother's attempt to take them away from Pierce.

Connie stares straight ahead, avoiding me. Her eyes are hollow, bloodshot, and loaded with grief. There actually are signs of guilt over her actions. Or it could be a mask to cover the humiliation of her children admitting to the officer involved, and a room full of people, they wanted to stay with Pierce indefinitely.

It could also be that they requested me to join Jill in getting them ready for bed. I tried to decline until Pierce shot me the most gorgeous look of appreciation and gratitude. Knowing her children chose me over her had to sting.

I didn't know the Webbers well all those years ago, but I'd run into them a few times. They, like everyone, thought I'd left town to nurse a broken heart, so they assumed Connie's pregnancy was the result of Pierce moving on to better things in life.

It is time to set the story straight. That is why I requested to speak to Connie. Pierce wanted her out of his house, Evin forbid me being alone with her, and Stephanie advised witnesses so she couldn't twist my words later. I thought it was overkill to have the audience, but no one agreed.

Connie doesn't deserve my secrets, but I'll do anything to end this for Pierce. And he'd never deceive my trust by outing the truth. It has to be me.

"Contrary to popular belief, I didn't run off on Pierce. I had my reasons," I start, and Pierce's head whips to me at the same time a breath hitches behind us.

"Don't do this, Darby," Miller grunts sharply.

I shoot him a thankful glare before continuing. "In May, thirteen years ago, Pierce and I found out I was pregnant. It was a beautiful surprise."

I may be ready to spill, but Connie is getting the clean and basic version of my story.

"We were already planning to get married, so that was simple, and I was going to move in with him and Miller until we found our own place. August of that year, I lost our son. It was an ugly miscarriage that neither of us knew how to deal with." Stephanie's hand lands on my shoulder, and Pierce slips closer, his hand covering my lower abdomen. Connie's eyes heat at him touching me with tenderness. She never got this. Even when fully round and carrying the kids, he didn't show affection.

"I didn't react well and, for the sake of privacy, left town to seek counseling. Only a few people knew, and Pierce was not one of them. He tried to track me down, find me, pull me back from drowning in misery. But I didn't allow it. He turned to alcohol and marijuana to dull his own grief. Nothing about him was stable or predictable, and his own family couldn't help. We all know you saw this."

Connie squares her shoulders, slicing her eyes to each side before landing on mine. "What are you implying?"

"I'm not implying anything, only stating the facts. Miller, Jill, and Warren were trying their best but couldn't break through. I was selfish and dealing with my own heartache. I live with that regret every day, not thinking about what was happening to him."

"That's enough," Pierce grates out.

"No, I want to know what's Darby's getting at," Connie says.

"We're sorry to hear about your loss, but I agree with Connie. Why are you telling us this, and what does it have to do with anything?" Mrs. Webber eyes me wearily.

"Because, while I was working on myself, Pierce was wallowing in self-destruction, and his senses were impaired. Connie was by his side, matching him hit for hit and shot for shot." I lock eyes with Connie, speaking directly to her now, ignoring our audience. "You encouraged him to bury himself in that dark place, and then you mapped out a plan to take advantage of him."

"You have no idea what you're talking about. What happened between Pierce and me is none of your business."

"You're right; it's none of my business. The only reason I'm telling you this is because, sometime today or tomorrow, I'll be making a formal statement as a character witness on his behalf. You chose to bring me into your custody fight, painting me as the reason he should lose his children. I can't let that happen. After today, it may not be necessary, but I'm hoping the judge will see your bitter battle started as a honeytrap."

At the term honeytrap, Mr. Webber bolts to attention, his eyes swinging between Connie and me. "That's a very farfetched accusation. Not to mention, now is not the time to sling insults after what we've all been through today. We've accepted the fact that Pierce is making life changes and settling down, even if he chose you over the mother of his children," he sneers as if the thought alone is repulsive.

"What we went through today could have been avoided if Connie would let go of her vindictive jealousy and accept the only thing she will ever get from me is my love for our children. And, yes, the timing fucking sucks, but it's time you both stop living in denial and accept the truth," Pierce snaps at them. "I know you expected me to marry Connie and make a home with her, and I know you've always been disappointed in my decisions. But Connie and I didn't have a relationship."

"But you have children together!" Mrs. Webber looks appalled. "Certainly, you had some sort of relationship!"

"Connie, you want to step in here and explain this?" The already thick tension in the room grows heavier as Pierce gives Connie the chance to explain in her own words.

Every eye in the room is glued to her. She looks between her parents and slumps deeper. She knows she's been beat. Pierce is about to expose her charade to everyone. "Pierce and I never had a relationship, but I thought getting pregnant would change his mind."

I blow out the breath I'm holding, hearing the same behind me. A low growl rumbles from him, but my focus is on the Webbers. They are horrified.

Pierce's suspicions are finally confirmed. She carefully orchestrated getting pregnant to trap him.

"The one thing you can't deny or question is my dedication to Maya and Cole. You were kept in the dark, but Connie always knew the score. She did try to trap me by using our kids as emotional blackmail. Out of respect for you, I've never spoken harshly about your daughter, always taking responsibility for my actions. She has her version of how things happened with us, and she's made me out to be a villain. But now you've seen firsthand how she's been behaving. She tried to take my kids from me because I'm marrying another woman, for fuck's sake."

With each word, his voice goes colder and sharper, his anger blistering through to them. I take his hand and bring it to my lap, squeezing gently. This conversation took a different turn than I intended, but he needs to get this out in the open and set the Webbers straight.

"Darby is a beautiful, kind, hardworking woman who loves with all her heart. Maya and Cole felt safer going to hide out in her house today than they did coming to either of our families. They heard their mother saying vast lies as she rehearsed for a performance in front of a judge. They heard her *LIE*, time after time, about the woman I've been in love with most of my life. She smeared her name through the mud any chance she got. My twelve- and almost ten-year-old kids have been manipulated to the point of danger. I lost a child once, and it almost killed me. Today, I went through the fear of thinking I'd lost two more. She's not going to get away with that."

The reality comes crashing down on everyone with the pain radiating in his words. Tears spring to my eyes. I've never been a violent person, but right now, I'd like to leap across the living room and bitch slap Connie's face.

"It's time for you to leave." Miller walks to the door and opens it, making a sweeping motion with his arm. "My family has gone through hell and dealt with your bullshit for the last time."

All of the Webbers jerk in disbelief, not moving from their spots. Connie opens her mouth, then snaps it shut when Miller lasers in on her. I've seen that look, the fire of righteousness that blazes right before he loses his temper. It's the same look that seared me the night at Rosen's, and right now, it's flaming ten times hotter. I take a sip of my wine, lean into Pierce's side, and prepare for the verbal lashing about to explode.

"Miller," Jill chides without an ounce of sincerity.

"Pierce is a hell of a lot more gracious than I am. You heard me. Get your asses up and get out of my brother's house."

Mr. and Mrs. Webber rise, but Connie stays in her seat with an increasing guise of defiance.

Poor decision.

"Connie, the only good thing that came out of this shit storm is that I can finally stop biting my tongue when it comes to you. You're a bitch, a plain-out, cold-hearted, jealous bitch. We've pretended all these years for the sake of keeping the peace between you and Pierce. You've desperately thrown yourself at us, thinking you could worm yourself into our family. It was never going to happen. You convinced yourself with all your trying that Pierce was going to come around. It was never going to happen. You wanted the money, the house, Pierce parading you around like you were a precious to him. It. Was. Never. Going. To. Happen. Your rap sheet of immorality is a mile long. If it were me, I'd destroy you publicly, but my brother has a nicer disposition."

I swallow my giggle, but Evin openly chuckles. Connie's mom pales, her face going white before she finally tugs Connie to her feet and hustles her out. They are on the porch when Miller delivers his kill shot. "You're a pathetic excuse for a mother. I hope it haunts you for the rest of your life they asked Darby to be with them tonight while you were five feet away. My family is fucking lucky to have Darby Graham agree to be a part of Maya and Cole's life." He slams the door but not before I witness Connie's face crumble and her falling into her dad.

For a brief second, I feel sorry for her, knowing the feeling of your world shattering into a million pieces when there is no more hope. Then Pierce scoops me into his lap, and all pity vanishes.

"I think she got the hint long before you eviscerated her parenting, but that was an exceptional show," Stephanie praises him.

"Since I'm not going to work, I'm having a stiff drink and sleeping here." Miller goes to the bar.

"Pour one for me," Evin adds.

"I think you all should stay here," Pierce suggests.

"Maya and Cole would love that," I throw in.

"Y'all can have your slumber party, but I'm taking my bride home to sleep in our own bed. We'll come back this afternoon and do dinner. Darby, how long are you here?" Warren asks.

"I left in such a hurry; things are up in the air. I'll shoot off a few messages to check in later, but at least the next two days."

"Dinner it is then." Jill and he go out the back door.

"Pierce, I suggest you call John right away. It's not my area of expertise, but my legal intellect says this little sham is over. Maya's statement to the police is enough to tank Connie's credibility. I doubt Darby will need to give any kind of character statement about your mental stability during the time Connie got pregnant." Stephanie's lawyer mode is in full force as she sits next to us.

"I'll do it in a minute." He folds me into him. "Right now, I need to kiss my fiancée."

I giggle to the groans around us when his mouth meets mine.

•—•—•—•—•

My eyes open to the bright light, but my line of vision is Pierce's face. The dark circles and deep lines are proof he's struggling.

I skim my fingertips along his forehead, over his eyebrow, and into his hairline, massaging softly. "It's over, baby. They're safe."

"Because of you."

"I still don't know why I had a hunch they were at the shed. It struck me on the way here from the airport that Cole thought it was cool we had a hidden key."

"I've only ever felt that helpless twice in my life. Both times, the outcome was crippling. You changed that today."

My heart leaps to my throat and breaks a little. He's thinking of losing our baby and my leaving. "You would have found them. Maya already admitted her choice to go to my parents in the morning. She was scared."

"Ten hours, Darby. They were missing for ten hours."

"I know."

"And you were missing for five of those."

"Only because I was on my way to you."

"You dropped everything and came."

"Of course, I did. You needed me."

"I needed you," he repeats. His troubled eyes glaze over, and I can tell he's having a hard time. After the events of the day, he could be reflecting on anything. I'm not prepared when he rumbles, "All those years ago, you needed me, and I let you down. I should have chased you, made you talk to me, and smothered you with the love I had bleeding through my veins. You were four fucking hours away. Instead, I fucked up and let that woman into my life. Today, you stepped in and gave me something I can never repay you for."

"You don't need to repay me. We're a team," I whisper tenderly.

"My kids are upstairs, safe, and under my roof until this thing with Connie levels out. I should be content, relieved, even happy, but all I can think about is how I lied to you."

"What did you lie about?"

"I've been working hard to convince you we can put the past behind us, but it's not possible for me. I'm never going to forgive myself for being the arrogant, cocky, untouchable boy who let you go. You came face-to-face last night with a woman who made your life hell, all because of me. I didn't shield you from her."

"I'm not scared of Connie Webber; therefore, no one needs to shield me from her. As for the past, you can't take all the responsibility on yourself. I played a huge part in that."

"You were hurting."

"I was, and you know what came out of it? Tons of therapy. Maya and Cole's disappearance triggered how you felt when we suffered our loss. You're going through some personal reflection now, but let it go."

"How?"

"I have a suggestion, but it's going to sound a bit unconventional."

"I'm listening."

"If I didn't leave, you wouldn't have Maya and Cole. Can you imagine your life without them?"

"No, but it's no consolation on my regrets and what I missed out on with you, with us."

I rack my brain with how to get through to him, and my solution is going to put me in the hotseat, but it's not like I can avoid this subject much longer. "Do you want more children with me, Pierce?"

"Almost as much as I want us married and you here on a daily basis." He doesn't hesitate.

"How many?"

"As many as you'll give me."

"Realistically, how many?"

"I'd like four but could be convinced to stop at three." His features soften, a little of his sadness easing away. He's catching on.

"Good Lord, are you serious?"

"I could also be convinced to keep going past four."

His expression shows a hint of humor, but otherwise, he's serious. I swallow hard, knowing I'm signing an invisible contract that is probably going to bite me in the ass.

"If it's possible, I'll give you three. We'll get back what we lost. Having babies, living in pandemonium because the children will outnumber us, fighting off our families who will undoubtedly intrude every chance they get. Our lives will be chaotic and crazy, and we'll never retire because we'll have five college tuitions looming over our heads. Do you think that could help you move on from these feelings of regret?"

"Raise that number to four, and I'll find a way to forgive myself." He grins smugly.

"Where the hell are we going to fit six children?"

"That's my area of expertise. You won't need to worry about that."

I let out a *hmpf*, knowing he would find a way to move mountains if I agree to give him what he wants. "We will start with one." I give a little.

"Today."

"Today, what?"

"We will start working on that first one today."

"Nope! I draw the line at that. I've dreamed about my wedding to you for far too long to miss the festivities. Endless champagne and martinis, dancing until dawn, spa treatments, and girl's trips to shop for dresses. My menu includes an ice sculpture that holds a full oyster bar and seared ahi tuna that melts in your mouth. I have my eye on a wedding dress that will not work with a baby bulge. A shotgun wedding would not be conducive to any of my plans."

As I speak, his eyes grow wider and wider in shock. He has no idea how much time I've spent with Renee, going over the finest details. "You found a dress?" is the only thing he says.

"I think so."

"And it won't work with a bulge, so does that mean it's tight?"

"It's fitted, not tight. Tight would indicate tacky."

"How fitted?"

"You'll have to wait and find out."

"If I'm hearing you right, I'm going to get a night with endless amounts of you drinking champagne, eating oysters, and dancing around in a tight dress that molds to your curves, ass, and tits. All in exchange for waiting to try and have a baby?"

Like I said, I knew this would bite me in the ass. "Yep."

"You drive a hard bargain."

"Don't forget, you'll get your wife, too." I throw his words back at him from the night by the fire in Aspen.

"I'll get my wife." He seems to process this, sucking his bottom lip between his teeth, the wheels in his head spinning. "How long until the wedding?"

"Not long at all. Just a few months."

"Get yourself sorted, see your doctors, get off the pill, purge your system, or whatever it takes to be ready, and I'll agree to give you until May eighteenth."

"Why don't we see how things go living together, get through the wedding, and—"

"You're backtracking," he growls.

I hold my breath, but it's useless. A small peep escapes right before my outburst of giggles. Pierce rolls on top of me, bracing his elbows by my neck to hold some of his weight. My hands still frame his face, and I pull him down for a quick kiss.

"Tonight, when everyone is gone, and once Maya and Cole are asleep, I'm going to show you what teasing feels like."

"You make it too fun."

"How do you do it? How can you take me from the darkest thoughts and turn it into something beautiful?"

"We do it for each other. You're no longer alone in this life, and you're not responsible for always being the hero."

"May eighteenth, Darby. You'll be mine forever, and we're going to start the life we were meant to have."

"May eighteenth," I agree.

His lips cross mine as a little voice calls through the door, "Dad? I heard laughing. Are you up?" Cole knocks.

"Shit," Piece utters. "Yeah, buddy. Give me a second." He rolls off, grabbing his pajama pants from the chair in the corner. "I can't believe I'm being cockblocked by my nine-year-old."

I sit up and straighten my pajamas, retying my hair on top of my head. "You may want to think about that as you start your mission to add four more to the mix," I taunt.

He flashes me an evil look. "I'm upping it to five."

My jaw drops as he unlocks the door, Cole and Maya stumbling in sleepily. They drop at the end of the bed, fanning out. "We're here for our punishment," Cole draws out dramatically. "Sock it to us. No electronics, clean the house, take away our lives... We're ready for it."

Pierce's eyes fly to mine, and I burst into laughter again. "I'm sorry. I can't help it. He's too damn cute."

His little face lights at the compliment. Maya giggles with me.

"We're not talking about punishment today, but I'd suggest you both be on your best behavior," Pierce grumbles.

They nod.

"Is anyone else up?" I ask Maya.

"Uncle Miller and Evin are on the sofas snoring, but I think Stephanie is in the shower."

"I have an idea if your dad agrees and can make it happen."

He comes to sit next to me. "I usually make things happen."

"Since everyone is off work and out of school today, and while Stephanie is here, can we take a quick look at the progress of the Brasher Gardens?"

It's a good thing I'm sitting because the expression that takes over his face would knock me off my feet. He brings my hand to his mouth and kisses my ring. The truth is, I do want to see the progress and get a visual of the layout, but this is for Maya and Cole. They need to be included as much as possible. They have a lot to work through when I leave, but today needs to be filled with love and support.

309

"That's not a problem. I need to make a few calls before we leave." He's referring to touching base with John and whether I need to go talk to him. "You two go get showered and ready."

They scramble away, Pierce's gaze staying on them until they're around the corner. He hefts me out of the bed, pressing me close. He doesn't speak, but his body and the racing of his heart say it all.

Chapter 36

Pierce

The engines of the jet cut off as the door opens, and a man in uniform appears with Runner on a leash. The dog bounds down the stairs, and when he spots me, the man's arm jerks with the pull of the dog's excitement.

I clap loudly, flicking a wave, and the man releases the leash so the dog can race to me. Like the times I've watched him with Darby, Runner leaps with the force to rock me back on my heels. His energy is ratcheted up, even for him, and I wonder if he knows he's finally home.

Man after man files off the jet, ten in total. Jealousy stirs in my gut, knowing Darby has been on a cross-country flight with all these men. She can live in denial all she wants, but I call bullshit. I've witnessed the attention she gets. Every male in her presence is immediately taken with her. Married, gay, young, old—it doesn't matter—she's a magnet and totally oblivious. It's one of the millions of reasons I wanted that ring on her finger. Even when the band is added, I'll still be a jealous fucker.

To everyone's surprise and elation, Brasher on Atlantic was completed on schedule. But due to complications out of my control, Darby had to stay in Aspen for a few extra weeks. Each of those days stung like hell as I waited for her to finish her projects. My mood was shit, and I threatened more than once to fly out and drag her back myself. As a consolation, she agreed to transport her vehicle and most of her things and fly on the jet for the next trip. Five days on the road, driving her back, wasn't a problem with me, but this was simpler.

She steps into view, and I swear my world shifts with the impact of what is finally happening. The instant her foot hits the pavement, I'm moving. A few of the men wave, shouting their hellos, but I'm too focused to respond with more than a chin dip. Her face lights up bright, and behind her sunglasses, I can feel her eyes glowing into my skin. There are no words before my mouth lands on hers, and I'm lifting her off the ground. She giggles down my throat as I curl my tongue around hers, covering every inch of her mouth, and grumble in appreciation at the taste of chocolate and cinnamon.

"Hey," she whispers breathlessly against my lips.

"Why does it feel like I spend most of my life waiting for you?"

"I'm here now."

"Let's go home."

"Home." She repeats the word in a hushed sigh. I take her hand and walk us to the back of the plane, where the flight attendants unload bags. This time, I do speak to the few people I recognize, and Darby introduces me to those I haven't met. This crew is the first round to arrive for the grand opening event scheduled in a few days. Several full-size SUVs pull up, ready to transport them to the hotel. She confirms we will be at the dinner scheduled for tomorrow night while I load her bags and Runner into the truck.

"What did you work out with Connie?"

I frown at the mention of her name. "I didn't work out anything. I told her to have the kids at the house on Saturday morning by nine. If she's even a minute late, we're going back to court."

"They'll be at the ribbon-cutting ceremony?"

"Yes, and if she does anything to screw it up, she's fucked."

Stephanie was right; Connie held no credibility after what happened. The judge granted me seventy-five percent custody, and Connie lost all financial support. If I have any suspicions of her manipulating the kids or backhanded activity while they are with her, she's losing them for good. We tried to keep what happened back in January quiet, but it was impossible. Connie received most of the backlash. On top of losing her kids, she ruined her reputation and found herself dropped from all social circuits. Plus, her lavish lifestyle came to an end.

Connie's scheme was eventually fully exposed for what it was all those years ago and leading up to trying to destroy my relationship with Darby. She came after me with intentions of getting pregnant and took measures to help that along. All our families, including hers, know the truth, except for the part of how Cole was conceived. That is a secret that will never be disclosed.

I didn't give a fuck. What I did care about was the kids' transition, but Cole and Maya had no problems. I worried how Darby would adjust, moving into a house that was insta-family, but she was dead set this is what she wanted. And now we'd have a whole new set of grandparents to step in when needed.

"We're going to make a detour. If you need to make any calls or texts, I suggest you use this time to do it."

"What detour?"

"I have something for you."

"You mean our families aren't already waiting to swarm us when we drive up?"

"Not unless they're aiming for a death wish. Today and tonight are mine. We made a compromise."

She lets out a laugh. When I glance over, she's turned in her seat, facing me with raised eyebrows. "Compromise? When did you learn to compromise?"

"I'm a very reasonable man."

"Liar."

"I'll amend. I'm a very reasonable man when people see things my way."

"That sounds more like it."

"Make your calls."

In the twenty minutes it takes us to get to our destination, she speaks to her parents and Evin, who didn't put up an argument about postponing Darby's homecoming once they knew my plans. My secret can't stay hidden for much longer, not with our families bursting to squeal. Especially Cole and Maya. That's why everyone agreed to give me this time.

That and I threatened to physically remove anyone that stepped foot on my property before tomorrow afternoon.

"What did you do exactly? Even my mom didn't give me a hard time. That's highly unusual." Darby drops her phone in her purse.

"I didn't do anything," I reply with my best innocent face.

She eyes me skeptically but is distracted when I pull up to the familiar brick building. "Why are we here?"

I don't answer, getting out and whistling for Runner to follow. He sniffs around while I go to help her out. She takes in the few changes from the outside. "New landscaping, fresh asphalt, a delivery bay," she assesses.

"I thought you might want to see what the new owner did."

"Okay, but we're the only people here."

I shrug, leading her by the elbow to the door, taking her finger in mine to punch in the code on the security pad. Her sharp intake of breath is all I need to know she recognizes the number sequence. It's the date I walked up to her in that gym years ago.

"We can change it to whatever you want, but it stuck with me," I whisper into her ear.

"You bought this building?"

"I have an investor."

"Why?"

"Open the door, baby. You'll see."

Her hand trembles in mine as she twists the handle and nudges it open. The smell of new construction assaults us. Paint, drywall, sawdust, grout, all of their smells mingle together in the newly renovated space.

"Oh my God," she gasps, now clutching my whole arm.

"Welcome home, beautiful."

"You bought me a bakery as a welcome home present?"

"No, I bought this as your wedding present then decided it wasn't nearly romantic enough. It'll have to do as a welcome gift."

She swivels in all directions, her eyes scanning rapidly, her lips parting in awe. Walls that once separated this building are open to make it one large workspace. The old bathroom that was on her side has been renovated for her personally. The other bathroom was enlarged to accommodate separate men and women's facilities. I took every conversation and observation Dad, Miller, Evin, and I had with Darby into consideration while in the construction phase. The walls are painted a warm blue-grey, and the white cabinetry and open shelving are topped with the grey-veined marble Darby once mentioned she had in Charlotte. The industrial appliances were supplied by Brasher and resemble what they have in their kitchens. The prep tables are larger, and the small sitting area she once had is twice its size to accommodate more people.

It's ready for her to move in and add her own special touches and decorations to make it hers. Runner scoots by, sniffing at the new tile, wandering the room. He finds the bed I placed in the back corner and plops down.

"I can't believe this," she marvels, eyes still sweeping around. "It's everything I've ever wanted."

"Believe it."

"But why?"

"Because DG Creations was technically established in Charleston, and you needed a place to reflect that."

"But I have a kitchen at the resort."

"You have a small space for limited quantities. This is where you'll spend the majority of your time. It's built for you to have staff and also serve as a training facility if needed."

Her nose scrunches in confusion, and she opens and closes her mouth a few times, still surveying. "Is Brasher your investor? This had to cost a fortune."

"Not exactly. Evin is the investor until I buy him out."

"Why is Evin involved?"

"It goes back to him and Stephanie brainstorming last summer. He knew about Brasher's resort expansion, knew Mr. Baldwin wanted to sell, and he saw an opportunity. After Stephanie witnessed you and I that morning on your porch, she saw the bigger picture that included me in your life. She worked the legal side of things and made this possible. When Evin shared with me, I purchased the building. I bought it for you."

"We weren't even together! There's no way you could have known what the future held for us."

I wrap my arms around her waist and hold her so she can't squirm away. It's my turn to cock my eyebrows with an amused grin. "We were together, and I knew exactly how things were going to work out."

She's not nearly as amused. "That's the craziest thing I've ever heard!"

"Depends on who you ask. I think it was brilliant."

"I work for Brasher Resorts."

"No, you work with Brasher Resorts. You've proved your worth to them a thousand times over. They're not going to do anything to jeopardize that partnership. But in the off chance you want out, this will always be yours. In the meantime, they're paying rent for you to keep creating masterpieces for their resort."

"They're paying for me to have my own space outside of their building?"

"Another perk Stephanie worked out."

"I can't believe this."

"I told you thirteen years ago I'd build you a bakery. Hopefully, it's up to standards."

"Pierce, I love it, but I think I'm in shock." One side of her lip quirks, and her eyes gleam the shade of copper. "You built me my bakery," she repeats, her voice husky and filled with emotion. "Guess this explains all the questions and unusual interest in my workspace over the last few months. I can't believe I didn't catch on."

I skim my mouth across hers, kissing the corner of her lips and walking her backward. "There's one more surprise."

"Is this where everyone jumps out cheering?"

"Fuck no, and in case they got any ideas, I changed the code on the lock so they can't get in."

My foot kicks open the door, and I spin her to the room. This is the only place where I added personal items.

She walks to her desk, zoning in on the frame I took the risk of putting there. It's at her and Evin's graduation. I'm holding her in the air, and we're smiling at the camera as our parents took endless pictures.

"I can't believe you still have this." She skims a fingertip along the glass.

"It's one of my favorite things in this room."

315

She raises her gaze to mine, and I know she's remembering that day and moment. "I love it all. It's perfect."

"It'll be perfect when you get done with it."

She nods, putting the frame back, and slowly strolls around, taking in the details. "Did you make this shelf?"

"Yes."

"Hmmm," she mutters, kicking off her heels. "And where'd you find these?" She motions to the articles and write-ups hanging.

"Annie got them to me, and I had them specially done."

"And all these other ones?" She waves to the other frames of her with family and friends placed on various surfaces.

"Some of them I took; some of them I found."

"Very thoughtful." She stops, this time eying the corner bench seat. "Is this custom, too?"

"Yeah." My answer comes out rough as she does something with her hands at her hips, and a scrap of pink tumbles down her legs. My cock springs to life, growing rock hard as I catch onto her game.

"Is it sturdy?" She props a foot on the bench, her dress riding up and exposing her inner thigh.

"Absolutely." I tear my shirt over my head, ready to tackle.

She flashes a coy grin, wrenching her hand behind her back. The unmistakable zing of her unzipping pounds in my ears. Her dress pools at her feet, and she breaks our stare to step over it.

I toe off my shoes and socks, rip off my shorts, and zero in on the curve of her ass as she continues her strut around the room in only a bra. My dick now screams for relief, all the blood in my body racing to my cock and balls. It's been a long time since he's felt the soft, silky heat of being inside Darby. My visit over spring break seems like a year ago with the way my body is reacting. She turns, running her hand over the back of her sofa.

"And what about this? Last time I knew, it was in storage in Charlotte, along with several items in this room. How'd it get here?"

"I went and got it all," I bite out, palming my dick through my boxers.

"You did all this for me?"

"I'd do anything for you."

Her eyes roam over my body, an appreciative shine forming when they meet mine. "You know it is a sofa sleeper?"

"I'm aware. I moved it in here for a reason."

With a flick of her finger, the front of the bra is unclasped and gone.

"Darby." Her name comes out gruff as my cock thickens, pulsing against my hand.

She comes to me, moving my hand and replacing it with hers. "You're a little wound up." She grips me tighter, rubbing her chest to mine.

"I'm about half a second from fucking you."

She leans up, nipping my lip and stroking down my shaft. "Are you finally learning the art of self-control?"

"Teasing me isn't a good idea. Hope you're ready," I grind out.

"I'm ready, dripping, hot, wet, whatever you want to imagine. I want it hard, fast, and wild, but I want it all night, so I should start by taking the edge off."

She lowers down, taking my boxers with her. Her tongue darts out, licking the crown, circling the rim, and running up and down the entire length before she sucks me in as far as she can. My hands fist through her hair, tugging and flexing as she works me with her mouth.

My eyes drop in time to see her angle her head and take me fully down her throat. A low animal growl rumbles from my chest. She hums, the vibration shooting to my balls, making them grow heavy.

Jesus, Pierce, don't fucking pump and dump.

I tense, holding back as long as I can until she glances up at me through hooded, glowing eyes. Her lips are wrapped around me, her head moving up and down, and her jaw is tight with the right amount of pressure as she swallows my dick with each bob. Her hand snakes up my thigh slowly and then clasps around my balls, rolling them between her fingers.

Dripping, hot, wet rolls through my brain. That's all it takes to shatter my discipline. Feral need scorches through my bloodstream, and my hands grip her scalp as I drive into her, fucking her mouth without reserve. She notices the change, scraping her nails against my sac and increasing her speed.

I've relied on the image of Darby sucking my dick to get me through countless nights. The years without her, I learned no one could give head in a way that could drive me insane.

This is proof. It's not the fact that I haven't had a release from anything other than my hand for over a month. It's the fact that Darby knows my body, knows how to work me, worship me, and bring me to the brink of madness by working her mouth around my cock like it was made for her.

I pump in and out, and she moans her approval, stroking, rolling, sucking, and opening wider so I can drive harder. Through my haze, I spot her free hand sliding down her torso and disappearing between her thighs.

Dripping, hot, wet... The hitch in her throat awakens the beast in me. I'm the one to take care of her, and that's happening now.

I tear my hands through her hair, wrap my hands around her biceps, and yank her high in the air. She smirks knowingly, hooks her ankles around my hips, and throws her head back when I impale her. I get us to the sofa, collapsing on top of her, and drive in harder.

"Every surface, every wall, every single inch of this space needs to have our mark on it," I ground out.

"I assumed as much." Her hips arc, bringing me so deeply, I know I've found her spot.

She writhes with the recognizable signs of struggle. She's holding back, waiting for me. I'm ready, right there with her, but I want more. With superhuman effort, I find the ounce of willpower left and slow my strokes. She whimpers at the change of pace, locking her ankles around my back. "Every time I slide inside you after being apart for so long, I'm a madman with no restraint. Today, I want more."

Her lips part, and the wild hunger in her eyes melts. I rise, gliding my lips over hers, kissing a path down the column of her throat and chest. Her nipples are hard, begging for attention. I run my cheeks and chin over one, using the bristle of my stubble to taunt her. My palm covers the other, rolling the stiff peak with my fingers, mimicking what she did with my balls. She arches her chest, silently begging for more, and when I close my mouth and suck, she grips my head, holding me in place.

I lick, nip, squeeze, and savor, worshipping her tits and leaving my mark. My tongue craves the taste of her, but there's no way I can pull of out her. I know my limits.

"Pierce, please," she whines desperately, bucking up.

I lean back, glancing over her naked body in front of me, and grin proudly. She's going to be pissed when she sees the purple and blue splotches, but I don't give a fuck. I spread her thighs so I can watch myself thrust in and out of her. She reaches behind her, gripping the arm of the couch, powering against me. Possession fires through my veins, and I increase my speed, ready to hear her scream.

"Do you have any idea how fucking sexy it is to see your pussy stretched around me?"

"Mmmmmm," she moans, lifting her ass in the air and ramming up.

I circle her swollen clit, tracing the nub with feather-light touches until Darby is writhing and panting. Her face is flushed, her eyes are wild, and her body strains as she meets my strokes.

"Come for me." I roll her clit with my thumb, and she flies apart, crying out. A gush of wet heat coats my dick, and my eyes dart between her face and her pussy. Once again, my mouth waters to taste her, feel her squirm against my face.

This thought annihilates my control, and I thrust harder. Her eyes lock with mine at the same time she clenches her muscles, closing around me. She grins smugly, releasing the couch and trailing her hands down to cup her tits. My cock thumps and throbs, swelling inside her.

"Give me another one," I demand.

She shakes her head defiantly, caressing her nipples, playing with herself.

My pace quickens, and I try to grind my way out of her clutch, but it's useless. She's holding me in.

"Darby," I growl, plunging until I hit so deep her chest curves.

The sound of our bodies slapping together fills the air, and her eyes begin to glaze. Shockwaves fire off, my balls tightening. This time, I know there's no stopping, no turning back.

"Baby, I need you with me."

"Yes! God, yes!" she answers with a stuttered cry.

I grind my teeth as sweat drips down my chest, my heart thundering against my ribcage. My thumb swipes back over her clit while I rock into her. She curls up, screaming so loud the walls echo. I follow, exploding inside her with such force it sends tremors down my spine. My cock throbs with each pulse jetting inside her body.

Darby's body spasms against mine, our hearts racing in sync. "It's fucking great to have you home," I tell her.

Chapter 37

Darby

"Any reason you're hovering?" I don't have to open my eyes to feel his body heat above me.

"You're burning. I should rub some suntan lotion on your back."

"I'm not falling for that again. You rubbed lotion on my back an hour ago, and I still have sand in private places."

"Let me carry you to the ocean, and we can rinse you off. Or, better yet, let's go shower."

"Don't you need downtime?

I roll to my side, raising my glasses, and almost swallow my tongue. Pierce looms over me, dripping wet, muscles rippling, his bulge outlined in his swim shorts, and he's glaring at me with raw hunger.

"Did you take a pill? The kind that has warnings about erections lasting more than six hours should contact a physician?"

He rocks back, clenching his fist with no hint of amusement. "I don't need a goddamned pill."

"There's no shame in it." I wink.

"I can fuck on demand when it comes to you."

"Oh, I know."

"I have a fucking job to do, and I'm not going to fail."

"We're on our honeymoon. Neither of us is supposed to be working," I throw back, enjoying the way his jaw sets and his eyes slit.

"Dammit, wife, I gave you the wedding. I fulfilled my end of the deal. Now, you have to fulfill yours."

I smile, reaching my left hand to the sky. Diamonds sparkle so brightly I drop my glasses. He's right. He gave me the wedding.

He gave me the most spectacular, outrageous, talked about wedding of the decade. Possibly the century. It had everything any bride could dream of. Brasher Resorts pulled out all the stops and created the perfect wonderland—dancing under the stars and twinkling lights, endless champagne, open bars with every martini ever made, anything and everything I could ever want.

It was beyond remarkable. Hundreds of people agreed.

Pierce takes my suspended hand and crouches next to me, bringing the diamonds to his lips. "What are you thinking?"

"I'm having flashbacks. Trying to figure out my favorite part of the wedding."

"You've been doing that a lot."

"There's a lot to reminisce over. I think I've narrowed it down."

"Why don't you share them with me while I'm balls deep inside you?" He tugs.

"We have this private house for a week, and you've barely let me outside in two days. Let me enjoy the Costa Rican sunshine for a while."

He glances up at the house, scans the property, and dips his chin. My jaw drops when he tears his trunks down and climbs on the bed of the cabana, pulling the back curtains to shield us from view behind us.

"Those are sheer. Anyone looking can make out body forms." I gawk at his boldness.

"They see my ass, no big deal. I'll handle hiding you." He covers my mouth with a quick but wet kiss, stirring up the already active butterflies in my stomach. "Like you said, this is a private house. We are alone except for the women prepping for our evening."

It would be useless to deny him, considering he had me on my back under the hut an hour ago. I was less inhibited because that was completely hidden from view, but this is much more open.

"Let's go back to talking about our wedding." He takes my hand back to his lips. "I had many favorites, but one sticks out the most."

"Ripping my dress to shreds the minute the hotel door closed?"

He smirks. "That one's at the top but not exactly number one."

"Almost flattening my dad to get to me before he could officially give me away?"

"That should have been expected. One look at you, and he should have known to stand back."

I grin with him, thinking of one more possible instance. "Was your favorite part being able to usher the kids down the aisle?"

We—well, mostly Pierce—decided to have an all-adult wedding party. Stephanie and Renee stood with me, while Miller and Evin were at his side. Renee was a new addition to our group since she decided to transfer to Charleston. During the months leading up to my wedding, she and I had grown close. She was the polar opposite of Stephanie in personality, but when those two got together, it was like the three of us fit.

I was scared Scottie would have his feelings hurt that we didn't have him at the altar, but he was honored to usher the moms down the aisle and sat proudly by my mother's side with his partner, Billy, next to them.

Pierce's decision to have Maya and Cole sit with Jill and Warren was solely his. I'd mentioned having them as attendants, and it was the only source of tension that ever came up during our planning. Finally, it became clear he was protecting us all in his own way, with a few selfish motives.

He wanted it to be him and me, with no trace of Connie while we said our vows. At the same time, he found a sliver of sympathy left in his soul for Connie. He knew how badly it would sting her for their children to stand in support of him marrying me. He didn't want that for them or her. Thankfully, the kids didn't care because they were included in every festivity leading up to the event. And it worked out beautifully.

"Ushering them was a memory that'll stay with me forever, but my favorite part was slipping that band on your finger and getting mine in return." He brings my hand to his chest.

"Yes, that was a good part." I visualize the moment. "And it's very close to my favorite, too."

He rolls us over, positioning on his knees between my things, and slides his hand into my bikini bottoms. A whimper escapes when a finger slips inside.

"You're ready." He pulls the material to the side and thrusts in. "Okay, now that I'm balls deep, tell me what you've decided on."

"When the minister announced us husband and wife. Before you kissed me, you whispered Darby Kendrick to my lips. It was official."

"Yes, it was." His eyes soften, remembering along with me. "And when we get home, there's going to be something else that's official, too. I can't fucking wait."

He rocks in and out of me slowly, holding our stare and clenching my hand to his heart. I no longer care that we are out in the open, and I'm letting him have his way with me under the sun.

Epilogue

Pierce

3 Weeks Later

"Pierce, stop pacing. You're making me dizzy." Darby covers her mouth and stands, rushing to the bathroom.

I'm at her side, holding her hair back as she bends over the basin. Nothing happens, and when she looks up, her face is flushed.

"It was just a wave of nausea. It's probably nerves."

"We're going to add that to the list of things to talk to this doctor about," I grumble, helping her back to the table.

"Honey, the test this morning was positive. We already have our confirmation. These things are expected."

"You didn't have morning sickness the first time."

"I was a younger woman. Things change."

Before I can respond, Dr. Jenkins walks in, her blinding smile set on Darby. "It's about time you come back. I've been waiting a long time for this." She looks over at me, flashing me the same smile of recognition.

I haven't seen her in years, but it's impossible to forget how comforting she was to us throughout our ordeal. She also probably knows the events that happened afterward and leading up to our wedding.

"All right, let's get to the good stuff. Tell me what you know."

"I took a test at home this morning that was positive, and my overexcited, impatient, and out-of-control husband insisted we see you immediately. We think I'm still early, possibly seven weeks," Darby fills her in.

Dr. Jenkins reviews the folder in her hand, flipping through what I assume are labs. Her lips pinch together as her eyes move furiously. An uneasy feeling twists in my gut, and I sit on the table behind Darby. "Is there something wrong?"

"Why do you think you're so early?"

"My last period was around May fifth," Darby answers.

"I assume you're off all forms of contraception?"

"Stopped taking the pill back in January. I was told it could take a year for it to work out of my system." I drop my eyes to her, wondering why she didn't share this sooner. A year? If I'd have known that, I'd have increased my efforts.

"And what happened afterward?" Jenkins goes on.

"I had unpredictable cycles, mild cramping, and random bleeding."

"All that sounds normal and an indication of why your timing is off. Our labs show you are much farther along. I'm going to estimate closer to eleven weeks."

Darby's whole body tenses, and she gasps. I can't help the chuckle that slips out of my mouth. Soon, I'm flying off the bed and stumbling to catch myself as Darby shoves me off the table.

"Eleven weeks! I was pregnant at our wedding? I was pregnant on our honeymoon?"

I throw up my hands in defeat, having the sense not to gloat... too much. Although I do feel a touch guilty for not letting her sleep a full night.

"I've eaten forbidden foods and drank alcohol. How could I not know I'm pregnant?" she screeches, clawing the table and looking desperately at Dr. Jenkins.

"Have you had a lot on your mind?"

"In the last eleven weeks, I've uprooted my life, again, created a top-to-bottom business plan for a brand new hotel, moved in with Pierce, planned a wedding, had a wedding, went on a honeymoon, and came back to working twelve-hour days."

Dr. Jenkins squeezes her knee in support. "I think that's exactly how you may have missed the signs. You may have thought you had a cycle in May, but it was probably something else."

I'm at her side again, this time standing with her curled into me. "Baby, you have to calm down."

"How can I be calm? I may have done it again!"

The weight of her words slams into me, and she's in my lap before she can lose it. "You didn't do it again because you didn't do it the first time."

"How can you know?" The panic in her voice kills me.

"Because I know."

"Pierce is right. All your labs look on track, and I think taking a look will help with your concern." Dr. Jenkins gloves up and grabs the long wand attached to the machine at Darby's side. I've been through this before and know I have to let her go to lay back, but fuck if I want her out of my arms right now.

Reluctantly, I slide away, laying her down and keeping her hand tucked in mine.

"Relax, Darby, and you shouldn't feel much pressure if we're right about our timing."

I wince watching the wand disappear under the cloth, knowing where it's going.

"We could do an abdominal ultrasound as well, but this could tell us what we need to know right now," Jenkins rattles on as my heart rate soars. This may be common to her, but our world is about to change.

Her voice fades off as a loud *whoosh-whoosh* fills the air, and it all comes into view. Our child. So small and so beautiful at the same time. A racing heartbeat thrums through the room.

"Yep, the baby looks fine," Dr. Jenkins confirms, leaning toward the screen. "Wait." She clicks a few buttons, zooming in and squinting. "Never mind."

"What the hell?" I roar. "Never mind what?"

"I thought I saw another ticker, but it is a finger. I can never be too careful, knowing Darby has a high chance of carrying twins.

I glance down at her and wink. "Maybe next time."

I howl when Darby wrenches her hand free and punches me low, grazing close to my cock.

"Don't even joke. Pierce, I'm serious. This will be our only one if you start thinking about twins."

I don't stop the smile that spreads, not replying.

"Can you stay for a bit? I'm going to get the sonographer in here for a more detailed exam. Plus, you need to set up a series of appointments."

She talks to Darby, and I recognize a few of the terms, but it's like a whole new experience. Staring at what she's pointing to on the screen, I fall into the chair, laying my chin on Darby's shoulder and paying close attention.

"In my medical opinion, this fetus is around eleven weeks, three days."

"How can you be so precise?" I question.

"Because I've been doing this long enough to pinpoint within a few days."

I mentally calculate back and know exactly. "April eighth." The day Darby came home. We married six weeks later.

This most likely happened in her new office.

I glance at her and can see she shares the thought.

The next hour is a whirlwind of ultrasounds, more blood tests, and a long session assuring Darby the baby seems fine. But it isn't until I mention our active sex life that Darby's worry lines ease, and she bursts into laughter. As we leave the office, I'm ready to conquer the world.

"When we get home, you're going to lie down, and we're going to talk about your schedule. You're going to have to cut back," I tell her when we're in the truck.

"We can't go straight home. We need to swing by the resort and the bakery."

"This is what I'm talking about. You can't keep these long hours and grueling days."

"We have plenty of time to argue about my schedule over the next few months. For today though, I need to grab my laptop and get an idea of the event schedule. Renee keeps a master calendar. With this baby due during the holidays, I've got to get my life in order."

I nod and pull her to me for a quick kiss before driving in the direction of the bakery.

"How do you want to tell our families?"

"I want to wait," she surprises me.

"Why?"

"Just until after the testing comes back. I'll pay for a rush on the results, but we have to be able to keep the secret for at least another few weeks."

I study her, understanding why. She wants to pass the fourteen-week mark. "Whatever you want."

"And I'd like you to bar our doors and keep my parents away. Mom is going to know the second she sees me."

"You got it."

She holds my hand and stares at the dozen pictures. "This time, it's different," she admits softly.

"How so?" I have a feeling what she's going to say but need to hear it.

"The baby actually looks developed, healthy, strong."

"I agree."

"Is it stupid to think he's smiling?"

"He?"

"Uhhh, yeah. Did you not catch the little rod in this picture?" She waves the grainy shot at me.

No, I didn't catch it because my eyes were glued to my glowing wife. "I can promise you, if it's a he, it's not a little rod."

She throws her head back, shaking until tears run down her face. "You are such a guy!" she gasps.

"I'm a man, baby, and in about five minutes, I'm going to be the man buried inside you."

She laughs harder, clutching the pictures to her chest. "I'm in so much shock that I can't even be mad at you for knocking me up, again, before we were married."

"I'm ready to scream it from the rooftop."

"Such a good baby daddy."

We both remember that day from long ago. I'm floating on a high when Miller calls.

"You're on Bluetooth with both of us," I greet him.

"Great, where are you?"

"Headed to the bakery."

"Where have you been?"

"Why?"

"You not showing at work this morning has everyone scrambling."

"I'm a newlywed and spent the morning with my wife. That should speak for itself."

"I get it, but this baby watch gig is serious business."

Darby covers her mouth to muffle her laugh.

"Do you know how fucking crazy that sounds?"

"Not my fault. You're the one who committed to five more kids, and you're not getting any younger."

This time, Darby gasps. "You did what?" she screeches. "Five? I agreed to three!"

"Oops, take it you haven't let her know?" He chuckles.

"I'm hanging up now, asshole." I punch the button on my steering wheel and feel the heat of her stare.

"If I wasn't so happy, I'd strangle you."

"Lucky for me, you're happy."

A few minutes later, I'm pulling into the bakery. "What the fuck?"

Miller is leaning against his truck with Evin at his side. Then, I figure it out. He tracked my phone.

"Oh no," Darby whispers.

"What?"

"Evin knows."

"How? There's no way—" I shut up when she quirks an eyebrow and purses her lips.

The twin thing.

I'm barely parked when they're opening Darby's door.

"What have you got there?" Miller motions to the pictures in her hand, smirking.

She hands them over without a word. I crowd into her, resting my hands on her stomach, and watch our brothers scan the pictures.

"I know nothing about babies, but is this normal size?"

Darby tilts her face to me, her eyes shining bright, and gives me a quick nod.

"The growth is normal for almost three months."

Their heads jerk, eyes flying between Darby and me. "Three months?" Evin questions.

"Eleven weeks to be exact," she clarifies.

"Holy shit. You didn't know?"

"No. Let's just say my body was going through changes, and I didn't have any signs."

"Is everything okay?" he asks with concern written all over his face.

"Yes. As you know, we were trying, so I stopped drinking when we got back from our honeymoon, thank goodness. All signs show the baby and I are healthy."

"Come here." He holds out his arms, and she falls into his embrace.

"Congrats, brother." Miller offers his hand, and I take it, pulling him into a one-armed hug. "You have to be fucking excited."

"You have no idea."

"This time's going to be different, and I'm glad to be a part of it."

I step back and read the meaning in his words. This time will be different for many reasons.

"Seeing as she's so far along and neither of you knew, I can assume you took my advice?" He wiggles his eyebrows, speaking low enough for only me to hear.

"Pleading the fifth."

"When are you going to tell everyone?" Evin asks.

"We're going to wait until we hit the—"

"Actually," she breaks in, coming back to my side and curling into me. "I changed my mind. I don't want to wait. Let's give our families another reason to celebrate."

"Are you sure?"

"I'm not scared anymore."

"All right, your choice. When?"

"Right now." She looks to her brother. "Evin, can you send a text to everyone to meet us here? Since they're all on baby watch, I'm sure it won't take long."

He takes out his phone and types.

"I think it's appropriate we announce it in the place it all started, don't you?" she teases.

"It's the perfect place."

"Here? It happened here?" Miller's eyes fill with shock, and

Darby throws her head back, laughing.

I take the opportunity to kiss up her neck, placing my hand back on her stomach. It may be my imagination, but I swear there's a ripple against my fingers.

My wife and my baby are happy, and that makes me feel like a fucking king.

•—•—•—•—•

"Proud of you, boy. It took longer than I wanted, but you came through." Edward hands me a fresh beer.

"Do not let her hear you say that. She's already strung up about us not knowing earlier. I promised her a wedding."

He grins, but it doesn't reach his eyes. Silence lingers, and I wait for him to work through whatever is bothering him.

"I took a chance that morning, coming to your house, knowing I'd kept quiet for too long. Many times, I wanted to track you down, but life got complicated, and my allegiance was with Darby."

"We've covered this ground and moved on. No need to talk about it again, especially today."

"Today's exactly the day to talk about it because I owe you an apology, and I want to thank you. You slayed those demons I couldn't. You brought my daughter back, and she's getting the life she was meant to live."

"She brought me back, too. We're living the life meant for us."

This time, his grin takes over his whole face. "Guess you are. I'm going to go find Annie and see if she's ready to dance." He pats me on the shoulder, heading toward the pack of women.

I zone in on Darby, who's right in the middle. Today is my parents' annual July Fourth celebration, and the party is in full swing. She's lying on the new lounger I bought for their patio specifically for her. It's the size of a queen bed with a retractable canopy. One look at it, and she rolled her eyes, telling me I was ridiculous and that my parents' furniture was fine. She is right. Their furniture is top of the line, but the lounger allows me to lie next to her while we watch the kids swim. And next year, she will have a comfortable place to hold our son if she wants to be poolside.

Darby was right. We confirmed yesterday that she's having a boy. Another son. The thought sets my heart racing. She keeps reminding me that, when he gets here, we'll be outnumbered. I can't fucking wait.

She catches me watching and pats the spot next to her. I start her way and feel a shot of cool water soaking my side.

"You coming in, Dad?" Cole shouts from the pool, spraying me with his super soaker. Scottie is next to him, taking aim at me as well.

"I'll jump in after I check on Darby."

"She needs to come in, too. The baby needs to cool off."

"I'll mention it to her," I chuckle, making my way around the pool.

Maya and Cole didn't blink when we told them Darby was having a baby. She was nervous they'd be upset, but it was the opposite.

I wade through the group and bend down for a quick kiss.

"Fair warning, we're baby crazy over here," Stephanie tells me.

"Got it." I settle next to Darby, right as Runner hops on her other side, laying his head on her barely-there baby bump. He's been doing this a lot lately, and Darby swears his dog intuition knows she's carrying a baby.

"Want to fill me in on what baby crazy means?"

"Well, between Mom, Jill, and Lynda, we're covered on childcare when I go back to work. Maya has chosen the room for the nursery, and Stephanie and Renee have planned the baby shower."

"Don't forget me. I'm all about planning a party," Andi pipes in.

I give her a grateful nod. Andi still works for Kendrick Construction, but we promoted her to the project management team a few months ago. She was a great assistant, but she is a hell of a project leader.

"I'm going to help Darby paint the nursery." Maya smiles wide.

"We'll do it together. Darby's not painting anything."

"Told you that's what he'd say." Maya directs this to Darby.

"We'll talk about it when we don't have an audience." Darby pokes my side.

"Talk all you want. You try to lift a finger, and I'll lose my mind. "

All the women find this humorous, except for Darby, who scowls. "We'll see."

The music starts, and Edward leads Annie to the dance floor.

"I'm going to get another margarita," Stephanie announces.

"That sounds good," Mom agrees, and the crowd breaks apart, everyone going in different directions.

"I'm going back into the pool." Maya runs off, jumping with a splash big enough to spray us.

I drape an arm around Darby, tugging her close and kissing her again.

"You taste like beer." She licks her lips.

"Does it bother you?"

"No, I like it. The thought of drinking a beer isn't appealing, but the taste on your lips is delicious."

"I'll remember that."

"You also smell like summer." She nuzzles into my neck.

"You do, too."

"Hmmm," she sighs.

"You still feel like taking the boat out tonight?"

Her head pops up. "Of course, it's our tradition."

Our tradition. A tradition we got back. This year will include Miller, Evin, Stephanie, Scottie and his partner Billy.

"Cole and Maya are staying here tonight, and Runner can stay, too. I thought, once we drop everyone off at the dock, we could spend the night on the boat."

Her eyes glimmer with excitement. "I'd like that, but we need to make a deal."

"Anything."

"This year, we have to get to the bed. I'm not sure it's safe to drop naked and have sex on the deck in my condition."

I roll to my side and smile wide. "You've got a deal."

●—●—●—●—●

I lean on the railing, sipping my whiskey and staring at the band on my finger. My wife and unborn son are tucked into the bed below deck, sleeping soundly.

There was a time I thought this was impossible, but now, my life completely makes sense. It was a hell of a ride, but Darby and I finally made it full circle.

Acknowledgements

There are a lot of people behind the scenes that keep me going, and when the time comes, help me prepare the roll out. Thank you to my editor, graphic designer, and the group of women that throw in your advice and wealth of knowledge to encourage me. My insanity can only be appreciated by a select few and luckily, I found them.

A special *THANK YOU* to you- the reader-for purchasing, downloading, and reading this book. Without your support this would not be possible. Hope you are ready for the ride as this series continues. Miller and Evin are up! Their bachelor days are coming to an end and I can't wait to watch how it all unfolds.

It's been over six years since I published my first book and I can't tell you how much has changed. Call it courage, or call it crazy— either way, I'm still here and writing romances that hopefully fill your heart with happiness. And I love doing it!

Cheers to many more years!

About the Author

Ahren spent her formative years living in an active volcano. There her family made collectible lava art. She studied rock collecting at the Sorbonne in France. There she met the love of her life-her pet pig, Sybil. She returned to the states and started writing. She is happily married to a guy who used to live under a bridge, who she met while pole-dancing.

Now, meet the real me. I grew up in the south and consider myself a true Southerner. Most of the special locations mentioned in my books are reflections of my favorite places. Living on the Florida coast, my family spends a lot of time at the beach, which is where I usually can be found with a book in my hand.

For more information on my books, please visit *www.ahrensanders.com.*

Bonus Extravaganza

The Marriage...

The Wife...

The Baby on the way...

You'd think that Pierce would settle into his new life and finally calm down... Not a chance. He's got his hands full, and not just with his stubborn wife.

Darby's up to something, and this time, it's Miller's world that is about to explode.

Stay tuned for Miller's story— Book two in the Southern Charmers Series coming soon!

Printed in Great
Britain
by Amazon